Crime Books by Caroline Roe

CONSOLATION
for an
EXILE

Caroline Roe

BERKLEY PRIME CRIME, NEW YORK

THE BERKLEY PUBLISHING GROUP
Published by the Penguin Group
Penguin Group (USA) Inc.
375 Hudson Street, New York, New York 10014, USA
Penguin Group (Canada), 10 Alcorn Avenue, Toronto, Ontario M4V 3B2 Canada
(a division of Pearson Penguin Canada Inc.)
Penguin Books Ltd., 80 Strand, London WC2R 0RL, England
Penguin Group Ireland, 25 St. Stephen's Green, Dublin 2, Ireland (a division of Penguin Books Ltd.)
Penguin Group (Australia), 250 Camberwell Road, Camberwell, Victoria 3124, Australia (a division of
Pearson Australia Group Pty. Ltd.)
Penguin Books India Pvt. Ltd., 11 Community Centre, Panchsheel Park, New Delhi—110 017, India
Penguin Group (NZ), Cnr. Airborne and Rosedale Raods, Albany, Auckland 1310, New Zealand
(a division of Pearson New Zealand Ltd.)
Penguin Books (South Africa) (Pty.) Ltd., 24 Sturdee Avenue, Rosebank, Johannesburg 2196, South
Africa.

Penguin Books Ltd., registered Offices: 80 Strand, London WC2R 0RL, England

This book is an original publication of The Berkley Publishing Group.

This is a work of fiction. Names, characters, places, and incidents either are the product of the author's imagination or are used fictitiously, and any resemblance to actual persons, living or dead, business establishments, events, or locales is entirely coincidental.

First edition: November 2004

Library of Congress Cataloging-in-Publication Data
Roe, Caroline.
    Consolation for an exile / Caroline Roe.
        P.   cm. — (The chronicales of Isaac of Girona)
    ISBN 0-425-19837-5
    1. Isaac of Girona (Fictitious character)—Fiction.   2. Teacher-student relationships—Fiction.
3. Spain—History—711-1516—Fiction.   4. Jewish physicians—Fiction.   5. Gerona (spain)—
Fiction.   6. Jews—Spain—Fiction.   7. Blind—Fiction.   I. Title   II. Series : Roe, Caroline.
Chronicles of Isaac of Girona.

    PR9199.3.S165C66   2004
    823'.914—dc22

                                                                                          2004054426

                    10   9   8   7   6   5   4   3   2   1

FOR SHAUDIN MELGAR-FORASTER
professora sense rival i amiga
with gratitude

LIST OF CHARACTERS

From Girona:

THE JEWISH QUARTER

BENIAMIN, 3 months, Isaac and Judith's son
DANIEL, newly wed husband to Raquel
ISAAC, a physician
JUDITH, his wife
MIRIAM and NATHAN, 9, their twin children
NAOMI, LEAH, IBRAHIM, JACINTA, 10, and JONÀS, 9, their
    servants
RAQUEL, their second daughter
YUSUF IBN HASAN, 13, Isaac's pupil, a Muslim boy from
    Granada

MORDECAI, a prosperous bootmaker and banker, friend to
    Isaac

THE CATHEDRAL

BERENGUER DE CRUÏLLES, Bishop of Girona
BERNAT SA FRIGOLA, his secretary
DOMINGO, the sergeant of his guard
GABRIEL, soldier in the Bishop's guard.

THE *FINCA*

ESTEVE, Raimon and Marta's steward
JUSTINA, 20, their housemaid
MARTA, wife to Raimon Foraster
PAU, 26, Marta's son by her first husband, Gregori

RAIMON FORASTER, 50
ROGER BERNARD, Raimon and Marta's son, 15
SANXA, their kitchen maid, 19

THE CITY

FAUSTA, servant to the Manet household
FRANCESCA, 26, wife of Jaume Manet
JAUME, son to Joana and Pons Manet
JOANA, wife to Pons Manet
PONS MANET, a prosperous wool merchant
ROSA, 40, nurse and trusted servant to Sibilla Lavaur
SIBILLA LAVAUR, 20, Francesca's impoverished cousin

BERNADA, 50, a fortune-teller
GUILLEM DE BELVIANES, 35, a stranger resembling Raimon Foraster
NICHOLAU MALLOL, cathedral scribe and Rebecca's Christian husband
REBECCA, Isaac's eldest daughter, a Christian convert

GRANADA

ABDULLAH, 10, servant to Ibn al-Khatib
FARAJ, the vizier's least important clerk
IBN AL-KHATIB, the Emir's secretary, advisor, historian, and physician.
MARYAM, step-mother to the Emir
MUHAMMED V, Emir of the kingdom of Granada, 16
PRINCE ISMA'IL, 15, Maryam's son
PRINCE QAY, 5, her second son
RIDWAN, the Emir's vizier

LADY NOOR, Yusuf's mother
ZEYNAB, 12, Yusuf's sister
AYESHA, 10, Yusuf's sister
HASAN, 6 ½, Yusuf's brother

NASR IBN UMAR, Yusuf's tutor, engaged to marry Zeynab
in a year or two

ON THE ROAD

AHMED, a guide, member of the Emir's private guard
ALI, a helpful traveling companion to Yusuf
IBRAHIM IBN UMAR, Nasr's brother
JABIR, a prosperous farmer
MARIA/AMIRI, a helpful innkeeper, perhaps Ali's mother
SALIMEH, Ibrahim's wife

ESTELLA, a horse breeder near Lleida
FELIP, her servant

THE DEAD

RAIMON LAVAUR, Sibilla's grandfather
MATHELINE, Raimon Lavaur's wife
CECILIA, Matheline's sister
BERNARD LAVAUR, Raimon Lavaur's son and Sibilla's
father
RAIMUNDA, Raimon Lavaur's twin sister
ARNAUD, her husband

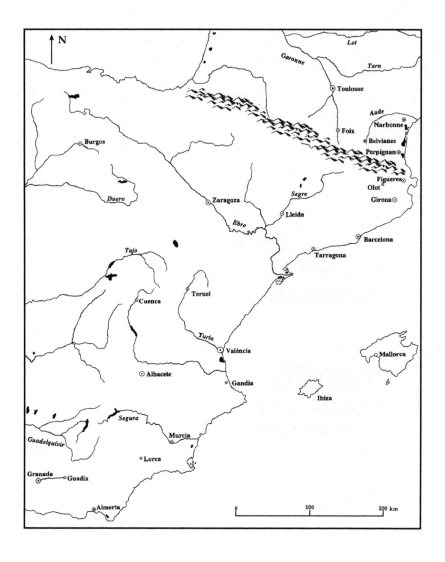

HISTORICAL NOTE:

Cathars and Catharism

CATHARISM as a religion in the area in and around Catalonia lasted from the beginnings of the twelfth century until the early fourteenth. The last Cathar Perfect, Guilhem Bélibaste, was burned at the stake in the autumn of 1321. With his death, the religion could not continue.

During that time, it was a powerful force, spiritually and politically, in Occitania (in the south of present-day France), Lombardy, Tuscany, Catalonia and surrounding areas, as well as in many other areas in Europe.

The events in this book take place in 1355, twenty-four years after the death of Guilhem Bélibaste. But the after-effects of the devastating crusade against the Cathars, familiarly known as the Good Men/Good Women or the Pure Ones (from the Greek, *katharos,* pure), lasted long after those who had taken part in it were dead.

The growth of the Cathar faith was a startling phenomenon, shocking the Catholic Church into a variety of actions in order to counter it. The Order of Preachers—the Dominicans—was founded to shore up the untaught and often corrupt local clergy. The Inquisition was established to search out the areas where the new faith had taken hold. Both of these institutions, as is the way of institutions everywhere, survived long after their initial mandate was over: the Dominicans as a religious order fulfilled many other functions, and the Inquisition as a feared and powerful instrument that, not answerable to the local Church hierarchy, hunted out heresy in villages and universities alike and monitored the conduct of converts after the forced conversions of the late Middle Ages.

Catharism (like Zoroastrianism) was a dualist religion, which viewed the cosmos as a continuous struggle between two equal, or almost equal forces, good (the Good God) and evil (the evil God, or Satan). Good is the spirit; evil is the flesh. Heaven is the place of the spirit, and earth of the flesh. A person consists of spirit trapped in flesh, seeking to return to heaven. Cathars believed in the transmigration of souls as a spirit was reborn again and again in the struggle to purify itself and become one with the Divine Spirit, God, the Good.

This upward path was gained with the renunciation of the evils of the flesh through the single sacrament of the Cathars, the Consolation (*consolamentum*) before death. The Consolation consisted of the laying on of hands by a Perfect, one who has himself received the Consolation, and who thus passes on the divine spirit to the newly consoled. The Cathars believed that Jesus, a divine messenger or angel of God, passed this spirit on to the fourth Evangelist, St. John, and that it had come down from him in an unbroken chain to them.

Once a person had received the Consolation, that person had to live a pure life. This meant abstaining absolutely from sex, or from eating anything that was connected with sexual reproduction or the flesh—meat, eggs, milk. (Fish was permitted, since at the time it was not clear that fish eggs had to be fertilized. Because of this, many Cathars were trapped by observing their eating habits.) In addition, a Cathar Perfect could not kill, was not allowed to have wealth, must dress simply, could not fight in a war, and was expected to work.

Most Cathar adherents received the Consolation when they were near death. Those who were consoled during a serious illness and went on to recover were expected to live a pure life from then on, or to allow themselves to die, usually of starvation, in an act called the *Endura*. Since the conditions for living the pure life were difficult for most people, only a relatively small number of Cathars became fully initiated long before they could reasonably expect to die. This was the group of Perfects upon whom the existence of the faith depended.

Since this one act of dedication wiped out all the sins of the flesh at once, and since as far as a Cathar was concerned, sex was evil whether a couple was married or not, a side effect of the religion, it was claimed, was a great deal of sexual license in Cathar communities among those who had not as yet been consoled. There is considerable evidence for that, as there is for the fact that a number of important Catholic nobles and members of the Catholic clergy sent in haste for a Perfect when they felt death was approaching.

The Catholic Church drummed up support for the suppression of the Cathars in the so-called Albigensian Crusade (named for the city of Albi in France), promising that those who defeated the great Cathar lords would be given land and wealth seized from them. The French responded in force, and in the carnage that followed, the independence of the Occitan-speaking world was doomed.

I
Sibilla

Girona, Friday, March 13, 1355

"YOU down there!" said the young woman on the gray mare. "Boy!"

Yusuf shifted his admiring glance from the mare—she was small, almost a pony, with neat hooves and a pretty head—to her rider, who was also rather small, he noticed, but otherwise enveloped in a fur-trimmed cloak that concealed both leg and head. He frowned, silent, having appreciated neither her tone of voice nor her mode of address. Then after a considerable pause, he said in neutral tones, "Señora?"

As if belatedly aware of her rudeness, she shook her head in exasperation. "Excuse me, young man. Señor," she said. She pushed her hood back a little and smiled. "Can you tell me where to find the house of Pons Manet? We have ridden far, my friend and I. The porter has disappeared from the gate, and the only other person we saw seemed to be as new to the city as we are."

"I can do more than that, señora," said Yusuf. "I will take you there. It is not out of my way."

"Thank you," she said. "You shame me with your courtesy."

Yusuf caught the mare's bridle and led the small procession across the square at the foot of the cathedral hill, passing by the wall of the *call*, or Jewish Quarter, where he lived.

"Is it far?" asked the young woman, pushing back her hood and revealing a tired face and a mass of dark curls in wild disarray, as if she and her mare had been propelled to the city by a high wind. "I had not expected it to be so warm today."

"It's not far at all, señora, and it will be much cooler when we reach the shade up ahead. Have you come down from the mountains?" asked Yusuf.

She nodded. "When I left there was heavy snow on the north slopes still, although it was already beginning to melt."

Yusuf led them up a curving street and stopped in front of a solid wooden gate. "Master Pons and his family live at this house, señora. Shall I ring for you?"

The sturdy young man who was riding behind the young lady jumped down to help her and her silent female companion dismount. He unloaded the baggage from the donkey and set it on the doorstep. The young lady reached for the purse hanging from her waist, removed a few coins from its very slender store, and gave them to him. He bowed and left, taking the donkey, the companion's mule, and his own horse with him.

A breeze struck the young woman; she shivered and pulled her cloak around her again as Yusuf rang the bell. "You are most kind, young man. May I—" She reached again for the purse, then looked at his bearing, his face, and his clothing, and turned the movement into a graceful gesture in his direction. "May I ask who has been assisting me so gallantly?"

"My name is Yusuf ibn Hasan, señora. I am of the household of Isaac the physician." He caught the look of confusion on her face as she tried to place him. "A student, you might say, from another country, learning something of the ways of the kingdom."

"And I am Sibilla Lavaur," she replied. "I, too, am from another country, and like you, I have traveled far to see what or whom I can find in this one."

"Madame," said her woman attendant in shocked tones.

"I jest, Rosa, that is all," she said and turned to look directly at Yusuf. Her eyes, gray like the stone walls of the city, darkened to purple, then she smiled and they narrowed to crescent-shaped slits through which she appeared to be searching his most private thoughts. "Fortunately," she continued more cheerfully, "I am a cousin of Mistress Francesca. She will be of great assistance to me, no doubt.

"Then you are in excellent hands, señora," said Yusuf.

The door opened, a gawky, timid-looking housemaid looked out, saw Yusuf and smiled, and then curtsied to the lady.

"The señora Sibilla Lavaur to see Mistress Francesca and Mistress Joana, Fausta," said Yusuf, with all the polish and elegance his thirteen years had given him. He bowed to the young lady and took his leave, hastening to the physician's house for dinner.

"MY dear Lady Sibilla," said Mistress Joana, rising to her feet. "I am delighted you are here and safe. And the Lady Matheline? I know that you can only bring us sad news—"

"Yes," said Sibilla abruptly, her eyes bleak and face expressionless. "My grandmother died on the feast of the Purification. Her last instructions to me were to come to you in all haste."

"Then sit by the fire and rest for a moment," said Mistress Joana. "You must be weary."

Sibilla sank into a carved chair lined with cushions, feeling as if she had just thrown off an enormous burden. She had been uncertain just how she would be received when she arrived. She was the only daughter of Francesca's cousin, Bernard, but Francesca was just Mistress Joana's daughter-in-law. Sibilla and Francesca had barely heard of each other before this, and certainly had never met. And yet, Mistress Joana seemed honestly pleased to have her arrive on the doorstep without warning, at dinnertime, bringing a country-bred servant with her and expecting to stay for an indefinite period of time. The gentle fire on the hearth banished the chill that had struck her as they approached the house and from somewhere close by came the smell of roasting lamb perfumed with herbs. "I am very glad to be here," was all that she could think of in reply. "It is most kind of you to take me in."

"Nonsense," said Mistress Joana. "I will be glad of your company, and so, I know, will your cousin Francesca."

"We have never met, you know," said Sibilla. "Francesca's mother, Cecilia, and my grandmother, Matheline, were sisters. But when Cecilia was born, my grandmother had already married. Or so she told me. And then Cecilia married and moved to Mallorca long before I was born."

"It was in Mallorca that our son Jaume met her," said Joana. "Until I heard from your grandmother, I had thought her family had been there many generations. But Francesca never speaks of her family. Some people are like that, I have found. Even so, she is a very sweet girl, most affectionate, and my son adores her." A fleeting expression wiped the pleasant smile from her features. "That is one reason more that we are pleased to see you. We worry about her a little. She is timid and nervous, and cannot stand much solitude."

"Is Francesca ill?" asked Sibilla.

"No, not ill," said Joana carefully. "I believe Francesca is quite well. It is just that she finds the world—well—difficult. An arrogant shopkeeper or an impertinent servant can send her into a fit of weeping in a moment. Jaume—my son—spends all the time he can spare with her, either here or in her sitting room, but he has his responsibilities. I think she will find you a great comfort."

"I will do the best I can, Mistress Joana," said Sibilla. "Although I cannot imagine anyone kinder and more reassuring than you are."

"I am her mother-in-law," said Joana dryly. "She feels she must live up to some standard of accomplishment that I—all unwittingly—have set. If she had not lost the child she was carrying last year—as if I have not lost several, myself—things might have been different, but now she feels she has failed us all. Silly child, when all we care about is Jaume's happiness and hers. But what am I talking about? You must be very tired and hungry after your trip."

"I confess that the enticing odor from the kitchen has made me aware of how hungry I am, Mistress Joana," said Sibilla.

"Wonderful," said Joana. "If you bring a good appetite as well as your pleasant manners to our house, you will be welcomed here by everyone with great enthusiasm. Our cook becomes discouraged if we don't appreciate her efforts. Fausta is preparing a chamber for you," added Joana. "It should be ready, and when you have had a chance to wash the dust of travel away, we will dine, and then you may rest as long as you wish. Supper will be whenever you like. I have sent the boy to rout Pons out of his study and away from his accounts. Jaume has just come in, and Francesca will join us any moment, I expect, my lady."

"Please, Mistress Joana," said Sibilla in some distress. "Do not call me that, especially not here in Girona. I am not entitled to it, and it could prove an embarrassment. Since I am younger even than your daughter-in-law, could you not bring yourself to call me Sibilla? It would be a comfort to me."

"I am so sorry," said Joana. "I must have misunderstood. The truth becomes sadly distorted at a distance, doesn't it? Sibilla it shall be, as if you were our own daughter." She embraced the young woman and took her to her chamber, where a fire had been lit and hot water for washing set conveniently out on a marble-topped dresser.

"Well, my dear, what is our visitor like?" asked Pons Manet as he came into his wife's sitting room.

"Charming," said Joana, "and down-to-earth and I think very strong-minded, but with perfect manners. She is not to be addressed as 'my lady', nor is she to be called 'Lady Sibilla', as we were told."

"Why ever not?" asked Pons. "If I were a lord, I would insist on your being called 'my lady.' "

"And never care what men called you," said his wife, smiling. "She is a tiny thing, smaller than Francesca, and she has one of those thin, curved noses designed to look down at lesser folk. She doesn't need to be called 'my lady.' "

"Does she look down on lesser folk?"

"Without a doubt she could," said his wife. "But she didn't. She reminds me of an elegant cat, very quick, very determined, and very charming. I like her tremendously, Pons. I told her about Francesca."

"What did you tell her about Francesca?" asked a hostile voice from the doorway.

"Jaume," said Joana. "Thank you for coming early to dinner.

I told her that Francesca became nervous and melancholy when alone right now, and could use a friend of her own age and sex."

"Are you sure that's all?"

"What else is there to tell her? Except that I said that her cousin was very sweet, and we all loved her."

"And what did she say?"

"She asked if Francesca were ill. I said no, and she said she was glad, and that the smell of the lamb roasting was making her very hungry, so I sent her off to wash and change."

"Oh, Mama, you didn't," said Jaume.

"Much more politely than that, of course, on both sides, but we were in perfect accord. She is not to be addressed as 'my lady'. Apparently that was an error in the letter that Francesca's aunt wrote. She apologized."

"I am glad of that," said Jaume. "I could not imagine a pampered lady lolling about the house complaining all day."

"She's not that," said Joana. "Is Francesca dining with us today?" she asked.

"I don't know, Mama," said Jaume. "She's nervous about meeting Sibilla, or rather, about you meeting Sibilla. She's worried that you won't like her and will blame her for bringing her into the house, since she is her cousin. How old is she?"

"Judge for yourself, my dear," said his mother. "Here she comes, and if I'm not mistaken she is bringing Francesca with her."

FRANCESCA toyed with a pair of grilled fish the size of her little finger, nibbling some of the sweet flesh off the tiny bones and leaving the rest. Pons helped her to a portion of roasted lamb, and she stared at it as if someone had placed a large rock in front of her.

On the other side of the table, Sibilla looked at the fish. "You don't see fish like this where I come from," she said. "Up in the mountains,"

"I'm not surprised," said Pons. "These are from the sea and are a great delicacy. It is not every day that we can find them at the market. You eat them just as they are," he added, dismayed at the prospect of their guest trying to fillet a sardine with her teeth like their daughter-in-law.

"Our cook must have known you were coming," said Joana. "She said that the birds woke her early this morning, and in honor of spring, she headed out to the market just as the fish were brought in. You have to be first there to find them."

"You could move to the sea," said Pons.

"And face all those pirates and storms and . . ."

"They are delicious," broke in Sibilla. "Our rivers have lovely trout, but nothing quite like this. It's sad, isn't it, that no matter where you live, you miss wonderful things that other people have. Of course, they miss the wonderful things you have, as well. There is something about the area around our village that makes delicious cheeses," she went on, "although neighbors who have traveled say that our wines are merely ordinary."

"It is the air and the earth, which are different in every place," said Jaume, who was becoming interested in what his wife's cousin was saying. "Francesca has often said that the flavor of the oil and the wine in Mallorca is—if not superior—then at least quite different from ours here."

Francesca blushed. "It is," she said. "The oil has a taste of sweet olive. It's delicious with a dish of rice or chick peas, and transforms greens. But I think I prefer our wine here."

"The next time someone we know sends for goods from Mallorca, we must get him to procure a small barrel of superior oil for us," said Joana. "It sounds excellent."

"I wouldn't want you to do that just for me, Mama," said Francesca, looking upset.

"I was thinking quite selfishly of myself, Francesca. I would love to try it, since it is not likely that I will ever go to Mallorca. And think, my dear, it might keep our cook happy. I live in fear that she will go to live with her prosperous widowed sister in Figueres," said Joana to Sibilla. "She really is an excellent cook, and they are very hard to find."

"That, I think, must be true all over," said Sibilla. "One of our neighbors went all the way to Montpellier to find a cook. He had heard that there were many excellent ones there."

"And was he successful?" asked Pons, amused.

"Oh, yes. She was wonderful. But she couldn't bear to be surrounded by foreigners, she said, and left. Are there many foreigners like me in the area?" asked Sibilla as soon as Pons had stopped laughing. "Or are people going to stare at me as if I were some strange creature you might see at a fair?"

"We are quite used to foreigners," said Joana cheerfully. "Especially those who can speak as we do, even if they do it rather oddly. But I assure you that the first time we all go to mass, every person in the cathedral will be craning his neck to get a look at you. I fear we have as much curiosity as any other place."

"But it is a friendly curiosity, I think," said Jaume. "No one will find you odd. After all, we have several priests and clerks from Valencia," he added, "which is farther away than Foix."

"I dispute that slightly," said Sibilla good-humoredly. "The first person I met as I entered the city was a man who stared at me as if he had never seen so strange a creature. I asked him where I might find your house, and he behaved as if he had never been in the city before. He shook his head and said that although he had heard the name, he didn't know where the house was. He is a big man," she added, "very courteous and pleasant, if not very well-informed, with a splendid black horse. He was accompanied by a younger man who looked well able to tell me what I wished to know if he cared to. But evidently he did not, and so he kept his silence."

"Light brown hair and a long face with a very solid chin?" asked Jaume. "And speaks like one from Lleida?"

"Yes," said Sibilla, "except that I don't know how one speaks in Lleida. He did not sound like anyone here at the table."

"Master Raimon," said Jaume. "And that would be his son, Pau, with him. He is a very pleasant man," said Jaume. "But rather shy, especially when faced with beauty."

II

Raimon

THE FIRST DREAM

He is standing in a cold, dark mountain pass, all gray and black: gray rock, bare black trees, gray sky, gray leaves catching at his feet. The wind screams about his ears. He must run. If he does not run, some horror will overtake him. He tries, but his legs are too weak to carry him; the rocks under his feet are sharp and steep. He cannot climb over them. Even if he could move, whatever rushes through the wind behind him is too terrible to turn and look at. He crouches down with his hands around his knees and his head tucked down as far as it will go and waits for the end.

1.

Wednesday, March 25

RAIMON Foraster arrived at the gate to Isaac the physician's house and met a scene of barely controlled chaos. Somewhere close by a very young baby was screaming with rage and dismay at the discovery that he was awake and hungry. Adult voices, louder but less penetrating, added to the din. Raimon rang the bell a second time, long and loud.

The adult voices ceased. The baby, apparently having achieved his goal, was silent. He heard muttering and footsteps shuffling over the courtyard stones and at last the sound of the gate opening.

"You can't see the master now," said the man who was blocking his entrance.

Raimon looked around, considering what to do next. To his right, the stone house rose three stories high, with attics on the top. Ahead of him was a smaller two-story wing and to the left, a wall. In spite of all the noise he had heard, the courtyard, stairs, and passageways were deserted. Before he could compose another request, a door at ground level directly facing him was flung open. "Who is it, Ibrahim?"

"I don't know, master."

"Well, ask him in and find out," said the physician, sounding exasperated.

"I am Raimon Foraster," said the man, raising his voice a little. "I am here to consult your master. However if this is a difficult time . . ."

"All times can be said to be difficult," said the physician philosophically, striding with confidence across the courtyard in spite of his blindness.

"Master, that chair," said Ibrahim in alarm.

Isaac stopped. "Which chair?" he asked, reaching out a cautious hand and then moving a leg forward until it touched the edge of a heavy bench. "Has everyone gone mad, Ibrahim?" he asked. "Are there any more stumbling blocks about the courtyard? I am sorry, Master Raimon. My wife has recently presented me with a son, and the household is behaving, not as if we have been blessed, but as if the end of the world were in sight. Is it safe to take Master Raimon to the sitting room?"

"I will show him the way," said a small serving maid who had come darting down the steps leading from the main section of the house into the courtyard.

"Thank you, Jacinta," said the physician. "And please warn me if anything else is lying about in my path."

ONCE the two men were settled comfortably by a pleasant fire, the physician turned to his new patient. "Now, Master Raimon, what has made you ride such a distance to see me?"

"You know who I am?"

"Perhaps not. I know only that a family by that name

inherited a fine piece of land near to Sant Martí, and I thought perhaps the head of that family might be you."

"It is. Although in truth the land belongs to my wife, Marta. She inherited it in her own right from an uncle, and a great stroke of luck for us it was, too. I must apologize for troubling you, especially now," he continued with some hesitation. "But I have heard much of your skill as a physician. I have never been to see you before, as you must realize, but we are a very healthy family as a rule."

"There is no need to apologize for that," said the physician.

"I agree, of course. Usually we are attended by a pleasant herbalist who lives nearby, but his remedies . . ."

"Let us talk of your problem first of all, Master Raimon, before considering his remedies. Mine may be no better, you know."

"My problem is simple. I have trouble sleeping," he said.

"That can be dealt with, usually. For how long have you suffered from this?"

"This has been a bad winter, as everyone knows, and toward the end of it, a month or more ago, I came down with lengthy cold and cough. The cough still troubles me in the night sometimes and keeps me awake."

"Is that all?"

"Well—recently, in the last week or two—it is becoming worse . . ."

"The cough?"

"No. Sleeping. Or not sleeping. When I do fall asleep, I have disturbing dreams. They wake me up, and when I fall asleep again, the dreams continue and become worse, until I am forced to rise in the dark and the cold and dress myself and go down to the kitchen and stir up the fire. I can't keep on this way, Master Isaac."

"I have had cases like this before," said Isaac calmly. "The causes are varied, but there is usually a cause."

"What do you mean, a cause?"

"Have you particular worries about yourself or your family?"

"No," said Raimon, puzzled. "None that I can think of."

"Money?"

"Not at all. Both our children are well provided for, since Marta's son, Pau, inherited a farm near Lleida from his father. The farm is rented because he prefers to live with us, but it is a considerable property. We are a fortunate family."

"Perhaps you suffer from fears or misdeeds that weigh on your conscience. We are alone, and whatever you say will go no further."

"There is little to tell. I am an ordinary, happy man, no doubt happier than I deserve. I come from near Lleida, I am married to an excellent woman—in addition to turning out to be an heiress, she is exceptional in every way, I assure you— and I lead a most contented life. As I said, my stepson, Pau, and my own son, Roger Bernard, both live at home. We have ordinary problems—too much rain or not enough rain or one of the animals falling sick—but our estate is productive and I have no financial worries."

"Nothing? No neighbor you have mistreated who might resent you? Your children are not causing you worries? Do you work so hard that you cannot rest when you stop?"

"None of those things. Not only am I an easygoing man by nature, Master Isaac, but my wife is affectionate and capable, and our children are a great joy to both of us. I could wish a good wife for our eldest son—he had promised himself to an excellent young woman who died before they could be married—but otherwise I have little to vex me. I have not knowingly harmed any man—or woman. Any small misdeed on my conscience is not the sort to keep me awake."

"Then just one moment." The physician rose and went over to the door. He called out, "Raquel!" and returned to his place.

In a moment, the door opened and a young woman slipped into the room.

"This is my daughter, Raquel," said the physician, "she is my eyes, and sometimes, when I am too lazy, my feet. My dear, can you fetch me the ordinary syrup for coughs and the medium herbal mixture for sleeping? Enough for three weeks, I think."

"Certainly, Papa."

"If what you say about your circumstances is true, then it seems likely that you suffer from the aftereffects of your illness. These winter colds can set the humors seriously out of balance, and that can cause fearful dreams. Unfortunately some sleeping compounds seem to worsen this condition. The one I will give you should not have that effect."

"I have tried several," said Raimon, "without much relief."

"Try this one, and remember that to sleep well you must also take care of how you eat. I have two suggestions. Add an abundance of fresh young herbs, dressed any way you choose, to your diet. And eat sparingly at night. Have a good dinner, but once you have eaten it, for the rest of day, confine yourself to light, easily digested food. For supper I suggest soup, with bread, dried fruit, and a little wine, and then a cupful of this herbal mixture that Raquel is bringing. She will explain how it is to be prepared. And if you begin to cough, put some of the syrup into a little water and drink it. It will soothe your throat. Come back and see me in a week or two if you can— even if just to tell me you are better," he added.

WHEN Raquel came in after showing the new patient out, she sat down wearily. "I am back, Papa."

"Good. Now tell me what he is like."

"He's a big man, Papa, but not at all fat. He has a great deal of brown hair and a long, rather fierce-looking face, with hollowed cheeks—he looks more like a northerner than someone from around here. But they do say he is a foreigner."

"From Lleida. Lleida, my dear, is not in the north. And I was more interested in whether he looks ill or not."

"I'm sorry, Papa, I wasn't thinking. But he does look as if he comes from the north—from France or somewhere way up there. He seems strong and healthy, although he is pale and has dark hollows under his eyes as if he lacks sleep," she said.

"He walked with more spring in his step leaving than he did when I caught a glimpse of him coming in, so I think that you must have relieved his mind."

"I am glad of that," said the physician. "He is an odd case, I think. How is your mother?"

And they returned to the topic that had been engaging the house for the past two weeks.

AND in the bishop's palace, His Excellency's neat and efficient Franciscan secretary, a man of humble mien but great power in diocesan affairs, slipped into his superior's private office. "A dispatch has arrived from Cagliari, from His Majesty, Your Excellency," said the bishop's secretary.

"Don't stand there and look portentous, Bernat," snapped Berenguer de Cruïlles, Bishop of Girona. "Read it."

There was a pause as the secretary broke the seal, glanced through the covering page, and then took out an enclosure. "His Majesty sends you a translation of a letter that he received from Emir Muhammad V of Granada. Shall I read everything?"

"Start with the emir's letter. Then tell me what His Majesty thinks of it and what he wants. After that, I will read it, no doubt, to make sure you have not misinterpreted anything."

"Very well, Your Excellency," said Bernat, raising an eyebrow. " 'To his Imperial Majesty Pere, Count of Catalonia, King of—' "

"You may omit the titles and compliments."

"Very well, Your Excellency. 'Your Royal Highness may remember the unfortunate death of Hasan Algaraffa, a man as wise as he was noble and courageous, and cousin to our royal father, Yusuf, may God take pity on his soul. Hasan's death occurred seven years ago, during a most lamentable disturbance in Valencia. At that time Hasan was an emissary from Our court to Your Royal Highness. We believed, as indeed it seems that Your Royal Highness also believed, that Our cousin's son, Yusuf ibn Hasan, perished with his father. Recently, however, a traveler of little importance in the world, but known to Us as an honest man, brought Us news from Valencia that was of some interest to Us. If this man has not been deceived, it would seem that Hasan's son survived the cowardly attack upon his father, and after many perils and difficulties, reached Your Royal Highness's court. We are further told that he resides there still.

We write to inquire what status Our beloved cousin has in the court of Aragon, and for what reason he has been so long detained there. He and his father were very close to Our Royal Father's heart, and also to Ours. It would be of great consolation to Us for the loss of Hasan to see his son once more.' And then the usual compliments," said Bernat.

"That is a most carefully crafted letter, Bernat," said the bishop to his secretary. "The new emir of Granada may be a young man, but he seems remarkably wise."

"Or he has wise advisors who draft his letters, Your Excellency," said Bernat sa Frigola dryly.

"You do not give him credit for his accomplishments, Bernat. It takes great wisdom to accept the advice of one who, although wiser than you, has less power."

"I wonder when he heard about Yusuf," said Bernat.

"Undoubtedly when the scamp was in Sardinia and then in Valencia on his way home," said Berenguer. "That was several months ago. The emir must have considered for some time whether to raise the issue or not."

"It seems a moderately friendly letter," said Bernat.

"It could be construed as such," said Berenguer, "but it could also be construed as a challenge. After all, Yusuf might have been sent to the court as a slave, which would not improve relations between our two kingdoms. I have heard that young Muhammad is even more inclined to support Pedro of Castile than his father ever was. What does His Majesty have to say?"

"He asks after his ward and expresses a desire to have your opinion on the emir's letter," said Bernat. "Soon."

"Then we must settle down and draft a reply," said Berenguer.

2.

"THE rain has stopped," said Sibilla the next morning, turning away from the window where she had been peering through the slats in the shutters. "I was afraid that it would last for weeks and weeks. Do let us go out, Francesca. Surely there are errands that we can look after for Mistress Joana."

Her cousin put down her needlework and looked up.

"There. The sun has come out," said Sibilla, throwing open the shutters. "It is a splendid day for March."

"It is cold," said Francesca.

"That's because you've been sitting still all this time. You'll soon warm up if we move about. Run and get your shawl while I ask if there is anything useful we can do."

And borne up by the force of Sibilla's determination, Francesca went up to her room and fetched her shawl.

"I'VE never been to the saddler's before," said Francesca. "It seems a very odd place for a lady to go."

"I don't see why," said Sibilla. "We ride, our horses have saddles and bridles, and so why should we not have an interest in whether they are well made? Anyway, we're not expected to know anything; we're just delivering a message from Master Pons."

At that, Sibilla swept into the shop, trailed by Francesca. After a nod of greeting, the newcomer explained with precision and force exactly what Master Pons wanted in the way of a new bridle. The saddler grinned and nodded; Francesca stood silent by the counter, looking at samples of leather and trimmings.

"You'll be a good deal more demanding than Master Pons, mistress," said the saddler placidly. "He just says to me, Pere, do what you think best, you know more than I do about harness, and I do my best. It's hard, though, if you don't know what he wants. I'll make him a fine bridle here," he said. "Just you see, mistress. He's too easygoing a man, he is."

"Who is, Pere?" asked a voice from the doorway.

"Master Pons," said the saddler. "Good day, Master Nicholau. And good day to you, Master Pau. Lovely day, isn't it?"

"Except that I was drenched in the rain riding into town, yes, it is," said a square-shouldered young man with black hair and a sweet smile.

"Mistress Francesca," said Nicholau. "I didn't see you over there in the dim light. What brings you to the saddler's?"

Francesca was struck mute by the question.

"I'm afraid I did," said Sibilla. "I am her cousin, and I am carrying out a commission for master Pons regarding a splendid bridle. And you," she added to the square-shouldered young man, "are the person who doesn't know where Master Pons lives."

"Nonsense, Pau," said his friend. "Of course you do."

"I beg your pardon, mistress," said Pau, taken aback at the sudden attack. "I don't understand what you mean."

"I assure you," said Sibilla, "that you will soon enough. We have been promised a visit from you. But now, we must take our leave, mustn't we, Francesca?"

"Yes, indeed," said Francesca, and scurried out of the shop.

"I am so very glad to be out of there," said Francesca. "Let us go home right now."

"Why?" asked Sibilla. "The sun is shining and it's beautiful out. No one will need us for at least an hour. I'd like to walk down to the river. I expect it's very different from the streams I'm used to. Come, Francesca, why can't we do that?"

"What will Jaume think?" asked Francesca.

"I have heard him say to you half a dozen times since I arrived that you should get out more. Jaume will be pleased."

This was so clearly true that Francesca paused. "Every time I go out people stop me. They say hello and ask me things, and I don't know what to say to them."

"Are they people you know?" asked Sibilla. Francesca nodded, pale and miserable-looking. "Then your problem is gone. Introduce me to them, and I will be the subject of conversation. Now—where is the river?"

"You must know where the river is," said Francesca.

"How could I? I've scarcely been out since I arrived."

"The nicest bridge is down this way," said Francesca.

"Then let us look at it while the sun is still shining," said Sibilla, heading off in the direction that Francesca had indicated.

Shortly after they had started off, Francesca stopped suddenly. "Wait, please, Sibilla," she said, sounding somewhat distracted. In front of them stood a tall woman with a weather-beaten face, dressed in a coarse but respectable dark gown with a black shawl over her shoulders. Her graying hair was tied back in a kerchief, in the manner of most countrywomen. All in all, thought Sibilla, she seemed too ordinary a person to stop Francesca in her tracks. Then she turned her glance to Sibilla.

Her eyes were pools of darkness that seemed to radiate their own brilliance and in doing so, to pierce in a most unsettling way the thoughts and feelings of each person nearby. Sibilla shivered and turned to her cousin.

"Mistress Francesca," said the stranger, "It is such a long time since I have seen you that I was afraid you might not be well. Why do you not come and visit me? Not today, for I am afraid that I will not be home, but perhaps tomorrow. Bring your charming friend."

At the sound of that harsh voice, so different from the usual soft speech of the inhabitants of the city, Sibilla was prompted by some impulse to pull her veil more completely across her face. She turned again to her cousin.

"Sibilla, this is an acquaintance who has been very helpful to me in the past," she said, as if the words were being dragged from her. "Mistress Bernada."

"Delighted," murmured Sibilla, with something between a nod and a curtsey in acknowledgment.

Mistress Bernada responded in kind and turned to knock at the door nearest them.

"Let us go to the river," said Francesca.

"Who is that woman?" asked Sibilla. "I couldn't tell from your introduction whether she was a valued acquaintance or a money lender you dared not insult," she added with a laugh.

"Oh, no," said Francesca. "She is not. She is—she is a very wise woman. She knows things. She can tell what is going to happen, and she prepares me to deal with it. I don't know what I'd do without her. But she is not of our class, and there are people who disapprove of her."

"You mean that she is a fortune-teller?" asked Sibilla.

"Not in the way you mean!" said Francesca with more animation than Sibilla had yet seen from her. "She is no common fairground creature who coaxes money out of the gullible; she is thoughtful and helps me so much. But you mustn't tell Joana or Jaume or my father-in-law that I have seen her, for they get very angry when I do."

"Do you pay her?"

"Not very much," said Francesca defensively. "No more than they pay the physicians who come to see me and do me no good at all. She knew that I was going to lose the baby," she whispered to Sibilla, "and she prepared me for it so it wasn't such a great shock. But I must go and see her again. Will you come with me? Because they never let me out alone, for all that I'm a married woman," she added resentfully.

"Where does she come from?" asked Sibilla.

"I don't know," said Francesca. "Somewhere in the country. She's a widow. After her husband died, she came to the city to earn a living."

"I hastened over as quickly as I might, Your Excellency," said Isaac, later that day. "What is troubling you?"

"Nothing to do with my health, or anyone else's," the bishop replied. "I would like you to listen to a letter that was sent to me by His Majesty."

"A letter from His Majesty?" asked Isaac, with growing alarm. "Concerning the community?"

"You will understand once you hear it. Read it to us, Bernat," he asked.

And Bernat read the letter from Muhammad V, Emir of Granada, to Pere, Count-King of Aragon.

"May I ask if Your Excellency has replied?" asked Isaac.

"I have. It was clear from His Majesty's accompanying letter that he wished to hear from me without delay."

"It was bound to happen," said Isaac. "The world is not so large that word of Yusuf's survival would not get back to Granada. He must be returned," said the physician, "But we will miss him sorely."

"You in particular," said Berenguer. "Still, His Majesty may decide to ask the emir if he can be kept here. Let us wait and see what happens. I think it best that no one else but the three of us in this room know of this. Say nothing to the boy."

"I agree," said Isaac. "It is best not to."

BUT when Isaac left the bishop's palace, instead of returning home, he went to the house of his friend, Mordecai, an excellent bootmaker who had used the profits from his business to become a prosperous banker.

"Isaac," said Mordecai, "How pleased I am to see you. I am glad to hear, as I did this morning, that your young son seems to be thriving."

"He is indeed," said Isaac. "Beniamin appears to be strong and lively, if I may be allowed to say so."

"And what brings you here?" asked Mordecai, "or are you simply escaping from the world of womenfolk and babies?"

"I am quite used to that," said Isaac, laughing. "But I am here on a particular errand. I have come to ask a favor of you—or of someone in your household. I need a letter written and I do not wish any member of my household to discover what is in it. I cannot think of anyone I can trust to assist me in confidence more than you, Mordecai."

"Is this letter . . ." Mordecai paused.

"It is nothing at all to be ashamed of, my friend," said Isaac, following his friend's train of thought. "It is merely that I do not wish my family to worry needlessly over an event which might not happen. You will understand in a minute."

"In that case," said Mordecai, "I will write it myself. My secretary is very discreet, especially about financial matters, but I suspect if it were something else—"

"It is."

"Then he might be tempted to tell a friend. I am all prepared with mended pens and fresh ink, for I had some work to do on my own account. Let me get a clean piece of paper and we can start." He pushed his chair back and Isaac heard him rustling through some papers. "There. I am ready."

"The letter is to go to the most distinguished physician, Nisim of Montpellier," said Isaac. He leaned forward in his chair and dictated slowly and with great deliberation. "My honored friend, I write at last in reply to your letter concerning your son, Amos. At that time he was seeking a position as an assistant, hoping to practice his skills and perhaps learn new tricks and methods from another. Well, my esteemed Nisim, it seems that I will soon be in dire need of an assistant. My daughter's marriage, long planned, is to take place in six weeks. She will take her skills off to a new household, and my young friend, Yusuf, it appears, may be returning to his family.

"If your son still seeks this position, and is even half as skilled as his father, the city and my patients will be the richer for his presence for as long as he wishes to stay. I would not concern yourself with the little disturbance that has caused him to wish to leave his native city. Such things occur and often teach valuable lessons." He stopped, and waited until the pen ceased its scratching across the paper.

"Shall I end it with the usual compliments?" asked Mordecai, "or do you wish to say anything else?"

"I think that will be sufficient," said Isaac. "I greatly appreciate your willingness to return to the labor of your childhood for a friend."

"I had a better hand when I was that child," said Mordecai,

casting a critical glance at what he had written. "But I understand now why you were reluctant to let others know of this request. Is it true that Yusuf is to be sent off? I thought His Majesty had granted him permission to stay in the kingdom for as long as he wished."

"He has. Yusuf is not being sent away; the emir has discovered that he is alive, and is demanding his return, I believe. Although there is much that is not clear to me as yet."

"Does the boy know?"

"He does not," said Isaac. "Until it is absolutely settled that he must go, I would not like him to be concerned with the possibility."

3.

THE next morning was windy, with rain that poured out of the heavens, and then gave way to gray skies and biting cold. To Sibilla's astonishment, breakfast had hardly been finished when Francesca showed a keen interest in going out to look for cloth for a new gown, and perhaps to order a new pair of gloves.

"It is very cold and wet, Francesca," said Joana.

"I will feel colder staying inside," she said sulkily. "Will you come with me, Sibilla?"

"Of course," said Sibilla, thinking mostly of her boots, her only pair, and how wet they would be after an excursion today. "I would like nothing better. Shall we take Rosa with us?"

"If you think so," said Francesca, giving her a meaningful look.

"I think so," said Sibilla. "She is very useful for carrying packages, if nothing else, and her advice is often valuable. We will be ready in a moment."

As soon as Francesca was out of the room, Joana looked in amazement at Sibilla. "I cannot believe this," she said. "You seem to have given Francesca a taste for exercise that can only be good for her."

"I only hope it doesn't make her ill," said Sibilla. "This is not a day I would have chosen. But I will bring her back as soon as possible, and we will be inside the shops some of the time."

The three women, led by Francesca who moved with unusual eagerness, headed back to the street where the saddler's shop was located. "This is where she lives," said Francesca and knocked on the door.

"This is where who lives?" asked Sibilla.

"Mistress Bernada, of course. Do you want to come in?" Something in the way she said it gave Sibilla to understand that an audience was the last thing she wanted.

"If you wish me to, I will," said Sibilla, "but I really was very anxious to visit the bootmaker."

"Excellent," said Francesca. "I will be no more than half an hour."

"We will come by then," said Sibilla.

At that moment, the door opened on the tall form and formidable face of Mistress Bernada. She nodded to Sibilla and held out a welcoming hand to Francesca Manet.

"Who is that woman, mistress?" asked Rosa.

"She is, to put it plainly, Rosa, a fortune-teller. And I suspect that my cousin Francesca spends most of her dress allowance on her."

"Where is she from, do you know?"

"No. But to judge from her speech, somewhere not too far from us."

"I thought that might be the case," said her maid.

"Do you know her, Rosa? That would be interesting, if you did."

"I might. It was difficult to see her, because I was standing behind you, mistress, and she was in that dark doorway. I would like to hear her speak and to get a better look at her before deciding. Without her getting a better look at me," she added cryptically.

THE SECOND DREAM

He is standing in the doorway of a vast hall. Its roof is as high as the clouds and the gray stone walls loom over him. Standing on the other side of the room is a woman in a white dress, very tall and very beautiful. Her hair hangs loose in dishevelled curls about her shoulders, as if she has just come from her bed. She is surrounded by people, but he can see her eyes darting everywhere around the hall, looking for him. She catches sight of him and cries out, very clearly, "He is here. When he grows older, he will protect me. I will be safe." Then the hair begins floating out from her head, as if she were lying in the water. Suddenly it catches fire; her screams echo through the hall. He races, panic-stricken, across the room, through the silent crowd that towers over him, pushing people aside, trying to come close enough to stamp out the flames. But when he reaches the place where she was, he finds nothing but a pile of ashes and a skull.

1.

Saturday, May 2

"IS there anything else that we must look at?" asked the young man standing behind Raimon Foraster at the entrance to draper's shop.

"I don't believe so," said the other. "Esteve and the lad are taking everything else back with them. They left before the bells for sext." He counted out a stack of coins and pushed them towards Vincens's assistant.

"I trust that your wife will be pleased with the silk," said the assistant. "It is a beautiful color and will make a handsome summer gown." He handed him a package wrapped in linen and tied with ribbon.

Raimon took the package and headed out into the bright sun of the cathedral square. "If we start now, we will be back in good time for our dinners."

"Why, there's Nicholau over there," said the young man. "I didn't expect to see him today."

"Where?" asked Raimon, looking up, his eyes narrowed against the brightness. Then he took a gasping breath, stepped back uncertainly, and laid a hand to support himself on the young man's arm.

"What is it, father?" he asked. "Are you well?"

"Well?" Raimon said after a long moment. "Yes. I am well. Only a trifle giddy," he added. "I must sit for a moment, that is all. Don't worry, Pau."

"What happened to you, Papa? You have turned white as piece of cloth."

"Nothing at all, my son. It will pass in the time it takes to tell about it. Stepping out into the brightness of the sun after being so long in the dark shop must have caused it."

"Here," said Pau, pushing him gently but firmly over to a bench in front of a wine shop. "Sit here in the shade and rest. I will fetch you something to drink before we ride back. You have been working too hard, Father. Perhaps I should send someone for the physician. In truth, that is the physician's lad over there."

"Not at all," said Raimon. "It is Saturday, and whatever his lad may be doing, Master Isaac will be celebrating the Sabbath. It is not as if I were dying, Pau. I will go to see him next week."

On the other side of the square, a man and a boy who had been deep in conversation were following the drama with interest. The man looked to be in his early thirties, with a square jaw and strong cheekbones underneath a shock of light brown hair. The boy was Yusuf, out, as he usually was on the Sabbath, amusing himself. The man pointed over to Raimon and Pau and said, "That man seems ill. I wonder if he needs help? Perhaps I should go to see . . ."

"Master Raimon?" asked Yusuf. "I wouldn't think so. He has his son with him, and if he needed help, Pau would be seeking it. I expect he is hot, tired, and thirsty," he added confidently. "I met them on the road when they were riding into town very early this morning. Poor Master Raimon has likely not had a moment to break his fast since he left his *finca*."

"Do they have far to ride?" asked the brown-haired man, a look of concern on his face.

"No more than an hour," said Yusuf. "They live up that way, near Sant Martí. A very pretty *finca*, well looked after. I ride out there often to talk to Esteve, the steward. He knows a great deal about horses, and he speaks my language—he learned it from a stable lad when he was a boy."

"You're probably right," said the man. "They're getting up."

"Master Raimon looks fine," said Yusuf. "Just as he always does." Which was an indication that Yusuf had not learned as much medicine as he thought he had.

BUT it was not until the following Wednesday that Raimon Foraster sought his physician's advice once more. "After talking to you, Master Isaac, and doing what you suggested, I soon began to feel much stronger and better," said Raimon Foraster, who was sitting once again in the physician's house, a cup of cool wine mixed with water at his side. "I was able, with time and the return of the warm sun, to spend a good part of every day in hard work among my vines and trees. I thought that would cure me."

"And it has not?"

"No. I fall asleep more easily, but once I am past my first sleep, the dreams begin again. Especially recently."

"What are these dreams?" asked Isaac. "Are they always the same, Master Raimon? Or are they different each night?"

"Neither of those," said Raimon thoughtfully. "Each dream is different, but they seem to be related to each other. I see the same two or three places and events each time, but each time I see them, they are different."

"Can you tell me what places and events you see? For when we search for causes, it is one thing to have bad dreams in general, but quite another to have the same dream, over and over."

"They grow worse, that is one thing," said Raimon. "And more frequent. But as to what they are about, that is difficult.

There is a woman in many of them—in most of them. She is tall, very tall, and beautiful, dressed in a white gown, with her hair hanging loose about her shoulders. It has occurred to me from time to time that she might be my mother."

"Does she look like your mother? Or do you simply know, the way one does while dreaming, that she is?"

"Master Isaac, I can scarcely remember my mother. I think I remember a woman, but I do not know. I have no idea what she looked like—"

"She is dead?"

"She must be. The people who raised me told me I was an orphan."

"Tell me what happens next in the dream."

"As I just told you, her hair is loose about her shoulders and it catches fire. She screams for me to help her." His voice tightened with panic. "I try desperately to reach her, but there are crowds of people between us. When I finally break through, there is nothing there but a skull on the ground." He took a deep, sobbing breath. "Then I dream of a narrow, dark mountain pass. It is cold, very cold, and windy, and wet. I am trying to run, a voice behind me is crying at me to hurry but I cannot, and I am caught by a tall man in a dark cloak. His hand is cold and bony and it digs into my shoulder. At that point I usually wake up, although the dreams seem to get longer and longer as time goes on." He stopped, as if to catch his breath after a steep climb. "I am not sure that I can bear much more of this, Master Isaac. I am being tormented."

"Are you a child in these dreams that everyone surrounding you appears to be so tall and powerful? For people tell me you are a big man."

Raimon looked at the physician with interest. "I must be, although I have no sense of being a child in the dream. I'm just me."

"What do you know about yourself?" asked Isaac. "And your family and background?"

"I know my parents were not from the village where I grew up. But as far back as I can remember, I lived in that village."

"What about your last name, Foraster? Was it common in the village?"

"Not at all. It wasn't a name, really, it was a description. My father and I were the 'foreigners,' and so they called us Foraster. Just the way one calls Joan the carpenter, Joan Carpenter."

"But that suggests that you—or your father—came from elsewhere—farther, for example, than the next town."

"That may be, but I don't know where. I cannot remember living anywhere but in the province of Lleida and here. We moved from Lleida because I had the good fortune to marry a lovely young widow with an infant son. As well as having control of her husband's property in Lleida, now belonging to her son, Pau, she inherited land here in her own right. We rented out the vines and fields in Lleida until Pau should want them and came here."

"And you never asked about your parents? What had happened to them?"

"Never. It seems odd to me now, but I was happy in Lleida and happy with the good couple who raised me. Perhaps I thought if I mentioned my family, I would be sent back to some cold dark land where life was not so pleasant."

"Like the cold dark place in your dreams," murmured the physician. "I will give you another mixture," he added, without waiting for a response, "in the hopes that it might help. You must eat well and take long, pleasant walks, and absorb yourself in the ordinary tasks of the day. That, too, should help."

ISAAC walked down to the courtyard with his patient, made sure that he was supplied with a new herbal mixture to calm his spirits, and joined his family where they sat in the sun. "And how is my son?" he asked.

"He grows hungrier and more demanding every day," said Judith with some complacency. "Hold him and feel how heavy he grows in just a few weeks. He will not wake up now until afternoon," she added. She placed the well-wrapped bundle on

Isaac's arm and settled back. "How is your new patient?" she asked quietly. "He looks to be better, but there is an air about him that I do not understand."

"He is a man who is puzzled because he believes he has all that a man needs to be happy, and yet, for no reason that he can tell, suddenly he is not."

"Then something has changed in his life," said Judith. "That seems clear to me."

"I had thought of that," said her husband, trying not to sound condescending, "but he swears nothing has happened to disturb his existence."

"Whether he knows it or not," she replied firmly, "there has been something. These things do not appear out of nowhere."

"Why is the courtyard so peaceful?"

"Raquel is at the new house, looking at what needs to be done and where things can go. As for the twins, Nathan is at school, and Miriam is so jealous of Jacinta's skill that she has decided to learn to cook. Beniamin, as you know, is asleep in your arms. Soon they will all be hungry, except Beniamin, and the noise will start again. Mordecai sent a message asking you to come to see him in the afternoon. What is going on, Isaac? I know there is something. I can feel it."

"Perhaps nothing, perhaps something, but whatever it is, it is not serious. Do you understand me? Raquel will still be married to the man she loves, Beniamin will grow bigger and stronger, and you will still be my most beloved wife. If you can wait until I return from Mordecai's, we may find another moment of quiet, and I will tell you what I can of it."

"TELL me, Francesca. What was your mother like?" asked Sibilla, as they bent over their needles in the sunny courtyard.

"My mother?"

"Yes—after all, she was my grandmother's sister, and my grandmother was like a mother to me. I wondered if they were alike."

Francesca began to tremble and stabbed her finger with

her needle. "Oh," she said. "I will bleed all over my work."

"Then put it down," said Sibilla. "Let the blood drop on the courtyard until it stops, and then I will wrap this around it." She tore a strip from some extra cloth in her workbag. "Did you know your mother?" she asked.

"Yes, of course," said Francesca. "She brought me up."

"Did she look like you? Or are you more like your father?"

"I'm not sure," said Francesca. "My finger . . ."

"There," said Sibilla, tying the cloth neatly around it. "Because my grandmother always said I looked much more like my father's and grandfather's side of the family than my mother's, or my grandmother's. So I didn't expect to look much like you. And we don't. You have such lovely, smooth, glossy hair."

"That's like my mother," said Francesca, distracted by questions of beauty for the moment. "Mama was very pretty."

"Her name was Cecilia, wasn't it?" said Sibilla.

Francesca nodded and reached for her embroidery. Sibilla gently took it away from her. "How did your mother end up in Mallorca? It seems a long way from where we lived."

Francesca mumbled something indistinct.

"What did you say?"

"I said that my father took her there, after they were married. For her health," said Francesca.

"What was wrong with her?"

"Wrong with her?"

"With her health—that he felt he should take her to Mallorca?"

"Oh—how foolish of me. She—" Francesca looked around for her needlework. "She had a weak chest," she said in a muffled voice.

"It is a better climate, I have heard, for those with weak chests," said Sibilla. "And he prospered there in the sun," she added, "for Joana mentioned your excellent dowry. And that certainly didn't come from our side of the family, as I'm sure you know." She laughed ruefully. "I'm pleased for you. It makes life simpler."

"Actually," said Francesca, "It wasn't Papa. He died quite soon after we arrived, and Mama married a nice gentleman, a merchant, who was as kind to me as if I were his own daughter."

"Until Jaume arrived and whisked you back here. You have been very fortunate in people," said Sibilla.

Francesca picked up her work again, clutched it too tightly in her hand and left a small bloodstain in the middle of it.

2.

Friday, May 8

YUSUF was walking up the hill toward the bishop's palace when he caught sight of the physician walking slowly but confidently through the gate, his staff in his hand. He ran lightly up the rest of the way and fell into step beside him.

"You left the house this morning, lord, before I had time to get back and accompany you," said the boy in reproachful tones.

"I admit to arising early this morning," said Isaac. "I was suffering the consequences of partaking too liberally of the wedding banquet."

"It was a magnificent feast," said Yusuf. "And Mistress Raquel shone like a lily among thistles."

"As I was recovering peacefully," said the physician, "I received a message from the bishop that could not be ignored, Yusuf, and hurried over. After all, before you arrived I used to walk all over the city with only my staff to guide me."

"But you said that it took you much longer."

"It did, and it still does, but I like to reassure myself that I can still do it," said Isaac. "But now we need to take some time for thought and discussion, and so let us walk slowly together, because what the bishop summoned me for concerns you."

"In what way, lord?" The boy spoke warily.

"Do not speak as if you feared a mighty blow," said Isaac. "The news I have for you is most joyful. The new emir of Granada, your cousin Muhammad, has discovered that you did not perish in the attack on your father and greatly desires that you return home. It troubles me that when we discovered who you were, we did not think to inform him, but I had not realized that you were so closely linked to the royal house."

"Where I come from, lord, we call everyone 'cousin' who is even remotely connected to us. I am sure that half of Granada is my cousin," he said. "But I think I remember the prince, Muhammad. Why does he want me to return after all this time?"

"For all the emir knows, Yusuf, you could have been sold into slavery. It would be a great insult to him if one of his kin were a slave at His Majesty's court. But His Excellency, the bishop, and I have little to do with this. The emir wrote to His Majesty, and His Majesty has made up his mind what is to be done. I will tell you now what he said, and then we will tell the others together."

"THERE are difficulties on the frontier with Granada right now," said Isaac carefully, once he was seated with his family in the courtyard. "Especially since there is talk of war on our frontier with Castile. His Majesty and the Emir Muhammad are anxious to conclude treaties of peace and cooperation, but until last spring, Granada had been constrained by the terms forced upon it in the treaty the emir's royal father signed with Castile after the siege of Algeciras. That treaty has lapsed. Until it did, the emirate was bound to keep peace and to pay tribute to Castile."

"Then if there is war," said Raquel, who had dropped by to visit with her very new husband, Daniel, "Granada will be against us?"

"Not necessarily," said Isaac. "Young Muhammad is a careful

and clever ruler, and is attempting to secure peace with us before any war can break out."

"And His Majesty?" asked Daniel.

"I am sure that His Majesty would also be greatly pleased to secure peace on his border with Granada," said Isaac. "They tell me that he is already concerned about the loyalty of the nobles and the landowners in certain frontier districts. To have secured the southwestern borders would be advantageous. Yusuf is to bear messages for him to Granada."

"I do not like it," said Judith. "It sounds dangerous."

"He will not travel alone, my dear," said her husband. "And embassies between kingdoms are treated with respect." He rose to his feet as if to conclude the discussion. "A small embassy will accompany him, and they will bear proposals to be discussed with the royal house of Granada. Whether he returns or not will be something to be decided between the emir and Yusuf himself. He has permission to return to the kingdom if he wishes."

"But what if he does not wish to stay, and the emir will not let him go?" asked Judith sharply.

"He has accepted that possibility," said Isaac. "Have you not?" he continued, turning to the boy.

"I have, lord," said Yusuf. "I cannot say what will happen, because I do not know," he said. "But I think if my family has asked His Majesty to send me back, I should go."

"And so do I," said Isaac. "He will suffer all his life if he does not risk this voyage."

"Suffer?" asked Raquel. "From what will he suffer?"

"From disloyalty to those to whom he owes everything. I have seen enough of it these days to know what suffering it can cause."

"What do you mean, Papa?" asked Raquel.

"Nothing that concerns this family," said the physician.

"But what will you do, Isaac?" said Judith suddenly. "How will you manage without Yusuf? Now that Raquel is married, and gone away—"

"Mama. I am not gone far, and as soon as the new house is ready, which will be very soon, I will be just on the other side of this wall," she said, pointing. "With a gate between us."

"Still, it is different, with you married," said her mother. "And although I will do my best, Beniamin takes much time and . . ."

"Judith," said her husband, "do not distress yourself."

She paid no attention. "There is only Naomi, Leah, and Ibrahim left. And Jacinta, but we need her, and she is still learning. But there is Jonàs. With Jacinta in the kitchen, we have not such a need for a kitchen boy, and Jonàs is coming along fairly well . . ." Her voice faded away as she contemplated reality. "He might not be able to find herbs the way Yusuf can. But you may have Jonàs."

"Mama, I will come in every day to help Papa," said Raquel firmly. "Daniel always understood that, didn't you, Daniel?"

"Of course," he said. "I always knew that your father would need you."

"Raquel, Daniel is your husband now," said her father, "and your first duty is to him. And besides, you will likely have children who will need you, so make no rash promises. I accept your offer for now, but I believe that soon we will be able to organize things quite satisfactorily."

All three who were seated there stared at the physician. "How?" asked Raquel at last.

"We should prepare ourselves for the arrival of my new pupil and assistant, Amos, son of Nisim of Montpellier."

"New assistant, Papa!" said Raquel. "When did you decide on this?"

"When His Excellency first warned me that inquiries were being made about Yusuf," said her father calmly. "I realized that the time had come to do what I have always known I must do. After all, Raquel, you reached the age of marriage two or three years ago, and Nathan and Miriam have yet to learn their letters and numbers well enough to study the rudiments of herbs and treatments. Soon they will be able to start, but it will take them some time to be of use. I knew that Yusuf's position here with us was precarious, and that I would probably need a pupil. I had not thought it would be so soon, but it is. If Yusuf returns, all the better. If, for some reason, he cannot, we will make do without him."

"I will return," said Yusuf.

"Wait before you decide that," said Isaac. "You have a family that wishes to see you again, a family that has long mourned your loss. Wait until you speak to them again before you decide what you wish to do. And then you must argue your case before the most Royal Emir. We will be delighted to see you again if you can and wish to return. There will always be a room for you here."

"When does he leave?" asked Judith.

"In three days time, at dawn. He will ride to Barcelona and sail from there."

"Alone?"

"No. He will be well protected."

3.

Saturday, May 9

THE sun had burned clear and hot that May day, and by dinner time the streets and houses felt more like summer than late spring. The city drifted gratefully into its afternoon rest, and did not stir itself until the sun began to move into the west.

Sibilla Lavaur sat in her room and considered her position. She had been in the city for two months now and had accomplished nothing. She had met many pleasant people; she had accustomed herself to the idiom of the town, and could understand everyone, even the boy, and make herself understood by almost everyone. She felt a member of the household, although her promise to help relieve her cousin's fears troubled her conscience still. She had not achieved much in that direction.

She got up from her chair, washed herself, tidied her hair,

and put on a fresh gown. She considered summoning her maid, and decided against it. Rosa had blended into the household and was occupied in the kitchen.

The sound of voices in the courtyard drew her down the stairs and out into the slanting sun of late afternoon. Two men were deep in conversation with Pons, and seated by Joana was a young woman with a child of about three or four years at her side. Jaume was sitting on a bench with Francesca, who looked pale, chilly, and miserable.

Jaume was the first to catch sight of Sibilla. He rose and took her by the hand, leading her into the group. "Sibilla," he said, "I would like to present some friends to you who have long wished to meet you."

"We have indeed," said the young woman, who was small, with thick dark hair and a fair complexion. "A fresh face and new conversation are greatly appreciated here."

"Mistress Rebecca," said Jaume, "may I present you to my cousin, the—my cousin Sibilla." Rebecca curtsied slightly. "And Nicholau, my cousin Sibilla." Nicholau bowed. "And Carles."

The little boy looked around and bowed as best he could.

"What a charming child," said Sibilla to Rebecca. "I am enchanted to meet you, Carles," she said.

"And Sibilla, may I present Pau, a friend of Nicholau and Rebecca, who has just ridden into town." Pau bowed as well.

"I am delighted," said Sibilla, "to meet you for the third time, now. I have heard much of you," she said, and turned to Rebecca. "Meeting Master Pau has been long promised to me as a treat for my good behavior."

"For the third time, mistress?" asked Pau. "I remember well having the honor to be presented to you at the saddler's one sunny morning a month or more ago."

"But you have forgotten the woebegone young lady who had just come through the city gates and asked directions to the house of her kinsman, Master Pons? The gentleman with you at least had the courtesy to respond, although he seemed quite at a loss."

"Mistress Sibilla, I am sorry beyond belief," said Pau, his

face reddening. "I remember the occasion very well, and I also remember being struck dumb by my father's reaction to it. I was so concerned with him that I, too, must have failed to answer you."

"You are forgiven," said Sibilla with a magisterial wave of the hand. "What struck your father so about my question?"

"I don't know," said Pau. "I asked him, and he could not tell me. He asked me if I had seen you, and I had to admit that, wrapped as you were in your cloak and hood, I only caught a glimpse of you. Then he said that you were a pretty thing, and he thought it odd that you traveled alone from foreign parts—which we could tell from your voice," he added. "I had been afraid that he was ill again, for he had been troubled by a cold that most of the town has suffered."

"Oh, yes. Several people have spoken of it," said Sibilla. "But I had decided that my new family did not wish to risk the introduction of a stray waif like myself to their friends. And no one has mentioned Master Pau's existence. I had to discover it for myself."

"Alas, it was not that," said Rebecca, laughing, as Pau retreated in slight confusion to pay his respects to Joana. "We have been anxious to meet you, but first Carles had a cough that troubled him, and then he generously gave it Nicholau, and finally to me. We thought it would be an ill return for the pleasure of meeting you to then infect you with our family cold."

"And are you better?" asked Sibilla. "You seem to be blooming with health."

"We are," said Rebecca, with her eye on her son, who was edging his way over toward plates of cakes, fruits, and nuts that sat on a table.

"I envy you your charming child," said Sibilla, seating herself on the bench beside Rebecca. "And your pleasant husband, whose wit and charm are much prized by Pons and Joana, as well as by Jaume. I have learned to trust and admire their judgment."

"They have cost me dearly," said Rebecca quietly, looking over at them.

"Dearly? And how, if it is not a secret?"

"If it is, it is a secret known to the entire city. To marry Nicholau, I gave up my father and mother, my sisters and my brothers, one of whom I have never seen," she said seriously. "My sister was married a week ago, and I was not at her wedding."

"Life can be hard," said Sibilla, staring off into the distance. "I have no sisters or brothers, and death has taken all my family—parents and grandparents and all their kin, some of them most cruelly. Francesca is my only relative that I know of."

"She is your cousin?"

"She is the daughter of my great-aunt—my grandmother's youngest sister. When my grandmother was dying, she wrote to her and asked her to take me in, as there was no one else."

"Did they die in the great plague?" asked Rebecca.

"No," said Sibilla. "Through some strange twist of fortune—or perhaps through God's mercy—that touched our village but slightly. Our great plague was more—shall I say—political."

"Ah—war," said Rebecca. "I understand. It is hard enough to escape the common scourges of humanity without adding to them what man can do to man."

"You are from a village nearby?" asked Pau, drifting over closer to the two women and shaking off his initial embarrassment.

"Not nearby, no," said Sibilla. "Do I sound as if I come from nearby?"

"No, but my ear is not attuned to the variations of speech here. I am from somewhere else as well. What village has the good fortune to claim you?"

"No village, really. I am from a small estate—or to be honest, from a place closer in size to a poor peasant's smallholding. It is to the northwest of here." She waved her hand vaguely in that direction. "Where I come from, a man can go for years without hearing any news of the world."

"Surely you exaggerate," Rebecca said. "The remotest village is not that far from the rest of the world. Fairs and peddlers must come by with news every year at least."

"Perhaps I exaggerate a little," she said. "There are fairs and peddlers. And shepherds, moving their flocks twice a year, pass not far from us, and other strangers come by for one reason or another, bringing news. I have even heard of the kingdom of Castile. I know the name of its king and his reputation."

"And what is that?" asked Pau.

"Oh—they say that he is a very harsh man. Except for the people who admit to having heard that he is just and fair, but harsh. And of course others who speak highly of him, calling him generous and kind."

"You laugh at us, mistress," said Pau.

"Not at all. Every word I say is true," said Sibilla, raising a finely arched eyebrow.

"Then Don Pedro of Castile must be much discussed," said Rebecca.

"Everything is much discussed," said Sibilla. "Once we had three spies from Castile in the next village, but it was such a bad place for them to hide, that they had to leave."

"Why was that?" asked Pau, laughing.

"Everyone there knows the family history not just of each neighbor but of every goat. Within minutes they had traced the poor men's lineage back to three of the king's men from Burgos."

4.

THE following day, Sibilla failed absolutely to tempt or bully Francesca out of the house. She was fatigued, she said, or ill, or too busy even to attend mass. If she went out, she would be fit for nothing for days. Yesterday's small gathering had taken all her spirit out of her.

Sibilla wished her a refreshing rest and collected Rosa from her newfound tasks in the kitchen.

"If I had known you were at heart a kitchen maid, Rosa,"

she said, "I would have left you behind and found myself a proper lady's maid."

"You wouldn't have been able to do without me," said Rosa, throwing her shawl over her shoulders. "And here, you don't need me, with everyone in the family rushing about to do your slightest bidding."

"You just enjoy talking to the cook."

"She's livelier than that Mistress Francesca you talk to all the time. Cook says she always was a nervous thing, jumping whenever you spoke to her, but now she seems to be getting worse. It comes from staying in and not seeing anybody, Cook thinks."

"Cook's probably right," said Sibilla. "I tried to get her to come to mass, but as I was pulling on one hand, I swear she was clinging to the bedpost with the other. I decided that we would both be better if we had a day free of each other."

"Where are we going?" asked Rosa.

"To mass," said Sibilla.

SIBILLA, followed by her maid, came out of the cathedral by the west door and started to walk briskly across the square. "Look over there, mistress," said Rosa suddenly, grabbing her arm and pulling her over to the side. "Over there must be the meadow where the fair is held. Let us walk down and see. They say it's not far. Out that gate, down the hill, and across the bridge."

"Perhaps," said Sibilla. "It's early yet. What are you doing?" she added, for Rosa had taken a great length of her mistress's veil, and was starting to arrange it over her face.

"You were about to lose your veil, mistress," said Rosa. "And the sun is very bright. You know what happens if too much sun falls on your face."

"Very well," said Sibilla, turning her head back to see what the maid was doing. She gave a little start and stood still, facing forward. "You are too clumsy, Rosa," she said. "Let me do it. Then we will walk over there, as you wish." She pulled the veil over her face, covering it completely. "But for the length of the walk you must try to behave as if I were mistress and you were maid. Just because when I was a little girl you always chose the walks, doesn't mean you can do it forever."

"If I weren't here to stop you, mistress, the Lord only knows what you would do," said Rosa. "Speaking to strange men and wandering off on your own whenever you liked."

"Then you behave like a maid, and I will promise to behave like a modest, innocent young lady," said Sibilla.

They walked down the cathedral hill and out through the splendid north gate of the city, Sibilla nodding shyly at people she had already met. As they came near the great church in Sant Feliu, the bustling suburb just outside the gates, a pleasant male voice hailed them. Both turned to look

"Mistress Sibilla."

"Master Nicholau," said Sibilla, glancing around and throwing back her veil. "And Master Pau. What a happy coincidence. How did you know who I was under all this disguise?"

"You cannot hide that graceful walk," said Nicholau.

"He recognized that gown," said Pau, "but doesn't like to admit what a keen eye he has for fashion."

"Where are you headed?" asked Nicholau with a grin.

"Over the bridge to the meadow and back. And you?"

"I have a basket to deliver, but we will accompany you as far as the bridge, won't we, Pau?" he asked, turning to his companion.

"We will indeed," said Pau.

Their conversation was nothing but idle chatter about the weather and commonplace events in the city until they reached the bridge. "I must leave you here," said Nicholau, raising the basket in his hand and bowing, "or I will be late for dinner, and Rebecca will never forgive me. Until the next time," he added, and strode away.

Pau, apparently forgetting that he had been with Nicholau, continued on over the bridge with the two women. Sibilla picked up her skirts to keep them out of muddy patches in the roadway, moved forward to the edge of the meadow, and stopped. She surveyed the area—the confluence of the two rivers, the patch of marshland and sandy spit, the fast-growing grass at her feet—with the focused regard a general might give to a site of great strategic importance. "It looks very green and pleasant here," she said, "but I would not come here again for any reason beyond the wish for a pleasant walk."

"I confess that it is more interesting at fair time," said Pau, as they turned back toward the bridge. "I'm sorry that you're disappointed."

"Don't listen to me," said Sibilla, and then immediately contradicting herself. "I'm not disappointed. But I find this land very strange. It's not like mine at all."

"Where is your land?" asked Pau.

"Do you know Foix?" asked Sibilla, as they wandered slowly back to the bridge.

"I have heard it spoken of," said Pau.

"I lived a day's ride into the mountains from Foix. Girona is different," she said, stopping at the middle of the bridge. "Very different. Here, too, there are hills all around us, but they are gentler hills. Our mountains are sharp and steep, like huge walls." She stared down into the water, watching the fish move lazily about in the shadows cast by the bridge. "There is a great difference," she continued, "between being protected by rock, and being protected by walls made from pieces of rock, no matter how finely shaped and how massive. Can you understand that?"

"I think so," he said cautiously.

"It is like—" She paused to think. "It is like the difference between being protected by God and protected by man," she said. "Our walls, where I come from, have crevices and niches that only we know, where we may hide when our enemies come up the passes." She fell silent. After a moment or two she straightened up and turned, looking intently into his face. "I must apologize. I am behaving like those unlettered philosophers who expound deep notions over their wine, a position most unsuitable for a young lady." She laughed and shook her head. Her curls tumbled down, and she attempted to push them back into order.

Pau stared at her oddly. "I do understand something of what you say. Our *finca,* where we live now, is most unlike my own little estate."

"Where is that?"

"To the west."

"You do not live on it?"

"Clearly not, or I would not be here. It is many hours ride away. It was my father's and became mine when I reached the age of sixteen. Some uncle or cousin farms it now."

"But isn't your father the man who didn't know . . ."

"That is my stepfather," said Pau, smiling. "My father died when I was a baby. The man you spoke to is my mother's second husband, Raimon Foraster. But in him, I have had as kind and generous a father all my life as any man has had."

RAIMON Foraster, his wife, and their younger son strolled up the road after mass in companionable silence. "You are feeling better today?" asked his wife, with the air of one who was trying to look calmer than she felt.

"I am," he said. "Today I shall do nothing but eat and sleep and enjoy myself. By tomorrow I will be fine. What the devil?" he said suddenly. "Why is Esteve rushing down here to meet us?"

"Oh, dear," said Marta, his wife. "That bodes ill. I wonder what it is now?"

"Who is that behind him?" asked their son. "Good God, Papa!" he said. "Look at him!"

Striding down the path from the house was the stranger who, a week before, had observed Raimon's attack of giddiness in the cathedral square in Girona. As he approached the three family members, silence fell on the entire group.

The first to break it was Esteve. "Master Raimon," said the

steward, "this gentleman arrived some half-hour ago. I thought you might wish to speak to him and have prevailed upon him to stay until you returned from mass."

"I should think we would all like to speak to him," said Raimon's wife crisply. "I am sure, sir, that we are very interested in hearing who you are and where you come from."

The stranger bowed to each in turn. "My name is Guillem," he said. "Guillem de Belvianes."

"The devil it is," said Raimon, staring at him.

"How come you to be here, sir?" asked Raimon's son.

"Roger Bernard!" hissed his mother. "That is not a polite greeting, no matter who he may be."

"That may be, Mama," said the young man, "but given his appearance, it is a question that must be asked."

"My appearance?" asked the stranger.

"You are as like my father as two peas in a pod," said the young man, "as I am sure you know."

"He is?" said Raimon. "I admit he has a very familiar look, but I had not seen myself in him."

Everyone stared at the two men. The thick, light brown hair, tall stature, the rough-hewn features with their prominent cheekbones and jaw were the same.

"Except for this Guillem being younger than you by several years, Papa, and not as thin, and your noses not being the same," said Roger Bernard coolly. "Papa's is stronger and thinner, and the eyes are somewhat different as well. But the general air of likeness is very strong. Who are you, sir, and how came you to be at this house?"

The stranger looked from one to the other and then addressed himself to Raimon. "My name is Guillem," he said. "I am a notary and have come from the lands of my lord the Count of Foix, north of the mountains, having business in Girona to execute for a client. Several people stopped me on the streets and told me that they had thought that I was you, Master Raimon, until they realized that I was, indeed, the wrong age and somewhat different in appearance. I had heard rumors at home that I have family here in Girona, and thought that you must have been the person of whom they spoke. I am sorry if I am mistaken. I had no intention of trespassing on your good nature in any way."

"In what way are we supposed to be related, Master Guillem?" asked Raimon.

"On your father's side of the family," said Guillem awkwardly.

"My father's side?" asked Raimon. "That is all you know?"

"I have heard many odd rumors," said Guillem, "which I would be loathe to repeat, since I doubt that they are true."

"Are you staying long in Girona?" asked Raimon.

"I have not decided," said Guillem. "There is little to draw me back north of the Pyrenees at this moment, although doubtless I must make the journey at some time." He smiled brightly and winked at Roger Bernard, who recoiled.

"Perhaps you would care to dine with us," said Raimon. "That will give us time to accustom ourselves to this new idea. For as far as I have ever known, I have no family. I was told that they had all perished when I was a child. You come as something of a surprise to me."

5.

THE next morning, the atmosphere at the physician's house was gloomy indeed, not even enlivened by the arrival of Raquel and Daniel in time for an early breakfast. "I will miss you, Yusuf," said Raquel. "Now that I have learned my letters and many words in your language, without you to keep teaching me, I will forget them all."

"Raquel," said her father softly. "Do not make Yusuf's voyage home more difficult for him. He is going to see his family, and I am sure that he will return. He will not forget us. And if you weep over breakfast, he will not be able to eat, and I will be angry."

"I am not weeping, Papa," said Raquel, surreptitiously mopping up a few tears with the end of her sleeve. "I wish I could go to Granada," she said to the boy. "I have heard that it is a city of beauty beyond belief."

"I remember only the courtyard," said Yusuf. "And the sky. And my mother combing her hair by the fountain. I fear that when I arrive my mother will be dead," he said, dropping his voice to a whisper. "I fear it in my heart. For if she is, I do not wish to know."

"You have a sister, at least," said Raquel. "You have spoken of her. Won't she want to see you? Do you think she has not missed you? Now eat your breakfast, or Naomi will make you take it with you. Until she hears you are well and safe, she will not stop fretting over you. Mama," she said, trying to turn the conversation, "have you heard of this man who has come to the city who is supposed to look the very image of Master Raimon?"

"Dolsa said something of him," said Judith. "She suspects him of being a fraud. She is sure he does not look so near to Raimon as people say, and that he is trading on a slight resemblance."

"No, mistress," said Yusuf. "I saw him. He looks very like Master Raimon. He pulled me aside in the square and asked me many questions about Master Raimon."

"Did you answer them?" asked Isaac.

"I answered those that he could learn from any housemaid or kitchen lad," said Yusuf. "The others, I said that I did not know. And all the time he was talking, Master Raimon was sitting on a bench in front of the wine shop, looking pale and rather ill from the heat, I think. But this Master Guillem never looked directly at him."

Before he finished, hoofbeats and a jangle of harness outside the gates brought Yusuf to his feet. He took some fruit, cheese, and a piece of bread and wrapped them in a small cloth. Isaac rose as well and walked over to the boy. He murmured something in his ear. Yusuf bowed, clasped his hands over the blind man's, and said, "I will, lord. As long as there is breath in my body. Thank you, and farewell."

The sergeant of the Bishop's Guard, Domingo, came into

the courtyard. "Are you prepared to travel, Señor Yusuf?"

"I am, Sergeant. And I will never let down my guard."

"I hope not. After all, you have been trained in warfare by me and by my captain. Seize your bundle, say your farewells, and let us go. The sun is almost up and your mare is waiting for you."

"IT doesn't seem right, Papa," said Raquel. "He was so happy here and learning so much from you."

"My dear daughter," said her father. "All this is true, but it is not right. The city needs at least one more skilled physician to meet its needs. It is now seven years since the plague started; we have recovered from the devastation and the city is growing again. We need another person here whose profession is that of physician. Jonàs can be trained to do the work that Yusuf was doing, which was not at all fitting for a boy of his state in life. Yusuf must learn to take his rightful place in his rightful society. His Majesty was correct when he insisted that his time be spent on study both in Latin and Arabic, and on learning courtesy, swordplay, and horsemanship, as well as strategy and diplomacy. But he will never leave us altogether, my dear. I am sure of that."

"I hope not, Papa. Perhaps the emir will allow him to return."

"Perhaps he will," said Isaac. "But if he does, it will be as an equal to His Excellency, not as a gatherer of herbs in this household. Now, if you will take pen and ink, and write a letter for me, I will ask this Amos, Nisim's son, why it takes so long for him to travel from Montpellier to here."

THE THIRD DREAM

He is sitting in a great hall, near the hearth where a fire blazes. He is surrounded by friends and good fellowship. As he picks up his cup, someone throws a burning torch; it flies over the assembly and

suddenly there are flames everywhere. In the middle of the confla-
gration he sees his mother. She is fighting her way through the crowd
with her arms outstretched toward him. The flames catch her. He
turns his head, searching for help, and sees her again, in another
part of the room, trying to reach him and finding only the flames. He
turns around, and wherever he looks, she is there, always in danger,
and always dying.

1.

Tuesday, May 12

"WHERE is this hall?" asked Isaac as Raimon's voice faded
away.

"I do not know, Master Isaac," said the patient. "I don't remember. But I always dream about the same hall. Each time I
have one of the dreams the people in it are different, but the
hall itself is the same. I am convinced it is purely an invention
of my own mind."

"How do you know that?"

"I am sure I have never seen it before."

"Do you still have the other dreams?"

"Of mountain passes and wind screaming about my ears?
Yes, I do, although not as often as the dream of the hall and
the torch."

"And this woman? Does she still seem to be your mother?"

"I don't know, Master Isaac. I know that she is in terrible
danger, her distress cuts through me like a knife, and yet I
have never seen her before."

"Come, Master Raimon. Let us walk in the courtyard. It is
a fine day, warm and sunny, I believe. It is time we talked
about many things."

Raimon followed the physician down the stairs to the courtyard. It was filled with the scent of flowers and ripening fruit,
and songbirds, both caged and flying wild, chirped, twit-

tered, and sang in an ecstasy of spring. "This is a pleasant place," said Raimon. "Full of life. Your cat does not interest herself in the birds?"

"She has greater success with mice," said Isaac. "She discovered long since that birds are too agile even for her quick leaps. My daughter Raquel used to patrol the courtyard when the fledglings were trying their wings; now little Miriam is taking over that task, trying to save the mother birds any anxious moments. How and when did your mother die?" he added with no change in tone or manner.

"I do not know," said Raimon, startled. "For all I know, she may be alive still."

"Do you think that is possible?"

"No. I suspect she died when I was very young. Why else would I have been turned over to the care of strangers, even good-hearted ones?"

"There are other reasons," said Isaac. "But that is the most likely, I agree. When did you last see her then—under what circumstances?"

Raimon halted his leisurely stroll around the courtyard. "I can't remember that either. I have memories of her, but they are just moments, all mixed together," he said. "Of suppers by the hearth, songs she sang, walks we took up the mountain path."

"Mountain path?" asked Isaac.

"Yes," said Raimon, in surprised tones. "We lived in the mountains. I do not know which ones. In a big house. Or it seemed big to me."

"Is that where the hall was?"

"Oh, no. The house wasn't that big. The hall, if it exists, must be somewhere else."

"Do you know of any cause for these dreams to have started?"

"What do you mean?"

"We know that dreams have many causes. Some are caused by diet, some by a disturbance in one's life, and some by illness. There are also dreams that seem to be granted by the Lord Almighty as prophecies or warnings."

"Do you think my dreams are prophetic?" asked Raimon.

"That I cannot say. Prophetic dreams do not lie in my province," said Isaac. "I have no cure for them."

"Some dreams are snares laid by the devil, they say," said his patient.

"That, too," says Isaac. "But those are beyond my competence as well. It is best to assume a more ordinary cause first, and to start with simpler remedies. When did the dreams start?"

"I am not sure. Two or three months ago? Maybe less? It was gradual."

"Nothing happened just then?"

"Nothing. The only strange thing to have happened to me recently occurred just two days ago," he said slowly.

"What was that?"

"I discovered that I have a relation that I had never heard of—a nephew or a cousin. I have always believed I had no family, except for a father who left me with the family who raised me and then disappeared. But this man had heard some rumor of my existence and came to Girona to find me. He was directed to the *finca* and rode out to see me."

"I do not wish to seem suspicious," said Isaac, "but are you sure he is related to you?"

"You could not be more suspicious than my good wife, and even she admits that we must be closely related to look so very much alike. Although, I admit, I do not see the resemblance as clearly as my family does."

"He could not have caused your dreams."

"No. Not unless they prophesied his arrival in my life."

2.

"PAU!" said Nicholau. "What are you doing in the city today?"

"May I not come into the city when I please?" asked the young man wryly.

"Of course, and I am heartily glad to see you whenever you arrive. But you are not usually here on a Tuesday. Where do you dine?"

"I had not thought of dinner," said Pau. "I had just finished my business with the cooper and was about to ride home."

"You will starve by the time you get out there. Come and dine with us. Rebecca spoke most promisingly of a baked fish and a piece of stewed mutton, and no one could surpass her in the matter of stewed mutton. She will be delighted to see you. Where is your horse?"

"Up the valley in old Pere's meadow, a quarter of an hour away. She will be safe until I come to fetch her."

"Excellent." And the two young men strolled across the square and down a short distance to where Rebecca and Nicholau lived, in the modest suburb of Sant Feliu.

"Tell me about Mistress Francesca's pretty cousin," said Pau as they entered the house. "What do you know of her? Where does she come from?"

"Hasn't she told you?" asked Nicholau.

"Only very vaguely," said Pau. "She waved a hand in the air and said, 'I come from north of here,' which could be anywhere from Figueres to the frozen ends of the world. Although she did admit it was in the mountains, a long way from Foix."

"She has been asking Rebecca about you," said Nicholau. "Hasn't she, love?" he added, turning to his wife, who had just entered the room.

"She has," said Rebecca. "But I must admit she has been asking about other people, too. Still, she seems very interested in you, for some reason."

"It is not difficult to understand the reason," said Nicholau. "Look at him. A handsome man with excellent prospects."

"She was also asking very pointed questions about the man who went out to visit your place," said Rebecca. "The one who looks so much like Master Raimon. He has caused much talk, I can tell you. Who is he, Master Pau?"

"Guillem," said Pau shortly.

"Guillem?" asked Rebecca. "Do you know where he's from?"

"He says he is from near Foix," said Pau. "And he says he is related to my father. My father knows nothing of any connection he has with Foix, or the count, or someone called Guillem. But they do look alike."

"What brought him to Girona?" asked Nicholau.

"Business, he said," replied Pau. "But I think he is here to improve his fortunes. He has extracted an invitation from my parents to stay with us as long as he is in the neighborhood, and now he is talking seriously to my father about how fitted he is to be a manager of an estate like ours. He has seriously upset my good friend Esteve, our steward."

"Is he?" asked Nicholau.

"Not at all, I think. He claims to be trained in the law, and that might be so, but it's clear that he knows no more about vines and orchards and herds than he does about life in a convent. It would double my father's work to lose Esteve."

"Would Esteve leave?" asked Nicholau.

"He has threatened to. He has no desire to be placed under some man who knows nothing and yet has the power—because of his family connections—to give him orders."

"I can understand that," said Rebecca. "It is a matter of pride in one's work. But come. It is time for dinner."

"But why is Sibilla interested in Guillem?" asked Pau.

"I didn't say that she was interested in him," said Rebecca demurely. "It is his resemblance to your papa that, for some reason, fascinates her."

"The resemblance? How?"

"That's very clear, Pau. You have two men. They know nothing of each other—or so they both claim—they look so much alike, yet they come from two different parts of the world, and they turn up in the same city. Is it chance? Or is it not? And if not chance, what is it? Now, please, sit down and help yourselves to the fish."

⊹⟫⟨⟫ ⟨⟫⟩⊹

THE two friends sat long over the dinner table until Nicholau could no longer think of reasons for not returning to his tasks at the cathedral. "I must leave you," he said. "I am needed at a meeting that will begin shortly. If I am not there to copy down the proceedings the meeting will have no real existence, and no doubt," he added sardonically, "the diocese will collapse."

"I will walk with you as far as the cathedral," said Pau. And instead of heading out to fetch his mare and riding home, Pau walked into the city with Nicholau, left him at the cathedral, and carried on past the *call* to pay a visit on the Pons family.

Sibilla was out with Francesca again, but instead of excusing himself, he sat down in the courtyard near Mistress Joana with the air of a man who had hours to waste in conversation. She picked up her needlework, commented on the weather, and fell silent. "Mistress Francesca's cousin is not in?" he asked, although the maid had already told him that.

"She has gone for a walk," said Joana. "I think they are headed out the south gate if you wish to look for them."

"Oh, no," said Pau. "I was just passing by and thought how pleasant it would be to see you. I hope your guest is settling into her new surroundings."

"Pau," said Joana. "When did you start coming into town at the beginning of the week and coming over to talk to me?"

"I had business in town," he said.

"And now I would have expected you to be riding home for your supper before darkness fell." She leaned forward and touched him lightly on the arm. "Tell me. What did you want from me, if not to ask me how to find Sibilla?"

Pau smiled. "You see straight through one's sad little subterfuges, Mistress Joana. What is a poor ordinary man to do?" He spread his hands in front of him in surrender. "I want to know who Mistress Sibilla is," he said.

"She is Francesca's cousin," said Joana.

"I apologize for my bluntness," said Pau, "but I do not know how to put this more delicately and still hope for an answer. Who is her family? Who is her guardian? If she wished to marry, for example, whom would she have to ask for permission?"

Joana tilted her head and looked quizzically at him. "That is a most interesting question, Master Pau," she said. "She will know that better than I. I must ask her when she returns from her walk. As far as I know, Francesca is her only relative still living. She was raised by her grandmother, a woman of excellent—indeed noble—family, now dead. I believe that her grandmother wrote to His Excellency at the same time that she wrote to me, commending her grandchild to our care, in different ways. I think you would do well to address your question to him, since you are reluctant to ask Sibilla herself."

"You mock me, Mistress Joana," he said.

"Not at all. Or at least, only very little, and with great affection. All I ask is that you not trouble Francesca with questions about the family background. It seems to disturb her to talk about her family, and she has enough worries at the moment."

"Thank you. And I will do as you ask."

But as Pau was gathering himself together to leave, his parting compliments were interrupted by a stir at the gate. Francesca entered, nodded to Joana and Pau, and hastened into the house. Sibilla and Rosa came in after her.

"Is Francesca well?" asked Joana.

"I think she is tired from the walk, and a little upset," said Sibilla.

"I will go to her, mistress," said Rosa.

"No—I will go," said Joana. "Perhaps you could bring her some mint tea, Rosa."

"How are you, Mistress Sibilla?" asked Pau. "Although it seems an unnecessary question. You look very well."

"I am," she said. "But then I am rarely ill. Although I fear that if I continue to keep close to the house and never walk anywhere too far for my cousin's taste, I shall soon become feeble and nervous. How are you, Master Pau? You, too, look well, although a little cross, I would say."

"I am never cross," said Pau. "I am known by all to have the most even temper of any man in the district, although I admit to being somewhat irritable at the moment."

"Tell me about the stranger who has come into town and caused all the stir," she said abruptly.

"Stranger? Do you mean this Guillem who has turned up at the *finca* and shows no signs of going away again?"

"Really?" asked Sibilla. "That sounds most unpleasant for you."

"He has moved in, bag and baggage, saying that since he has very few relations, he wishes to help those whom he has."

"And does he help?" asked Sibilla. "As someone who is doing much the same thing to my own distant kin, I am most interested."

"Since he knows very little about running a farm, managing livestock, or taking what we produce to market, he finds it all endlessly fascinating, he says. He spends half his day following Esteve about and asking him questions, and so preventing him from working."

"And the rest of the time?"

"As far as I can see, he spends that attempting to seduce the maid, Justina. And that makes Mama very cross, since Justina, who did little enough work before, is so distracted by the attention that now she does nothing at all. I'm not sure what he sees in her—she's too tall and ferocious-looking for my taste. And yet our sweet-faced little kitchen maid accomplishes three times the amount of work in a day."

Sibilla laughed. "I am sure it is not at all amusing," she said, "but you have a gift for describing things so as to make them sound comic."

"Life has its comic moments now," said Pau.

"I would like to see the estate," said Sibilla, "if your mama would not object to a visit."

"I am sure that Mama would be delighted," said Pau. "And I know that I would be even more delighted."

"Then Rosa and I, and perhaps even Francesca will ride out some day soon."

3.

SIBILLA stood in the courtyard for a very long time, staring at the gate through which Pau had left. She had a great deal more to think about than she could comfortably manage, she reflected, starting with Pau.

"Why do you stand there staring at the gate, Sibilla?" asked an amused voice behind her.

"Joana!" she said. "I'm sorry, but you startled me. I was lost in thought, I'm afraid, and did not even realize that I was admiring your excellent gate."

"Were you thinking of Master Pau, perhaps?" she asked, sitting down on the bench under the pear tree, and patting the place beside her in invitation.

"He was one of the things I was thinking about, yes," she said, sitting down. "One of the more pleasant things, in fact."

"I'm glad you find thinking about him pleasant. I think he has fallen in love with you, Sibilla."

"Wait, Joana," said Sibilla. "Why do you think he has fallen in love with me?"

"Because he wanted to know who you were—who your parents were, who your guardian is—"

"What are my prospects and how generous is my dowry?" added Sibilla, flatly.

"No. Not even a breath of that. He wanted to know to whom he should apply for permission to court you."

"To court me?"

"Sibilla, if he does not interest you, please tell me, and I will drop a word in his ear. You must know that for all his good humor and wit, he is a serious man, and somewhat shy. He would be devastated if he misinterpreted your jests and laughter as encouragement."

"He has not misinterpreted anything, Joana, but I fear that when he discovers what my circumstances are, his ardor will cool."

"I don't think so," said Joana. "He already owns a valuable property in Lleida, I have never noticed him to be a greedy man, and if dowry were important to him, you would have known about it already. He is painfully honest, my dear. It is one of his great drawbacks."

"Surely there must be worse drawbacks a man could have," said Sibilla, laughing, "but I can imagine that painful honesty could be uncomfortable at times."

"It's better than lies and deceit, which are what many men bring to marriage," observed Joana. "But what else were you thinking of so gravely?"

"My cousin Francesca," said Sibilla.

"Oh, dear," said Joana. "What is wrong now?"

"I'm not sure you can say that anything is wrong," said Sibilla carefully. "And all that I am saying to you involves my breaking a solemn promise to keep silent. But I cannot sit back and see possible harm come to her through my silence, so I enlist you in this uncomfortable conspiracy."

"What are you talking about?"

"Francesca is pregnant again."

"Excellent. Does Jaume know?"

"She believes that he does not. Whether he does or not, I suppose, depends on how attuned he is to his wife's behavior and such."

"Why keep it a secret?"

"Fear, Joana. Fear of losing this baby, and of I do not know what, but it all centers around a crazed fortune-teller, who is giving her insane advice and collecting vast sums of money for doing so, saying that otherwise she is sure to lose the baby."

"Bernada!" said Joana. "That witch! Sibilla, she has been a curse to this household ever since Francesca discovered her—or she discovered Francesca. I am not sure how it came about. I count it my fault. If she had felt that she could confide in me, she would not have needed someone like that to soothe her fears."

"She doesn't soothe her fears, Joana. She stokes them. Francesca visited her today and I think that the fortune-teller told her something that has driven her out of her mind with fear. She came out of the house trembling and wiping tears from her cheeks, but swearing that nothing was wrong, nothing at all."

"What could that foul woman have said?"

"I have not the slightest idea what it could be."

"I shall go to the bishop," said Joana. "I swear it. I shall denounce her as a witch. She should be hanged, Sibilla, before she can do any more damage. You know, my blood has always turned cold at the thought of poor, mad souls burning at the stake for nursing terrible errors, but in the case of Bernada, I think I could almost approve the stake."

"And what would that do to Francesca, who seeks her out and follows her advice?"

"Almighty God," said Joana. "Why has my family been so afflicted?"

"There may be one way to stop her, Joana. My Rosa has discovered that—"

"And what are you two plotting out here?" said Pons Manet in his liveliest voice. "Jaume and I have negotiated a contract that deserves a cup of wine. Francesca declines to join us, saying she is feeling a little chilled after being out, but surely you will join in?"

"Of course, my dear," said Joana, smiling as if nothing in the world could possibly be wrong.

THE FOURTH DREAM

Once again he is standing in the doorway of the vast hall with its roof as high as the clouds and its towering, gray stone walls. He sees the beautiful, tall woman, who he now knows is his mother, standing in the same place on the other side of the room, still wearing the white dress, her hair again hanging loose in dishevelled curls. She looks directly into his eyes and cries out, very clearly, "He is here and he will save me; I know that he will save me." He rushes toward her to prevent the tragedy, but once more her hair floats out from her head and catches fire; her screams echo through the hall. He races, panic-stricken, across the room, throws his arms around her, and she crumbles into ashes.

1.

"THAT is indeed a horrifying dream," said the physician.

"But wait, Master Isaac. I have more to recount. I rose from my bed, put on a warm robe that I keep by me for these times, and went down to the kitchen as I often do. Shortly after I had stirred up the fire, my cousin—or whatever he is—Guillem, came into the room."

"That could have been a very innocent occasion. Your moving about may have disturbed him."

"Not if he were in the chamber we had assigned to him," said Raimon. "He was more likely in Justina's room—she's our maid—which is near the kitchen. But that is of little importance compared to our conversation."

"What did he say?"

"He said that he had much to tell me and had debated long over whether he should. I told him that if he had something to say, he should say it. He put a little more fuel on the fire, set his feet comfortably on the hearth and began. Shall I tell it to you as he said it?"

"If you can."

"I can. He said, 'First of all, I am not a distant connection, but your brother.'"

"Indeed, not distant at all," said Isaac dryly. "But were you aware that you had a brother?"

"This was the first I had heard of it. But he continued, Master Isaac. 'Or half-brother,' he said, 'for we had different mothers. Our father was a Cathar, one of the "good people," as they were called, who so abounded in the part of the world where both of us were born. I speak of a time when you were a small lad, when there was, as our father told me, and others as well, a final effort to wipe the Cathar heresy out of the count's lands, and at the same time, enrich the Church and those who helped her by seizing the lands of all those who followed the Cathar faith. Our father, whose name was Arnaud, told me that he was willing to die at the stake for his faith, but he had you to think of. Then he learned from a loyal housemaid that your mother intended to denounce him to the Inquisition. He decided that it would be better to take you and flee through the mountains to the south. The two of you rode through those mountain passes in winter, barely escaping with your lives. Our father left you with a family in Catalonia because he was being pursued. He told me that they were willing to raise you, and he left a sum of money with them for that purpose.'" Raimon paused, breathless.

"And did he?" asked Isaac.

"No," said Raimon. "After I had been there for a year or so, I overheard them having a serious conversation about me. I think it was a hard year, and money was scarce. They were speaking of their nephew, who had been their heir, and how my arrival had affected his prospects. My foster mother said that she knew my actual father would never send the money that he promised, and that their plans for me should not depend on that. In the end they left me three hundred *sous,* and the land and little house went to the nephew. I cannot imagine they were lying, for they thought they were alone in the house."

"The interesting question is whether your father lied to your brother, or your brother is lying to you. But please, continue. This is an interesting tale."

"He went on to say that he did not know where our father went in the seven or eight years between leaving me in Catalonia and meeting Guillem's mother in France, but that his life was one of a man in hiding from an implacable enemy."

"Who was his implacable enemy?" asked Isaac.

"My mother, one Raimunda, he told me. Apparently she sent out men to find him, gain his confidence, and then bring him to the Inquisitors. He went on to explain that certain valuable family property had been seized by Raimunda's family to which I have the clearest claim."

"And he wishes a sizeable share but cannot claim it as younger son?"

"He cannot claim it because he is a bastard son," said Raimon. "This so-called brother of mine, Guillem, tells me he is trained in the law and could help me claim my property. He was hoping that if he were successful, I might consent to allow him to stay there with me—perhaps make him steward of the property. Such a responsibility would be most satisfying to him, he says."

"I am glad to have heard this story," said Isaac, "for otherwise I was being asked to believe that two men who were completely unconnected resembled each other like two seeds in an apple, and that it was by sheer chance that they arrived in the same city at the same time. If, however, they were brothers, and the poorer one had means of knowing the richer one's whereabouts, it was not such a mystery."

"You think he sought me out?"

"I am sure of it," said Isaac. "What do you know of your family?"

"Nothing. My father was known as Foraster, the foreigner, and I was called Raimon Foraster. My mother he called by everything but her name, although he referred to her most often as 'that rich harlot, your mother.'"

"You didn't ask your foster parents what they had been told about your parents?"

"Not that I remember," said Raimon. "I remember being happy living with them even though one day my father disappeared."

"Were you upset by his disappearance?"

"I don't think so. I became as it were my foster parents' son, although the name Foraster stuck to me. After a while, I think I stopped trying to remember the old life and concentrated on making something of the new. Three years before the death of the old king, before His Majesty took the throne, I married a young widow with a small son. I had known her since I arrived in the town and would have married her earlier if her parents had allowed it. She was a good and lovely woman, and owned some meadows and vineyards. Ten or twelve years later she inherited property around here. Since it had been long neglected and was more in need of work and attention, we leased the land we had in the west and we came here. We worked hard, and we prospered. I never thought of my original family, or my early life until these dreams started."

"Have you considered the consequences of your history, supposing that it is true?" asked Isaac.

"I have thought of it," said Raimon, "but my conscience is clear and my behavior can withstand scrutiny."

"Could your father be alive?"

"He would surely be an old man if he were."

"There are old men," said Isaac. "But I would suppose that if he were still alive he has come to some settlement with the Church. Might the people who raised you be suspected of heresy?"

"How could they be? They were pious folk and took me off to mass every week without fail. I suppose they knew of my background, and wanted to make sure that no one suspected me of being an infant heretic."

"I think you are vulnerable to such accusations now that this Guillem has arrived in your life. I think also that you need a better confidant in these matters and a stronger protector than I am as you wade into this swamp."

"What do you suggest that I do?"

"If I were you, I would talk it over with the bishop, who has a very keen sense of the politically possible. And in the meantime, we must try to restore your strength to you. I can tell from the touch of your hands and from feeling your arm that you have lost weight. And there is a tremor of exhaustion in your body—I can hear it in your voice as well as feel it. Things grow worse, do they not?"

"I feel ill, Master Isaac. Or weary, too weary to live, as if these terrible dreams will pull me down to my death. The arrival of my brother with his foul tale has been the last blow. How could my dreams be that wrong? In them, she is the betrayed, the helpless, the one who reaches for me. It is he who is the pursuer, the one who terrifies me. Is it not?"

"It would seem to be," said Isaac. "Think of other things and I will try a new mixture to improve your appetite and soothe your spirits."

＊＝＝ ＝＝＊

2.

"HOW is Your Excellency this morning?" asked Isaac when he had been ushered into the bishop's study.

"My knee troubles me again, in spite of the fine weather," said Berenguer. "Bernat seems to think that I spend too much time sitting and talking to people with complaints, and not enough out in the good air."

"Father Bernat may be right," said Isaac, "but let us examine that leg and see what it tells us."

The bishop's attendant appeared out of the shadows with a footstool for the bishop and a low stool for Isaac to sit on. Isaac found his way to the low stool, reached for His Excellency's foot and began a process of probing and massaging his leg that started with his toes. "They say you are treating Raimon Foraster, Isaac," said the bishop.

"They say true, for once, Your Excellency."

"I came to know him very well when he first moved into this province," said Berenguer. "And as I knew him better, I came to consider him a good man. A pleasant fellow, as well, but a good man. I liked him, Isaac. And I do not like every man I meet in this world. For one reason or another, I have not seen much of him recently," he added. "But I cherish a regard for him."

"I find him a most worthy and upright man, as well," said Isaac. "And an interesting one."

"Did you know that they also say that he is the grandson, or the great-grandson, through his mother's side, of the old Count de Foix? This is not a claim he makes, I hasten to add. We never discussed such things in our conversations."

"And is he?" asked Isaac, working his fingers deep into the muscles of the bishop's calf.

"I did ask him once, and he said that he has no idea. He seemed amused at first, and then perhaps annoyed. He pointed out that as he remembered his father, no count in Christendom would have given his most ill-favored and rebellious female relation to such a man, unless he had been immensely rich, of which Raimon says he saw no sign at all."

"I have suggested to him that he come to see you, Your Excellency," said Isaac. "A man claiming to be his bastard half-brother has turned up on his doorstep, with wild tales of his background. Nothing about the Count de Foix, though."

"Are they true?" asked Berenguer.

"Not entirely, I would think," said Isaac. "Although they might be."

"Perhaps tomorrow, if the weather remains fine, I will ride out to see him," said Berenguer. "On the combined advice of my secretary and my physician."

"Surely not before we are finished looking over the diocesan accounts," said Bernat.

"You are the one who wanted me out in the fresh air, Bernat."

III

Granada: Day One

1.

THERE was little for Yusuf to do on the ship during the seven days it took them to sail to the kingdom of Granada under an embassy flag. Even though they were following the coastline, there was nothing to look at but the dim outline of the shore to starboard from time to time. The members of the Valencian delegation retreated into their cabins in rough weather and spent fine days in earnest discussion with each other. Idle as he was, Yusuf leaned over the side for days on end, attacked alternately by boredom and apprehension, yet they seemed to get no closer to their destination.

In spite of all his hours of watching, when the lookout's cry came, Yusuf was asleep. It jerked him awake, his heart pounding and his stomach lurching uneasily. He rolled out of his hammock and dressed as neatly as he could in the dark. Out on deck, he could see vague shapes on the horizon against the paler sky. It was at once the end of night and the barest beginnings of day. On land, the first bird would be stirring on its perch before breaking the silence of the night; at sea, the sky was beginning to lighten in the east and swallow up the stars, one by one.

"We're almost there," said the junior ship's officer from Valencia with whom he shared a cabin.

"How far is it from the coast to the city?" asked Yusuf.

"You're the one who comes from the city," said the officer. "I've never been there."

"I haven't been there for seven years," said Yusuf. "And when we left we went by land."

"I don't like land journeys," said the officer, speaking with the full world-weary experience of his fifteen years in the world. "I'll be staying with the ship. But I think it's a day or two's hard ride to get there."

"I hope the ambassador knows the way," said Yusuf.

"You'll be met," said his informant. "They'll have a crowd of guards and high officials in fancy clothes waiting at the port to take you up there. And I'll be sitting here until the rest of you come back. With my luck they won't even let me go ashore," he grumbled and went off to see to his responsibilities.

Yusuf considered this information with some alarm. He straightened the tunic he was wearing for travel, brushing it vigorously with his hands to remove the dust and dirt. It didn't help. He knew that he looked more like an impoverished student than a member of the royal court. Any royal court. And the sword hanging at his side looked very much at odds with his unwarlike garb. In his chest, stowed away somewhere beneath the decks, he had some better clothing, but it would be impossible to find it now.

He wondered if they would bring him a horse. With great misgivings he had left his mare at the royal stables in Barcelona, to be returned to Girona as soon as possible. He had been advised by his trusted friend, the sergeant, that even though no one would object to her being transported all that way to Granada, she would not enjoy the voyage, and if it were too long or stormy, she might not survive. "Leave her," said Domingo, "as a pledge you will return, at least to see us. And perhaps the next time you go back to Granada, it will be by land."

Or if they did not bring him a horse, he hoped it would at least be a respectable mule. He saw himself, at the back of the procession, riding a baggage donkey all the way to Granada.

His family will be expecting a courtier from His Majesty's palace to return to them and would wonder at his shabby, clerklike appearance, he thought. If he still had a family, he added to himself, and fought back a sudden rush of tears to his eyes. "Please," he murmured to the wind that buffeted the ship's side, "let them not all be dead, let Zeynab still be alive, and my mother." But standing in this galley flying the flag of an Aragonese royal embassy, fast approaching Granada, the country of his birth, he hardly knew to whom he was praying for mercy.

As they approached nearer, the land he saw rising up in front of him looked strange and forbidding. Cliffs jutted out of a sea that seemed somehow unrelated to the one he had left. Then the first officer cried out; his command was echoed back by the boatswain, and Yusuf, now experienced in these matters, headed back to the officer's quarters in the stern. Sailors who had been lounging peacefully, talking, laughing, and in some cases occupied in small tasks suddenly leapt to their feet and tightly controlled chaos broke out. The sails were lowered; the crews set their oars and the steady pull into port began.

Yusuf went into the cabin he shared with two junior officers and packed his few loose possessions into a bundle. He was going to wait in here, safe in the stuffy darkness, until the sound of oars being shipped and anchors hitting the water told him that they had arrived.

WHEN he ventured out, the world was filled with silver light, and the sun was near the point of rising. The ship was riding at anchor and a small fleet of longboats were approaching rapidly. He looked over the side to watch them, and as the first boat executed a neat turn and pulled up alongside the ladder, one of the oarsmen looked up. "Welcome to Al-Andalus," he said with a grin.

"I thank you for your courtesy," replied Yusuf, stumbling slightly over the unaccustomed words. "I am glad to be home."

His reply was greeted with a shout of appreciation and amusement and drew the attention of the ambassador's secretary. "Are you sure, my lord," he murmured, "that you should be joking with common sailors now that you are home?"

"My lord?" asked Yusuf, effectively silenced.

Their arrival in the city of Granada took as long as the junior officer had predicted. Yusuf's chest, containing his extra wardrobe and his books, some of them gifts from Isaac, and some from the bishop, was loaded safely on a donkey, as were chests of gifts from the king for the emir. It was a large group by the time they set out. Along with Yusuf were the ambassador, an august nobleman from Valencia, and his small train as well as a party of royal officials from Granada and their guards, whose task it was to conduct them safely to the emir's palace. The nobleman was there officially to escort the boy, but the king had entrusted other matters to be dealt with to him as well. As soon as they were on their way, the ambassador fell into conversation with the head of the royal officials from Granada, so as to waste as little time as possible.

Yusuf found himself riding beside a young man from Granada who looked at him oddly from time to time. "I know you," he said at last. "You are Yusuf ibn Hasan."

"I am," said Yusuf, looking warily at the young man.

"I'm sorry that I don't remember you, but everyone assures me that I know you."

"That means that I must know you, too," said Yusuf. "But you don't seem familiar. May I ask who you are?"

"At the moment, who *I* am is very unimportant," he said, smiling to take the sting out of his words. "You are the important person here today. You speak our language rather oddly," added the young man. "One moment you sound like a scholar and the next like a common soldier."

"Where I have been, I had little choice in the people I could speak to in our language," said Yusuf. "I was close to forgetting it when a very scholarly man helped me with it. Otherwise, unfortunately, it is the language of slaves."

"I am sure that His Highness will forgive you any slips in your speech. But what an interesting and difficult life you must have had in the past seven years. Tell me—how did you manage to save yourself? We were all told you had been killed."

"And have you been sent to find out what I have been up to?" asked Yusuf. "Do I really know you?"

He burst into laughter. "You really do. And yes, of course I was sent to find out what you have been up to. My lord the Emir Muhammad, like his honoured father before him, may Allah smile upon his face in heaven, has many enemies. Although we are concerned lest you might be plotting against us, we do not wish to plot against you. You are among friends and family now."

Yusuf was to remember those words with uncomfortable clarity.

THE sun was rising into a cloudless sky when they had left the coast, heading inland for the city of Granada. But as they climbed the road northward, a fresh breeze sprang up and banks of dark, rapidly moving clouds rolled in. "Did you bring a cloak?" asked the young man, after surveying the skies around them.

"It is tied to the back of my saddle," said Yusuf. "But surely I will not need it." As he was speaking, the first of a series of rainstorms hit them.

"I think you might," said his companion. "I will help you untie it."

"I remember my homeland as warm and sunny," said Yusuf, a little while later. He was shivering with the cold in spite of his cloak, and bending his head down into the wind and the rain.

The young man laughed in genuine amusement. "Sometimes it is," he said. "In the summer, especially. Very warm and very sunny, as you will see. In spring, though, even this late in the year, hardly a day goes by without at least one shower. And it can be very cold. But children often remember the good days better than the bad."

The road wound upward, twisting and turning along the slopes leading up to the mountains that loomed ahead of them and disappeared in the distance away to the east. When the clouds blew away from the face of the sun, Yusuf looked around him with astonishment. "What is that?" he said, pointing at the mountains to their right.

"Snow," said the young man. "They say that there was a heavy snowfall up there a few days ago. You never noticed the snow on the mountaintops before?"

"I must have been a most—" He searched for the word. "A most unobservant child. I remember flowers, and a fountain with a big pool in the courtyard, and lemon trees, and figs, and other wonderful things. My mother, and my sisters."

"All Granada knows of the Lady Noor's beauty, wisdom, and kindness. I have met her many times. What did your sisters look like?" asked the young man casually.

For a while Yusuf could not answer for the relief that washed over him like a warm ocean. For the first time since he had heard that he would be coming here, someone had casually confirmed that his mother was still alive. "Ayesha is young," he said at last, "smaller than I am, and very serious. She has long, dark hair that even then—and I think she cannot have been more than four or five when I last saw her—was very long and shiny. My other sister is a little younger than I am, and very clever and beautiful." He closed his eyes with an effort at memory. "Zeynab has big eyes. They are light in color, like the color of new leather or the carved wood screens over our windows, and she has long hair that curls all over her head if she does not remember to oil it carefully when she bathes, and then my mother gets cross at her and says she will never have a good husband. I wonder if she did? No—she would still be too young to marry."

"I think she will have a good husband," said the young man with unabated good humor. "Allow me to present myself. I am Nasr ibn Umar, I am of your family as well, on your mother's side, and as soon as may be permitted, I am to be Zeynab's husband and your brother-in-law. Welcome home, brother."

THE afternoon was well advanced when the road made its final turn on the climb up the side of the hills and began its descent into the plain. "Look," said Nasr, bringing his horse to a halt and pointing straight ahead of him. A river glinted in the sun as it wound through the plain, and on its far side, another hill rose sharply upward. On its westward and southerly sides, a city clustered at the foot of the hill, and on its summit stood a fortress of splendid towers and solid walls, looking red in the afternoon sun. "Is it not marvelous?" he asked.

"What is it?" asked Yusuf.

"'What is it?'" repeated Nasr. "The name of the splendid hill is Sabika, and on top of it is the most magnificent fortress in the whole world. It is the Alhambra. It is home, Yusuf."

"And the river?"

"That is the Genil. As we ride down and closer, you will see the Darro. It comes down from the far side of the Sabika, from the northeast, as this does from the southeast, so that the city and the fortress are bathed in water."

"How long will it take us to get there? It seems only a minute's ride away."

"It is longer than that," said Nasr. "But we will be there long before they have to come to seek us with torches. If we are too slow, we will stay down in the city and enter the Alhambra in the morning. But I think we will be there before sunset."

"Why does it look so red?"

"Because the soil here is red, the towers are built of stone and brick, and the bricks are red. But now that we have reached the plain, let us go ahead a little toward the city gates and let our horses stretch their legs. That is my brother's horse you are riding. He has another, and you are welcome to this one as long as you need him."

But it had been a very long day already, and Nasr's joking manner of speech and rapid delivery required a great deal of concentration to follow. "Certainly," said Yusuf, yawning, not at all sure what Nasr had been talking about.

Then his companion's mount surged ahead as if he had been fighting his rider all through the day of intermittent rain, treacherous, narrow mountain paths, precipitous climbs, and even more precipitous descents in order to have a chance to gallop at his fastest pace.

Yusuf's horse lowered his head, stretched out his neck and went in pursuit, intent on catching up. They passed the Aragonese ambassador and the grave men who rode with him, almost knocking them onto the ground; they flew by the courtiers who had come down to escort them; but when they passed the advance guard, Yusuf heard the bark of a command, and four horsemen galloped up beside them. With the rush of wind in his ears and the noise of hoofbeats drowning out their words, Yusuf had no idea what they were saying, but what they meant was clear enough. Nasr reined in his mount, and Yusuf followed suit.

"I am sorry," said Nasr, laughing. "I meant no harm to my cousin. I wished only to see how he would react to a challenge such as this."

"I am sure Lord Yusuf will race you as often as you like," said the captain. "Closer to the city and where the ground is more suitable for such pursuits. Fortunately he seems to have become a skilled horseman while he has been away. I would be interested in knowing what you were hoping to do, aside from forcing some rather weary travelers to move at speeds they were not expecting at the end of a long day." He gathered up his reins and rode back to speak in low tones to the ambassador.

"Who is he that he speaks so plainly to you?" asked Yusuf.

"He is another of the family," said Nasr. "A cousin of mine, certainly, and perhaps of yours as well. He will be leading our royal lord's armies one of these days. But he must learn like everyone else the trials of being a junior officer." Nasr shook his head. "But he is right. I had not thought that the entire group would hasten to keep up with us. It was ill done on my part."

But Yusuf thought that the discomfort written momentarily on his face was anger rather than remorse.

NONETHELESS, the group moved at a slightly faster pace after that, and the distance across the fertile river valley melted away before them. They wound their way somewhat westward, into the sun that now slanted into their eyes, dazzling them. Then the road turned north and suddenly the city walls were straight ahead. Yusuf looked up and gasped. The hill and the fortress were scarlet in the light, as if they had been hung with brilliant red silk.

"It is astonishing," said Yusuf, but Nasr seemed to be concentrating on his own affairs, and appeared not to hear him. The captain of the guard took over his education, as it were. He led them through the streets of the city, pointing out the old royal palace, and the stronghold that had been built by former rulers.

"You must wonder," he said, "why they chose to build on these small rises of land when they had such an excellent defensive hill right in front of them."

"Indeed," said Yusuf.

"But those men, who were not of the family of the Nasrids, our great sovereigns, had never applied themselves to the problem of how to bring water to the top of a hill that had none except for what can be collected from the rainfall."

Yusuf blinked. It had been a long day, and while water was an important subject, the language of water engineering was not part of his Arabic vocabulary, and the effort of trying to understand what the captain was saying was the end of him. His eyelids drooped, the clamor and activity of the city faded from sight and hearing, and he began to dream that he was riding through a land where the trees were bright blue and red, and the pavements yellow and purple.

"And this is the Darro itself," said a voice loud in his ear. He straightened up with a jerk. The horses were crossing a solidly built bridge over a fast-moving river toward a massively steep slope that had been cleared of anything that could be used by a hostile invader as cover. Their path led up to the fortress on top of the hill and was protected by a solid wall that rose above them on their right. The wall was further protected by a

hexagonal guard tower at the river end of the hill. As their train
of horses, mules, and donkeys toiled up the slope, a cry went up
from the western tower. The captain acknowledged it with a
silent wave of his hand.

The wall and the pathway they were following ended in a
ramp leading up to a gate in the side of a massive tower in the
north wall of the stronghold. Yusuf was now following along
behind Nasr; his weariness had fled, replaced by a feeling of
sick apprehension. Nasr rode through the open gateway and
disappeared; Yusuf felt as alone as he ever had been in his
short, eventful life.

2.

THE interior of the tower was lit by defensive slits set high
up in the walls. Once his eyes had adjusted to the relative
dimness, he saw that two heavily armed men were standing in
front of him, one at each side of his horse's head. He was in a
rectangular space just wide enough for his horse to turn comfortably to the right and walk two paces forward, turn sharply
to the left and stop beside a stand for dismounting. Disdaining
the proffered hand of assistance, Yusuf jumped down, valiantly
pretending that he was not stiff and sore from a hard day's riding. The men who had brought him thus far backed away with
the horse, and two more escorted Yusuf forward around another
bend toward a gate leading into the fortress.

No one would enter this tower without a great many people
knowing he was there, thought Yusuf, decidedly impressed by
the display. The heavy door ahead swung open, and he was outside again in the red glow of the evening sun, surrounded by
very military-looking towers, high walls, and a camp full of
soldiers, busy at their everyday activities. It was a good-sized
army camp, but he was puzzled by where the palace could be
hidden—not to say the house that he had lived in with his family, which he remembered as being quite large.

"Is the palace in here?" asked Yusuf.

One of the guards escorting him looked baffled by his question, but the other one shook his head and pointed at a farther tower in the wall just ahead. This one was somewhat easier of access, although Yusuf noted that the entrance door and the exit were staggered so that an arrow fired into one could not possibly pass through the other. He half-expected to pick up two fresh guards as he came through this one, but the two stayed with him, down a few steps, and across an open space planted at the edges with trees and bushes. Somewhere behind those trees, he could hear bursts of laughter and sounds of conversation. It was the noise of normal life, and it was reassuring.

Then they climbed more steps into a paved garden filled with scented flowers and fruit trees, some still with a few blossoms clinging to their branches. "We must leave you here, Lord Yusuf," said the guard on his right, bowing low and backing away a step or two before turning and marching smartly out. Yusuf watched them leave with a sense of dismay.

"And you must be the lost one who has been restored to us," said a voice that seemed to tinkle with laughter like small bells.

He whirled around in the direction of the voice. "I am Yusuf ibn Hasan," he replied, at a loss for a better answer. "Sir." Standing in front of him was a young man, or perhaps a boy, dressed in the somewhat long tunic and trousers that many in his escort had been wearing. They looked very warm and comfortable on this distinctly chilly evening. His dark hair was long and he wore it neatly dressed, hanging down his back.

"I need no titles," he said with a giggle. "I am, perhaps, almost of your rank, or perhaps the same, but certainly not above you. But come, this is a distinctly public sort of place, and His Majesty is almost ready to receive you. We had better move on." He turned and headed toward another set of stairs that led to a patio with fountains and an elegant pool, and once again, flowers and trees. "There now, we're almost in the palace," said the lad, trotting up another set of stairs, down a paved path, and entering a magnificent hall. "My lord Ridwan will meet you here," he said. "You are greatly honored, since no one is completely sure—well, I shouldn't gossip."

"Is this where His Majesty . . ."

"Oh, no. His Majesty sees ordinary citizens in here twice a week, just as if he weren't a great king, and listens to their complaints and gives judgment. Important people are seen right in the palace itself." Suddenly he straightened up. His mocking grin was replaced with a look of grave contemplation, and he bowed low.

"Do I?" whispered Yusuf, not sure who this was.

"It would be tactful," murmured his guide.

Yusuf followed suit.

"Faraj, I told you to send someone to me as soon as our guest arrived. This is our guest, is it not?"

"May I present Yusuf ibn Hasan, Lord Ridwan?" asked the young man. "He has only this moment arrived through the gate."

"Excellent," said Ridwan. "I am fortunate enough to be His Majesty's vizier, Lord Yusuf."

Yusuf bowed again.

"His Majesty has asked that you be brought to him at once."

"But, my lord," said Yusuf, stammering slightly over the words, "I am in no fit state to approach His Majesty. I have not even had a chance to wash."

"I am glad to discover that you have not lost your sense of what is owing to one's family and one's ruler," said Ridwan, smiling benevolently. "But His Majesty understands that you have just dismounted. Follow me."

And the little procession of three, Ridwan, tall, well fed, and splendidly dressed in silks; Yusuf in a dark, dusty, mud-splattered tunic that at its best could never have been considered magnificent; and the enigmatic young Faraj, looking rather like a small peacock, made its way past guards and servants, through corridors, in and out of another patio lined in marble that glowed in the low rays of the sun, and into the last, and most beautiful patio of all, with its perfectly proportioned pool and plantings of lemons. But Ridwan had seen it all before, as had Faraj, and they hastened along until they reached the hall where Muhammad V sat in state with some of his advisors.

The sun, now very low in the sky, poured in the windows to the west and straight into Yusuf's eyes. He blinked and narrowed his eyes to control the dazzling effect of those rays. It did not help. To his great distress, he could not, in that high-vaulted splendid hall, see who might be his cousin. But under his feet was a welcoming carpet, richly colored, and having no other option, he flung himself down on it onto his knees, with his forehead touching the ground, his hands forward, and prayed that someone would rescue him.

Then he heard an amused voice saying, "And everyone assured me that you would walk in here in your boots like a Christian barbarian and try to take me by the hand, Yusuf. Rise, cousin. You are somewhat late in returning from your voyage to Valencia, but we forgive you. Come forward. We wanted to see you before anyone else had a chance to do so, but were kept here by business of the state."

Yusuf rose as gracefully as he could and moved forward.

"Stop there. Now turn your head a little toward the sun. There, you see, Ridwan? Is it not as they said?" He turned back to Yusuf. "Can you speak?" he asked.

"I can, my lord emir, although I do not speak with the grace and dignity of Your Majesty. I have had little chance to speak our tongue in the last seven years."

"They tell us that you sound either like a scholar or an old soldier when you speak, but we will go into that later. You will dine with us, but first, you will be given a chance to bathe and change into clothing that is more suitable."

"Thank you, Your Majesty," said Yusuf, bowing, and was hurried out before he had a chance to say anything more.

FARAJ scooped him up as the doors to the throne room closed behind him. "I will show you to the baths," he said, snapping his fingers. A boy of about ten, who had been sitting in a dark corner of the room, scrambled to his feet and came over. "This is Abdullah. He is yours, a gift of the emir. He knows the court and will keep you from getting lost."

"But my mother—" said Yusuf.

"You will see the Lady Noor tomorrow," said Faraj. "She has been told that you are here. She sends her greetings and wishes you to know that your arrival brings her great joy. But you will be staying here in the palace for now."

"And my clothing—"

"That is taken care of," said Faraj. "The baths are through that corridor and down a few steps. Abdullah will take you. My lord Ridwan needs me."

"What is your position?" asked Yusuf.

"I am his secretary," said Faraj. "Well—actually I am assistant secretary to his secretary. It is a very busy post," said Faraj, and hastened away.

"And you are to be my assistant, Abdullah?" asked Yusuf.

The boy bowed.

"I am certainly in need of assistance. At the moment I am very confused."

"Lord Ridwan, who is vizier, has several secretaries," observed Abdullah. "Faraj is the least important of five assistants to Lord Ridwan's least important assistant secretary. People see so much of him because he is the fastest on his feet, and so he runs all the errands, Lord Yusuf."

"I can see that you are going to be extremely useful, Abdullah. Now, where are the baths?"

Almost two hours later, Yusuf emerged from the baths. He had soaked in hot water, been scrubbed with rough towels, dried, refreshed in cool water, dried, then his tired body was massaged with sweet oils and wrapped in a sheet. They left him stretched on a bench lined with soft cushions in a quiet nook and he promptly fell asleep.

He was awakened by an urgent voice in his ear and a hand shaking his shoulder. "Lord Yusuf, you must wake up. It is time."

"Time for what?" he said groggily.

"Time to dine with His Majesty."

At that, he remembered. Where he was, what he was doing, who he was staying with. And he sat up, blinked, and focused his eyes on the small boy in front of him who was holding an armful of brilliantly colored garments. Abdullah.

"Your clothes, lord," said the boy.

"Those aren't mine," said Yusuf.

"I was instructed to give them to you and to help you put them on," said Abdullah. "And to hurry you, if I could. His Majesty is ready to dine."

"And I am ready to die of hunger," said Yusuf, getting to his feet.

THE meal was, Yusuf decided, something between a state banquet and a cozy supper at home. It was held in the hall of a palace that had been built onto the official residence of the emir, adjoining the patio of the pool, but this hall looked onto its own courtyard. The doors onto the courtyard were open, allowing the guests to see its intricate and beautifully shaped fountain. The flagstone paving was interrupted by broad sunken flower beds filled with heavily scented flowers, forming a brilliant carpet that perfumed the cold, night air. Braziers had been placed discreetly around the hall for warmth.

The lavish tunic and trousers that Abdullah had supplied him with were as warm and as comfortable as Yusuf had enviously supposed when he had first seen men wearing them. The dishes that were laid out for them were delectable, and the splashing of the fountain was joined by the music from a group of skilled performers.

Once he had satisfied his first hunger, his natural curiosity returned and he set himself to studying the guests and the ways of the court. The diners were arranged, more or less, in a semicircle with the emir in the center, facing the courtyard directly. Yusuf had been placed directly opposite the Aragonese ambassador, who was there with three lesser nobles, all chatting together in Valencian-accented speech, as if no one else in the room could understand them. He assumed that they had been placed in seats of honor, but until he could verify that, he would simply wait and observe. The vizier, Ridwan, he recognized, of course. He was too striking a figure to have forgotten within a few hours. He was placed close to the emir, and seemed to feel that a state banquet was a perfect opportunity to discuss matters of state. On the other side of the emir, not far away from the ambassador, was another distinguished-looking man, soberly but richly dressed. He held a cup containing wine mixed with water, but did not drink; he listened intently to the conversation between the emir and his vizier, without taking part, and otherwise his eyes, sharp and keen-looking, darted from person to person around the table, as curious as Yusuf's, until Yusuf felt them locked on his face and person, and turned away in confusion.

"Yes, lord?" whispered a small voice beside him.

"Are you still here?" asked Yusuf in an equally low voice.

"Yes, lord," said Abdullah. "I thought your lordship looked as if he desired something."

"Only to know something," said Yusuf. "Who is that keen-eyed man in the dark green tunic, who holds a cup of wine but does not drink?"

"It is His Majesty's secretary, he who holds the keys to all the records of the kingdom, and all the petitions and legal documents, and makes sure that His Majesty sees everything that he needs to see. There are those who say that if he were not here, the kingdom could not be ruled. He knows the history of every man in the kingdom, and they say he is writing it all down," whispered Abdullah.

"And his name?"

"Ibn al-Khatib. He is very famous, lord."

"Why does he not touch his cup?"

"His Majesty the emir knows well the stricture of the Prophet against wine, but allows himself a small amount of the substance mixed in water on these occasions," said Abdullah piously. "They say he dislikes drunkenness profoundly, and prosecutes it strongly among the people. See how he frowns that the Christian ambassador calls for wine and refuses the pitcher containing the water."

At this the music changed, and a troop of dancers entered the patio and began to form sinuous patterns back and forth around the fountain. Abdullah retired into the shadows again, and Yusuf watched the display with fascination. First one, and then another would step forward and perform the complicated movements of the dance; it was as if, thought Yusuf rather sleepily, the luxuriant spring blooms of the flowers in the sunken beds had leapt out of their moist soil and danced.

A voice murmured in his ear that His Majesty would like a word with him if he would come this way. Yusuf scrambled hastily to his feet, rather like Abdullah, and followed the dim figure ahead of him to the place next to the ruler.

"You look much cleaner, cousin Yusuf," said Muhammad. "And smell much better, too. When you entered our court, you seemed to have brought your horse with you."

"It was to my great shame that I was brought into the court in no fit condition to pay my respects to my lord and emir," said Yusuf.

"What do you think of our court, Yusuf?" asked the emir.

"I am overwhelmed by its splendor, Your Majesty," said Yusuf. "I have never seen anything like it."

"Is it more splendid than the court of Aragon?"

"It is," said Yusuf. "I have been in four palaces in the kingdom of Aragon: Barcelona, Perpignan, Vilafranca, and Valencia, and although they are buildings to be marvelled at, never in my life have I seen such beauty, grace, and splendor as I have seen here."

Muhammad looked pleased. "That is gratifying to hear, cousin. The splendor is not ours, of course, but our father's, and our uncle's, and all the kings of the Nasrids before us who built these, but we shall try to maintain the work they have started. We are building a new palace around this courtyard—it is a pretty courtyard, is it not? Although it is rather small. We particularly like the curious fountain with its charming lions. It will be the center and the inspiration of the new palace. The work starts soon. We are now in discussion with the architects."

"I am sure that it will be a more beautiful edifice than those buildings it replaces, Your Majesty," said Yusuf.

"We shall not destroy, except for a wall here or there," said Muhammad. "That palace must stay," he added, pointing to a structure beyond the courtyard, "for that is where we keep our brothers and their mother, where their every move can be watched. We have an obligation to protect our father's second wife, even if she seems to feel that her only duty in life is to replace us on the throne with one of her sons."

"It is noble of you to treat her well, Your Majesty," said Yusuf.

"There are monarchs who keep wild and ferocious beasts. We keep Maryam. Besides, she is very rich and wields a certain amount of power among the people. Some of the people." He paused and suddenly burst into a flow of speech so rapid Yusuf could scarcely follow, except that he was speaking as one boy to another, rather than as monarch to subject. "I remember you now, Yusuf. I have been thinking and thinking since I first heard you were alive. You were the quiet little boy who rode well, and listened to everything, and asked questions I couldn't answer." He frowned and resumed his invisible mantle of power. "Now that we are emir, no one dares to question us, but you still listen as if your life depended on it," he added, and smiled sweetly.

"From time to time, Your Majesty, it has. I do not remember being like that when I lived here, in this paradise, but what you say must be true, and it has been very helpful for me."

"Will Aragon attack us?" asked Muhammad in the same quiet tones. "Here in our paradise?"

"I do not know, Your Majesty. Aragon is much occupied with troubles in Sardinia, and is concerned about her borders with Castile. His Majesty Pedro of Aragon made great haste to summon me as soon as he received the news of your letter. As quickly as it could be arranged, I was on a ship to Granada. I know little of his mind, but his actions seem to be that of

a monarch who wishes to improve his relations with the kingdom of Granada."

"Then why did he not send you home before?"

"He has known of my existence for less than two summers,
Your Majesty. He knew that I had come with my father to Valencia, for I was to be a page at his court, I believe, but he, too,
had been told that I had perished in the attack on my father."

"But your father did die in the attack?"

"Oh, yes, Your Majesty," said Yusuf, turning pale. "My father died right at my feet, holding me behind him with his
arm. The floor was wet with his blood. The attackers must
have been interrupted, because they fled, and my father gave
me a letter for the king of Aragon that he had written at your
royal father's command, Your Majesty. He told me to deliver
it, but it took me a very long time to find the king. It was not
until I was able to give His Majesty the letter that anyone
knew who I was, except that I was a friendless boy named
Yusuf. They had apparently searched for me, but I had run
away, as my father told me before he died that I must."

"You are possessed of a priceless quality, Yusuf."

"A priceless quality, Your Majesty?"

"Something that, if it accompanies virtue and courage, is
the most valuable gift that God grants to a man. My good secretary, who has been listening to this conversation while pretending to sleep, knows what it is, do you not, Ibn al-Khatib?"

"Pure luck, Your Majesty," said the pleasantly grave-looking
man at his side.

IV
Granada: Day Two

1.

YUSUF awoke the next morning in a strange room with sunlight pouring in on his face. He sat up and winced. Yesterday's fourteen or fifteen hours in the saddle, with only the briefest of rest stops, had left his back and legs stiff and sore. He looked around. He was in a tiny, luxuriously furnished, completely unfamiliar bedchamber. The last thing he remembered clearly was sitting at the banquet, suffering from an overpowering desire for sleep, but knowing that he would have to wait until the emir retired from the festivities before he, too, could find himself a bed. Abdullah must have brought him here, but he was not sure exactly where this bedchamber was.

A hanging that seemed to double as a door and a wall for his chamber was pushed aside by a small hand, and Abdullah came into the room. He was carrying a pitcher and a bowl from which a most appetizing smell arose. He set these down in the small space between the bed and the curtain.

"I bear a message, lord. When my lord has had a chance to wash and dress and break his fast, his noble mother would be honored to receive him," said Abdullah.

Yusuf laughed. "I cannot remember my mother ever speaking quite like that to me before," he said.

"But in those days Lord Yusuf was only a little boy," said Abdullah.

"I can see that whoever chose you to look after me did so because he thought you would make a good teacher for me."

Abdullah looked momentarily confused and then smiled and bowed. "Your clothing is in the other room."

Yusuf looked around the hanging and saw that he had been sleeping in a small alcove of the chamber, and that by his standards he had been assigned to a spacious apartment. A suit of clothes in a darker shade of blue trimmed with dark red had been spread out to wait for him to awaken. He looked at them uneasily.

To be offered a clean set of clothing suitable for dining with the emir had seemed reasonable to him last night. He did not know where his box had gone, he was unquestionably dirty from travel, and it may have occurred to someone that there was nothing in his box worth considering. Perhaps they had searched his box while he was in the bath and found nothing worthy of the royal court. But who had provided this morning's suit of clothes? What was his status here? Had he a position? Was he to be a student again? Could his mother afford to supply him with food, drink, and clothing? Somehow these questions seemed to be beyond the reach of the little slave, wise as he seemed to be in the ways of the palace.

YUSUF followed Abdullah down a set of stairs that took him out a side door and onto a paved pathway. "Where have I been staying?" he asked.

"At Lord Ridwan's palace," said Abdullah. "But tomorrow, when the Christians leave, you will move into the guest quarters at the palace where they are staying."

"Why am I staying at Lord Ridwan's?"

"I do not know, lord. Perhaps he wished to entertain you."

Since Yusuf had seen almost nothing of the vizier, that seemed unlikely, but he made no further comment.

The Lady Noor now lived with her children and servants in a house not far from the palaces. It was built up against the north wall, a most favored position, Abdullah had assured him, and was only a few minutes walk away from the palace complex.

Those few minutes, however, were the difference between the suffocating formality of the court and the bustling life of a city. For out here, although there were splendid houses here and there, there were also modest ones, and there was a street filled with people. This was where the huge number of civil servants lived required to run the kingdom as well as the even larger numbers of servants, gardeners, craftsmen, and workmen of all kinds needed to run the palaces. There were markets and vendors of grilled meat, syrupy, flavorful drinks, sweetmeats, and honey-filled pastries. Yusuf's spirits rose.

He heard hoofbeats behind him, turned, and saw the emir riding at a fair pace along the road to the east, smiling and waving at the people. "Where is he going?" asked Yusuf, without expecting an answer.

"Riding, to take some exercise," said Abdullah. "His Majesty often rides up to the Generalife on a fine day." He pointed to the northeast. "Your lordship will remember that it is outside the walls."

"I remember no such thing, Abdullah," said Yusuf crossly. "Now where is my mother's house?"

"It is right here, lord. We are outside the door. Shall I knock?"

Yusuf nodded and braced himself.

THE door opened with suspicious promptness. A tall, broad-shouldered man, powerful-looking but running to fat, filled the doorway. "Lord Yusuf," he said, "you are welcome home, master."

His eyes dazzled with the bright light of the street outside, Yusuf could barely make out the features of the man in front of him in the dark hallway, but the voice was one he still heard in his dreams, he realized. "Ali!" he said. "You are still here."

"Where else would I be?" asked the big man. "Who else would protect the Lady Noor now? And what are you doing here?" he added, looking down at Abdullah, who had crowded around his temporary master to clear his path.

"Lord Yusuf has come to pay a visit to his honored mother," said Abdullah.

"Enter, Lord Yusuf," said Ali, and stepped back into the dark hall to allow them to do so.

He was facing, at the other end of the hallway, a brilliant rectangle of light. "So early," said a voice from that direction and a dark shape filled the dazzling rectangle. "Yusuf, my son? Is it you?"

He moved forward, still unable to see anything but a shape outlined in light in front of him. "It is so dark in here," he said at last. "I cannot see you."

"Then come into the courtyard," said the voice, gentle and sweet. "And we can see each other."

IN the sunfilled courtyard, with its small fountain and pretty pool, Yusuf turned to look at his mother. He remembered a tall, slender woman, filled with laughter, delighting in all his accomplishments, and taking great joy from the small matters of living. She was still slender and graceful, but they were now of equal height. Time and sorrow had planted dark hollows under her eyes and thinned her cheeks, but it had not destroyed her beauty.

At that moment, a child, a small, frightened-looking girl dressed in a coarse brown tunic, hurried in, holding a great pitcher with some difficulty in her small hands. As soon as she set it down, his mother gestured at Abdullah and waved her away.

"Now we will have a few moments of peace. Why do you look at me like that?" she asked. "Have I changed so much?"

"You have not changed at all, Mother," he said. "Except that you look a little weary, and you are not nearly so tall."

She laughed, as she always had at his conversation. "I am a little weary. I have been awake most of the night praying that you would remember me. I am as tall as I ever was, Yusuf, but you have grown. What a fine young man you have grown into.

I can hardly see my little boy in you, except that in some ways you have not changed." She regarded him seriously. "You look more like your father than you did before. And that is excellent, for he was a handsome man. Come, sit with me by the fountain and we will talk. Then I will allow the others to come in and share my delight in your company."

There were rugs along with large and comfortable cushions by the pool, where someone could sit at ease and dabble his fingers in the water. They settled next to each other. Ali looked into the courtyard and was sent off again with a whisk of his mother's hand.

"I had thought that when I returned I would stay here with you," said Yusuf. "But I was given no choice. I was kept at the palace until we had eaten, and then taken to Lord Ridwan's house."

His mother's voice dropped. "They are not sure what to make of you, Yusuf. At first they feared that reports that you were alive were part of an elaborate trick, for one of the members of your father's party had brought back a most touching account of your poor body lying there, your throat cut, beside your father. When they heard that you were alive and well, and apparently living in the court of the Christian king, I did not know what to think. Nor did the emir. The man who testified to your death swore that you must be an impostor, who used this trick to obtain a position in court."

"Who is he?" asked Yusuf. "I would like to speak to him."

"Unfortunately, he is dead," said his mother fiercely. "For I, too, would have liked to speak to him, and to accuse him, and to know that he suffered a sore penalty for his lies. But God who is the great judge of all will judge him not only for his betrayal, but for the agony he made a mother suffer."

"Dead?"

"So says his widow. Perhaps he has merely fled, and his family has buried a sack of refuse. But you can understand that they wished to see you, and speak to you, and make up their minds whether you are indeed my Yusuf."

"And have they?"

"Abdullah, who is very clever and has sharp ears, told Ali that the emir is impressed with how awkwardly you speak. If you had been sent here by the Christian king to spy on us, he believes that you would have been better coached."

"Once he decides, will I be able to move into the house here with you?"

"I am just a woman, a poor widow, with no power, my son," said his mother, sounding neither uncertain nor downtrodden. "But I think His Majesty wishes to keep a close eye on you, and on those who approach you. His excuse is that he does not want you to become as weak as his own two brothers."

"What is wrong with them?" asked Yusuf. "In the Aragonese empire, the king is plagued by having strong brothers, not weak ones."

"Well, the emir's brothers by Queen Maryam have always lived with their mother, even after their father, Yusuf, our most royal and open-hearted emir, died. When Muhammad inherited his throne, he decided that it would be best to keep them all together. Now they are all locked up in her palace to keep them out of trouble. But the emir says that it was living with the women all these years that made Isma'il so effeminate, and that he would never allow a boy to stay in the women's quarters until he was thirteen."

"What happened to his father, the Emir Yusuf?" asked Yusuf. "We heard many different accounts of his death."

"Our great emir died a martyr's death through assassination while he was in the mosque, at his prayers, on the day of the feast of the breaking of the fast," said Lady Noor in a troubled voice. "It was a great blow for us, since he had always been a steadfast friend."

"Who would do such a thing?"

"They say it was a madman. There are those who prefer to see someone else's hand guiding the knife, but such things are said whenever an act of this kind occurs," she added. "If someone of the court had a hand in it, most people would pick the old queen, the Lady Maryam, who must have hoped that with the help of her powerful relatives, her son Isma'il would become emir."

"Is he effeminate?"

"A little, they say. He has long, beautiful hair that he wears straight down his back, plaited with silk of the most brilliant colors. But many men are proud of their appearance and what else has he do with his time? He is no scholar, they say."

"I cannot imagine a life like that," said Yusuf.

"Nor could I," said his mother. "Of course, I think it is more likely that it is living with Maryam that makes the boys like that, not just living around women, but then, my opinion counts for little in this new world."

"Is she so terrible?"

"She is horrifyingly terrible. And rich. Too rich to ignore, with powerful brothers, and a son-in-law who is related to the emir through his uncle. If he were as wise as he is merciful," she said, "he would execute them all. They will cause him nothing but trouble."

"He mentioned the same thing to me, and I don't understand it. It seems to me that his claim to the throne is as clear as a claim can be."

"It is indeed. Not only did his father, Yusuf, pick him as heir, but he also explained why and had it written down and proclaimed. He is the firstborn legitimate son; he has the wisdom and judgment to rule, and at the time of his father's death, he was of an age to take the throne without a regent to rule for him. It could not be clearer than that, could it?"

"How old am I, mother?" asked Yusuf, abruptly, for suddenly it seemed the most important question in the world.

"How old? Don't you know? Oh, my poor darling Yusuf."

"I'm sure I must have known how old I was before I left, but in the years that I was lost, travelling from Valencia to the north, I forgot, and now not only do I not know the day, I do not know the year, either, of my birth."

"My poor Yusuf," said his mother, looking down into pool, as if her life were transcribed on its rippling waters. "You were born on the sixteenth day just before the dawn in the eighth month of the seven-hundredth and forty-second year of the Hegira. The moon was just past the full, but the night was very dark, for there was a terrible winter storm and your father was away all the day and into the night at the palace, not knowing that his son was about to be born. And that means, by our reckoning, you are close to your fourteenth year, although I believe that in the Christian reckoning of the years, you would be considered somewhat younger."

"How much younger?"

"A few months, my love. When the decision was made that you should leave Granada with your father, you had just completed your sixth year of life and were young to be sent away. There was much discussion over it, I can assure you. There was another storm during that winter, just as fierce as the one when you were born, and during the day and the night that it raged, the idea was born of sending emissaries to Valencia."

"I was just six when we left?"

"No. By the time you left, spring had come and you were six years and a half, almost. It is a miracle you survived that terrible voyage and its aftermath."

"Why did you send me off so young to a foreign court?"

"My dearest, it was not I who sent you away. I wept for weeks before the final decision was made, trying to make them change their minds. But the emir, our royal Yusuf, and our kinsman, had done much for your father, and it was he who wished for a pair of acute ears and of sharp eyes in the Aragonese court. It seemed perfect to them—you were exceptionally clever and observant and the queen, for you were to go to the queen, you know, was delighted. You were to come home after a short time. The emir hoped that the queen would want you back, and that would have been even better for their scheme."

"I was to be an infant spy," said Yusuf, laughing. "I don't think I would have been very useful."

"Perhaps not the first time you went, but then if you had gone back, you would have been even better. But when you reached Valencia, the queen was dying. The next queen hardly lived a year, but by then everyone knew that you were dead."

"How terrible for you," said Yusuf, in a low voice. "But I, too, was convinced that you would be dead by the time I arrived here. Or that you would not know me."

"We will talk of that later," said the Lady Noor. "Now where are your sisters?"

"Here, Mama." A clear voice rang across the courtyard, and his two sisters came in, one near his age and the other slightly younger.

Yusuf rose to his feet. "Zeynab," he said, "I was afraid that I would never see you again," and embraced her.

"You have learned odd ways in the Christian court," said his sister, freeing herself after a few moments.

"At least you have learned to look after your hair," said her brother in a teasing voice. "But you have grown to be a great beauty. And so has Ayesha," he added, turning to her. She giggled and stepped back, revealing a boy of six or seven years of age, who was staring up at him in amazement. "Who is this?" he said, turning to his mother. "Have you married again?"

"This is your brother, Yusuf. Hasan. And his name is from his father and yours. He was born at the end of summer in the year you went away," she said. "I have not married again. Unimportant as I am, I still have enough influence that I cannot be traded like a pawn at the whim of others. But look at him, Yusuf. No one could think he was anything but your full brother, surely."

"They are like twins, only one is much taller than the other," said Zeynab. "Ayesha is ashamed because she cannot remember you," she added in a very low voice. "Do not tease her about it."

"It shall not be spoken of, ever," said Yusuf.

Zeynab clapped her hands and the small servant came in with platter of things to nibble on, followed closely by a boy carrying a low table to place it on. These were set down by the cushions near the pool, a jug of a sweet fruit drink was carried in, with cups, and the family was left alone again.

"I rode from the port to the city with a handsome young

man who seemed to think that he had a claim on you, Zeynab."

"Nasr?" she whispered, blushing fiercely. "What is he like?"

"But surely you have met him?"

"I knew him when we were both children, and played together with other children," she said. "And I have seen him since then, but not alone, or to speak more than a few words to."

"He is full of himself," said Yusuf. "He had the ill judgment to challenge me to a horse race after we had been riding all day over the mountains, but I had been mounted on his brother's horse, who had no wish to left behind."

"Who won the race?" asked his mother.

"No one, unless you can call the arrogant captain of the guard who made us stop the winner," said Yusuf, laughing. "But I enjoyed Nasr's company. He had much to talk about and is a witty sort. But with my woeful skill in speech, I had to work very hard to understand him."

"I meant to remark on that," said Zeynab. "We have had country slave girls who spoke more elegantly than you do now."

"I sound better than I did yesterday," said Yusuf. "I am remembering more and more as the day progresses."

"Good," said his mother. "We look forward to when you can speak like a civilized man. But now you must go. I have won you for an hour or two every morning or afternoon, but that is all. The rest of the time you must stay where they tell you at the palace, at least for the first little while."

His sisters crowded with him toward the door. "I am sorry we had so little time together, Zeynab," he said. "But mother wanted to have me to herself at first."

"She did," said Zeynab. "And remember, until she was sure that you were our brother, she was not going to allow us the freedom of the courtyard with you. As if you could be anyone else and know about my hair, you wretch. Did you tell Nasr?"

"Of course I did. But I also told him you were of unsurpassable beauty, and I was right. Until tomorrow, then."

2.

WAITING outside in the street for Yusuf was not only Abdullah, but also Faraj. "I thought that you would never come out of there," said Faraj. "I was about to have your slave here beat on the door and rescue you from the clutches of your womenfolk."

"I was not there long," said Yusuf, rather coldly. "And had not requested your assistance." In his irritation, words that he had not known he knew bubbled up and slid easily off his tongue.

"You seem to be quick at learning a language," said Faraj.

"I already knew it," said Yusuf. "But I have hardly spoken it in the past six years."

"I thought you had been away seven years," said Faraj.

"I was. My first year was spent with one who spoke our tongue. It was not until after that that I learned the language of the Valencians. To what do I owe the honor of this visit to the street in front of my mother's house?"

"Lord Ridwan wishes to talk to you," said Faraj.

"Where?"

"At the palace," said Faraj. "Where else would he be at this hour?"

"That is not something I would know, would I?" asked Yusuf. "I have only been here since last night."

"We must hurry," said Faraj. "Lord Ridwan is a very busy man, and he is to see a group of merchants who are waiting for him now."

"Merchants?" asked Yusuf. "Does Lord Ridwan himself see merchants?"

Stung, the young man turned to Yusuf. "These are very rich and powerful merchants. They come from Fez, and are more important even than the ambassadors that wait upon the emir."

"How interesting," said Yusuf. "Where I have been living, there are rich merchants, but none who are more powerful than royal ambassadors. I would like to meet these men.'

"Well, you cannot," said Faraj. "I assure you that they are not here to see you."

LORD Ridwan looked anything but busy. He was seated on a couch of generous proportions, well heaped up with cushions, in a room that led off from the area where his secretaries and their assistants seemed to be working at high speed. A young man seated on the floor nearby with a fat scroll in his hand, was reading from it in a light, clear voice. It sounded to Yusuf very much like poetry, rather difficult poetry, and he stood in silence until the reader paused.

"Welcome, my young lord Yusuf," said Ridwan. "My tasks for His Majesty are never-ending. The poet who created these verses wishes a post in the court, and I am forced to listen to them to judge if he is worthy of such an honor. Do you enjoy the beauty of love poems, Yusuf? Perhaps you would like to continue with the reading."

"I apologize profoundly," said Yusuf, "but I would not be able to do them justice."

"That is a pity," said Ridwan. "I think his work is more suited to be enjoyed by the young than by an old man like me."

This was an unanswerable comment, and Yusuf did not attempt to answer it. Servants brought in another couch, a smaller one, with cushions piled up on it as well. He sat down and prepared himself to listen.

"Why has the Christian king sent you back to our court after keeping you for so long?"

"I have not been at his court, Lord Ridwan," said Yusuf. "I have been living in the city of Girona, pursuing the cause of learning."

"Under whose tutelage?"

Yusuf paused long enough to draw breath, organize his thoughts, and then answered smoothly. "Under the tutelage of the Lord Berenguer de Cruïlles," said Yusuf, "and various tutors in his employ."

"And what did you study?"

"Various things, Lord Ridwan. The physical arts—swordsmanship, riding, and the like, as well as philosophy, mathematics, and the natural sciences."

"The law?"

"No, Lord Ridwan. I have not yet studied the law."

"And yet your studies are singularly deficient in the area of your own language."

"They are, Lord Ridwan, through a lack of tutors in the city where I was living."

"I am puzzled to know what to do with you," said the vizier. "Had you been studying the law, you could have followed in your illustrious father's footsteps, but you say you know nothing of it. Well, I shall think about it before making my recommendation to the emir."

"Has His Majesty placed my fate in your capable hands, Lord Ridwan?" asked Yusuf.

Ridwan looked sharply over at him, at his tranquil face and relaxed pose, and smiled. "Not as yet, but I have no doubt that he will, and when he does, he will want an instant answer. He is a very impetuous youth."

"But one of great wisdom and judgment," said Yusuf. "That is apparent after the briefest conversation with him."

"Without a doubt," said the vizier. "You will want to say your farewells to the noble ambassador and his train who accompanied you here. Faraj will take you to them. They are leaving tomorrow morning at first light."

The ambassador was in the courtyard beside which they had dined the night before. The sun was pouring in, and after yesterday's cold wind and rain, and the stiffness in his legs, the warmth was welcome.

"They tell me you will be returning soon to the kingdom of Aragon, my lord," said Yusuf. "I would like to thank you for your kindness and courtesy in allowing me to be part of your embassy for the voyage here."

"I think it should be the other way around, my young lord," said the ambassador. "I believe that I was allowed to come here on delicate business because you were traveling and required an escort. But we have both benefited, and therefore, although farewells are certainly in order, the thanks should be on my side. I hope that everything goes well for you here."

"I have been away for a long time," said Yusuf.

"When I heard you chatting with Ali, that tall sailor with the red beard, you know, I realized that we should have shipped someone who could speak proper court Arabic so that you could use the hours on shipboard to improve your skills."

"It may have been better in the long run that you did not. It would have seemed odd to everyone if I had arrived after living in Girona speaking perfect court Arabic."

"You have a properly suspicious mind, Yusuf." He dropped his voice. "You are well-placed here. Should you hear of anything that we should know, there is a man in the city by the name of—" He broke off with a smile, grasped Yusuf's hand in both of his and looked guilelessly at him. "We will be very grateful," he whispered. "May you enjoy your life here in this beautiful city," he added, taking his hands away and leaving a piece of folded paper in Yusuf's hand.

"Please convey my gratitude to His Majesty when you report to him on your mission," said Yusuf. "It grieves me that I was not able to take my farewell from him."

Yusuf adjusted his sash slightly and slipped the paper into it. He stood perfectly still, considering what was best to do, and then looked around. Abdullah appeared at his elbow— silently and suddenly—like a shadow when the clouds cover the sun.

"Where have you been?" asked Yusuf.

"Close by, lord," said the boy. "Watching you, lest you needed me."

"I think I would like to visit my mother again," said Yusuf.

"Lord, I think that would be most unwise," said the boy, distressed. "While I have been watching, others have been watching you as well, and so I have watched the others watching you. They would decide that something the Christian had said was so secret and so deadly that you had to hide it in the Lady Noor's house. It could bring great sorrow to her and to your family."

"Then what do I do?" he asked.

"I will fetch Faraj for you."

"If you are finished with your farewells to the ambassador," said Faraj, who appeared almost as quickly and almost as suddenly as Abdullah, but not quite, "there are other amusements you might wish to consider after your meal."

"Where am I dining?"

"At Lord Ridwan's table," said Faraj. "In a half-hour."

"Then I must go and make some adjustment to my dress," said Yusuf. "Abdullah," he said, in questioning tones, looking around, and the boy appeared again.

"You must visit my master, lord," he murmured, "but first, it is true that we should make some adjustment to your dress. Come this way."

"So the truth comes out at last, and you are not mine," said Yusuf, as they left the group in the courtyard. "I thought you were too good and clever and efficient for anyone to give away. Who is your master?"

"You will see."

+‡══· ═══‡+

THE boy looked narrowly at Yusuf when they reached the chamber. "Your hair is somewhat in disarray," he said, wielding a comb to good effect, "and you have picked up the dust of the street." As he passed a rough piece of cloth over the dusty patches, Yusuf was aware that the piece of paper had been neatly extracted from his sash.

"That is better, lord," said the boy. "Now there is one more person who has begged for a chance to meet you, since he was a dear friend of your father. I will take you to him. We have just enough time before dining."

+‡══· ═══‡+

"SO my little Abdullah has brought you to me at last," said the serious-faced man in the sober suit of clothes.

Yusuf bowed low. "I am honored to be presented to you, my lord."

"Everyone calls me Al-Khatib," said the secretary. "To be called anything else startles me. What have you to tell me, Abdullah?"

"I have no doubt he wishes to tell you that the piece of paper that the Valencian ambassador slipped into my hand, and which, in my panic, I slipped into my sash, is now safely in his sash," said Yusuf.

"It is rare for Abdullah to be caught," said Al-Khatib, smiling. "You must be a master of the arts."

"I survived on the road from Valencia to Girona for more than five years," said Yusuf. "I learned many things."

"And yet you remember your childhood here."

"I remember some of it. The city astonished me. I could swear I had never seen it before. Yet my mother's courtyard, although it is not in the same house, I believe, seems to me to be exactly the same—the same sun, the same fountain, the same flowers. And my mother has not changed at all, except that I used to have to look up to her. I have tried not to forget my language, but it has been difficult."

"I can understand that. We must find you a tutor at once. It will not take long for you to regain your proficiency. You are speaking much more fluently today than you were last night. Can you read and write?"

"A little. I knew some of my letters because my father had taught me, and so did the first man who rescued me on the road from Valencia. And then last summer, on a ship to Sardinia, I met a learned man who taught me a great deal and gave me a book so that I could take it back with me and practice."

"A Christian?"

"Yes, Al-Khatib. Or one who is now a Christian . . ."

"What they used to call a *muladí*, Lord Yusuf."

"Please do not call me that, sir."

The secretary nodded. "Then when we speak together like this, as friends, I shall call you Yusuf. And are you now a Christian?" he asked, without pausing.

"I am a follower of the one God of my father and my mother, and of all my family," said Yusuf, looking up helplessly. "But I know little of my faith except fragments that I remember from babyhood. I have not become a follower of any other faith. No one has even suggested that I should do such a thing," he added.

"Something must be done about that part of your learning as well," said the secretary, as if he were making a list of necessary repairs to a neglected building. Then he looked at Yusuf as if summing up all that could be read in his countenance. "Now can we speak of your conversation with the Valencian?"

"I must speak of it with someone," said Yusuf. "I do not know what to do."

3.

YUSUF had hardly wiped his fingers clean when Abdullah whisked him back to the secretary's office. "I have found you a tutor for now," said Ibn al-Khatib. "He is one of the most promising young men working under my control, as well as one of the most pleasant. It may be that your skills will grow beyond his power to assist you. I would be surprised if that were the case. But if it is, we shall consider the arrangement once more." The secretary nodded to Abdullah who trotted out of the room and returned with a familiar man in tow.

"Nasr!" said Yusuf. "I had wondered where you had disappeared to. Are you to take me to my tutor?"

"This is going to be difficult, sir," said Nasr, not sounding at all distressed.

"Nasr is your tutor," said al-Khatib. "Few speak Arabic more correctly, or with greater elegance and style, than Nasr ibn Umar. And while he is no *imam,* he certainly has a firmer grasp of his faith than you do, and he will not be shocked at your ignorance. Now you must find yourself a quiet corner of a pleasant courtyard for your first lesson, for I understand there is a race between you two as soon as the sun is lower in the sky."

"A race?" asked Yusuf.

"I leave Nasr to explain," said al-Khatib.

Nasr led them out of the palace complex, past the houses that connected to it, or were very close to it, and up a slope to a vast garden. "We will be peaceful and uninterrupted here," said Nasr. "All we need is . . ." He turned thoughtfully toward Abdullah. "I don't suppose that you could fetch us something to nibble on and a pitcher of something cool, could you?"

"No, lord," said Abdullah firmly. "I was to stay here with you until the lesson was over, and then to make sure that Lord Yusuf had riding clothes." To illustrate his determination, he sat down cross-legged on the flagstones and began to draw pictures in the dust and sand that had gathered on top of them.

"When he gets like that, there is no moving him," said Nasr. "We will have to suffer. But perhaps he will deign to fetch us a pair of twigs, and we can follow his example, only we will draw letters in the dust."

"What do we do?"

"We talk. And when you meet a word you do not know, or there is something you cannot say, we will write it down."

"When were you chosen to be my tutor?" asked Yusuf, determined to start with something he knew how to say.

"When we first had word that you were coming. His Majesty consulted al-Khatib, who was a close friend to your father and knew something of what you were like then, and al-Khatib suggested that your first difficulty would likely be language."

"Was it not the vizier who was charged with taking care of my education?"

"In court there are many factions." He caught the look on Yusuf's face and wrote a word in the dust. "Groups that compete for favor, that follow one or another powerful courtier."

"Every court has them," said Yusuf with assurance. "I understand."

"His Majesty left this in al-Khatib's hands because he is very learned and knew your father well. They decided that if you spoke like one of us after seven years—the years when you should have been learning—then we would know you were an impostor and a spy. It was with great relief that he discovered how primitive your speech was, and how peculiar. He would not have received you with such warmth in that case."

"How did he know before I got there?"

"I told him," said Nasr. "Did you not notice how slowly your attendants brought you to the palace? I had already been chosen to be your tutor, since my poor skills in speech and writing have been much praised, and also because I was of your family, and have dim memories of you as a child."

"And are to marry my sister."

"If God so wishes it," said Nasr. "Do you think she is as lovely as you remember her?"

"Lovelier," said Yusuf. "And filled with grace and wit. You must treat her well, Nasr."

"How could I not?" he asked. "Now it is time for you to talk as much as you can, and I will correct your errors. Tell me how you escaped assassination and found your way to the court of the king of Aragon."

"That would take days and days of explaining," said Yusuf. "It is a long and complicated story."

"I love long and complicated stories. I shall listen like a monarch being amused by his favorite storyteller."

"My father and I rode from here up through many long roads, over hills and mountains, and across long and dusty desert areas until we reached Valencia."

"Just the two of you?"

"No," said Yusuf. "That would not have been possible. There were others, soldiers and guards, as well as men my father talked to. It took a long time, but I cannot tell you how many days. I remember a scene here, and a scene there. I remember my horse and my little sword—I was very proud of them.

In Valencia we stayed in a great palace. It was blue inside—everything looked blue. It was filled with people whom I could not understand, but always I stayed with my father."

"Did your father speak the language of the Christians?"

"I don't know," said Yusuf. "I couldn't understand anything that was going on, so I didn't listen unless he was speaking to me."

"Of course," said Nasr.

"Then one day—it was very bright and sunny and hot—there was noise, people running, screaming, doors banging. We were in a huge blue room, my father and I, and some men came in. My father spoke to one of them, quite calmly, and I stopped being frightened, I remember. Then more men came in. They shouted something, and the man my father was speaking to pointed to my father. I remember that now. My father thrust me behind him and said that I must run and take the letter to the king. He must have told me about the letter because I knew where it was. The men attacked my father and then ran away. I took the letter and ran." He was shaking now. "I was covered with blood, but so were many other people."

"And did the fighting stop?"

"No, but I stayed away from groups of people fighting. I asked everyone I met where the king was, and finally someone understood me and pointed to another street and said that he had gone out there to the high road to the east. So I went out of the city that way and started walking. A man spoke to me in our language and then took me as his servant. I stayed with him for a long time because he was going east, but then he decided to go inland, and so I left him. I still didn't know the language of the country, but I knew that boys like me could be sold."

"Are you sure about your father speaking to someone he knew?"

"Yes, I'm sure. I felt safer as soon as the men came in the room, because I knew them."

"*You* knew them?"

"Didn't I say that? I knew them, and I knew they would help us, but they couldn't because the other men came in."

"We must continue this conversation tomorrow," said Nasr. "But now, let us talk about the race."

"Why are we racing?" asked Yusuf.

"Because our cousin the captain insists that it was all organized yesterday for an hour before sundown, and that honor demands that we race. He told everyone that he had arranged it all long before he mentioned it to me. And so we will race part of the way around the perimeter, with everyone standing on the towers and the walls to watch us, and then up to Generalife and back. I'm not pleased. We had a hard ride yesterday, and my horse will likely pull up lame if I race her today."

"But we did not agree to a race," said Yusuf. "Mention was made of one in jest—"

"Who spoke of racing first?"

"Our cousin the captain. He said if we wished to gallop our horses like madmen then we could race them in front of the city where the troops exercise, but that we should not race along a crowded road through a group of eminent court officials and upset their horses."

"That is how I remember it, too. But I am afraid it is too late now. It has all been arranged."

"What horse am I to ride?"

"My brother's horse is still at your disposal, although I am sure a fresh horse can be found."

"But you will not have a fresh horse, so we must both ride our mounts from yesterday. If we hold them back, they should not be injured."

"Can you do that?" asked Nasr. "How good are your skills?"

"Quite good," said Yusuf.

"Abdullah has found you riding clothes to supplement your own," said Nasr tactfully. "You will find them in your chamber. I will come by to get you before the race."

⊹⇒═ ═⇐⊹

WHEN Yusuf arrived back at the apartment that had been set aside for him by the vizier, he stretched out gratefully on the comfortable bed. The pleasant courtyard where they had been studying was delightful; Nasr was as pleasant a companion as one could wish for, and he had understood him much more clearly today than yesterday; but the exercise had been exhausting. He fell at once into a light sleep, filled with odd dreams.

When he awoke, the flawless weather they had enjoyed throughout the day had begun to shift. The morning's light breeze gathered strength and became a wind; the sketchy white trails across the sky had been replaced by thick banks of gray and purple clouds. Yusuf leaned out the window. There was a definite uneasiness in the air. He saw people putting on cloaks; he saw mothers rushing their children into houses. Somewhere in the distance a bolt of lightning pierced the sky, and after a while, a rumble of thunder spoke of distant storms.

He washed his face and hands to wake himself up and inspected this third suit of clothes. Most of it, including the riding boots, were his own. But there were unfamiliar-looking padded trousers and a padded hat, of the sort that he had seen several horsemen wear.

"What is this for?" he asked Abdullah, who was sitting on a cushion, polishing Yusuf's riding boots with a cloth.

"Should your lordship be so unfortunate as to fall against a tree trunk or onto a sharp rock, such hats protect the head," he said. "They are comfortable and are not readily dislodged. I believe the Lord Nasr will be here very soon, lord," he added.

"Life in this place requires a great deal of work," said Yusuf, stripping off the clothes he had put on that morning and getting into his riding habit.

"That makes an interesting combination," said Nasr in his most mocking tones from the doorway. "I suspect it will become the fashion here as soon as you are seen."

"The tunic is rather tight," said Abdullah in worried tones. "Perhaps I should have found him one that matched the trousers."

"I am perfectly comfortable," said Yusuf fiercely. "I shall ride as I am. I could not have worn the harness for my sword and scabbard over a larger tunic."

"Indeed," murmured Nasr. "But I must teach you how to handle one of our swords as well, if you will teach me the use of yours. Being skilled with both would be a great advantage to a man. They are quite different and require quite a different approach, I suspect. But come—we must head for the stables."

"YOUR brother's horse appears rather edgy today," said Yusuf, as his mount danced its way along the path after Nasr and his steady gray mare. "Will your brother be there, at the race?"

"I doubt it," said Nasr. "At the moment, I believe he is still in Guadix, on a mission for the emir. But if he knew, he would approve of your having Falcon for the time being, I am sure. He is a generous fellow, and, as I said, he has another horse. This fellow suffers from lack of exercise, I suspect."

At that moment, a bolt of lightning struck the mountain ahead of them along with a ferocious crash of thunder. Startled, Falcon whinnied and reared up. Yusuf pulled his head down firmly, murmuring into his ear. The horse flicked his ears irritably and settled down a little.

It began to rain ferociously, and by the time they reached the gate that led to the stretch of road they were to race on, they were both soaked.

"I say we call this off," said Nasr, raising his voice to be heard over the beating of the rain, as they passed through the gate and onto the road.

"I couldn't agree more," said Yusuf, turning so that Nasr could hear him better. As he shifted his weight, Falcon went berserk.

The horse leapt up, twisting in the air, rearing and kicking, and then bucking with frantic determination to rid himself of the rider who seemed to be tormenting him. Suddenly he bolted.

Nasr's horse set out after him.

Falcon tore around the perimeter of the wall and headed into a gulley, lost his footing and slid down in the mud, landing on his side.

Nasr was not far behind, closely followed by two mounted guards. Yusuf was in the mud as well, but not under the horse. For the moment, Falcon lay still.

"Yusuf, speak to me," said Nasr.

"As soon as I get the mud out of my mouth," said Yusuf.

"Are you injured, my lord?" asked one of the guards.

"I fear I have—I don't know how to say it—my arm and my shoulder are away from each other. Otherwise I think I am fine. But the poor horse?"

"Which arm, lord?"

"The one below."

"Fetch the physician and the bonesetter," said Nasr.

"They are on their way," said the guard.

One of the guards came down into the gulley with Nasr. They helped Yusuf to get on his feet and clear of the horse. Then Falcon shuddered, tried to move, and shuddered again. The guard moved forward and with his knife, cut through the girth and gently lifted up the saddle.

"Look at his back," said Nasr after a moment. "Who has done this thing?"

The flesh under the horse's saddle was a bloodied mass.

"I have seen such things done before to horses that were racing," said the guard. "When I saw blood seeping from under the saddle, I suspected it."

"To make them run faster?"

"No. To madden them enough to kill their riders and disqualify them," said the guard. "There will be some sort of rasp fastened into the saddle. It drives into his flesh when the girth is tightened and the rider mounts."

"Poor Falcon. My brother will not be pleased. How is he?" asked Nasr. "Can you tell?"

"If he has not broken a leg, he may be fine," said the guard. "Let us see if he will try to stand."

Once the saddle had been removed, Falcon waited for a moment, shook his head, and began the complicated effort of getting to his feet. The gulley was now running with water. With much splashing and snorting, he achieved it on his second try, earning cheers from the spectators. He shook the water from his coat and looked around, deciding where to go next. There were people everywhere by this time, except for on the road behind him. He scrambled onto the bank of the gully and walked peacefully back onto the road. Two more guards appeared.

"His most royal Majesty would like to see the horse and the saddle," said one of the new guards, seizing Falcon's bridle. Another took the saddle, and they disappeared through the gate.

As suddenly as it had started, the rain stopped. The wind began to blow the clouds away, and the sun broke through.

Yusuf was still standing, up to his ankles in muddy water, holding his right arm absolutely steady with his left. He could see no possibility of scrambling up that slippery edge without using his hands. But the two guards, relieved of the responsibility for determining the cause of the accident, dealt efficiently with its second victim. The one who had scrambled good-naturedly down into the water with Yusuf grasped him around the waist and hoisted him up toward the other. Braced by the man behind him, Yusuf took a couple of steps up the sloping edge and then felt himself being pushed firmly toward the man above, who bent over and grasped him just above the waist and hauled him out and upright. "There you are, my lord," said the second guard. "The physician and the bonesetter are both here."

It was the work of one agonizing second to set the arm back in its socket. "Do not use that for a little while," said the bonesetter. "Let it recover a bit. I will bind it up for now." He whipped out a piece of cloth, wrapping it tightly and neatly around the arm to bind it closely to the chest.

"When can I use it?" he asked.

"In a day or two. Don't use it if it hurts," he said. "I will see you tomorrow. We will see you tomorrow," he emended it, with a nod to his colleague.

"I will have something brought over to you to dull the pain," said the physician. "And to promote healing." With that, they turned and left.

"I hope they spend more time over poor Falcon," said Yusuf.

"They will," said Nasr. "Poultices for the wound and then healing salves, soothing leg massages, and special hot mashes to eat. People can look after themselves," he added jokingly. "But let us get you into a warm place where you can rest quietly."

"Where is that?"

"We will take you back to Ridwan's little palace. Abdullah and I will take care of you for now."

YUSUF was shaking with cold by the time he reached his apartment in Ridwan's palace. Abdullah stripped off his wet garments, put him in a clean shift and into the bed with warm rocks at his feet. A brazier was already warming the room, and someone brought him a hot infusion of a mixture of herbs. He tasted it with professional interest, recognizing some of its ingredients as familiar standbys. As he puzzled over the formula for the infusion, a welcome sensation of warmth crept over him and he fell asleep.

When he awoke, it was dark. The curtain over his alcove was pulled back. In the principal room, an oil lamp was burning and he heard the scratching of a pen. Then he heard a murmur of voices and the door to his apartment opened and closed. For a moment he thought he had been left here alone, helpless with his sword arm bound to his chest, and felt a rush of panic.

He struggled to sit up, but was interrupted by the sound of someone moving about. He fell back, keeping his eyes fixed on the opening to the alcove. The other person looked in at the door; it was Nasr. Relieved, he feel at once into a profound sleep until the sun fell once more on his face.

V
Granada: Day Three

✣

1.

WHEN the physician and the bonesetter returned in the morning, Yusuf had shed the cloths that bound his arm tight to his chest, and was eating breakfast comfortably with his right hand, under the watchful eyes of Nasr and Abdullah.

The bonesetter's delicate fingers explored his shoulder joint. He pronounced himself moderately pleased with Yusuf's progress. "I do not object to your using the arm for such common tasks as eating," he said. "My own master long observed that such injuries healed better if they were not kept too long out of use. But if you go out in the city, or ride, or do anything where you might fall or be pushed or jostled, I must insist that you bind up that arm before you set out. It will be very poor if it is injured again in the same way in the next little while."

The physician peered in his eyes and his mouth, prodded him in the belly and looked at his urine with a judgmental eye. "You seem very healthy," he said. "Take more of that infusion if you are in pain and send for me. I am the emir's personal physician," he added.

"I am honored and grateful for the attentions of both of you," said Yusuf. "I feel completely recovered, although a little bruised and sore."

"That is to be expected," they agreed judiciously and left once more.

His other attendants prescribed a visit to the baths and a massage, and then a visit to the emir's brother, who was most anxious to meet him. "While you are occupied with those things," said Nasr, "you will be moved from here to an apartment in the palace. For a few days, Abdullah and I will have beds there as well, so that we can keep an eye on you."

"The emir's brother?" asked Yusuf. "Do you mean the one who is imprisoned?"

"It is hard to describe him as imprisoned," said Nasr slowly. "He is living in a smaller palace close by with his mother and his younger brother and sisters, with a large income and whatever he wishes in food, drink, clothing, and amusement."

"But it was His Majesty who described him as imprisoned," said Yusuf. "I did not wish to impute any . . ."

"Of course not," said Nasr. "And I would concede that if Isma'il requested permission to ride to Guadix or to Malaga, he might not receive it. In fact, he most certainly would not receive it. And for that reason he does get bored. I would say that he gets extremely bored. If he were a poet, or a scholar, he would be in an ideal situation, but then he is not. So it would amuse him greatly to have you visit him, for his favorite occupation is gossiping. It would be an act of great charity on your part."

And once more Yusuf could not decide whether Nasr was speaking seriously or in jest.

2.

"And how are you now?" asked Nasr, as Yusuf came out of the baths.

"Much better," said Yusuf. "The masseur is very skilled."

"He is," said Nasr. "They say his massages can raise the dead. I don't know if that is true, but I do know that if you are exhausted, bruised, and sore, he can work miracles."

"I'm not sure he has worked a miracle," said Yusuf pragmatically, "but I certainly feel better. When do we go to Isma'il?"

"Now," said Nasr. "I will come with you. Just remember that everyone in that house is a spy for someone, even the boy

who takes your shoes and the housemaid sweeping the courtyard. Don't say anything in that palace that you do not want
to be market gossip before sundown. If you are asked a question that is dangerous to answer, I will interrupt in some
manner or another."

"And if I am offered food or drink?" asked Yusuf, in mock
alarm. "Will it be safe to eat, or must I endeavor to exchange
cups with my host?"

"I don't think they would feel safe using poison in their
own house," said Nasr, quite seriously. "But Maryam is a dangerous woman. She is ambitious and ruthless and she is rich."

"You are at least the third person since I arrived to tell me
that," said Yusuf. "You make her sound quite alarming."

"I only wish to put you on your guard."

"Will I meet her?"

"She claims the right as a widow and as a queen to free-
doms that many women would not dare to wish for," said
Nasr. "You will probably meet her."

FROM the time Abdullah rang the bell, Yusuf felt as if he
had stepped into the world of women once more. A maid answered the door and showed them into a comfortable recep-
tion room furnished with thick cushions, marble benches,
bright carpets, and a variety of oil lamps. They settled themselves comfortably, prepared to wait.

"I wonder how long they will consider that those of our
lowly rank must be kept waiting," murmured Nasr.

"Have you waited on them before?" asked Yusuf. "Since
the death of the old king?"

"I have," said Nasr. "It is one of the courtesies that one
pays to the widow of the emir, the old queen, if she permits
it. And I am still alive," he added, his eyes dancing in amusement.

"That is reassuring," said Yusuf.

A burst of noise in the hall warned them of the arrival of

the old queen and the young prince. Nasr and Yusuf were on their feet, decorously bowing when the group swept in: a boy of four or five, two women, one middle-aged and plump, the other still in her twenties and of startling beauty, and a plump boy, hovering on the edge of manhood, with enormous eyes ringed with kohl, long glossy hair plaited with scarlet silk, and wearing a tunic of saffron-colored silk trimmed with green and gold thread.

"Highness," said Nasr, bowing to the plump young man, "may I present my cousin, Yusuf ibn Hasan, who craves to be made known to you? And Your Majesty," he continued, turning to the startling beauty, "may I be so bold as to present to you my cousin, Yusuf ibn Hasan?"

"We are pleased that you have sought us out," said Prince Isma'il, with a slight nod, and settled himself on a couch.

"I have been curious to catch a glimpse of a young man who has been so much talked about," said the beauty in a husky voice while she too settled herself into a heap of cushions on another couch. The woman with her fussed for a while with the arrangements of the cushions and then pushed the little boy onto a cushion on the floor in the pose of an adoring son.

"Mother, you know perfectly well that you have seen much more than that of him since he arrived," said Prince Isma'il. "You had a complete description of him before that miserable thief Ridwan had even laid eyes on him." He turned to his guests, waved at them to sit, and went on. "Our mother the queen has a tower room in this palace with windows that overlook the eastern sectors, the northern approaches, and the road to the Generalife—"

"Hardly. I would have to push aside the screens and lean way out," said Queen Maryam. "And I could never do that, could I?"

"You know you've done it," said Isma'il. "And she has a perfect view of the Alcazaba and the western approaches. She knows more of who is doing what than the watchmen on the towers," he added confidentially.

"Women always know more of what is going on than men do," said Nasr, laughing. "They watch what is going on, and they listen to what people are saying, and then they hoard information. We men listen for a moment and search for something more significant or important or wittier to say, and miss hours and hours of important news."

"Tell me, Yusuf ibn Hasan, what brings you back to Al-Andalus?" asked Maryam.

As soon as his mother started to speak, Yusuf noticed young Prince Qay glancing around. When he saw that no one was paying attention to him, he got up quietly and wandered off to a more interesting part of the house. Suddenly Yusuf realized that the silence in the room was because everyone was waiting for his response.

"His Highness heard of my unexpected survival and wrote to the king of Aragon, requesting my return," said Yusuf.

"Everyone knows that," said Isma'il. "We want to find out why, after all this time, you bothered to come."

"I hear there are great differences at the moment between Aragon and Castile," said Maryam. "Do you think there will be a war soon?"

"I have no idea, Your Majesty," said Yusuf. "I did not live in the court, but rather quietly in the city of Girona, pursuing my studies."

"When you were not with the king in Sardinia," said Maryam, tapping her foot in its tiny slipper against the end of the couch. "Why did he summon you to him then? We cannot imagine why such a powerful monarch would have need of a boy like you. Or is he fond of boys? That would be useful information."

"Has Your Majesty been well?" asked Nasr. "But I ask a foolish question, for anyone allowed into your presence can see that such blooming loveliness could not come from ill health."

"Nasr, you know you are not in the least interested in my health or my appearance. Stop interrupting me. I am having a charming conversation with this pretty creature. Whose side are you on?" asked Maryam, turning back to Yusuf. "The king of Aragon or the king of Castile? Is it not strange that they should both have the same name?"

"Pedro, or Pere, as he called in the province where I live, is quite a common name in the Christian lands, Your Majesty," said Yusuf.

"Like Muhammad," said Maryam, with venom in her voice. "I wonder if the king of Castile also likes pretty boys. Do you know?"

"I have never even seen the king of Castile and know nothing about him, but I can assure Your Majesty that the king of Aragon has no particular fondness for boys."

"Are you sure? Because a clever boy can learn an unbelievable amount from even the most discreet of men. They are so useful," she said, sighing. "Boys, I mean. They take a lot of training, though," she added, looking thoughtfully at Yusuf.

At that the doors opened and servants swept in with trays of sweet syrups and little cakes and sweetmeats. Yusuf looked at them suspiciously, and then took a date from one tray and tiny cup of syrup from the center of another. As he nibbled on the date, he noticed that the prince was watching him with interest. "I can see that you have lived at a court," he said.

"I expected an old woman," said Yusuf, once they had escaped the palace. "Gray of hair, with missing teeth and a wrinkled face. Why did you not warn me?"

"You knew she had a child who was under five and that her eldest is only fifteen. She is not yet thirty years of age," said Nasr, laughing. "I tried to put you on your guard."

"I suppose you did, but since everyone calls her the old queen, I was not expecting that."

"I will admit that she was even more outrageous today than she usually is," said Nasr. "For some reason she seemed to want to make you uncomfortable, and I find that interesting. She usually drowns her visitors in flattery and charm. What could she have against you?" asked Nasr.

"I cannot imagine what she would have against me," said Yusuf.

"It sounds unlikely, I know," said Nasr. "She cannot think that you conspired to keep her son from the throne," he added softly. "You were in another country and didn't know any of us."

"Why does Prince Isma'il refer to himself as 'we' half the time?" asked Yusuf. "It sounds very odd."

"Not at all. For years he was sure that he would be named the heir to the throne."

"Why would he think that?"

"The old queen convinced him of it," said Nasr. "And although he makes very pretty speeches to his brother the emir, it's clear to everyone that he still thinks it. He was practicing his royal speech and manner on you, that's all."

3.

"LIFE has been very interesting since I saw you yesterday," said Yusuf. He was seated by the pool beside his mother, watching as she combed his brother's hair, and then her own.

"So I have heard," she answered. "You hadn't told me you intended to race Nasr yesterday."

"I didn't know," said Yusuf. "Nor did Nasr. It seems a snatch of conversation on the road here was interpreted by others as a challenge to race given and accepted. The first we knew about it was some time after I had seen you."

"That is interesting, in light of what happened," said his mother calmly. "I hope you have recovered."

"I have."

"Good. I was told as much, but I wished to see you before believing everything they said."

"Other things happened yesterday in addition to the race," said Yusuf. "I wanted very much to see you again yesterday afternoon, to ask you questions—not only about the people involved in the race, but also about those other things—because

I am becoming rather confused. But little Abdullah, my slave, said that it would be most unwise. Did you know that he actually belongs to Ibn al-Khatib, who placed him with me?"

"I'm not surprised," said his mother. "He and your father were dear to each other."

"Is he there to spy on me, do you think?"

"I doubt that. Al-Khatib believed my assurances that you could not be anyone except my Hasan's son. And of course he has the evidence of his own eyes to help him. Abdullah is more likely to be there with you to keep you out of trouble. I expect that you can trust him."

"And Nasr?" asked Yusuf softly, for Zeynab was in and out of the courtyard, listening to their conversation.

"I hope so," said his mother. "Although no one can know what is in an ambitious young man's heart. He is likely to be more trustworthy than many. I hear you have met Maryam. Tell me what you thought of her."

"First, tell me why she appears to hate me, when she has never seen me before."

"I suspect she is now conspiring, or attempting to conspire, with the Christians to help place her Isma'il on the throne. She probably cannot decide if you will be a hindrance or a help in that cause." She put away the comb and sent little Hasan off to fetch his sisters. "Muhammad's accession to the throne was a bitter blow to her. You know that they say she talked our great king, Yusuf, into letting her wear many of the royal jewels, and that as soon as she had word that he had been attacked, she hid them away in a safe place. She is now fabulously wealthy. They say she has bribed some of the Castilian emissaries, and no doubt she made an attempt to do the same with the Aragonese who left this morning."

"But she cannot expect one of the Christian kings to invade the country only to put Isma'il on the throne, can she? If they invade, I assure you, mother, it will be to take over the kingdom."

"Of course, but she believes that she has solved that problem. She has married Isma'il's sister Zahra into a powerful family that is rumored to have useful connections with the Castilians. It seems that the only time the city is at peace these days is when she rides off to visit Zahra and her husband. Now, tell me what you thought of her."

Zeynab and Ayesha joined them, and Yusuf, much recovered from the first wave of shock over meeting the "old" queen, regaled them with exaggerated accounts of her outrageous behavior. The courtyard rang with raucous laughter, his the loudest of all. But when the laughter stopped, tears sprang to his eyes, and his heart ached for the lost years.

VI

Granada: Day Four

1.

HIS apartment at the palace, chosen to accommodate Nasr as well, along with Abdullah and a guard, seemed the height of luxury to Yusuf. It was also comforting to have an armed man inside their rooms, and to observe that there was another outside in the corridor.

"Where was His Majesty tonight?" Yusuf had asked Nasr after they had retreated to their apartment for the night.

"Dining elsewhere, I suppose," said Nasr blandly. "With friends, no doubt."

"His Majesty was dining with the ladies," said Abdullah quietly.

"You see? I am supposed to know all the gossip of the palace, and half of it I have to get from Abdullah," said Nasr. "That, of course, is why Ibn al-Khatib knows everyone's business, even more than the vizier does."

"And why are we so well-guarded, I wonder?" said Yusuf.

"Does it bother you?"

"After yesterday, not at all," said Yusuf. "But I didn't expect it."

"His Majesty was struck—almost more than we were—by the matter of the horse race," said Nasr. "It seemed to him to go somewhat beyond the normal high spirits among the stable lads."

"Was it one of the stable lads who did it?" asked Yusuf.

"That is who would have had easiest access to Falcon's saddle," said Nasr. "But a stable lad would have difficulty organizing a race without the consent of the participants. Let us say that the affair is still being looked into. But at least for tonight, we will be safe. What are you supposed to do tomorrow?"

"I don't know," said Yusuf. "I seem to be carried off by someone or other to unexpected places every time I look around. But I am planning to visit my mother in the morning. They cannot refuse me that."

YUSUF arrived at his mother's house in the middle of the morning on the fourth day of his stay. It was raining, but he joined her where she sat in the courtyard under the arches that supported the balcony above them, and watched the pattern of rain on the pool. When he first arrived, she sent away his sisters and brother for a while and talked—about his father, about Ibn al-Khatib, about the emir and his younger brother, about the vizier, Ridwan, and what the city thought of him, about Nasr, and about all the swirling factions of the court and how they combined for a while over this issue or that event and then fell apart again. She pointed out each man—or woman—who could be dangerous, and how she herself, as the widow of a man who had been admired and feared and hated by some, had avoided disaster to herself and to her children.

"How do you know all this?" asked Yusuf. "Living in the house, rarely going out, seeing few people?"

"What an odd life you must think I lead," said his mother. "I have stayed at home every day since you arrived until your visit, certainly, lest I miss you, but I have many friends, both women whom I go out to see, and many respectable men who pay calls upon me.

"I am interested in the political life of the court," she continued. "Your father, a wise man, and a great jurist, taught me all the subtleties of law and custom that govern us that my own teachers when I was a child had not. Even if I am not in the councils of the powerful," she said in a much lower voice, "the husbands of my friends are. What we hear and discuss is what the men call women's gossip," she added in her normal tones, smiling. "But you will find it is mostly accurate."

"Are you not nervous speaking like this?" he asked.

"Would my son betray his mother?"

"Never. You know that. Besides, you have said nothing treasonable. But some of it is perhaps—indiscreet."

"True. But there are no treasonable thoughts in my heart, and therefore no words of treason on my tongue. But what I have just told you is important for you to know for your own safety and prosperity. I have not spoken of it before because very little that is said in this house is not known to several interested people. But on a rainy day, here, away from the servants, it is difficult to hear what people are saying. I have waited for the rain before mentioning these things to you."

"You think there is a spy in your house?"

"Everyone has spies," said his mother. "You have to learn how to keep them from doing too much damage, that is all."

"You make them sound like mice," said Yusuf.

"They are very like mice," said his mother. "And, like mice, you wouldn't know you had them except for the telltale click of their little claws on the tiles in the night and a few droppings here and there in the morning. With slaves, you hear them opening the shutters and creeping out in the night, and they leave little signs of their wealth around. They're your spies."

"Then you need a cat," said Yusuf, and his mother burst into a crow of delighted laughter.

"Perhaps I do. Now I am the cat. I always get double work out of the spies since they are being paid so much anyway. Your best servants are almost always spies; they don't want to be sold or sent away, and so they put up with anything."

2.

FARAJ was waiting outside when Yusuf and Abdullah finally emerged from his mother's house. Although he had been sheltering as best he could in the doorway, he looked distinctly damp. The rain had stopped as they were leaving, with that abruptness that Yusuf had begun to expect, but the emerging sun hadn't seemed to cheer the sub-sub-secretary of the vizier, Ridwan.

"What brings you here, Faraj?" asked Yusuf.

"I am to bring you to the vizier's table," said Faraj. "He regrets that he has been too occupied to see as much of you as he would like, and hopes that you will join him now."

"I would be delighted," said Yusuf, his heart sinking.

NASR was present, as were Ibn al-Khatib and two of his assistant secretaries, the physician who had treated Yusuf, and other men who were probably, Yusuf thought, assistants to the vizier. Faraj, Yusuf noted, was not of the group.

The food, a variety of spiced delicate dishes and broiled meats, was delicious, and Yusuf ate well, although he was hampered by having to observe the manners and customs in eating of the others with great care. Occasionally he asked Nasr, who had tactfully been placed close to him, what to do with this dish, or that one. Otherwise, he imitated those nearby.

When they had reduced the amount of food placed before them to a fraction of its original size, servants brought around chilled silver goblets of *sharbat* to drink.

"Sometimes I think that Ridwan goes above himself," whispered Nasr.

"Why do you say that?"

"Even the emir rarely serves dishes made with ice, and for Ridwan to do so at an informal meal such as this, at which the emir was not in attendance, is overreaching."

"He must be very wealthy," said Yusuf.

"Beyond belief," said Nasr. "If I were Ridwan, I would not advertise it in such a blatant manner. It will be all over the city before nightfall. But, since it is here, let us enjoy it."

Nasr drank heartily and turned to see how his friend reacted to the extravagant treat.

Yusuf was holding the goblet in his hand and sniffing it carefully. "Nasr," he said softly, "take this one—and on your life do not taste it, seriously—do not taste it. Just smell it, and let me see yours for a moment."

Yusuf sniffed Nasr's, and his face cleared. "It seems fine."

"It is delicious," said Nasr. "And it had better be fine. I've drunk half of it." He sniffed the full goblet in his hand. "Yours doesn't smell quite the same as mine, but it seems all right. Well, there's a sort of odd—even unpleasant—smell in there, perhaps. As if your serving had a piece of overripe fruit mashed into it."

"It's more than that," said Yusuf. "I recognize that smell. It is a virulently poisonous plant with an awful smell. A few drops can kill you. Someone thought I wouldn't taste it in with all that lovely fruit and syrup."

"You can't taste cold things as well," said Nasr. "That's why a chilled *sharbat* has to have so much sugar syrup and fruit pressed into it."

"You do know everything," said Yusuf. "Is the *sharbat* really good?"

"It is, as I said, delicious," said Nasr. "But I'm not certain that I want to finish mine. I seem to have lost my thirst."

"What should I do?" asked Yusuf.

"We must tell someone of this."

"Who?"

"It would seem indelicate to tell our host that he has tried to poison one of his guests. If it was by his order, he will be very annoyed that you noticed, and if it was without his knowledge, he will be very disconcerted that you were threatened. Where is Abdullah?"

"Close by," said Yusuf. "He is always close by." He twisted around to look for him, and suddenly Abdullah appeared.

"Abdullah," said Nasr. "This cup, which was served to your temporary master here, contains poison. He has not drunk any of it, but he smelled a poisonous ingredient."

"Are you familiar with poisons and their smells, lord?" asked Abdullah seriously. "Or is it just that it had an unappetizing smell?"

"I am familiar with poisons. In my studies I have had to learn about herbs, both beneficial and poisonous."

"Thank you, lord," said Abdullah. "I am sure that information is important. If you will guard the cup, lord, I will return soon."

ABDULLAH returned in less than a minute, bowed low, seized the offending cup, and with another reassurance that they would see him in moment, disappeared again.

This time he did not return. The conversation, the eating of sweetmeats, and drinking of various sweet drinks continued with unabated good cheer. At last one of the servants discreetly handed a small, sealed scroll to Nasr. He glanced at the seal and then hastily broke it, spreading out the sheet it held together.

"This is really for you, my friend," said Nasr. "I think they were perhaps worried that you would not be able to read it."

"A natural worry," said Yusuf. "Some letters I find difficult, and I do make many mistakes."

"Not as many," said Nasr distractedly. "You are improving. We are to go at once to His Majesty. He is in a room off the throne room where he prefers to do his most important work; it is a place where he can have real discussions with his courtiers."

3.

THEY arrived panting and out of breath at a room that overlooked the precipitous slopes to the north and east. Al-Khatib was there, speaking in a low voice to the emir. Muhammad was sitting in the center of the room, apparently paying no attention. Behind him sat three scribes; several armed guards stood at strategic points around the room. In front of the emir was the silver goblet.

Muhammad was seated in a low chair, his legs stretched out comfortably in front of him. He was frowning, and barely acknowledged the entrance and the kneeling bows of the two young men. With a flick of his hand he directed them to a pair of thick cushions. They sat down. Al-Khatib sat down not far from them.

"His Majesty the Emir of Granada, Muhammad V, wishes to know how you knew what is in that cup," asked al-Khatib in a very neutral voice.

Yusuf took a deep breath. "I studied the natural sciences under the direction of a skilled physician who understood them well. He was much interested in the beneficial as well as deadly effects of herbs and plants, and in his youth studied here in Granada with the great Ibn al-Baytar."

Muhammad flicked his hand again.

"And where did you study with this man?"

"The city of Girona." Yusuf looked nervously at the emir, but he was apparently waiting for him to continue. "When one of my teacher's patients was poisoned, he taught me—he attempted to teach me how to recognize various poisons and identify them without actually poisoning yourself."

"And how was that?"

"The first test is to place a drop of undiluted poison in a cupful of water and try to catch its scent. The second is to taste with the tip of the tongue the diluted mixture. The third is to place a drop of undiluted poison on a piece of cloth and heat it over a lamp. My nose is quite keen, and I was able to catch the scent of the poisons that we were testing, my lord. One of them was the scent in the *sharbat* that overlay the smell of fruit and flavorings."

"I would be interested in talking to you at greater length about your studies and how you came to suspect the *sharbat*," said Ibn al-Khatib. "I knew Ibn al-Baytar well—he was a great man, and his books are beyond price—but I also know something of herbs and poisons."

Muhammad listened with almost professional interest but declined for the moment to interfere.

"Has it been determined that the *sharbat* was safe, Your

Excellency?" asked Yusuf. "If that is so, I cannot express my great misery at having caused such trouble."

"Oh, no," said the secretary. "It was poisoned. That is quite clear. There was enough in that cup to kill several men. It is a very rapid poison."

"We shall speak apart with Yusuf ibn Hasan," said Muhammad. "You will stay," he said to al-Khatib. "Everyone else will wait outside the door."

The room cleared in a moment.

The emir's gaze was fixed on the window to his left. Yusuf opened his mouth to speak, and closed it again at a warning touch of al-Khatib's hand. "The man who placed the extra flavoring in your serving of *sharbat* was able to tell us very little," said Muhammad. "We know that he was well paid for his service—the coins he received were among his possessions. When he saw that he was to be taken and questioned, he produced the small flagon containing the substance and drank. He is dead, after swearing that he does not know who gave him the poison or the money. It was careless of the men who went after him to allow that, but they were not expecting to find the culprit so easily." He tapped his foot irritably on the ground. "Except, as you have no doubt noted, he is no more the culprit than is the arrow that kills a man. At the moment, I seek the archer who launched him toward you."

"I regret, Your Majesty, that I have caused so many difficulties for the land of my birth," said Yusuf. "And I cannot imagine any way in which my death could benefit anyone in this great kingdom. I am a person of little importance and until three days ago, I knew no one here."

"The continued existence of your revered father's son clearly troubles someone," said Muhammad. "It has been suggested that someone in this kingdom had a hand in your father's assassination. That person—if he exists—might wish that you had not survived. The question is being looked into. But for now, it will be better if you leave our kingdom until this difficulty is resolved. It grieves me to send you away; you are not exiled; you will be invited to return when all is settled. But the next little adventure might be your last, and I would like to see you live to fight, and if need be, die for a greater cause than allowing a traitor to sleep better at night."

"When would it please Your Majesty that I take my leave of your court?" asked Yusuf. "I will go at once, or tomorrow, if it so pleases you."

"No," said the emir. "You will leave the city in absolute secrecy, and until you go, you must behave as if you were staying for a lifetime. Therefore, tomorrow you will spend at the mosque, in prayer and study, as is fitting, for it is Friday. It will not harm you to learn more before you go."

"In this, as in all things, Your Majesty knows what is right," murmured Yusuf nervously.

"Al-Khatib will tell you all that you need to know and will explain the arrangements to you. Letters will be sent to inform you when you may return. Will he be able to read them?" asked the emir.

"He can, Your Majesty, but he must continue to practice," said al-Khatib.

"That then is our word of farewell," said Muhammad. "May God go with you on your journey, and practice."

"Your Majesty," asked Yusuf in a panic, "may I visit my mother one last time?"

"It sounds unwise," said Muhammad, with uncertainty in his voice, glancing toward al-Khatib.

"A thousand apologies for intruding into your thoughts, Your Majesty," said al-Khatib, "but may I suggest it might look odd if the youth did not visit his mother tomorrow? Perhaps if he swore not to mention his departure, it could be permitted. Then Your Majesty might permit a message to be conveyed to the Lady Noor once the city is aware that he has left."

"Any message you wish will be conveyed to her," said Muhammad.

"Your Majesty—I do not know how to say this, and it is not in any way meant to be—" Words failed him.

"Speak, Yusuf," said the emir coldly.

"Your Majesty, if the message could be conveyed very discreetly, for I fear my mother's house contains a—" He couldn't say the word.

"A spy?" asked Muhammad, laughing. "Of course it does. And if there is only one in your mother's house, I would be surprised. Whoever delivers the message will be well aware of the situation. Farewell, little cousin. We are happy that you were able to visit us. We will be delighted when you return. Now go with our secretary, who has much to tell you."

4.

"WHAT we are convinced of now," said al-Khatib, "is that someone has heard you speak of your father's death and of how you were saved. You were asked this many times, were you not?" asked al-Khatib.

"I was, Your Excellency, many, many times. I have told all of it to my mother, much of it to Nasr, some of it to Her Highness, the Lady Maryam, and perhaps to others. Everyone seemed to want to know."

"You also told me, and what struck me the most about your account was that you knew the men who came into the room after the fighting started, and that one of them identified your father to the Christian assassins, who then killed him."

"I told you that, Your Excellency? I was not aware of doing that," said Yusuf. "And I'm not sure that is what happened."

"I think it was," said the secretary. "And I'm sure the whole city knows it by now. Have you seen that man?"

"No, and I don't remember anything about him except that I knew him."

"I have no doubt he does not know that. And he may be someone who has avoided being seen by you since you arrived, in case your memory is stirred by seeing his face. I think it would be interesting to have you stay, but neither His Majesty the emir nor I wish to see you dead, and so you are to go. Now, listen carefully, for this is how it will be done."

"AND so, Nasr, you are to come with me. We will go to Guadix first to get your brother, who will also accompany us, and then carry on to the border. We leave in the middle of the night with a guard to protect us, and two men who know the road well to guide us. We should reach Guadix by first light. When we arrive at the border, you and your brother will return with the guard and the guides. Someone will be found to take me to Valencia."

"There are many *mudéjars*—our people who have been caught now in Christian lands as the border changes—who perform these services for the emir," said Nasr. "How I would love to cross the border with you and to see for myself the state of things in those lands."

"Zeynab would never forgive me if I left her again and this time took her betrothed with me," said Yusuf.

VII
Granada: Day Five

1.

"I hear you have been at the mosque all morning," said his mother. "Poor Yusuf. Could you understand any of it?"

"Some," he replied. "Nasr has been going over the prayers with me, and al-Khatib has given me a copy of the Qur'an to read from every day. They keep saying that I should have been doing all these things every day for years, but that doesn't help."

"Don't complain," said his mother, looking shrewdly at him. "It was not by a fault of your own that you were left among the unbelievers. It is greatly to your credit that you studied your language as much as you could. And should you ever be in the position again of having to live among the unbelievers, now you have the means to carry on with your studies."

"True," said Yusuf. "And I have a book of poetry, too."

"Excellent. Then let us talk of less gloomy subjects. When do you think that Zeynab should marry? She is quite enamored of Nasr, you know," said Noor, "but she is only twelve. I married your father when I was thirteen—I was a fearful, but happy bride—but I wish I could spare her the fears."

"Aren't all brides nervous?"

"Perhaps," said Noor. "Your father was so sweet and kind and gentle with me, that I quickly forgot my fears. As my mother assured me I would. You must remember that, when you marry, Yusuf, unless you should happen marry a bold widow who has long since cast her fears aside."

"I think she should marry as soon as she wishes," said Yusuf. "But perhaps not until she is thirteen or fourteen."

"Where is Nasr?" asked his mother.

"I expect he is on his way here," said Yusuf. "He was to fetch me for more lessons as soon as we had our little visit."

At that, the bell at the gate rang.

"That will be Nasr," said his mother. "Come, let me embrace my tall, handsome son—you are so like your father, you make me weep to see you." Then with her arms around him, she murmured in his ear, "Remember all I have told you and take very great care. Don't forget your prayers, and may God go with you."

"Who told you?" asked Yusuf.

"Al-Khatib," she murmured, pushing him away with a laugh. She dried the tears on her face with her silk scarf and called for Abdullah. "I shall see you tomorrow," she said. "We will have a better chance then to talk about the wedding."

As they walked across an almost empty plaza, Yusuf whispered very quietly to Nasr, "I think my mother knows all our plans."

"The Lady Noor knows everything," said Nasr. "Just like Her Majesty the Lady Maryam."

2.

THE night sky was filled with fast-moving clouds. The crescent moon, just past the quarter, appeared fitfully, like a dying fire that flares up and dies down again. Around midnight, the clouds began to disperse. Yusuf and Nasr, dressed in warm clothing against the chill of the night, were sitting in the dark in their apartment, talking very quietly, when Abdullah came in.

"It is time to go, lord," said Abdullah. "You are expected at once." He bowed and disappeared, leaving Yusuf with his words of farewell and thanks unspoken on his lips.

They moved silently down the stone staircase that led to the garden outside. The door at the foot of the stairs lay open, and as soon as they stepped outside, the moon cast off her veil and shone directly on them. Yusuf froze. But the two guards whom they had to pass were apparently suffering from temporary loss of sight, for they neither blinked nor moved a muscle.

A third guard stepped out of the darkness and beckoned them to follow. He led them, not back to where Yusuf had entered the fortress city, but in the opposite direction, toward one of the eastern towers. It, too, had two sets of massive doors. In each, the postern gate stood wide open, so that no sounds of opening or closing would betray their passage. The guards on duty ignored them as completely as the guards to the palace had.

They made their way as quietly as they could around the perimeter of the city until they came to a road that led down to the river. There, six men were waiting, mounted and ready to leave. Another was holding two riderless horses and a baggage mule. The guard who had brought Yusuf and Nasr there raised a hand for them to stop and went forward to hold a moment of whispered conversation with the man holding the horses. "My lord," he murmured, returning to them, "They would be pleased if you were to hasten to mount. The moon will set in an hour or two and that will slow your progress."

"Then by all means let us hurry," whispered Nasr.

"You will follow that horseman," continued the guard, "and ride in single file until you are told otherwise. Lord Nasr will ride behind you. It is necessary to maintain absolute silence until you are far from the palace."

IT was fortunate, thought Yusuf, that his horse appeared to know the road, because as the moon sank lower and lower into the western sky, its light became more and more unreliable. They plunged down a slope into total darkness, eased up a little back into the light and then began to move at a steady trot. Somewhere, the sound of running water promised that they were indeed following some river or other, and from the confidence of their movements, Yusuf decided that they must also be following a road, although he wasn't quite sure that he could pick it out.

Suddenly they were on what was definitely a road. The moon lit up a pale line that snaked through dark patches of what was probably farm land. Occasionally he saw the faint twinkle of an oil lamp and knew that somewhere around there must be a tiny farming village, where a child was sick in the night, or a woman was in childbirth, or a man was dying.

These thoughts plunged him into a deep gloom, and he shivered. It was cold out here, and fog clawed its way up to them from time to time, slowing their progress and caressing them with its clammy fingers.

At that point the moon dropped below the horizon and they were plunged in real darkness. The horse ahead slowed down, and so did Yusuf's. He had long since stopped trying to help her find her way. She seemed to have a much better idea of what she was doing than he did.

"We will be in Guadix before dawn," said Nasr from behind.

And Yusuf realized that the men in front of him had been carrying on a series of low conversations for some time. "Even at this speed?" asked Yusuf.

"Look ahead," said Nasr. "The sky is just beginning to lighten at the horizon. Soon we will be able to see the road quite clearly again."

THE next hour or two seemed to be a nightmare of visions and waking dreams. The pale road they were following in the blackness rose up and turned into a giant, silvery snake that was trying to wrap its coils around his body. He raised his hands to fight it off, and realized that he was grasping the reins as if trying to choke them. He could just see his mount's ears flick back in surprise at the unusual movements. "Sorry," he murmured, and she settled back into her gait, which he now realized was as somnolent as his own state.

Suddenly they were climbing up again. The sky had become

almost light, and the road was clearly visible. Yusuf fought off the last remains of sleep and for the first time was able to see his horse. She was a dark chestnut—almost black—mare, and elegantly formed, as far as he could see while seated on her. He turned back to comment on her, and discovered Nasr slumped in his saddle with his chin on his chest. "Nasr," he hissed, "wake up!"

"I'm not asleep," said his prospective brother-in-law. "I could not be wider awake. And see, did I not tell you it would be light soon? Guadix is not that far away now."

"Where did this horse come from?" he asked.

"The emir's stable."

"You mean it's his?"

"I don't think he rides it," said Nasr. "And don't worry. He won't miss it."

Every time the road leveled out, the procession speeded up to a lively pace, eating up the miles. As they went up a particularly fierce ascent, Nasr pulled up beside him. "How are you?" he asked.

"Starving," said Yusuf. "I could almost eat one of these lovely beasts, I am so hungry."

"Once we are over this little pass, we should be able to see the walls of Guadix."

3.

IF Ibrahim ibn Umar had been surprised to see his younger brother, Nasr, his future brother-in-law, Yusuf ibn Hasan, and six horsemen outside his door before sunrise, he had covered it with true diplomatic skill. "Nasr," he said, once they had managed to awaken the household sufficiently for him to be summoned to greet—or perhaps identify—the guests. "How delightful of you to pay a call. Where have you ridden from?"

"From home," he said, as if this were the most normal thing in the world. "Our mother is well, as are the rest of the family,

and I am sure that if they knew that I was here, they would send you their greetings."

"May I ask if all is well with you? I mean that you have undertaken this ride at this particular time?"

"Oh, yes," he said. "Although we are all rather hungry, having ridden all night."

"Then I suggest that we all take this opportunity to wash and prepare ourselves for morning prayers. After that we can all eat a hearty breakfast." He raised an eyebrow at a hovering manservant, who made a slight bow and disappeared.

BREAKFAST was laid out for all, Ibrahim, his young son, his wife, Salimeh, Nasr, Yusuf, and the guards. Once the guards had eaten, only the man who had led the troop along that long and very dark road remained; the other five went off to find some rest before starting again. Ibrahim's young son was taken off by a nursemaid.

"I have asked Salimeh to stay," said Ibrahim, "because she is a native of the lands that Nasr tells me you must pass through. She knows them well. She makes frequent trips through them to visit her family, and she also hears all the gossip about conditions on them."

"Where are you hoping to go?" she asked in a soft voice.

"Toward Lorca," said Yusuf cautiously.

"Across the border?" she asked.

Yusuf looked over at Nasr, then at Ibrahim and the guard. Their faces were expressionless. With an uncomfortable feeling that saying either yes or no could possibly mean signing a warrant for his death, he was silent for a moment. If he said "No," the next question would be, "Where are you going?" For that he had no answer. "Yes," he said. "To Lorca and beyond."

"I do not wish to force you to reveal anything that you do not wish to tell us," she said. "But some roads are at the moment rather difficult. Are you going alone?"

"We will find him a guide to take him to Valencia," said

the guard, showing no apprehension about revealing his final destination.

"Valencia," said Salimeh. "And you were thinking of travelling straight east from here and then heading up the coast?"

"More or less," said Nasr. "We are under orders not to cross the frontier except to find a reliable guide."

"I see," said Salimeh. "People have said to me that the best way to cross the frontier is now farther to the north. There has been trouble to the east."

"Christians?"

"They are men of no particular faith, I imagine," she said, with a ghost of a smile. "Thieves, bandits, murderers. The dregs of everyone's armies. They are more dangerous than regular soldiers, they say," she added apologetically.

"To the north?" asked the guard who brought them through. "Up to the Guadalquivir? It would take him days longer to reach Valencia."

"If you are set against that route," said Salimeh, "this is how I would proceed." She clapped her hands, and the manservant brought her a sharpened pen, a small pot of ink, and a piece of thick, well-made paper. With all four men crowded around her, she sketched out a map and a suggested route, talking in her gentle tones all the while.

VIII

The Road Home

1.

YUSUF stretched out on a thickly stuffed, comfortable pallet in a quiet corner of Ibrahim's house. Two more pallets had been set out for Nasr and their first guide, but they had elected to linger in the courtyard to talk further with Ibrahim. Yusuf was just trying to calculate how long it would take them to reach the border, going by Salimeh's map and instructions, when someone shook him roughly by the shoulder.

"Yusuf," said a familiar voice. "Wake up. It's time to move on."

He sat up groggily. "How long have I been asleep?" he asked.

"Almost half a day. Get up. There is water for washing in the little courtyard outside. We will eat after prayers and set out."

"Nasr," he said. "It's you."

"Of course it's me," he replied. "Come. Get up."

DISHES of many kinds had been set out in the main courtyard by a tall, stately manservant and a young maid. With little ceremony, everyone placed himself where he was most comfortable. Nasr and Ibrahim were next to each other, talking earnestly, when Yusuf came in. He looked around awkwardly, received a friendly smile from Salimeh, and found himself blushing, to his great embarrassment.

"You must eat," she said. "You have a long ride this afternoon and evening. The moon is with you tonight. Unless the weather turns dark and cloudy you will be able to carry on until midnight. Come, sit down, and enjoy one last meal in civilized surroundings for a while," she added, laughing teasingly.

That was to be a very prophetic remark.

WHEN Yusuf and Nasr came out of the gate to start on the next leg of the journey, there were seven horses and the baggage mule waiting for them, one horse fewer than they had arrived with. Four of the guards were waiting as well, already mounted. Ibrahim appeared at the gate, with Salimeh behind him. He turned to speak to her, she shook her head, smiled, and went back inside. The gate closed and, with a harsh screech, was locked behind her.

"What is happening?" asked Yusuf.

"Two of the guards were sent back with certain reports that His Majesty requires," said Ibrahim. "And I am ordered to accompany you to the border."

"I am desolated to have caused you such trouble," said Yusuf, uncomfortably.

"It is no trouble," said Ibrahim. "On the way I can make certain observations and reports for the emir. He feels that I can be of assistance to our guides, but I believe that in his generosity, he exaggerates my talents. You would be better off with my Lady Salimeh as guide. She knows every stone and every hollow and peak between here and the frontier. But she has other responsibilities, and therefore we must go without her."

"In that case, perhaps we should take the route suggested by the Lady Salimeh," said Yusuf. "She seems to be a woman of great wisdom."

"Ah—listen to the young man," said Ibrahim, laughing. "She has charmed him, too. Let me assure you, Yusuf, she casts a spell over every man she meets," her husband added. "It would trouble me, except that I swear she has no notion at all that she is doing it. She talks with all the innocence of a child, but the wisdom of a philosopher, and is the least flirtatious of women."

"How can one be sure of these things?" asked Nasr.

"So speaks the man who seriously desires to be married," said Ibrahim. "Believe me, there is so much gossip in a house like ours that no one has a moment of privacy without it being remarked upon and discussed. Like everyone else, we have malicious servants who would curry favor with me by denouncing my wife. I would quickly hear rumors of unwise conduct. But what they can accuse her of are entirely innocent matters, things that I have seen with my own eyes. She is not perfect, nor am I, but she is a jewel beyond belief."

"You are a fortunate man," said Yusuf.

"It speaks ill of your sister that you do not consider Nasr to be a fortunate man as well," said Ibrahim, laughing.

"You are both fortunate," said Yusuf. "I thought that was understood from the beginning. But we are not taking the northern route?"

"I think Salimeh suffers from a woman's fears that some evil will befall us," said Ibrahim. "I suspect she exaggerated the dangers of the route through Lorca in order to dissuade us. I have heard nothing of these bands of villains she speaks of. Perhaps the northern route is safer, but it would take longer, and all of us have good reason to wish to be home." Ibrahim spurred his horse and rode ahead to have a word with the guide.

THEIR progress was slow. The track they were following through the hills and mountains was narrow in some places and treacherous in others. There had been recent heavy rains in the area, and here and there, a sudden rush of water coming down a normally dry riverbed had washed out the road.

And in spite of Ibrahim's professed desire for a speedy trip, he insisted on stopping at every tiny collection of houses they came to. Sometimes this led to useful information on the state of the road ahead, or the presence of groups of unsavory characters. Mostly he seemed to be checking on the probability of having good crops of various grains and other important commodities this year. "You must forgive me," he kept saying.

"I have reports to submit to the emir in addition to assisting you."

TOWARD evening, they halted at a particularly large farmhouse. Ibrahim was received with great courtesy by the proprietor, who walked with him down a path leading toward an orchard. In moments they had both disappeared, leaving the others to be entertained by one of his sons.

"I hope you are not in a great hurry, my lords. They will be some time, I fear," said the son. "Lord Ibrahim comes by every two or three months, and he and my father have much to say to each other." He smiled shyly. "About what, I do not know, because they prefer to hold their conversations in peace. But I have ordered refreshments brought, and I would most earnestly invite you to dismount and rest and water your horses, as well as resting yourselves. Please, come into the shade of the courtyard, out of the sun and the wind."

Since it was becoming abundantly clear that Ibrahim was not simply pausing a moment to admire the orchard, they dismounted with a certain reluctance and accepted the youth's offer of hospitality. The guards seemed distinctly uneasy.

"My lord," said the guide to Nasr, "it might be wise to mention to the Lord Ibrahim that if we do not increase our pace, this journey is going to last several more days than we expected. It was impressed upon us most strongly that the young lord should be escorted to the border in safety with all possible speed. That was the only reason why I agreed that this route would be the wiser one. But we are losing our advantage with every unnecessary halt."

Nasr listened and nodded. Without a word, he rose to his feet and headed for the orchard. He did not have far to go, for as he walked through the arch leading in that direction, Ibrahim and Jabir, the prosperous-looking owner of the farm, opened the door in front of him and came into the house. Jabir murmured something to Ibrahim and left the two brothers in the passageway.

Yusuf watched them standing there, facing each other. Nasr was expostulating angrily; Ibrahim nodding his head peaceably, with an irritating, tolerant smile on his face. Finally they returned.

Little patches of color remained in Nasr's cheeks, and his eyes sparkled with anger.

"My thoughtful and conscientious brother reminds me of the haste that is enjoined upon us. And so I must ask you, my friends, to eat and drink your fill of this generous supper that has been set in front of us, but do not linger. The moon will be bright this evening, and we can ride far by its light." He smiled, speaking a word to his host and clapping his hand on the shoulder of his host's son, and found himself a place.

Shortly afterward, a new array of dishes came round, and then cups and a pitcher of a sweet, fruit drink. Yusuf raised the cup to his lips, sniffed as he now automatically did before eating or drinking anything, and paused. "Nasr," he said, "let me smell yours before you drink it."

Their guide, who had been observing all this with interest, put down his cup, murmured something to the guard next to him, and then simply watched.

Yusuf sniffed Nasr's cup, put his finger in it, tasted the liquid and grinned. "It's not going to kill us," he said, "but we wouldn't travel very far tonight with this in our bellies."

"A potion for sleeping?" asked the guide.

"And a good strong one," said Yusuf.

"Someone must have thought that we seemed very tired," said Nasr. "Thoughtful of them, don't you think? Nevertheless, we had better stop the others from drinking it."

"There is no point," said the guide. "Lord Ibrahim praised the quality of the beverage and exhorted everyone to drink deep. They did. How long before it sets to work?"

"It is a simple compound of poppy juice and another herb whose name I do not know in our language," whispered Yusuf. "The one is bitter and the other has an odd flavor, but distinctive. The mixture is not very strong, and so they will start to feel very sleepy in half an hour or so."

"Just long enough to get them mounted and on their way," said the guide. "There is more than one way to kill the fox."

Ibrahim rose to his feet, his cup more than half-full, and looked around to gather their attention. "Our host has suggested that, since you have all ridden long and hard since yesterday, that you rest for an hour or two before setting out. The night is clear, the moon is waxing and bright and will be high in the sky until well past midnight. He will make certain that every man is awake and mounted in no more than an hour or two. I think it is an excellent idea."

"Ibrahim," said his brother. "I beg you to consider . . ."

"Nasr, be a useful little brother, will you, and see that the men all have safe and quiet places to sleep."

"My lord Ibrahim, you may rest in my son's room. It will be quiet and away from the bustle of the house," said the host. "Lord Nasr and Lord Yusuf, you may take this room just off the courtyard. It is very comfortable and cool. The guards may rest above the stables or in the courtyard."

"I myself will go to my rest now," said Ibrahim. "For some reason, I feel quite tired."

The guards rose to their feet and made their way toward the gate. "I think that Ahmed and I will stay here with you lords," said their first guide very quietly. "Until we can see what is happening."

"The room is large," said Nasr. "Come in and spare yourself from the cold night air."

THEY stayed inside without talking until the house quieted down, and the light slowly began to fade in the room with its east-facing window. It seemed to Yusuf that hours had passed, but when Nasr opened the door to look around the courtyard, the sun had not yet set. The courtyard was empty. He looked up at the rooms above them and saw no sign of movement.

"I'm going out," he murmured. He walked around the courtyard, inspecting the rooms that gave on to the vaulted passage around it and came back in. "It's very quiet, except for a lot of snoring from one room or another. I think I will go and fetch my brother. I believe I know which room he is in, and I am sure that he drank very little of the drugged drink."

He slipped out. Not long afterward, he slipped back in. "Unless I climb to his window," he said, "and hang there singing to him, I see little chance of talking to him."

"What do you mean?" asked Yusuf.

"All the doors to upper floor are locked and barred. Most of the rooms down here are locked as well—except for this one."

"And the other guards, lord?" asked the guard, Ahmed. "Do you know where they are?"

"In the room next to us," said Nasr. "But I assure you that they will be of little use. They sleep like the dead, except that they are still breathing."

"One moment," he answered, and slipped out. In less than a minute he returned. "They too are safely locked in," he said. "And if they should wish it, the key is slipped under the door."

"Then may I suggest, lords," said the guide, "that the four of us take advantage of their oversight and ride out as quickly as we can."

The four men moved as quietly and as quickly as they could out to the stables and fetched the harness. Their horses were dozing in a treed paddock; only the mule was awake and alert.

"We will be faster without her," said Yusuf. "Since she must be led, and that will slow someone down. I can take whatever I value from my box and leave it here. What else is she carrying?"

"Water bottles," said Ahmed. "Twelve water bottles."

"We will take them, three each, and fill them before we leave the mountains," said the guide.

They went back into the dim light of the stable to fetch the rest of the gear. "Sort through your things, Lord Yusuf, and hurry," the guide whispered.

Automatically reacting to the urgency in the man's voice, Yusuf opened his box, took out his books and a few clothes, all of which he wrapped in his old cloak. He tied the bundle up firmly, pushed the box back out of the way, took some of the water bottles, and headed back outside.

When he reached the paddock, all the horses were ready but his mare; he picked up the bridle, had it snatched from his hand by the guide, who slipped it onto her head with one rapid gesture and then mounted his own horse, as Ahmed was saddling her.

"Put your sword with your bundle, lord," whispered Ahmed. "You will find this more useful in real danger." As he spoke, he was fastening a long dagger in its sheath around Yusuf's waist. Yusuf tied his bundle and his sword behind the saddle and mounted as quickly as he could.

As he left the paddock, their guide was already waiting at the road, with Nasr behind him. "Make haste," he hissed at them and set his horse to a gallop, with the others following through the clear evening light, toward the east.

All told, thought Yusuf, they had left the farmhouse in less time than it takes to walk calmly from the house to the road. The mule watched their departure with interest, but wisely kept silent.

2.

TOWARD the top of a rise well shielded by trees, the guide slowed his mount to a walking pace. They all followed suit and came to a stop near the height. "It would be good to know what is happening behind us," said the guide. "Should anyone seem to be interested in our departure, there is a different road on the other side of the hill that we could take. I suggest we go into the trees here so that we do not stand out against the skyline on the ridge, and I will see what I can see."

"The difficulty with being in this charming forest," said Nasr as they moved in among the trees, "is that we cannot see anything but each other and the trees."

"As soon as we are safely shielded from view, I will climb up on those rocks," said the guide. "The view is excellent from there."

"It will be faster if I climb up that tree," said Yusuf, pointing to a sturdy and thickly branched evergreen right next to them. "The view should be almost as good."

"And are you experienced at tree-climbing, lord?" asked the guide, somewhat surprised.

"I am excellent at it. Many times in my life my ability to hide in trees has saved me from capture," he said. "And I have good vision." He dismounted and began to climb like a monkey up through the branches. When the tree began to sway with his weight, he stopped.

"What can you see, lord?"

"I can see the farm, I think," said Yusuf. "It looks different from here, but there was only one other on the slope, much smaller, and I can see that one as well." He crawled farther out on the limb he was perched on. "Yes, there is the orchard. There are lights at the house," he said. "Or a fire. It moves from place to place."

"Is the house on fire?" asked Nasr, his voice very controlled and level.

"I don't think so," said Yusuf. "The light moves from place to place like someone carrying a lamp from room to room. It is not at all like a fire spreading. I think there are more lamps in the courtyard and people moving about in one or two rooms."

"Do you see horsemen?"

"I cannot see horsemen, but I can see a wisp of fog which may be dust rising. There!" he said, his voice rising. "Horsemen at a gallop. They were behind a rise," he added apologetically. "Six or seven—seven horsemen, on this road, coming toward us at a rapid pace." As he spoke he was dropping down through the branches as fast as he could, careless of scrapes and scratches.

"And that is our signal to leave," said the guide.

⊶═· ═⊷

THEY crested the height staying in single file, close to the trees, but as soon as they were over it they moved at a slow and careful canter down a steepish slope. "There, lords," said the guide. "That path to the left will take us to the frontier at a different point, farther to the north, but perhaps more safely. Much more safely."

"Will they not realize we must have gone in this direction, and probably down this road?" asked Nasr.

"Perhaps," said the guide. "And perhaps not. It can be confusing terrain. You will see."

The path plunged down through a forested area. As they descended, slowly and cautiously, darkness filled with vague shapes closed in around them. Suddenly, it ended. The slope flattened out, the forest thinned to nothing and in front of them they could see in the orange light of sunset a stretch of rough grassy land. Yusuf looked back at the hill they had just come down and shook his head in disbelief. On either side of the forested path they had followed, steep cliffs loomed with piles of broken rock at their foot. Every step now was treacherous.

"Here we must proceed at a walk," said the guide. "We stay as close to the line of cliffs to our left as we can. Don't fall behind, lords."

They picked their way through tough, bunchy grass, around masses of broken rock, and down into dry riverbeds that still had a trickle of water running through them. The landscape around them changed as they went, but they continued on through the rugged plain. The moon, riding high in the heavens, replaced the fading twilight. It was bright enough to light their way, and Yusuf reckoned that the night was at least half over. Their guide turned up a streambed and halted.

He signaled for silence, dismounted, and disappeared. The others waited, straining to hear, peering into the darkness. After several minutes, he appeared again, standing at Yusuf's stirrup. "We will spend the night here," he said in his normally soft voice. "There is water ahead of us, grass, and shelter under the cliffs."

"How do you know all this?" asked Nasr.

"I was born and grew up not more than a mile away from here. Move carefully. In front of us is a deep pool. The water is good, but cold for swimming," he said, and Yusuf could not tell if he were serious or gently mocking them.

YUSUF slept heavily until the sound of birds preparing themselves for the day nudged him awake. He rolled onto his back. Something hard and sharp dug into him. Something irritating tickled his cheek. He opened his eyes and saw the faint outlines of rock above him.

He sat up cautiously and looked around. He seemed to be in a shallow cave. To his right was the opening, a largish oval of silvery light, and between him and that opening lay Nasr, sleeping peacefully on his side. Yusuf got up very carefully, bending over to avoid hitting his head, and stepped over his prospective brother-in-law. He crouched down to make his way out and dropped down the short distance to the ground.

The guide and Ahmed, their remaining guard, were seated between the pool and a small iron pot from which emanated a very appetizing smell. "Where did that come from?" asked Yusuf.

"The kindness of neighbors," said the guide. "They live not far from here. I also have bread, curds, and fruit that a nearby farmer let us have. We have water for washing and for drinking, and the horses have grass. It is a pity we cannot stay here, but it would be most unwise."

"What would be most unwise?" asked a voice from above them.

"Staying here much longer, Lord Nasr," sked the guide. "I am not the only person who knows about this place."

THEY ate a substantial amount of the food that the guide had managed to scrounge from the vicinity, keeping only some bread and fruit to eat later. "What about the pot?" asked Yusuf, well aware of the trouble a missing pot could cause in a kitchen.

"It will be rescued by the kind people who let us have it for a while," said the guide. For a moment a grin flashed across his face. It disappeared and his serious demeanor returned. "Let me explain to you what I had in mind, and you can of course make what decisions seem best to you." He smoothed out a patch of dry earth and picked up a twig. "Here is the road that we were on, and the farm that we left," he said in a very neutral voice. "We would have joined up to the road toward Lorca, which more or less runs through the valleys, perhaps an hour's ride or less if we had not come down here. I do not know the nature of the people who seek out the young lord, but it occurs to me that going straight north and seeking help from the strongholds there might be as unwise as seeking rest and comfort from Jabir seemed to have been."

"You are a master of diplomacy," said Nasr. "And I agree with you. If you do not know the face of your enemy, then you cannot know the face of your friend. But I interrupt you."

"Yes, lord," said the guide, his twig working quickly. "I suggest that we ride to the north and the east here, where there is a river crossing, and then we head straight for the pass in this line of hills. It is not much frequented, since it is easier to go around the hills than through them, but on that route we will have water, food, and at least one or two trustworthy friends, I think."

"More trustworthy, you mean, than my brother, Ibrahim," said Nasr bitterly.

"We do not know what was in Lord Ibrahim's mind, lord," said the guide. "This may have been a plot hatched by Jabir, the farmer, at the instigation of others."

"Which others?" asked Nasr.

"Anyone who observed our arrival in Guadix," said the

guide, "and realized that we would most likely head for the road to Jabir's property."

"I wish I could believe you," said Nasr. "But it was my brother, who when ordered by His Majesty to move with all haste, deliberately stopped at every settlement, giving enough time for all of Granada to arrive at Jabir's before we did. I believe he sent messages back with those two guards. I was told, on the highest authority, that they were to stay with us until we reached the frontier. And when those horsemen arrived at the farm, to a house full of sleeping people, all safely behind barred doors, they should have found one room with the door left unlocked, and the four of us in it, sleeping like the dead."

"No," said Yusuf. "The other two guards were also sleeping in an unlocked room off the courtyard, were they not?"

"They were," said the guide. "But, lord, if you remember, Ahmed, here, locked their door and somehow pushed the key into the room so that they could let themselves out when they woke up."

"It was a badly fitting door," said the guard. "And since the horsemen were apparently not intent on firing the property, then I expect they are sleeping there still."

"Since we do not know the cause of any of these misfortunes," said the guide, "except that I would stake my life on the truth that it cannot have been on orders from the emir, whose voice I can still hear in my head, then I think that we had best avoid people as much as we can."

"When we cross the pass, we will pick up another river and follow it upstream until we come into a stretch of land that I know well," said Ahmed. "I have friends there who will not question why we are riding toward the frontier. People have many reasons for doing so, and some of those reasons are less noble than others. Therefore, we who live there do not ask unnecessary questions."

"It was very good fortune that you two were picked to accompany us," said Yusuf.

"It was not good fortune," said the guide. "His Majesty sought out three reliable men from three areas of the eastern frontier to accompany you, and ordered us to stay as close to you as a tick to a donkey."

"Who was the other?" asked Nasr.

"One of the two who were sent back. The emir will know when they return that something has gone wrong."

"How long will this new route take us?" asked Yusuf.

The two men bent over the map drawn in the earth and murmured to each other.

"After today? Two days," said the guide. "Maybe less. It is not that far, but the terrain is often difficult, hard on the horses. In places water will be scarce, and because of the heat, it will be best to ride by moonlight and in the cool of the morning."

"Unless it rains," said Ahmed wryly. "Then we will have to be careful of flooding."

BUT it did not rain. They filled their water bottles with cold water from the pool, packed up their food, and set out. They passed through land that was a patchwork of rock, forest, and dry gulleys, and by farms rich with wonderful things: olives, almonds, pears, and countless numbers of vegetables, all growing in flat steps of land cut out of the steep hills and mountains, shored up with stone or log walls, and irrigated by tiny streams of water that ran along each step and then down to the next.

They forded the river with no difficulties and found themselves on an excellent track, shady and cool, along the bank. "This is better," said Yusuf. "All we need now is a great dish of rice and chickpeas to sustain us."

"With grilled mutton," said Nasr, laughing.

At that moment, their guide turned abruptly to the right up a rocky pathway back into the the burning sun.

"Is it not easier to keep by the river?" asked Nasr.

"Everyone finds it easier to keep by the river," was the reply. "And look over there. That is where the river, in its own time, would take us." To the northwest, on their left, on a rise of land in the distance, they could see fortifications. "We are heading for those hills," he said, turning toward the north-east.

Yusuf's heart sank. They seemed very far away.

The day grew hotter and hotter. When the sun was right overhead, and they were toiling up a particularly hilly section, their guide stopped. He scanned the landscape and pointed over to a largish outcrop of rock. The horses picked up their heads and began to move faster. Ahead there were trees and a small stream, patches of grass and shade. "We will rest until the sun hits that point," said the guide, gesturing to the west.

They unsaddled the horses, shared out the food, and stretched out on their cloaks to sleep.

3.

AS Yusuf was still riding, somewhat uncomfortably, across the rugged landscape of eastern Granada, hoping that they could find a cool place to stop, Isaac was lingering over his breakfast in his courtyard. It was a very pleasant day for late May, neither hot nor excessively cool, and he was enjoying the relative peace and calm around him. Birds, both wild and caged, sang from their perches. Somewhere his little son slept, dreaming whatever babies dream of. Now that was a question for pondering, thought Isaac idly.

But he was not left idle long enough to consider it. A clanging of the bell at the gate brought him to his feet and heading for his study. At the same time, he shouted for Ibrahim to admit the visitor.

"It is my master," said the boy at the gate. "Master Raimon. He is very ill and requires you at once. The mistress begs that you come out to the *finca* to see him. He cannot possibly travel."

THIRTY minutes later, Isaac, Raquel, and Jonàs the kitchen boy were following the messenger as quickly as they could manage out to Raimon's farm.

The day was becoming hot, and they were dusty from travel when they reached the *finca*. The gate lay open. As they rode in, the door into the substantial farmhouse also opened, and a man came out to greet them.

"I am Guillem," he said. "I am—" He paused. "Part of Raimon's family. Everyone else is with him at the moment. I said I would wait here for you and bring you to where he lies."

As he was speaking, a big man came quietly over and assisted Isaac and then Raquel to dismount. He turned their mules over to the messenger and stepped back.

"I am Isaac the physician," said Isaac. "And you, sir?" he asked, turning in the direction of the man who assisted him.

"I am Esteve," he said. "I have the honor of being Master Raimon's steward."

"Master Raimon has spoken of you, most highly," said Isaac. "Now, if someone could fetch us means of washing and towels, and take us to our patient, we will see what we can do. Jonàs, remember."

"Remember what, Mistress Raquel?" asked the bewildered boy.

"To bring all those things," hissed Raquel. "And carefully. I will carry this box," she said, taking a small cask containing vials of precious materials.

A hand was laid gently on Isaac's arm as he made his way into the house with his daughter. "Master Isaac, I am Marta, Raimon's wife. He is the room behind me."

"If it would not upset you," said Isaac. "Could you tell me exactly what has happened today? The messenger was rather incoherent."

"Certainly," she said quickly.

"Excellent. The more I know before I see him, the faster I

can work, so tell me everything you can, as quickly as you can."

"Let me say first that he was much better for about a week after the last time he went to see you," said his wife. "He told me about your suggestion that he visit the bishop and tell him what has been disturbing him. To our surprise, His Excellency came to the *finca* a few days later. They had a long talk, and he felt relieved by what he heard. I thought things were getting better.

"Then last night he could not sleep. This morning he ate a little breakfast, and about an hour later he became very ill, with pains in his stomach and all through his body. I sent for you."

"Has he vomited what was in his stomach?"

"Yes."

"Good. Let us visit him."

Raquel was with him, and as soon as her father came in, whispered her observations rapidly in his ear. Isaac leaned over, feeling Raimon's neck, listening to his chest, and then probing his abdomen with great care. "How are you, my friend?" he asked gently.

"Better than I was earlier," he whispered. "As soon as I felt the pain in my stomach, I made myself vomit until there was nothing left to bring up."

"That was a wise precaution," said Isaac.

"I reflected on your opinion that dreams rarely cause symptoms such as fever and chills or pains in the limbs, but that such things sometimes seem to cause bad dreams. I did not wish to suffer more of them."

"Your limbs are cramping?"

"They are," said Raimon.

"Raquel," said her father. "Take a cup of water and put a drop from the first vial into it. Let me smell it to make sure that it is the correct one."

She poured the water, took out the vial and uncorked it, holding it a few inches to her father's nose.

"That is the one," said Isaac, turning back to his patient.

"There are so many things we do not know," said Isaac. "But there is still much that we can observe and note."

"It is ready, Papa."

"Then I wish you to drink this whole cup of liquid," said Isaac. "It should ease the cramping. Raquel?"

"Yes, Papa."

"Please—would you now go to the kitchen and steep enough of the herbs against pain to make at least two or three cups. I would like you to do it yourself." Isaac stepped back from the bed and added, very softly, "While you are there, make note of anyone who approaches you, no matter who, or goes near the mixtures. And no one should be allowed close to the rest of the medications. Where are they now?"

"I had Jonàs bring them into the sickroom so that I could keep my eyes on them," said Raquel. "And Papa," she murmured in his ear, "that man who let us in really does look like Master Raimon, except not so pleasant."

"WE are preparing a mixture that will ease the rest of your discomfort and allow you to sleep a little. Then perhaps you will be able to drink some broth," said Isaac.

"My problems are not worth all this time and effort, Master Isaac," said Raimon. "No matter what is done, in the end it does not help. I begin to think that I suffer from a sickness of the soul that I do not understand, and since I do not understand it, I cannot overcome it."

"This is your indisposition speaking, Raimon, not your soul. I think it possible that you have eaten some food that was not wholesome. We will try to discover what it was," he said.

"I ate what was on the table," said Raimon. "As did everyone else. They are not ill."

"And you have eaten nothing else except for that which was shared by everyone?" asked Isaac.

"Nothing else," said Raimon. "Not to my knowledge."

"I cannot believe that melancholy is the cause of your complaint. I have seen strong, cheerful men before this who were stricken with melancholy, and it was a painful sight, but it did not happen in this way. You have no cause that I can see—hidden or open—to despair. You do not suffer so profoundly that you are deaf to your family's suffering. You know, I think, that they are distraught by your ill health. I surely can hear it their voices."

"I hear it too, Master Isaac," said Raimon. "Only my brother—my so-called brother—chips away at my happiness, watching me with eyes like a hawk on its prey. He murmurs that I harbor an enemy in the house, and that he must keep me well since I am the only family he has. It chills my soul to hear his words."

"People can feign tears, but they have difficulty hiding triumph or sorrow in their voices," observed Isaac.

"Triumph," said Raimon. "That is it. I hear triumph in his voice. He is winning, and I do not even know where the battle is being fought."

Raquel appeared at the door with the soothing draught for pain; she looked at the patient and then her father, and set it down. "It is cool enough to drink now," she murmured. "Will you take it now?"

Raimon nodded and allowed her to give it to him.

"What you were saying is interesting," said Isaac as soon as he heard Raquel closing the door behind her. "Who does Master Guillem murmur against?"

"Sometimes my steward, Esteve, who is surely the most upright man in the county, Master Isaac. And sometimes my sons, saying that they long for independence and control of my estate."

"Send him away," said Isaac. "Your health at the moment cannot withstand such worry."

"How can I send away someone whose every feature speaks of the closeness of our ties? Someone who otherwise would be bereft? Think of how fortune has favored me, Master Isaac, and disappointed him."

"Can you afford to settle a sum on him that will help him to live, even if he cannot earn his own bread? On the condition, of course, that he leave the province of Girona and not return?"

Raimon paused for a while, his eyes beginning to droop sleepily as his body relaxed a little from pain. But his voice, when he spoke, was firm and clear. "I can," he said. "Why did I not think of that before? That will banish at least one of my disturbances."

"And have you had more disturbing dreams?" asked Isaac.

"I do not know," said Raimon. "I cannot speak of it. Not now. It is all jumbled in my mind." His voice trailed off, and he slept.

ISAAC sat by his patient's side, listening to his even breathing, and thinking about everything that Raimon had said to him about himself. He was interrupted at last by Raquel again, who came in and murmured that dinner was prepared and on the table. Could he come down and have something to eat? She would sit with Master Raimon.

"I will. But first, my dear, please come down with me and choose one or two small dishes for our patient. He seems to be stirring a little; I think he will wake soon."

WHEN the physician and his daughter came into the room, the family, including Guillem and Esteve, the steward, were gathered around the table. Raquel cast a quick eye over the dishes that had been set out and went over to speak to Marta.

"We need a little dish of something very light that Master Raimon enjoys," said Raquel. "Could you help me to choose?"

"Certainly," said Marta. "The stirred eggs are his favorite dish," she said.

"Then we will start with that." Raquel spooned some eggs into a dish and carried it over to Marta. "Could you taste it, please?" she asked.

"What an excellent idea," said Marta calmly, and took a large spoonful.

"YOU have never met my family, Master Isaac," said Marta, when they were all seated and served with something to eat. "We are all here today, and although because of Raimon's illness, we are perhaps not our usual selves, still we are very relieved that he is improving. To be able to think about eating after this morning is a very heartening sign, is it not?"

"It is," said Isaac. "He is doing well."

"Sitting next to you," she said, "is Esteve, our steward. I don't know how we would have been able to do what we did with this farm without him, for when we arrived, we knew nothing of the weather and the crops that grow well here. They are somewhat different, as you probably know, and require different methods. In Lleida we battled wind and weather, not to say rain when it wasn't wanted, and sun when it dried up the crops—just as we do here, but in different ways. But Esteve knew everything and kept us from making disastrous mistakes. He still does. Next to him is our son Pau, who is his father's right hand."

"I have heard much about you, Master Pau," said Isaac, "all of it good, and from several sources, not just your father. I know you are a great help to him."

"It is our fear that Pau will do what we constantly urge him to do, which is to take up the farm in Lleida. It is his, but he leaves it leased and prefers to live here."

"And who would not, Mama," said Pau. "I am pampered and cosseted, and I have excellent friends here as well."

"Including some very pretty ones," a laughing voice said.

"And that nasty young thing," said Pau, laughing as well, "is Roger Bernard, my brother. But he is, Master Isaac, basically a good-hearted fellow."

"I am, sir," said Roger Bernard. "But I did want to point out that it was not just piety that keeps my older brother so close to his family's bosom."

"Roger Bernard enjoys the privilege of a youngest child to be outrageous," said his mother fondly. "And sitting across from you, next to Roger Bernard, is Guillem. He is the man who kindly waited at the door to make sure that you were admitted at once. He has been visiting my husband for a few weeks and has been a great help to us all during these difficulties."

"I am Raimon's half-brother," said Guillem.

His accent was odd and his voice light. There was nothing of Raimon in it, thought Isaac, but then if what Raimon had told him was correct, the two boys had been raised from infancy in completely different surroundings.

"Through the oddities of life," said Marta, "they had never met until a little while ago."

"I had heard on a visit to my childhood home that I had a half-brother in Girona," said Guillem softly. "Well—I always knew that I had a half-brother, but I did not know where he lived or under what name. And so having received a commission to negotiate some business in the area, I decided I would stay until I found him. I am a notary," he added.

"And are these the only people living in the house?" asked the physician.

"Except for the servants," said Marta. "You have met the boy who delivered the message. Otherwise there is the cook, our maid, Justina, and the kitchen maid, Sanxa."

"And how long have they been with you?" asked Isaac.

"Cook has been with us since a few days after we moved here, Justina came to us some eight years ago, and Sanxa—she is our second kitchen maid in this house—we found, I think, five years ago. But she isn't here right now. Her mother is ill, and she has gone home to see her."

"You have no new servants?"

"None. Even the boy has been with us for two years now," said Marta. "And we have known him for longer than that, for he is the son of our head farm worker and has always lived in a house on the estate. And now I must go to see my husband," said Marta. "If you will excuse me."

"I will come with you, mistress," said Isaac, "to check on my patient."

"I, too, must excuse myself," said Esteve, the steward. "I have my own patients in the barn. We have had some trouble with the livestock. I must see to them."

RAIMON was sleeping, having eaten a little of the dish of stirred eggs and drunk a cup of wine mixed with a great deal of water.

"I will sit with him for a while longer," said Raquel. "I have brought my work."

"Then let us go out for a stroll around the orchard," said Marta. "I find it easier to speak out-of-doors."

"What sort of man is your steward, Esteve?" asked Isaac, once they were near the orchard.

"Esteve? He is quiet and shy, very courteous, very helpful. He is also intelligent, skilled, and can be short-tempered when dealing with pompous fools. He has been with us now for ten years, and we have never had cause to mistrust him. The boys love him dearly. He is a widower—his wife and children died of the plague while visiting her family in the city—and I think he never recovered from the blow. He had a small holding, but lost it because he did not have the strength nor the will to save himself after the catastrophe. He was recommended to us by His Excellency, the bishop, and the Church has never done our family a better turn."

"Tell me," said Isaac, "do you trust your brother-in-law?"

"My so-called brother-in-law?" she said. "I realize that, looking alike as they do in so many ways, they must be related, but no two human beings could be so different in every other way. They cannot be brothers. Perhaps they are cousins."

"True," said Isaac. "I, of course, cannot see to tell. I can only hear, smell, and touch them. In those ways they are not the same. My daughter says they look alike in many ways. She does not doubt his claim to be at least a half-brother."

"That is what my sons say," said Marta. "I do not like him," she continued, "as you can no doubt guess, but, Master Isaac, if you are suggesting that he has caused Raimon's troubles, there are two reasons at least why that is impossible. First of all, they started before my husband had even met him, and for the second reason, he has no reason at all for harming my husband. He himself is not legitimate. He says that the grandfather or whoever it was left no will, and in the absence of a will, he has no chance of laying claim to a penny from the estate. To benefit in any way from the family property, if it exists, he has to count on my husband's generosity. Therefore he is very solicitous of his brother's welfare, spending a great deal of time with him."

"Does this property, if it exists, come down through Raimon's father's line or Raimon's mother's line?" asked Isaac.

"It must be through the father," said Marta. "Or Guillem would have no claim at all to it. Was the father not the heretic? It would have been his property, or his family's property, that was confiscated."

"I wonder," said Isaac.

BY late afternoon, Raimon seemed to be much improved. "Raquel," said Isaac, "I think we may safely leave our patient to the excellent care of his wife."

"Thank goodness for that," said Raimon. "I do not enjoy having the whole household tiptoeing about because of me. I thank you, Master Isaac, for your help.

"I will come out with you to the gate," said Marta. "I, too, am most grateful, but these episodes worry me.

"Mistress Marta," said Isaac, once they had left the house, "from now on, I want you to supervise every morsel that goes into the sick man's mouth. He is not to be left alone, and what he eats must always come from the common dish and be carried up to him by you, and you alone, until he is strong enough to eat with the family."

"I shall protect him in every way I can," said Marta. "And may Heaven call down its vengeance on whomever is doing this to my husband, for I am sure it cannot be a natural force causing this disturbance in his soul, nor could God wish such a punishment on a man as good as my Raimon."

"Now," said Isaac, as they rode away from Master Raimon's *finca*, "tell me, my dear, what you observed in the kitchen."

"About the infusion?"

"No—everything you noticed."

"If you wish. It was not a happy kitchen, Papa. Not like ours, for Naomi can be difficult, but she is fond of Jacinta and Jonàs, and she and Leah are friends. At the *finca,* the kitchen maid wasn't there, for some reason, and so the housemaid was helping, and it was clear they didn't like each other."

"The kitchen maid's mother is ill," said Isaac.

"I liked the cook. She was busy and impatient, like Naomi, but a good sort of woman, and clever. The housemaid, Justina, is a tall, striking sort of young woman, but she spent most of her time getting in the way, and a lot of it watching me. I couldn't tell if she was interested, or just lazy and avoiding her own work. Or if she wanted to interfere with the mixture."

"Do you think she might have been trying to do that?"

"If she was, she has a gift for deception. She seemed to me to be just sulky and lazy and more trouble than she's worth. I would get rid of her in an instant if I were Mistress Marta."

4.

YUSUF, Nasr, and their guides got up at about six in the evening and set out again, riding across difficult landscape until the moon drifted down below the line of hills. "We will stop here," said their guide, "and continue on when it is light."

Yusuf had barely closed his eyes when dawn arrived and, fortified with water and two or three hours of sleep, they set out again. The terrain became more and more difficult; their pace slowed to a careful crawl. The sun felt as if it had as much strength in the early morning as it had the previous day at noon. Then, as Yusuf was eyeing the water bottles tied to his mare and considering pouring some—just a little—of that water on his head, the guide turned and spoke.

"We go up here," he said, and turned onto a track that led them to a shabby farmhouse. The guide called out, and a small, bent man, one who looked as if he had labored hard all his life, came out from around the house. He greeted their guide like a long-lost son, with great cries and warm embraces.

The guide cut him short. "We need beds and food until it is cool enough to travel again, my friend. Can you supply them? And water for the horses? The gentleman will gladly pay whatever you ask."

The countryman laid out bread, cheese, olives, dried fruits, and nuts. "We will kill a lamb for you if you wish. I would give it to you, if I could, but . . ."

"No. You will swiftly die of starvation if you give away all your food," said the guide. "Can you have it cooked before evening? We will eat some then, take a little with us, and leave the rest for you."

"And if someone comes by and asks to whom belong these splendid horses?"

"A trader friend of yours, who is taking them to—wherever you wish—and will be annoyed if they disappear. Do you think it likely someone will ask?"

"Yesterday, someone came by and asked if I had seen you recently," he said. "I was very surprised. He gave me this," he added, taking a silver coin from a pot on his table. "And said there would be more if I had word of you."

"How interesting," said the guide. "My master has more to give than that thin coin."

"I am not so easily bought," said the old man. "In these times, friends are more precious and necessary than money."

THEY slept until the smell of grilling lamb drove them from their rest. They ate chunks of lamb wrapped in bread, more olives, and fruit. Then they wrapped a large piece of the remnants in a cloth, along with flat bread, nuts, and more olives. A generous amount of money changed hands, and they rode off. As they disappeared from sight, the old man was burying his unexpected wealth in a corner of the garden.

From the old man's house, the other guard, Ahmed, took over the direction of the group. He took them across a dry, dusty, windswept area, broken here and there by a fertile patch. When the heat became dizzying, they suddenly turned southeast. "We should pick up the river," said Ahmed. "And then I know someone reliable."

They had hoped to repeat the pattern of the previous day, finding themselves a safe bed with water and fodder for the horses for the long, hot afternoon, but when they rode up the track to a small farmhouse, he stopped. "It is very quiet," he said. "Stay there."

He dismounted and pushed open the door of the house. They waited. Finally their guide dismounted, drew his sword, and walked quietly up to the house. He went around the house toward the back. A few moments later he came out the door facing them with Ahmed. "Gone," said Ahmed. "They have all gone, and whatever was left in the house has been destroyed."

"It is not safe to stay here," said the guide. "We will continue on."

"He seems very upset," said Yusuf to the guide.

"He is. They were his aunt and uncle. In all likelihood they are dead, along with his cousins," said the guard grimly.

From there they followed the river down until Ahmed stopped them. "From now on, this area will be patrolled on both sides," he said. "We will go north again and cross where they do not expect it."

They crossed the frontier by the light of an almost full moon. There was no way that Yusuf could tell he had crossed the frontier, except that Ahmed, who seemed to know the land very well, told them that it was so.

"And so you must stay here and make no noise. I will go and find a reliable guide for Lord Yusuf."

5 .

YUSUF scarcely had time to say farewell to Nasr and to thank the guards who had brought him safely thus far, when he was thrust into the care of a thin, weather-beaten *mudéjar,* one of the vast number of Muslims who, with every turn in the fortunes of war, suddenly found themselves living under Christian rule.

"I am most grateful that you are willing to escort me across the territory," said Yusuf in Arabic. "My name is Yusuf ibn Hasan . . ."

"If you don't want to be arrested on sight," said his new guide, speaking in Valencian, "you had better change languages at once."

"Are there patrols in this part of the land?" asked Yusuf.

"Not many, but those that are here certainly know what Arabic sounds like. Where do you want me to take you?"

"To Valencia."

"It can't be done," he said.

"Why not?" asked Yusuf. "I am travelling legally, with papers, even though I had reasons to slip across the border unnoticed. I have friends in Valencia," he added. "Respectable friends."

"I'm glad," said the *mudéjar.* "But the problem is not that. It is getting through to the city. Your papers will do you no good if you cannot reach the city."

"What is to prevent us?" asked Yusuf curiously.

"There are various difficulties along here, friend," he said. "And you are dressed oddly for a Castilian or a Valencian. If we travel directly east, if the Castilians don't take us, the Valencians will. You may or may not have papers that someone is willing to look at, but I have none." He held up a hand to forestall Yusuf's objections, should he have any. "More likely, we will be taken by bandits, who are starving these days and care nothing for either king. Or the emir. Times are hard around here."

"Then how am I to get home?"

"Where is home?"

"Girona," he said. "Or even Barcelona. I have friends there, too."

He looked at Yusuf and then cast an eye around as if assessing the dangers around them. "I will take you north to Albacete," he said. "There I will find you someone to take you east to Gandia or somewhere else along that coast. From there you can get a boat to Valencia or a ship to Barcelona. Where have you come from?"

"Granada."

"You're mad," he said. "I don't know what you're doing here. You should have sailed from Almeria. Who could have suggested that you come this way right now?"

THE second evening, the moon seemed to hang bright, hot, and heavy up in the heavens. His mare was edgy and unlike herself, and the *mudéjar* was even less communicative than he had been. Up until this point none of the threatened dangers had materialized, and they were moving at a good pace on a reasonable stretch of road. Perhaps there was a storm coming from over the mountains to the west, thought Yusuf, because there was something in the air.

The *mudéjar* was riding ahead when he pulled his horse up and raised a hand for Yusuf to stop. Yusuf rather nervously guided the mare over to the side of the road, under some trees. His guide listened and then moved forward. Suddenly, he pulled his horse's head around, screaming, "Fly!" in Arabic. Yusuf caught a glimpse of a crowd of horsemen around the *mudéjar,* before he dug his spurs into the mare. She tore down the slope by the side of the road.

THE next thing he knew, he was lying on his side in a pool of wetness. He felt bitterly cold and in pain everywhere from his head to his legs. Unable to account for the way he felt, he moved an arm gingerly and then one of his legs. They were stiff, but not much more uncomfortable in movement than when lying still. He rolled over on his back, with no evil effects except for an increase in the pounding in his head. He sat up, touching his arm with one hand and looking around in horror. He was outside, alone, and sitting in a streambed carrying a trickle of water along its course. His clothes were gone. He was naked, stripped of everything.

Then memory began pouring back. He had been riding; the *mudéjar* was attacked. He had tried to escape, obviously without any success. It was odd that he was still alive.

And where was his poor little mare, who had brought him all this way only to fall into the hands of men like that? Something warm and damp touched his bare shoulder. He jumped with a yelp and a horse whinnied behind him. "How did you get here?" he said.

But she had no explanation.

What she did have, still fastened neatly behind her saddle, were his bundle and his sword. And in the bundle were the clothes he had been wearing when he arrived in Granada. He moved out of the stream and dressed. Lacking anyone else to consult, he looked the mare firmly in the eye. "I think we should wait until daylight, don't you?"

She nickered as if in agreement.

He took off her bridle and her saddle to allow her to graze in comfort, wrapped himself in his old cloak, and opened one of his new books to look at it by moonlight. His hand had found the one that al-Khitab had given him. It was the Qur'an—the holy book. Very slowly, he set himself to read the first page.

IX

THE FIFTH DREAM

The little boy is playing in the courtyard of his mother's house. When he looks up from his game, he sees the unmistakeable outline of his father's boots and hose. He shrinks back toward the shadow. It is a purely instinctive gesture, for he knows that he cannot avoid the man.

He is old enough to understand that his father lives somewhere else and is not welcome in the house. For that reason, the boy rarely sees him, and never with pleasure.

Although his mother never speaks of him, he thinks that she loathes and fears his father as much as he himself does. The man takes him by the hand and sets him on a large, broadbacked horse. He mounts behind him and they ride away. The man says that they are going to see the count. They wait in a bare foyer for an endless amount of time until a gentleman appears, smiles and winks at him, and says that the count will grant them an audience.

The count is sitting at table, having just dined. Some two or three men are sitting near him, all deep in conversation. At either end of the great hall fires burn brightly, and behind the long table, three narrow windows cast light on the scene. The count is a big man, dressed in a dark, red velvet tunic trimmed in fur. He expresses surprise at the sight of the boy's father. "I did not send for you," he says. "Why do you disturb my leisure?"

"My Lord Count, has Your Lordship had an opportunity to consider my petition? The boy grows quickly and will soon be old

enough to be influenced by his surroundings. Time grows short."
  The count frowns and taps his knuckle on the carved arm of his chair. "Approach."
  The boy's arm is jerked violently forward.
  "Leave the child," said the count. "He will come to no harm in his lord's hall."

The gentleman who brought them in takes the boy over to the hearth, where a woman brings a cup of something warm and sweet to drink, spilling a drop on his hand, and invites him to sit on a cushion. The concoction tastes of fruit and a little of wine. The hall beyond the fire is dark with shadows and he peers into the darkness curiously. He jumps up from his cushion at the sight of a tall, thin man in dark, plain clothes enveloped in a rough cloak of hunter's green like those the shepherds wear. The tall man turns his head, and the boy points at him and says to the gentleman, "That's Uncle Pere. He used to stay in our house sometimes. Why is he here?"

Then Uncle Pere lays his hand on his lips and smiles, and the boy falls silent. The gentleman smiles, too, and says, "Many men have business of all kinds with the count. But often that business is private, and we do not speak of it unless we know that it is permitted."

As they leave the great hall in the castle, the boy asks his father why Uncle Pere was at the count's, and his father shakes him violently and tells him to stop lying, that Uncle Pere and all heretical filth like him are not allowed anywhere near the count. Then his father takes him to the house where he lives. The next day he sets him on a mule, and they head for the boy's house.

The dreamer knows that this is the end of the dream, and shakes his head, trying to awake, trying to prevent the dream from continuing. This time he cannot.

His father leaves him alone in the courtyard and goes to the house. In a moment he returns with a bundle of the boy's clothes. He puts him back on the mule and takes him down to the river, where it makes a bend, and where you can walk into the water on the gravel and sand, and play. But no one is playing by the river. There is a crowd. It is silent. A man is speaking, but the boy does not understand him. He cannot see what everyone is looking at, but suddenly there is a great roar of fire. He hears a woman screaming. It is his mother's voice. He jumps down to run to her, is caught, and carried off to the long, dark, wind-filled mountain passes.

1.

AS soon as there was enough light, Yusuf went in search of water. A little way up the streambed, he found a small pool surrounded by slightly marshy ground with patches of grass growing around it. It was not a lush meadow, but it was enough to keep a horse interested for a while. He left the mare there and went cautiously over to the road to find out what had happened.

It was clear enough. The *mudéjar*'s body lay in a heap by the side of the road. His horse was gone, as were his cloak, his purse, and his bundle. A wave of anger and guilt brought a prickle of tears to his eyes. "I am sorry I brought you to this," said Yusuf to the lifeless form. "If it were not for me, you would never have been on this road."

As he debated whether it would be more seemly to try to bury him, or to leave him visible, so that his family—if he had any family still living—might possibly learn of his fate, the sound of hoofbeats in the distance made up his mind for him. He threw himself into the dry underbrush and began to work his way as silently as possible back to the mare.

He was hungry and tired and discouraged. He had a store of silver coins in a leather purse in his bundle as well as some gold coins sewn into his sash, but what good would they do him? In this strangely hostile territory it seemed unlikely that he would ever have a chance to spend them. He could not go back to Granada; traveling alone on this road was, it seemed now, sheer insanity. If there were farmers or herders around who were willing to trade a little bread for a penny or just for some conversation, he hadn't seen them as yet. He looked around in despair for a hint from the skies or the earth on which direction to take.

Then, on the principle that things were unlikely to get worse, he decided to continue on along the road the *mudéjar* had started on.

By the time the sun was high enough in the heavens to begin baking the dry hard earth even harder, a few respectable-looking travelers rode by in groups of two or three. He brushed the dust and dirt off his tunic, mounted, and headed up onto the road.

ACUTELY conscious of the possibility of danger, he let the mare find her own way while he watched the landscape around him. It mostly consisted of rolling hills, reduced in this dry season to a ruddy brown and gold of earth and dry vegetation. Here and there, however, he saw terraced farmland that had escaped the sporadic fighting in the area, but he felt no temptation to approach any one of the scattering of houses, in spite of his hunger and thirst. Every silhouette, every shadowy movement above him brought him to a state of full alert; every bush, tree, or rock seemed capable of concealing an enemy.

Far from being infected by his mood, the mare had apparently fallen into a semi-conscious state from the heat and the monotony. Inevitably, she stumbled on a particularly rough patch of road, lurched, recovered herself, and then tried to swerve off onto the verge.

Yusuf swore at her rapidly and fluently in the language she understood.

"*Hola*, friend," said a voice from behind him, very quietly, also in Arabic. "I would be a little more cautious traveling through here."

He whirled around and saw that he was being followed by a young man on a chestnut gelding. "In this territory, one never knows who is listening," he added. "Do you speak Valencian?"

"Well enough," said Yusuf shortly. He was feeling rather weary of being chastised over the language issue.

"Excellent," replied the other heartily, swinging at once into that language. "Where are you going? And what are you doing on this road? If we are heading in the same direction, perhaps we could travel together."

"Where are you from?" asked Yusuf.

"A village not far from here," said the other comfortably.

"Then I could benefit from your company along the road," said Yusuf. "These people are new to me."

"That seems clear."

"I would like to buy some food to break my fast," he continued. "But I have no desire to be seized or murdered while doing so. My contacts so far with the inhabitants have not been the happiest."

The young man laughed. "Perhaps that is because you were speaking Arabic, and for some reason, they believed you to be from Granada. You are likely to be either warmly welcomed or attacked with a long knife if you speak Arabic around here. Where are you from?"

"That's a very long story," said Yusuf.

"Good," said the young man. "That kind is best told over breakfast." He searched in the folds of his sash with his thumb and forefinger, frowning. "I have a penny or two in here, I think, which should buy us a small loaf and some cheese."

"I have a silver piece," said Yusuf, searching deep in his tunic. "Here it is. But not much else."

"For that, we'll get a large loaf, a cheese, some dried meat, and some fruit," said the young man. "What a happy chance that I should have fallen in with you. Just ahead of us there is a track on the left that leads to a village. If I am not mistaken, it ought to be market day, and food should be abundant."

"Should I accompany you?"

"Given what has apparently happened to you so far, I would not recommend it," said the young man. "You may be someone who by his very nature attracts trouble."

"Up until now in my life," said Yusuf, "I have been rather adept at avoiding trouble."

"Well, things are different here sometimes," he replied vaguely. "Wait for me here."

But Yusuf did nothing of the kind. He left the road, finding himself some shade and shelter with a view of the path the young man had taken, and waited, not quite sure what would happen, but prepared for anything.

A quiet half-hour passed by before he heard the sound of hoofbeats coming down the path and saw his companion bearing a basket that appeared to be filled with things to eat. "*Hola*," he called, looking around. "Did you give up on me?"

Yusuf rode out, feeling slightly embarrassed. "Of course not," he said. "My mare and I were resting in the shade of that little grove over there."

"You are a clever sort, then," he replied. "Come, your silver piece has bought us a feast, with a penny over."

"AND so," said Yusuf, "that is my story. I lost my father in these lands, escaping myself, and surviving until now up in the north. Having saved a little money, I bought passage on a ship for Granada to seek out my family, ran into trouble, and had to leave by the easiest way possible."

"Whose horse is that? Or should I not ask?"

"She is my cousin's," said Yusuf. "He will not be happy to lose her, but I will repay him her value. When I can. But in the meantime, I have her, some clothes, my sword and a little money. All I need now is to replace the dagger that was stolen from me. I would feel safer with it."

"If you have another silver piece," said the young man, "I have another dagger that would fit nicely into your boot."

"Excellent," said Yusuf.

His ingenious companion withdrew the dagger from someplace about his person and laid it flat on Yusuf's hands. "Is it acceptable?"

Yusuf examined it with great care, pronounced himself satisfied, took out another silver piece from his sash, and slipped the dagger into his boot. "What is your name," he asked, "and how came you to be traveling?"

"Let us say that my name is Ali," said the young man. "I, too, ran into a little trouble, although I don't think I will pay the man whose gelding this is his value. He cheated me, my mother, and my younger brother out of a good piece of land and this is the least that he owes me. Where are you headed?"

"To Valencia, to find a ship to take me to Barcelona."

"You'll not get through, I think," said Ali. "Not from what they are saying. You would need an escort with guards and soldiers to protect you. You're better off to stay inland for the moment until you find out what's going on. Ride with me," he said. "I'm heading toward Cuenca, where there are people who can give me some assistance. Come along, and you can go from there along the road to Teruel, which might get you safely to Valencia, or even up to Barcelona," he added rather vaguely, as if he little notion where such a place might be. "We have food here for a while, and I know people along the road as far as Albacete."

In spite of a strong feeling that he might be doing something very foolish, Yusuf smiled, and said, "That seems an excellent plan."

And indeed it was, until late the next day when they reached Albacete. The road was sufficiently well populated that they could fall in with various groups; an acquaintance of Ali gave them safe accommodation and plenty of clean straw to sleep on in his barn. Ali was amusing and bold, and Yusuf became more and more certain that his problem lay in the ownership of the horse, not of the "good piece of land." Whether or not his mother and younger brother were fictional adornments to give a touch of pathos to his story or real people, Yusuf had not made up his mind. It was the kind of story that when he was a waif, scrambling to live and to avoid being taken by slavers, he too had been clever at weaving.

When they arrived on the outskirts of Albacete, Ali stopped in front of a ramshackle building. "This is where we will spend the night," he said. "Get down and I will take the horses around to the stable. Wait here."

In spite of his misgivings at the sight of the mare disappearing around the building, Yusuf stayed in front. Under a grape arbor on one side of the structure was a long trestle table; seated on its benches were some eight or ten men. Loud talk and louder laughter filled the evening. Serving maids carrying fresh pitchers of wine moved back and forth between house and arbor; several of the seated men made half-hearted attempts to grab them as they went by. Sometimes one of the maids would fall into earnest conversation with one of the guests; she would leave, and a few minutes later so would the guest, into the house.

"I thought you would be in there, slaking your thirst," said Ali, appearing as suddenly as he seemed to do frequently.

"It's not my favorite sort of place," said Yusuf. "It looks more like a brothel than an inn."

"Well—there are some who might call it that," said Ali. "The landlady prefers to call it an inn. And it is entirely possible to obtain a good supper and a reasonably clean and comfortable bed here. More than that, you usually still have your possessions, including the horse that carried you here, when you leave in the morning. Unless you have been so generous and sentimental that you gave them to one of the girls."

At that moment the innkeeper bustled out of the door in front, wiping her hands on her apron. "Maria," said Ali, "I have come and brought a friend."

"My dearest, dearest boy," said Maria, clutching him to her

ample breasts like a long-lost son. She was a big, dark-eyed woman with sun-darkened skin, an abundance of flesh that struggled constantly to escape from her clothing, and an air of unshakeable good humor. "You have been away much too long. And look at the sweet boy you have brought me."

"He's not for you, Maria," said Ali with a grin. "We merely ride together, traveling along the same road, for amusement and company."

"Ah—how true," she said. "We all travel along the same road, for good or ill, do we not?" she said and winked. "But I see," she added, shaking her head. "He is heading for the same destination that you are. Poor soul. That is a sorry fate." At that, she burst into a peal of laughter, caught Yusuf's head and gave him a hearty welcoming kiss. "If you go to the courtyard," she said, "you will find as good a supper as you'll get in the entire province."

And indeed, there was a relatively quiet courtyard in the center of the house. As they sat down, their fellow diners nodded amiably at them. A young girl supplied them with two plates of lamb and lentil stew, a medium loaf, and a jug of wine. Yusuf was astonishingly hungry, he discovered, and silently applauded Ali's choice in stopping places. The various other travelers in the courtyard drifted off to their temporary beds, and soon Yusuf and Ali were left with a dish of fruit and the remains of the loaf.

Maria returned and sat down beside Ali. He addressed her quietly in Arabic, and they spoke for some time rapidly and softly. The effort of following the conversation, in a dialect very different from the polished Arabic of the court, became too much for Yusuf. He looked around and thought of other things. It occurred to him, looking at the landlady, Maria, and his new friend, Ali, seated side by side, that she treated him like a lost son because he probably was just that, and for some reason they did not acknowledge each other. As he played around with this idea, Ali turned to him, still speaking in Arabic. "Amiri tells me that your best route will be to head toward Teruel, but that perhaps you might wish to avoid the town itself."

"Amiri?"

"Or Maria, if you prefer. It is better for her, in this place, to be known as Maria."

YUSUF awoke early the next morning. He was alone in the small room they had been sharing; clearly Ali had risen earlier still. With a gloomy feeling that both horses might also have left early with his newfound friend, Yusuf straightened his clothing and ran downstairs. Maria was in the courtyard, supervising its sweeping, and helping to lay out a breakfast for those who had actually spent the night in her hostelry. "Will you take some breakfast now?" she asked.

"I had best see to my horse first," he replied, heading for the stables.

"I think you'll find that she has been well looked after," said Maria calmly, and returned to her tasks.

Yusuf returned, looking somewhat sheepish. For there the mare had been, looking clean, with all her harness polished and supple. He sat down, helped himself to a portion of the loaf and to more fruit. "You must have a very well-trained lad in the stable," said Yusuf, in the way of a peace offering.

"I think so," she replied. "But Ali, I'm sorry to say, discovered that he had unexpected business to attend to and had to leave the city at first light. He was very sorry that he was unable to say farewell to you. But there is a party of merchants who are heading in the direction of Teruel, and they would be happy to have along a pleasant-spoken young man who can handle a sword. I wouldn't mention to them that you're from Granada and have been living in Catalonia. I told them you were Castilian."

"How far is it to Teruel?" asked Yusuf.

"Not far. Four or five days," she said cheerfully. "Fewer

than that, if you're traveling with these gentlemen. But you had better hurry, because they're getting ready to leave."

AND so, on Saturday, the thirtieth of May, with half his breakfast as yet uneaten and wrapped in a kerchief, Yusuf set out for Teruel. The procession, four guards, eight servants, two wagons piled with goods and drawn by mules, and four prosperous and suspicious-looking merchants, plodded silently along. The first day, Yusuf had tried to strike up conversations with various people in the group. His tentative moves in that direction raised a good number of eyebrows and almost no speech. "Where do you come from?" asked a guard. "Nowhere around here."

"No, sir," mumbled Yusuf. "From the frontier," he added, since that seemed to him to cover a great many possibilities.

"You sound like someone I knew from Navarre," said the guard after thinking about this for a while.

"My mother was from Navarre," said Yusuf.

"And your father?"

"He was from—" Yusuf's mind raced furiously. "Tudela," he said, it being the first place in the north that jumped into his head.

"That explains it," said the guard, and rode on in silence.

THE road wandered through the plain mile after mile; they stayed away from villages, eating and sleeping by the side of the road, rising at first light of morning, and riding at the same steady pace until it was too dark for the beasts to see where their feet were taking them. They stopped from time to time to water the beasts and for an hour or two in the hottest part of the afternoon when they ate and slept, but otherwise they moved on in silence.

Yusuf had no idea where they were. They went from plains to hills and from hills to mountains and valleys. They crossed a multitude of dry streambeds and some rivers that were almost too deep to ford. They talked over the progress of their journey with each other in brief snatches of low-voiced conversation, mentioning names of towns and villages that he had never heard of, or lands belonging to lords whose existences were, for him, only rumors overheard at the bishop's palace or at the royal court, spoken between gentlemen plotting some diplomatic maneuver, or soldiers talking of old battles and new campaigns.

On the third day they were, he heard, well on their way to Teruel. It was getting late in the afternoon before they stopped that day, and it was hot. The road had been winding and difficult for some time; the mules and horses were flagging visibly, and the men were looking mutinous.

"We will stop here," said one of the merchants quietly.

They had reached a grove of trees by a river, high enough up to be somewhat cooler than the slopes they had been climbing. Yusuf rode over to a spot by the river apart from the others, intending, if he could, to wash, and to allow his mare to drink her fill. He found a place where they could both scramble down to the water, unsaddled the mare, stripped off his sweat-drenched clothing, and immersed himself in the stream. Greatly refreshed, he came out, threw on an old dry shirt and rubbed the mare down with handfuls of dry grass. "You stay there, old girl," he murmured to her. "I'm going into those trees to nap."

Barefoot and almost naked, he climbed quietly up the slope, and then stretched out on a bed of evergreen needles. He was just dropping off to sleep when a conversation, too low to hear easily but too close to ignore, woke him again. He raised his head sleepily and looked over in the direction of the voices. He could see no one, but the sound seem to come from the other side of a small hummock.

"We won't get through Teruel," said one voice. "We'll have to cut back south again."

"They're not going to be happy."

"They'll be getting more than they signed on for. They'll be happy."

"What about the boy?"

"So far, we haven't needed him," said the second voice. "I don't see why you wanted him along."

"We're two fighting men short," said the first man.

"That would be good if he were on our side," said the other. "But I doubt he is. If his mother is from Navarre, then I am from distant Cathay. I know where he comes from, no matter how much he tries to hide it."

"Where?"

"Valencia. I can smell it on him. The moment we set foot over the border, he will link up with his people and that will be the end of our mission."

"Are you sure?"

"I am. I've been listening to every word he says, and I have become more certain by the hour."

"Then we'll leave him behind."

"Good. Now?"

"No. When we stop for the night. I have something here you can put in his wine. He won't wake up before midday tomorrow."

Yusuf wriggled silently backward down to the river. He picked up his bundle, the saddle and the bridle from the river bank, clicked his tongue at the mare, and headed upriver toward a bend a short distance away. She followed him placidly enough. Beyond the curve of the stream, there seemed to be an excellent fording point. They would carry on from there while the others rested. But first he had something to do.

He put on his tunic, fastened on his sword, and followed the bank to the ford where the road and the river intersected. Drawn up beside each other were the two wagons. He sauntered over.

"Where you been?" asked a sleepy guard.

"Washing in the river," he said. "But it's hot down there. I thought maybe it would be cooler under the wagons."

"You're crazy," said the guard. "If I were you, I'd sleep under a tree, but I have to stay here. Orders."

Hardly had he spoken those words when he slouched down

onto his tailbone and fell asleep. His rhythmic breathing turned into a light snore; he turned his head to accommodate it to the side of the wagon and was lost to the world.

A second guard wandered over. He opened his mouth and Yusuf murmured, "Shush, he's asleep."

"How does he get to sleep on duty?" asked the second guard quietly.

"Why don't you wake him before the end of his watch and then get some sleep yourself?" suggested Yusuf. "I have my sword. I'll keep an eye on him and wake him if there's trouble."

"Well—" said the guard. "Don't you fall asleep, too."

"I was in the river—it's cold, and that woke me up all right," he whispered.

And so he was left alone.

HE untied one of the ropes holding the canvas covering on the goods inside the wagon and lifted it up very delicately. Almost instantly, he lowered it again, tied the rope once more and drifted very quietly back to his mare and his possessions.

"Come along, sweetheart," he said, "we're heading out on our own."

2.

Monday, June 1

IT had been a cold night. The sky was cloudless, but the winds were blowing straight down from the mountains, cold enough for Isaac to elect to breakfast indoors. As the June sun began to warm up the courtyard, the house sprang to life. Judith picked up her work and moved outside. Raquel arrived at the gate almost before her mother was well settled, looking rumpled and rather irritated. "Where have you been?" asked her mother. "You look as if you were interrupted in the middle of cleaning the house."

"At the house, Mama," she said. "Showing the workmen what is to be done. If you don't go over every day, you never know what will be done, or how badly." She brushed off her gown, straightened it, and then pushed her hair into some sort of order. "It's terribly windy out there," she added. "I'll be glad when they have put in the gate, so I don't have to walk all the way around to get from one house to the other."

"Tell them to do it now," said Judith.

"Certainly not, Mama," said Raquel. "It will be the last thing they do. You don't want the workmen able to come in and out of here any hour they please, do you?"

"Surely if they do it quickly and put in a stout lock, there won't be a problem," said Judith.

Jacinta brought them something to drink and to nibble on, and they argued the relative merits of easy access and privacy, until Raquel had almost regained her good temper. "You may be right, Mama," she was saying. "I'll talk it over with Daniel and the head of the crew," when another, more urgent clanging of the bell at the gate interrupted them. "I'll get it," said Raquel. "Ibrahim seems to have disappeared again."

"He's at the market," said Judith darkly. "I hope he understood what he had to buy."

But all small domestic concerns were buried in the news the lad at the gate was trying to communicate. "Master Isaac," he said to Raquel. "I was sent to fetch Master Isaac to come to see the master."

"Which master?" asked Raquel firmly. "Who is Master Isaac to visit?"

"Master Raimon," said the boy. "I have ridden as fast as I could, but the mistress said you must be quick."

"Papa," she called. "You are summoned to Master Raimon."

"I heard, my dear. Let me speak to the boy for a moment."

"Do you wish me to come with you, Papa?"

"I may need you," said her father, taking the boy to one side and speaking earnestly to him.

"Jacinta!" called Raquel.

"Yes, Mistress Raquel," said the child, running down the stairs from the kitchen.

"Run and tell my husband that Master Raimon is very ill, that I must go with papa to visit him, and that I may not be back for dinner," she said, and ran into her father's study to help pack the basket.

They rode as furiously as they could, but they were greeted in front of the house, not by a servant or even his half-brother, Guillem, but by his wife. Marta stood by the gate, waiting for their arrival.

"My Raimon is dead," she said, in a voice devoid of feeling. "They say, Master Isaac, that you possess sight that is clearer and sharper than the vision of those of us who can see with their eyes. You must look, then, and tell me who is responsible for his death. I must know."

"Responsible, mistress?"

"He did not die an ordinary death," she said, in a clear cold voice. "I know that as I know that the sun is hot and the rain is wet."

"Take us to where he lies, and we will attempt to determine the agent of his death," said Isaac.

3.

"I have not allowed anyone to straighten his poor body or to enter his room to tidy it," said Marta. "I wanted it left for you as it was."

"There is a curious odor in the room," said Isaac. "In addition to the odor of death. Take me to him," he said to his daughter.

Raquel led him to the edge of the bed; he bent down and ran his hands quickly over the bed coverings. He pulled them back and felt the limbs and then the body, twisted into contorted positions. When he finished, he gently straightened the limbs. "He has not died a peaceful death," he murmured.

"No, Papa. The bedclothes are much disordered. A cup of water has been knocked over. His face is mottled, and his eyes are staring."

"Close them," murmured the physician. "They will disturb his wife and children."

Raquel delicately closed the eyes.

Isaac leaned over and smelled the ghost of odors that still emanated from him. "He is not long dead," said the physician. "Not only is he not cold, but I can smell the odor of his breath still."

"As soon as we knew that he was gone," said a voice from the doorway, "I took my sons and left the room. I fastened the door shut and ordered them to stand in front of it and guard it closely. Then I came downstairs. I stopped for a moment to compose myself and walked out of the house toward the gate just as you rode up."

"And no one has been in this room between the time you left and we came in?"

"No, Master Isaac," said Pau. "Roger Bernard and I have been here at the door since it happened. And from the moment that we sent for you, mama has not left him, nor has she allowed anyone but us to come into the room."

"That is why I sent the boy for you, instead of one of my sons," said Marta. "I needed my sons to help guard their papa."

"Was he ill when he awoke this morning?" asked Isaac.

"He was," said Marta. "With stomach disturbances—mild, but enough that I made him stay in bed."

"And did he eat or drink shortly before he became worse?" asked Isaac.

"He did," said Pau. "He drank one of your soothing herbal mixtures to ease his discomfort."

"Where is it?"

"By the window," said Pau.

"I ordered it for him," said Marta. "It was the mixture you had given him to help him sleep. He had slept very little the night before, and I was afraid if he did not sleep that he would die of exhaustion. It was the same mixture that he had taken several times already, without any ill effects."

"Then it cannot have been the same mixture," murmured the physician. "Unless he took something else near the same time. Is there a table in the room, Raquel?"

"Yes, Papa," said his daughter. "Over by the window."

"Good," said Isaac. "Fetch me the cup he drank from, will you, Raquel?" he asked.

"It is on the table now," she replied softly. "It is about half-full."

THE room was silent, except for a faint rustle of breath and clothing that the living cannot suppress entirely. At intervals, Isaac murmured an instruction to Raquel, who then brought water, clean cups, and a candle for warming a few drops of the solution. At last Isaac turned toward the others. "Who has been in the house today?" he asked.

"Everyone," said Pau. "Except for Guillem. He left three days ago for Barcelona. In order to transact some business, he said."

"Then I would like to speak to everyone else who was here, if I may," he said mildly. "It would help me to have an idea of exactly at what time these events took place."

"TWO deadly herbs found their way into the mixture I gave your husband," said Isaac, directing his remarks to Mistress Marta. "Who prepared it?" Most of the household, except for some of the servants, was gathered together in the dining room, around the table.

"I did." The clear, young voice had a slight tremor in it.

"And you are?"

"I am Sibilla, cousin to Francesca, the wife of Jaume Manet."

"How came you to be here today, if I may ask?"

"I came to visit Mistress Marta and—and her husband."

Her voice broke slightly. She coughed and recovered herself. "I brought some dried fruit from Mistress Joana, along with their best wishes for Master Raimon. I fear that everyone here must have long wished for my departure, but I have stayed in case there might be something useful I could do."

"No one wishes your departure, Mistress Sibilla," said Pau quickly.

"Tell me, mistress," said Isaac. "Why did you prepare it, and not someone from the kitchen?"

"But Master Isaac," said Marta, "it was you yourself who said—"

"What reason were you given, Mistress Sibilla?" interrupted the physician smoothly.

"The kitchen was shorthanded," said Sibilla, "with only the cook and one maid—I believe the kitchen maid was ill."

"She had gone home to her mother, who was ill," said Marta.

"Can you tell me exactly what you did when you made it?"

"I took a small bundle of herbs tied up in linen—it was the only one in the bowl—placed it in a cup and poured boiling water on it. I let it steep until it was dark in color and had a pronounced odor, as I had been told. Then I took out the bundle of herbs and gave it to the cook."

"Did you hold the cup close to your nose to smell it?"

"Why would she do that?" asked Pau.

"Curiosity," said Isaac. "Interest. I would have, in her place."

"Yes, I did," said Sibilla. "After I gave the herbs to the cook, I handed the cup to Pau—to Master Pau—"

"Was he in the kitchen with you?"

"No," said Sibilla. "He was standing in the doorway, I think. The cook gave him a jug of cool water from the cellar, and he carried them up to his father."

"No," said Roger Bernard. "I was waiting with him. I carried the water."

"My daughter will bring you a cup of the infusion that Master Pau carried up to Master Raimon." Raquel got up and slipped out of the room. "It won't be exactly the same, for it is no longer hot, but I would like you to sniff it, and tell me if it is the same."

"Certainly," she said. "I will taste it, too, if you like."

"That won't be necessary. Smell will be sufficient."

"Here it is, Papa," said Raquel.

"Pour a little of it into a new cup and give it to Mistress Sibilla to smell."

Raquel found a clean cup on the sideboard and poured a little into it. She placed it on the table in front of Sibilla.

Sibilla picked it up, swirled it around in the cup, and then sniffed. She set it down. "Ugh," she said. "That isn't the same as the one I made up for Master Raimon. This one has an awful, musky odor. It's disgusting, not at all like something you'd want to taste."

"Sorry, Papa, I gave her the wrong cup," said Raquel. "Just a moment." She brought another cup from the sideboard. "Try this one."

"That is it," said Sibilla. "It smells like herbs, doesn't it." She stopped as a new thought struck her. "Is the first one the infusion that Master Raimon drank?"

"It is," said Isaac. "Is the cook here?"

"I will fetch her," said Roger Bernard.

The cook wafted into the room on a tide of garlic and spices. "Yes, mistress?" she asked.

"It was I who wished to ask you something," said Isaac mildly. "About that linen packet of herbs that Mistress Sibilla steeped for Master Raimon. Did it look like the other packets that I left for him?"

"I wouldn't know," said the cook, her voice quivering with annoyance. "The mistress made it quite clear that I was not to touch them. They were kept in this room, and I never looked at them."

"Were they locked up?"

"They were supposed to be," said Pau. "But the key was on the ring with the rest of the house keys—for the cellar, the larders, and the linen room. All the storage areas. And I'm afraid with all this going on, including being shorthanded, the key rings get tossed from person to person rather easily. We didn't think, especially with—with not everyone here today."

"Can you bring me the packet of herbs?" asked Isaac. "The one that Mistress Sibilla handed you?"

"Certainly not," said the cook. "I gave it to Justina to throw on the rubbish heap. Why would I keep it?"

"Of course not," murmured Isaac, almost to himself. "Why would you? And Justina is the other servant who is now helping you in the kitchen?"

"When she can find the time," said the cook sourly.

"Thank you. Master Roger Bernard," Isaac said, "perhaps you could find Justina and inquire about the whereabouts of those herbs."

"Certainly," said Roger Bernard.

ROGER Bernard returned some five or ten minutes later, bearing in his hand a small plate on which reposed a damp bedraggled-looking brownish packet. "I have it here, Master Isaac. Fortunately for me, it was on the top of the rubbish heap, with only a few kitchen scraps on top. I shook them off. I hope that was what you wanted."

"Indeed. I expect your kitchen scraps are much like anyone else's," said Isaac. "Raquel, would you look at that and see if it seems familiar?"

Raquel took the plate and looked at the thing on it. She flipped it over with her finger and examined the other side. It looks like ours, Papa," she said. "Jacinta has been making these little linen packages of our usual remedies. She folds them like an envelope and stitches them neatly where the sealing wax would go, leaving a long thread so that you can pull the packet out as soon as it's ready."

"Let me examine it," said Isaac. He smelled the packet, set it down on the plate again, and carefully pulled it apart. He rubbed the wet leaves and broken stems between his fingers, sniffing them as he went. Finally, he took out his kerchief, dried off his hands, and turned back to the others. "If this is the packet that was used by Mistress Sibilla this morning, it is innocent of any harmful substances," he said.

"Then how could it have harmed Master Raimon? And why did it smell that way?" asked Sibilla.

"I would like to ask this Justina if she saw anything," said Isaac.

"Justina was so upset that she has taken to her bed," said the cook. "Now, may I return to my cooking? For the poor mistress and her boys need to eat, no matter what has happened."

"Of course," said Isaac. "You have given me much to ponder, and I thank you very much. With your permission, Mistress Marta, I will return tomorrow. If you still wish me to do what you asked."

"I do," said Marta. "I will show you to the door."

"Let me do that, mistress," said a voice from the hall. "You are weary beyond belief, I think."

"Esteve, is that you? Thank you. I think I will sit in the orchard for a while."

"I will bring you a cup of wine," said Sibilla, "and then my maid, Rosa, and I will leave you in peace."

"Don't leave yet, Mistress Sibilla," said Pau. "I will take my mother to the orchard if you will bring the wine."

"THIS is a sad happening," said Isaac. "There are families in which the loss of a father and a husband is not an unmixed tragedy, but this, I think, is not one of them."

"You are right," said the steward, Esteve. "Mistress Marta is a remarkable woman of beauty, resourcefulness, and good humor, and her husband acknowledged and appreciated her."

"And the sons?"

"For high-spirited lads, they were remarkably fond of their father. They jested with him and enjoyed his company. This is a hard blow for them."

"Who could have done this, do you think?"

"One does not have to look far to see when trouble first entered this house, Master Isaac."

"The brother?"

"If he is a brother. He looks somewhat like him, except that he is sly and nervous, instead of straightforward and steady. The difference between them is as unmistakable as between a loyal dog and a weasel, both with coats of the same color—if you can imagine that."

"Then how did it come about? Master Guillem is in Barcelona."

"There are ways," said Esteve. "People can be hired; poison can be concealed for days in a sweetmeat."

"What could be his reason, though? He doesn't stand to inherit."

"He might wish to inherit the mistress, so to speak," said Esteve. "Marry her, dismiss me, and take over the estate—sending the boys, if they're wise, back to Lleida. Let me help you onto your mule, master."

4.

ISAAC sat in front of the fire in the common sitting room, thinking over everything Raimon had told him over the past few months. The household was quiet, either asleep or using the afternoon lull for their own private purposes, and it was a time that he found most fertile for thought.

A ring of the bell at the gate drew an exasperated sigh from him. It had been a delicate ring, too light to waken even Judith, and most certainly too feeble to rouse Ibrahim from his afternoon sleep. Isaac strode out of the room, down the passage with the wind whipping his tunic about his ankles, down the staircase to the courtyard, and over to the gate. "Who calls?" he asked without much attempt at good humor or courtesy.

"Master Isaac," said a soft, clear voice. "It is Sibilla,

Francesca's cousin. I am sorry to visit at such an inconvenient hour, but I wanted to be able to talk to you in privacy."

Isaac opened the gate with deft fingers and let her in. "There is a cold wind," he said. "Have you just ridden from the *finca*?"

"I have," she said.

"Then let us sit upstairs in front of the fire. If you wish, I can stir up one of the servants to prepare you something hot to drink," he added.

"Please, no," said Sibilla. "That would wake the entire household, I am sure."

"Possibly," said Isaac. "Although in all likelihood, only those members of it whom we didn't wish to awaken."

"Now," said the physician. "On the table you should find a jug of wine and one of water, along with several cups, and perhaps some fruit or nuts. Pour some—I can manage quite well, but I am slower than you would be—and bring us each a cup. When you have warmed your hands and feet and quenched your thirst, we can speak of what is troubling you."

Sibilla laughed. "I do not know how you knew that my hands and feet were cold, and that I was parched with thirst, but you are right."

"I live in a household of strong, lively, hardworking women, who do not shirk travel or effort, but they do seem to suffer from cold hands and feet, and thirst, when they are doing their utmost. I suspect that you are doing your utmost, and suffering greatly in the process. I hear it in your voice."

"Master Isaac, please, spare me kindness." Her voice broke, and she stopped to take a deep breath. "I have strength that enables me to carry on, but it is broken by kindness. I am fortunate that Mistress Joana is too worried about her daughter-in-law to notice me carefully, or she would have destroyed me weeks ago."

"I shall not mention it again unless you wish me to,

mistress," said Isaac. "Now—what do you wish to tell me? Surely not that you poisoned Master Raimon."

"No. I would never have poisoned him. Never," she reiterated. "Today was the third time that I had gone to visit him. My ostensible reason for visiting, of course, was to see Mistress Marta. Everyone assumed, and it is to some degree—some great degree—true, that I go to the *finca* to visit Pau. But my real object in going there was to become acquainted with Master Raimon."

"And for what reason?"

"It will become clear to you, I think. The first day, we chatted like old friends, for we felt very comfortable with one another right away. The second day, he asked me many questions about myself. Today, he spoke to me for the first time about himself. I sat with him a long time this morning, for he was interested in my history, and I was interested in his. At the end, he told me of his dreams, including his last one."

"When did he have the last one?" asked Isaac.

"Last night," said Sibilla. "And I think it is important. He dreamed he was a little boy, playing in his mother's courtyard, and his father took him to visit the count," said Sibilla. "While there he met someone whom he called Uncle Pere. He told his father, who called Uncle Pere 'heretical filth' and dragged him away in a rage."

"But there was no fire in that dream?"

"There is more. Before they left, his father collected a bundle of his clothes and took him down to the River Aude on his mule, to a bend in the river where the shore is a broad expanse of gravel, and the water on that side of the stream is very shallow. He used to play in the shallow water there with his mother and the nursemaid on warm summer days, in the same place where I, too, played on warm summer days with my nursemaid, Rosa."

"You know that?" asked Isaac. "Or do you guess that it must have been in the same place?"

"I know it, Master Isaac. I know it. It is well known. But on that particular day, no one was playing by the river. In his dream, there was such a crowd that he could not see what everyone was looking at. Then the fire went up with a great roar, and he heard his mother screaming. He tried to run to her, but his father caught him, and carried him off through the mountain passes into Aragon."

"But why did he tell you, and not his wife or his sons? asked Isaac.

"Because he could," said Sibilla. "Because I already knew the story in the dream. It is well known where I come from. Raimon's mountains were my mountains," said Sibilla. "In fact, we had a great deal in common, Raimon and I . . . But none of that matters right now."

"Why do you tell me this?"

"It is Guillem who is the vicious one in that household," said Sibilla. "Guillem who knows the truth and yet told his brother lies just to watch him suffer."

"But Guillem is in Barcelona," said Isaac. "Or so everyone tells me."

"I am confused," said Sibilla, and Isaac could hear the tears in her voice. "I do not understand how an honest packet of herbs could turn into a deadly mixture in my hands."

"There are ways, Mistress Sibilla," said Isaac.

"Even if there are, why would anyone want to kill Raimon? He left everything behind when he was taken away from his family as a boy; he made no claim on anyone. Only Guillem is vicious enough to kill him, but Guillem cannot profit in any way from his death. Raimon had no property to leave. Pau's inheritance is from his father who is long dead. It is his already. Marta owns the *finca* and will without a doubt leave it to Roger Bernard. What is there left for a bastard half-brother of a man who started with nothing? If anyone in the family were seeking vengeance it would not be on Raimon, who has harmed no one in his whole blameless life, but on Guillem and Guillem's father, Arnaud."

"Did Raimon know that his mother must have been a Cathar?" asked Isaac.

"He told me that his last dream was filled with unbearable

sorrow and fear, rather than the terror of a nightmare, and that he thought it was more likely a memory than a dream. He was sure that the visit to the count and to the river were all real, and that they were of the last day he ever saw his mother. We did not talk of religion," she added.

"That is understandable," said Isaac, and Sibilla gave him a curious look.

5.

"WHY did you believe that I would be concerned in any way—except that Raimon was a good man, and a part of my flock in the diocese—at Raimon Foraster's death?" asked Berenguer.

"I only feared that some religious issues might arise that could trouble Your Excellency," said Isaac.

"Those rumors," said the bishop in exasperation. "First I had thought that they had not spread at all, and then that they had been stopped long before anyone outside the palace could hear of them. But one cannot keep a secret here. Evidently even you have heard them."

"Not at all, Your Excellency. That is not how I came to hear of the possibility that Raimon, when he was a very small child, had been raised by a family considered to be heretics, Your Excellency. He himself knew nothing of it."

"How then did you know?"

"Raimon Foraster came to me because he could not sleep. He suffered from constant nightmares of people being burned, and of being pursued through dark, cold, mountain passes. That spoke to me of the events in France. He would have been a lad of four or five years of age when the last wave of condemnations of the Cathars began. And it was common knowledge that many of those who were under suspicion fled their villages and came down from the mountains into this kingdom."

"Indeed," said Berenguer. "It is not a problem that I would

like to see a resurgence of, Master Isaac." It was difficult to tell whether the bishop considered the problem to be the existence of heretics, their persecution, or their choice of refuge.

"Of course not, Your Excellency. But although Raimon may have started life among a group of adherents, and we do not know that, by the time he was four or five, as far as I know, he was living with a family that had nothing to do with them. He knew no other religion than his own until the day he died. His living here in your diocese should not have raised a problem."

"I admit to you," said Berenguer, "that when the Foraster family arrived in the district ten years ago, my predecessor wondered about their background."

"Why?"

"Because many of the Cathars who escaped from France settled in Lleida—once they had abandoned their heretical views, of course," he added blandly. "Raimon said he came from Lleida, and his name suggested that he was a foreigner. His Excellency, my predecessor, found nothing against them. And then a few years ago someone—I never discovered who— started the rumor again that they were heretics seeking refuge with fellow Cathars in Catalonia, and might still be practicing their faith."

"And were they?"

"There was no reason to suspect any such thing. We made discreet inquiries. His wife's family and the family he grew up in had no connection with the Cathars. It has been many years since there has been even a rumor of a Cathar Perfect in the province, and as you undoubtedly know, without at least one, the faith cannot continue, really. Did Raimon say anything to you about his religious beliefs?"

"Your Excellency, the last thing I would discuss with any of my Christian patients is their faith; the only thing that Raimon ever said to me on the subject of religion was that he had prayed for relief from his symptoms, and if that made him a heretic, then most of the rest of my patients are heretics too, including at times, I suspect, Your Excellency."

"Indeed, the most irreligious of men can be brought to his knees before God more certainly by an attack of gout than by one of my sermons," said Berenguer. "But I do not think that either one of us need worry about this issue, Master Isaac. But I grieve at Raimon's death. He was a good man. A very good man. What caused it? He seemed to be so strong and filled with life. But then, we do not know the hour of our going, do we?"

"No, indeed, Your Excellency. Usually not. But someone knew the hour of Raimon's going and planned it very carefully. He was poisoned. Of that I have no doubt.

lla to her cousin Joana, "his affection must have been sin-
arly selfless."

"What did Raimon think of him?" asked Joana Manet.

"He loathed him," said Sibilla. "Or so he gave me to under-
nd."

In the meantime, Guillem had edged over close to Raimon's
ounger son. "This blow has crushed me, Roger Bernard. Your
ather was so good to me," he murmured. "He swore to me that
ie would help with my claim against those who seized our
family's land—your land, now, Roger Bernard." He glanced
sideways at the boy and shook his head. "But this is no time to
discuss such things, is it?"

"I think not," said Roger Bernard. His voice was as cold
and controlled as his mother's. He nodded and walked over to
join her.

"I fear I must go now," said Guillem, to no one in particular. He took his horse from the village lad who was holding it,
gave him a halfpenny, and led it away.

The assembled company outside the church watched him
until man and horse disappeared around a bend in the road.
"Thank goodness," said Marta. "I am greatly relieved. I was
afraid he was intending to move back into the house. I don't
think I could bear that."

That was Wednesday. On Thursday, a clear, sunny day dancing with cool breezes, a young woman came to the bishop's
palace and demanded entrance. "I have some very important
information to give to the bishop," she told the porter.

"Tell me what it is about," said the porter, "and I will fir
out if His Excellency will see you. He doesn't usually, ˙
know," added the porter. "He's a very busy man. One of b˙
sistants might see you, if it's very important."

"I must see the bishop," she insisted. "And no o˙
And with a sudden shift of her body, she pushed pa˙
at the door and erupted into the hall, straight intr
Father Bernat.

"Who are you?" asked the Franciscan, halt˙
long rush along the corridor.

X

Justina

✛

1.

THE death and the funeral of Raimon Foraster ⟨
flurry of gossip and speculation, or perhaps even a brie⟨
of gossip and speculation, in the city of Girona. There ⟨
reason for him to die, some said, but then people often⟨
without much reason. The physician had been called out⟨
others, but then he was often called out. The cook would ⟨
had a fine tale of suspicion and false accusations to tell, ⟨
she was a close-mouthed woman, except with her friends a⟨
family. Since they all lived in Olot and she visited ther⟨
rarely, her tale was not told.

Whatever was being said, the preparations for his burial⟨
from the little church nearby, one that his generosity had
refurbished, went on. His family, his neighbors, and his friends
from the city came out to make their last farewells to him;
they condoled, wept, ate, and drank, as is often the way when
a good man dies. And then they left, scattering hearty promises behind them of comfort and assistance to come. Some of
those promises, like those of the family of Pons Manet, were
even sincere.

Much against their united inclinations, the family had sent
a message by the diocesan courier to the house in Barcelona
where Guillem, Raimon's half-brother, had said that he had
business. To everyone's surprise, Guillem appeared on that
Wednesday, just in time to form the tail of the procession
⟨arrying the body to the church. He wept over the grave as if
⟨e two brothers had lived side by side all their lives.

"Considering what Master Raimon thought of him," said

"It's a woman who claims she has something she must tell directly to His Excellency," said the porter, catching up to her and laying hold of her arm.

"I am Justina," she said angrily. "And I assure you that His Excellency will want to see me. I'm housemaid at the *finca* of Master Raimon Foraster who was poisoned on Monday, and if His Excellency wishes to know how Master Raimon died, he will be very angry that you do not let me see him."

"You come with me, woman," said the porter, tugging on her arm. "His Excellency has no dealings with the likes of you."

But Father Bernat was standing quite still, looking at her, apparently lost in thought. "I will deal with her," he said. "She may have information for us. Go back to your door, if you would."

JUSTINA was taken to a small room on the ground floor of the palace and told to wait. Considering her station in life, her lack of an appointment, and her general behavior, she ought to have been surprised that four men swept into the room not long after and sat down, leaving her standing: Berenguer de Cruïlles; Father Bernat, the bishop's secretary; his scribe; and the captain of the guard.

She did not seem to be surprised. "What I have to say is private, Your Excellency," she said, with a glance at the others.

Of the modest number of people who dared to speak so assuredly to the Lord Bishop, very few were young women. He raised his eyes in her direction, startled, and then subjected her to a searching look, the same look that had caused many a powerful man to wilt. She returned it boldly, looking down at them all from her taller-than-average height.

The captain docketed her neatly as a potential troublemaker; the scribe, who had a weakness for softly pretty women, thought that her features would have sat better on a man. Bernat glared at her. He had much work to drag the bishop through that day and this woman, with her gray eyes and fierce expression, her darkish hair pulled back from her face and partly concealed under a kerchief, was an unnecessary distraction. But Berenguer de Cruïlles continued to study her. He had met many strong-minded women in his time; he had liked some and disliked others; but this one offended him in some way that he could not define.

"Mistress Justina," he said at last, "I only talk to one man in private, and that is my confessor. I certainly do not conduct diocesan business in private. Either you speak to me now about what concerns you, or you leave the palace."

"Very well," said Justina. "I am, as I said before to the man at the door, a servant at the *finca* owned by Master Raimon, my employer until he died. And on the day he died, I was working both in the kitchen and around the house, because the kitchen-maid wasn't there, and I saw Pau, my master's son, with his younger brother, Roger Bernard, add something to a cup of infusion that they were carrying to the master. I followed him from the kitchen, being curious about what he was doing. As they walked, Your Excellency, I heard them muttering incantations over the cup, back and forth, like two priests at mass. I thought I should tell you that."

"What do you mean by incantations?" asked Bernat.

"Pau was singing—or more like what the priests do—"

"Chanting," said the bishop, his interest captured in spite of himself.

"Yes, like a priest, and Roger Bernard was answering. When I first heard them I thought they must be saying prayers for their father's health, then I realized they weren't. Or not any kind of prayers that I had ever heard, anyway."

"What did Master Pau add to the cup?" asked the captain.

"I don't know, sir," said Justina.

"Could it have been Master Roger Bernard who added something?"

"It could have been," said Justina. "They were together."

"Well—was the thing he put into the cup from a vial, or another cup? Or was it something that he cast into the cup, so that it made a splash?"

"It made a splash, I think, sir," she said. "That was why I noticed it. I heard it and turned to look."

"So you didn't actually see whichever person it was putting something into the cup," said the captain. "You heard something like a splash—where were you? In the kitchen?"

"I was, sir," she said. "I was in the kitchen, helping Cook."

"And where was your mistress?"

"She was upstairs with the master, sir," said Justina.

"And was Master Pau not up with his father and mother?" asked Bernat.

Justina hesitated for a moment. "He was, sir, they both were, but they came down and asked Mistress Sibilla to make the infusion. And so she did."

"Who helped her?" asked the scribe, suddenly, who had perhaps spent more time in kitchens than the eminent gentlemen around him. "She is a stranger in the town, is she not? She cannot have known where things were in the kitchen."

Justina stopped again and looked around. "Cook did, I think. She fetched the herbs and the cup, and Mistress Sibilla poured the boiling water on them. While Master Pau and Master Roger Bernard waited."

"Tell me, Justina," said the bishop. "Who had the keys? At that moment, when you and Cook were in the kitchen with Mistress Sibilla?"

"Cook did," she said. "I think. I was fetching things from the larder and didn't see all the time, but I saw Master Pau put something in that cup. I did."

"That was after the infusion had steeped," said Father Bernat. Justina nodded. "And then Master Pau took something—or perhaps Master Roger Bernard?"

"It could have been."

"One of the two young men took something—we're not sure right now whether it was a vial or something else—" He looked at her.

Justina nodded again, with a slight smile as if she were pleased that someone was following her argument.

"Where did he take it from?" asked Bernat.

"Where?" asked Justina and stopped. There was a slight tremor in her voice. "From his sash, I think," she said at last. "I don't know. Perhaps he picked it up."

"Perhaps he did. Where did he get this substance, do you think?"

"Get it?"

"Yes," said Bernat. "Surely your house is not filled with deadly poisons, is it? Where do you suppose he got it?"

She looked down at the floor, and then shook her head sadly. "On one of his trips into the city, I suppose," she said. "They say there are places in the city where you can buy such things. I wouldn't know where they are, myself. All I know is that Pau and Roger Bernard killed the master, who was the kindest man in the world." She raised her apron to her face for a few moments in front of the silent group. "Young Master Pau and Roger Bernard killed him through sorcery and poison, and they are heretics and murderers as well."

"And why did you wait until now to tell us?" asked Father Bernat, catching a nod from Berenguer.

"Oh, Your Excellency, I was afraid of Master Pau," said Justina, shrinking back as if she were trying to squeeze herself into a smaller space of the world around her. "I thought if he knew what I was doing, then he would kill me. And I think he would. But I knew he had gone out this morning, and Master Roger Bernard had as well, and so I dared to come in, and besides I got a ride on someone's cart who was coming to market."

"You will wait here until you are told that may go," said Berenguer. "We must talk over your accusations before we can take any action."

"MY physician will be waiting for me in my study at this very moment, Bernat," said the bishop as they walked out of the room. "When the deposition is ready, please bring it up there. And you, too, Captain. I will expect to see you there shortly. I wish to know more about Mistress Sibilla."

Isaac was waiting in the corridor outside the bishop's study when he arrived. "Excellent," said Berenguer, whisking past him and leaving the door open. "Do something about this wretched knee, and tell me what you know about Mistress Sibilla."

"Nothing, Your Excellency," said the physician, settling himself on the stool from which he could conveniently massage and manipulate the prelate's knee. "Except that she seems to be in excellent health, and that she grew up in the mountains close to the place where our poor Master Raimon was born. She said that everyone in her village knows the story of Master Raimon and how he was snatched away from his family by his father and taken to Lleida. In fact, I suppose that she knows more of it than he ever did."

"Ah," said the bishop. "I can feel my temper improving with each movement of your clever fingers. That is Bernat at the door, and I would like you to hear what we have just heard, concerning Raimon's death. Bernat, have that deposition read out."

As the scribe read what he had written in his clear, unemotional voice, Isaac continued to massage the muscles in the bishop's calf and around his knees. When it was finished, he picked up the towel that Jordi, the bishop's personal servant, had draped over his knee, and used it to wipe the sweet oil from Berenguer's skin and then from his own hands.

"That woman is lying, I think," said Isaac. "Although it is possible that something like that might have happened."

"You do not think Pau and Roger Bernard were responsible?" asked Berenguer.

"It would surprise me," said Isaac. "Unless one or the other of them is a madman, and neither one gives any signs of it. But what good could Master Raimon's death have brought to either one?"

They were interrupted by a knock on the door, and the

quick entry of a messenger from the porter. "Please, Your Excellency," said the porter's boy. "Master Pau Foraster is in the palace, greatly desiring to see Your Excellency on a matter of great urgency."

"I don't know why I bother to travel," said the bishop. "If I sit in this room for a sufficient length of time, everyone I ever needed to see will arrive on my doorstep. Conduct the maid Justina to the larger meeting room," he added. "We will see them all there."

The boy looked around him panic-stricken. "I am very sorry, Your Excellency," he said. "But the maid Justina has disappeared from that room. No one saw her go, and no one knows where she has gone."

"Send me the porter," said His Excellency, his voice silky with rage. The boy promptly bolted from the room. "How could anyone be stupid enough to allow that woman to walk out of the palace?"

"She said that she was frightened of him," said Bernat. "Sometimes fear will cause people to do astonishing things."

"If that woman is not afraid of me," said Berenguer, "I doubt very much that she is afraid of Master Pau."

"Perhaps she is more frightened of what he might say," observed Isaac. "It is just possible that it will contradict some points in her tale."

2.

AT first, Yusuf tried to stay well away from the road, thinking that if his former travel mates were moving quickly they might overrun him. This way he could save himself from a possibly dangerous, or at the least, embarrassing encounter by maintaining a course parallel to it. His system, he soon discovered, had serious disadvantages. He had not taken into account that the road had followed this same route through the rocky countryside for as long as people had lived here because all the other ways through were extremely difficult.

He returned cautiously to the road again and urged his little mare to increase her pace.

The moon, only a night or two past the full, rose not long after sunset and was bright enough to light Yusuf's way. But as he continued, forested areas of varying thickness on both sides of the road obstructed the light, and as the lingering dusk faded slowly, the moon did little behind that canopy of wood and leaf to help him.

He slowed to accommodate to the darkness until the moon was riding high above them, casting more light on the road surface. He thought about picking up his pace and continuing for the entire night. But it was now at least two hours since a distant bell had rung for matins and his little mare was flagging. The road crested a small rise and he stopped. Ahead it plunged down a steep wooded slope.

"This is it, girl," said Yusuf. "We stop here before we both break our necks." He rode into the woods and dismounted. The mare nickered softly and then started moving with determination across the hill, between the trees. When he caught up with her, she had her head well down in a small stream. "This is as good a place as any," said the boy, and stretched out on the soft forest floor, his knife to his hand.

He was so weary that he slept heavily for two or three hours in spite of hunger. At first light he awoke, aware of the chirping of birds and some other sound, less readily defined. He raised his head a fraction of an inch and looked around. Except for the mare asleep nearby, he saw nothing. Then he heard the same sound again. "I think he's waking up," muttered a voice in Arabic.

"Kick him," said a second voice, coming from behind a nearby tree.

"Why would you want to kick me?" asked Yusuf. "I am a countryman."

OVER a meal of bread and chickpeas with olives that they shared with him, he told them his story—or as much of it as he thought they might appreciate. "The worst of it is," he said finally, "that I have have no idea where I am, and I cannot ask anyone, because the whole countryside seems to be hostile."

The two men laughed. "You are in Valencia. And we are not so much hostile as cautious—even suspicious, around here," said the first. "We have had a lot of fighting. Many have been killed. Our women and our daughters have been raped and murdered, or enslaved. It has not been an easy time."

"You are lucky you woke up when you did," said the second man. "We assumed you were a raider. There are some in the vicinity."

"I expect those were the men I left earlier," said Yusuf. "They are traveling with two wagonloads of arms."

"Arms?" asked the first. "I find that hard to believe," he added casually. "Are you sure it was not wool or leather? Merchants traveling through here most commonly carry wool or leather."

"They had so much wool as it takes to weave a sash, or enough leather to hang a sword from or to hold a coat of mail to the body," said Yusuf. "No more."

"You have seen these arms?"

"Before I left, I lifted the canvas to see what they were guarding with such care. It was enough weaponry and light armor to outfit a several hundred men. But it is no concern of mine. I only wish to reach Valencia and find a ship going to Barcelona."

"Not an easy thing to get to the coast from here right now," said the second man. "Not at all easy. You would be better to go overland."

"Someone else told me that," admitted Yusuf. "A young man who called himself Ali. He suggested that I head for Teruel. That is why I was with that group—they were going to Teruel."

"And from Teruel? Where then are you going?"

"To Catalonia. I thought that I could get to the coast from Teruel and find a ship."

"Where in Catalonia?"

Yusuf paused for a moment. "Girona," he said.

The two men moved back to hold a muttered consultation and then returned, sitting down beside Yusuf.

"I would not suggest the road from Teruel to the coast," said the first man.

"Not at the moment," said the second one. "Especially not if you were to travel alone."

"Why not?" asked Yusuf.

"Well, the road from here to Teruel is not a bad road," said the first man. He brushed away leaves, sticks, and needles from the ground, picked up a twig, and began to sketch. "You go from here, over, and then up. You will find enough other travelers on it with you to offer protection from thieves who might have their eyes on that nice little mare of yours."

"And then where do I go?"

"Well—if you were to take the road to Zaragoza you would be able to get from it over to Lleida. It is also possible to follow the shepherd's route through the mountains—they, too, head in the direction you wish to take, going up past Lleida. My friend tells me that Lleida is not far from Girona."

"Where do I go from here?" asked Yusuf.

"You go down this hill, and that puts you on the road to Teruel. So many people pass through Teruel that one more boy will not be noticed, I would think, as long as you take care not to do anything outrageous."

"Thank you," said Yusuf. "I wonder if the party I was with has gone by while I was sleeping. I have no desire to meet up with them again."

"I do not know," said the first man. "We have been here all night and have not seen them. I wish you a good journey." He nodded at the other man, picked up a large leather bag from the ground, and headed off down the hill.

"If you do not wish to stay in Teruel," said the second man, softly, when his companion had moved a certain distance away, "outside the city you will find a little group of houses quite close to the wall. Ask for Pere the cabinetmaker, and tell him that his shipmate, Joan, sent you. He will put you on the right road." He picked up another leather bag and set off after his companion.

THE next four days were a blur of heat, hunger, and weariness. Pere the cabinetmaker had obligingly taken him in, given him a straw mattress on the floor for the night, fed him, and looked after his mare, before setting him on the right road. "You'd best beware of the inns along the way," he said, slowly, as if such warnings came reluctantly from his tongue. "There's a few as are all right, but the most of the innkeepers are thieves as'll cut your throat for a halfpenny. Sleep in the fields alongside your mare out of sight of the road."

"I thank you, sir, for your wise advice," said Yusuf, to whom none of this had come as a surprise. "I shall follow it."

AND the inns along the road were indeed not of the best. He bought what food he could from farms along the road and looked for grassy patches somewhere off the road to sleep. He traveled with groups when possible—merchants, musicians, laborers—and alone when he had to, alert to signs of danger at every rise and every turn in the road.

The heat intensified with each passing day, and soon he was riding by night and into the morning, and catching what sleep he could in the scorching afternoons. He was exhausted; dust and sand along with the bright sunlight had left his eyes red-rimmed and sore. Every bone and muscle in his body ached from the effort of staying upright in the saddle. In the shimmering heat in front of him he began to see odd images of trees or pale buildings set right in the middle of the road. Sometimes he blinked and shook his head, realizing that they were not there; at other times he urged the surprised beast he was riding over to the verge to avoid them.

ON the fourth morning he awoke at first light, aching in every limb. He saddled his mare, noticing suddenly how dull and dusty her coat was, and that her head drooped in fatigue and discouragement.

"Poor thing," he said. "You've worked hard over these roads, and there isn't much grass here." He took out his remaining piece of loaf, broke it half, and gave her the larger piece. As soon as the sun rose over the hills, the temperature climbed. Not long after, the road started to climb as well.

Light bounced off the road, the outcrops of rock, and the occasional stream into his eyes until he thought it would blind him. His head began to ache. The road started its long descent, and the mare struggled to keep her footing as it plunged.

When they reached the level, she was drenched in sweat and barely picking up her feet. To his left a pale farmhouse shimmered in the sun, with an olive grove on one side and a fruit orchard on the other. Just as he decided that this was another trick of his heat-dazed brain, the mare stopped dead. She shook her head and stood where she was.

Two mules in the orchard were watching the road with great interest. One brayed, and the mare began to move toward them, her ears set back in a gesture of open rebellion. A door banged, and a sturdy, pleasant-looking woman came around the corner.

"Well," she said, "you do look tired and dusty, young man."

"Have you water to spare for me and my mare?" asked Yusuf. "And perhaps part of a loaf? I am more than willing to pay for any refreshment I receive from your hands, *señora*."

"That is as fair an offer as I have received today," she said, laughing. "Come 'round the house to the shade of the courtyard and I will see what I can do."

⊹≡ ≡⊹

3.

ON Friday of that same week, Isaac and little Jonàs, the erstwhile kitchen lad, were heading at great speed toward the house of Pons Manet. That is, Isaac was walking with the long-legged rapid stride that he usually adopted when his hand was on an assistant's shoulder. Jonàs was breathless with the exertion of following his instructions and keeping slightly ahead of his master.

Jonàs reached up and rang the bell, and then stepped back again, enormously pleased with himself. The door opened a little, the maid looked down at the boy and then up, and said, "Oh, Master Isaac. The mistress will be so pleased. She is ever so worried about Mistress Francesca. She said to take you up at once to her chamber."

"Certainly," said Isaac. "And what seems to be troubling Mistress Francesca?" he asked quietly.

"No one seems to be quite sure," said the maid. "She's upset again, I think."

SOME time later, Isaac emerged from the room. The entire household, including the boy, had gathered at strategic points outside the chamber in an effort to discover why Francesca had fainted in the cathedral square while walking with her cousin, Sibilla. Isaac ignored them all, asking merely if he might speak with Jaume Manet, Francesca's husband. The two men moved into another chamber where they held a conversation so quiet in tone that the eavesdroppers had great difficulty hearing more than the occasional word or phrase. Terms such as "strengthening food" and "cheerful distractions" drifted over to them, but since such things were to be recommended in a multitude of cases, no one was the wiser. At last the two men came out of the chamber and headed toward the stairs.

"The best thing you could do would be to encourage her to take more exercise, Master Jaume. She needs to be out in the fresh, good air, moving about, talking to people, or at least listening to them. The worst thing she can do is stay in the house out of fear of fainting once more. That would weaken her further and depress her spirits seriously. I would suggest most strongly that she stay away from the heat and bright sun of midday, take the air early in the day, and then again in the cool of the evening. If you could go with her at first, to calm these irrational fears, that might help. That and good, nourishing food will do more for her than any medication I can give her."

As he was being shown to the door, a hand was laid softly on his arm. "Master Isaac, it is I, Sibilla. Would you object if I walked a little way with you? There is something that I would like to ask you about."

"Not at all, Mistress Sibilla," said the physician. "I would be pleased to have your company."

"Then perhaps it would be even better if we were to sit in the courtyard, if you have moment to spare."

"Master Isaac," said Sibilla, once they were seated comfortably in the dappled shade of a pear tree, "I bear a message for you from Rebecca," she said. "Your daughter."

"I know well who Rebecca is," said Isaac. "Is she in difficulties?"

"Rebecca? No. She is well, as are her husband and little Carles. She begs to be remembered to her papa and says that she hopes that you will soon be able to come to visit her, although she realizes that in the absence of that scamp, Yusuf, you must have less time for frivolous visits."

"I wish that more people who bore me messages were that precise and accurate in their reporting of them," said the physician, laughing. "I can hear her voice in every line. But that cannot be the substance of the message," he added. "For she knows well that I will visit, if not today, then tomorrow."

"No—it is not. The message is—" Sibilla paused. "It is just that she and her husband are much concerned over the fate of Master Pau, who is one of their greatest friends. Rebecca does not know whether her papa has heard of the accusation against him." She paused again. "And his younger brother, Roger Bernard, of course."

"I have heard that such a thing happened," said Isaac. "And I was much distressed by it, for it seems to me to have no merit at all."

"Do you feel that as well?" said Sibilla eagerly. "I am glad— I mean Rebecca will be glad to hear you say it. And Rebecca has asked me to pass on to you her earnest wish, if you can, if it is at all possible, that you use your influence with the bishop to save Pau. You probably know how true a friend he is to her husband, Nicholau."

"Is he under arrest?" asked Isaac. "If so, I had not as yet heard of it."

"No," said Sibilla. "He is not under arrest, not yet but he knows of the accusation—the entire city knows of the accusation that spiteful housemaid lodged against him and his brother. And once an accusation has been lodged, it must be examined, must it not? And anyone looking at the situation must know that he could not have done this thing."

"My daughter pleads most eloquently for young Master Pau," said Isaac. "I only wonder why she did not speak directly to me yesterday when I visited her last. Is she aware that she is pleading for me to use my influence with the bishop?"

"She is perhaps not aware that I am speaking to you about it this very moment," said Sibilla evasively. "But she did mention the possibility that the bishop would intervene if you were to ask him," said Sibilla. "And that the next time she saw you, she told me, she would suggest it."

"And you wished to ensure that she would not forget to do so," said Isaac.

"I apologize for the slight deception. But Master Isaac, there are reasons, strong reasons, why Pau would not consider for a moment doing such a thing as murdering his father—when I say father, I mean Raimon, for he was indeed the only father Pau ever knew. He loved him dearly. He is devastated by his death. And even if he had the temper or the disposition to be a poisoner, which I cannot believe that he has, he cannot benefit from his death."

"I believe that even His Excellency the bishop knows that, Mistress Sibilla. That is one reason why, I think, he hesitates to move any further on this accusation. Since Master Pau's own father died when he was a baby, he already owns a considerable property, I believe. And the *finca* here is his mother's property, to be disposed of as she wishes. Murdering her husband is not going to affect what she does with it."

"You knew that?" said Sibilla.

"I think that many people know that. You must not be too oppressed by rumors. They come and go again and people forget them. It happens all the time."

"But Master Isaac, it is not enough to say that rumors are unimportant. Someone killed Master Raimon. That is not a rumor. And I do not understand why. All that I am sure of is that it cannot have been Master Pau, and I do not believe it was young Roger Bernard, either."

"But surely no one believes that Roger Bernard poisoned his father," said Isaac. "I would think it most unlikely."

"Unfortunately, he is the only person who could benefit from Raimon's death," said Sibilla. "In a material sense, I mean."

"What do you mean?" asked Isaac. "How does Roger Bernard benefit? Unless you believe that he could then be callous enough to murder his mother as well."

"I don't think he could possibly do either. He is so lively and friendly. And fond of his parents. Both of his parents."

"Then what do you mean?"

"I should not have said what I said," murmured Sibilla. "When I am upset, I speak heedless of the consequences. This kind of information can help no one, but if it were generally known, it could cause trouble."

"Then tell me, but keep your voice low," said Isaac.

"I happen to know about some property that could well go to young Roger Bernard on the death of his father."

"Considerable property?"

"I suppose so," she said. "Men spoke of it as considerable."

"What kind of property?"

"Land," she answered promptly. "On a good river. Some of it is mountainous, but there are also slopes planted with pro-ductive vines, as well as meadows and forest. Roger Bernard cannot have poisoned his father to receive this property," she added. "Not only did he love his father dearly, but how could he have done something like that to acquire property he knew nothing about?"

"What do you mean?" asked Isaac.

"This was property that should have gone to Raimon," said Sibilla.

"And why didn't it?" asked Isaac.

"Because he knew nothing of it and therefore did not claim it. And that means that he could not have told his son about it."

"How do you know that?"

"That was one of the things that we spoke of the morning of his death," said Sibilla. Her voice was low and very unhappy-sounding. "When I told him that I thought he had property waiting for him to claim, he scoffed at me, and said that his father was a poor miserable creature without a penny to his name, as far as he could tell, not a great landowner."

"How do you know all of this?" asked Isaac.

"Raimon's family came from the village where I was born," she said simply. "Everyone in the village knows that there is a farm, and that its ownership has not yet been settled."

"But this farm is not near Lleida," said Isaac. "For you do not speak at all like those who are from Lleida."

"No," said Sibilla. "We are not from Catalonia. We are from the other side of the mountains. But I know the family Raimon sprang from. Some of its members are related to my family by marriage. Of course, everyone in the village is related one way or another to everyone else—It's a small village."

"I shall pass this information—or as much of it as seems important—to His Excellency," said Isaac. "I am sure that he will find it helpful. And now I must leave, I fear. I have other patients to see this morning."

4.

"YOU are a sorry sight," the farm wife said to Yusuf. "You and your very dusty mare. When did you last eat, the two of you?"

"I had a piece of a loaf left over this morning at first light," said Yusuf. "I shared it with her, because the grazing was rather poor where we stopped."

"Well, dismount, before the poor creature falls over," she said. They were now around at the back of the farmhouse, where there was a swept yard, a barn in good repair, and a washhouse from which came the clean, unmistakable smell of boiling linen. Yusuf's hostess was a trim woman in her thirties, with strong arms and a pretty face. Her hair was tied back in a kerchief, from which it fell halfway down her back. She looked as if life had equipped her to deal with anything that came her way.

As soon as Yusuf's rather wobbly legs reached ground, she unsaddled the mare and threw the saddle over a railing, led her over to a trough half-filled with water, and called out, "Felip, you lazy beast. Come here!"

An overgrown boy, all arms and legs, came out of the barn. "Yes, Mistress Estella?"

"Once this poor thing has had some water, brush her down and turn her into the orchard with the mules. Then clean that harness."

"Yes, Mistress Estella."

"He's slow, but he's good-hearted and always does everything he's told to do," she said. "I couldn't get along without him. Now—you," she said, looking at him. "You're just a lad, aren't you? How old?"

"Thirteen," he said, blushing under her gaze.

"You promise well. And what's your name?"

"Yusuf, Mistress Estella."

"Interesting name," she said vaguely, giving him the same

rapid diagnostic look she had given the mare. "For now," she said briskly, "I would say you need a wash, some fresh clothes, and something to eat. Come in here." She took him in to a large, airy kitchen and through a door to a shed connected to it. In it was a table with a basin for washing and a ewer filled with water. "I'll bring you more water," she said. "Fortunately for you, we're washing this week, so strip off all those clothes and drop them on the floor. Do you have a change of linen?"

"Not a clean one," said Yusuf.

"Then give me the dirty linen from your bundle, and I'll do that, too."

"But then what do I—"

"I'll get you a shirt and a tunic. Will that do to save your modesty?" she asked, laughing.

"Thank you, Mistress Estella," said Yusuf, too tired to argue. As soon as she retreated, he stripped off his sweat-soaked, smelly clothes, and began to wash himself vigorously.

"Pay no attention to me," said a cheerful voice behind him. "I brought you more water and your clothes." The door slammed, and he was left alone.

When he came into the kitchen, there was a great soup plate of simmered meats and vegetables in their broth, rich with herbs and spices, sitting on the table. Beside it was a large loaf of country bread, and a jug of wine, with two cups. "I won't eat with you," she said. "I have too many things to do first. But I'll have a cup of wine to keep you company. And when you've eaten, you should have a sleep, before you drop dead of pure weariness."

HIS hostess took him to a shady chamber with a carved wooden bed, a chest, a table, and a chair in it. She pointed at the bed, stepped back, and closed the door. He kicked away the slippers she had found for him, took off the extralarge tunic he had been wearing, and fell on the bed in his shirt. When he awoke, slanting rays of the sun had found their way through the slats in the shutters, and he could hear people calling back and forth to each other.

He splashed water on his face, put on his borrowed clothes again, and headed back to the kitchen. There sat the mistress of the house, chatting with someone who, from the size of her powerful-looking arms, must have been the laundress who had been washing his linen and doing what she could with his tunic.

"*Hola*," he said to the two women.

"I'd best be back to my work," said the laundress. "Your linen won't be dry until tomorrow, young master. But it's wonderful clean, now."

"Thank you, mistress," said Yusuf.

The laundress got to her feet and headed back to the washing shed.

"I intended to ride out this evening, Mistress Estella," said Yusuf.

"Nonsense," said the mistress of the house. "You cannot leave yet. If you don't rest that pony until tomorrow morning at least, she won't recover."

"Recover?"

"She's footsore, and one leg is tender. If you ride out tonight, she'll pull up lame. If you take her out tomorrow she'll carry you, but you'll have to move slowly. She should rest until the next day at least."

"Where are we now?" asked Yusuf.

"Not far from Lleida," she said. "Four hours at a comfortable walk for a horse or mule. Perhaps five for a man walking, or six if he's slow. Where are you headed?"

"For Girona," said Yusuf.

"Do you need to go into Lleida?"

"No," said Yusuf. "I need to get home."

"There's a path through the hills that'll take you to the road east and save you some time," she said thoughtfully. "If you rest your beast for another day, she'll get to Girona in three days by that route. If you ride on tomorrow at dawn, it'll take her four, I should think."

"You seem to know a great deal about horses, Mistress Estella," said Yusuf, in irritated tones.

"I do," she said. "I've raised many a gentleman's—and lord's—fine mount since I was a girl of your age. This was my father's property," she said. "When I married, my husband moved in here and helped, although he never learned enough to be of any use. Then the plague came, and they died—even some of the horses died. And I was left with Felip, the head groom's son, who's slow, but reliable, and a few horses, and some mules. We're slowly building up a herd again. If you'd change your mind about going to Girona, I'd gladly take you on, along with that mare. She's a beauty, even after all this hard use she's suffered. She's young, you know, and hasn't the strength or endurance she'll get when she's older, but she has excellent bloodlines. Fortunately, you're light, or you would have ruined her."

"And I would gladly give her to you," said Yusuf, "but if I did, I would have no means of getting to Girona but my own two feet, and although I could do it, it would be slow."

"Where did you get her?" asked Mistress Estella.

"That's a very long story," he said. "And not all of it is mine to tell."

"Then come out into the orchard," she said, "and tell me as much of it as is yours."

She brought a jug of a cool drink made of crushed fruit, honey, and cold well water, and led him out toward the orchard. He looked around him. For the first time since his mare stopped on the road, he was clearheaded and awake enough to notice his surroundings. The orchard nestled under a protective wall of high hills to the south and west. To the north, the land rose to embrace the distant mountains. More hills to the east formed the last wall around them.

But in the orchard itself, under a large tree, a table and a bench had been set up with thick cushions. They settled down comfortably, and Yusuf began to tell his story.

He described himself as the son of a minor official with the government of Granada, who had accompanied his father on a mission into Valencia and been caught in the middle of the uprising that happened during the plague year. "Somehow," he said, "word got back to Granada that I was alive; my mother was told and convinced an official who had been one of my father's friends to request my return to the kingdom.

"Granada is a kingdom filled with little political plots," he continued. "People are always trying to create problems for other people in order to gain advantage for themselves. Unfortunately, once I was there, I was caught in the middle of one of these plots and was helped to leave the country by the man who is to marry my sister. He was the one who gave me his horse. I hasten to add that she is his second favorite horse."

"I would be interested in seeing his favorite horse," said Mistress Estella, laughing. "And so she has come directly from Granada, then," she added thoughtfully. "And from the emir's stable as well."

"I did not say that she was from the emir's stable," protested Yusuf.

"Listen, my friend, the mothers of stable lads and kitchen boys don't have access to those kinds of high officials in any government—the ones who will write a letter to His Majesty or one of his representatives here in Catalonia that will cause even a sweet creature like you to be shipped away instantly to Granada."

"She is not one of the emir's horses," said Yusuf, determined to stick at least to the literal truth.

"Probably not," said Mistress Estella. "That would be a gift for a king. Has she ever lived in the emir's stables?"

"Well," said Yusuf. "I suppose you'd have to say that she has. But I wouldn't want you to think . . ."

"I know what I think. I think that I have a sturdy gelding, well rested, that could take you to Girona in three days or less. His dam was sired by one of His late Majesty's courier horses. One of the best. He doesn't know the meaning of the word tired."

"I'd like to see him," said Yusuf.

"And after I've had a foal or two from your pretty mare, you can claim her back if you like. Someday you might have to prove to your unimportant brother-in-law that you valued his second-best horse as a gift."

"You're a very clever woman," said Yusuf. "Can you draw up an agreement?"

"I can. Can you read it?"

"In more than one tongue, Mistress Estella."

"Come to the stableyard, and I will show you Fletxa, because if you two don't like each other, then the trade is off."

She took him past the barn and through a line of thickly growing trees. Beyond them was a stable, a stableyard, neatly swept as well, and an enclosed paddock with a couple of horses in it. Behind the paddock was a large meadow encircled by trees, with a stream that tumbled down from the hills and settled into a steady course through the pasture. There were perhaps a dozen horses and mules grazing, including four or five mares with foals beside them. For a moment, Yusuf thought of Mistress Estella's offer of a place here and was tempted.

She whistled; several inquisitive heads turned. "Fletxa," she called, and held out her hand. A dun-colored horse with a pale mane and tail, a neat head held high, and a compact, sturdy body cantered over to the wall. "Have a carrot," she said in a crooning voice. "What do you think of him?"

"He's a beauty," said Yusuf. "How old is he?"

"Eight years. You think about it until supper. Watch him run," she said. "Right, little one," she said to Fletxa, "off you go."

The horse galloped off.

They went back to the orchard and sat down. "I know someone in Girona who grew up near Lleida," said Yusuf sleepily. "His is an odd story."

"Really?" she said. "Tell me then. I like odd stories."

"It seems his father brought him to Lleida when he was a just a little boy, all the way from the other side of the mountains and just left him there, with a family he had never met before."

"That seems to happen fairly often," said Mistress Estella. "We had neighbors who brought up a boy like that. Some man dropped him off, asked them if they would take care of him for a while, and never came back. Well—they say he did come back once but few people saw him, and then someone else came by to inquire after him and the boy, but he didn't really return for him. He told the neighbors that the boy must be guarded with their lives, for he was immensely rich, and when he grew up and was able to claim his estate, they would be abundantly rewarded."

"And were they?"

"Of course not. They knew from the start that these were all promises from a tale told over the hearth in winter to pass the time. We're a practical, hard-headed lot around here, and they never expected to receive a penny for taking him in. They treated him well and cared for him as best they could because he was a nice lad, and they were fond of him. He grew up with them and fell in love with Marta, the wife of old Gregori whose *finca* is an hour or so away from here. When Gregori died, he married her."

"What was his name?" asked Yusuf, suddenly alert again.

"Raimon," she said. "They called him Raimon the foreigner."

"Ours is called that, too," said Yusuf. "This must be where Raimon grew up. How very strange."

"Marta's baby inherited the *finca* when old Gregori died," she said. "Raimon used to run it, and then they leased it to a cousin, I think, who is still running it—and making a good living from it, too, in spite of the rent he has to pay. It must have been ten years ago when they left. How are they?"

"They were fine when I left Girona," said Yusuf.

"My mother would be very pleased to hear news of them," she said. "Do come and meet her," said Mistress Estella.

"There are more people living in the house?" asked Yusuf, who had so far not detected a sign of anyone but Mistress Estella, the laundress, and the reliable Felip.

"You don't think I live in this great place all by myself, do you?" she said, laughing again. "My mother lives very quietly in the other part of the house. The cook and the two maids are still helping with the laundry. My brother lives here, too, but he has taken some horses to a fair."

"I am glad you do not have all the work of this establishment to do yourself," said Yusuf.

"I could still use another man," she said slyly. "But we were speaking of my mother. She knew Raimon Foraster well—he is just few years younger than she is—and she was always very fond of him. I was just a little girl when he married Marta and moved to the *finca,* but my mother knew him well and still talks of him. He was such a sweet child, she said, with manners like a little lord, but as strong as a blacksmith—he could work like a whole team of oxen when he got to be a man."

"He hasn't changed," said Yusuf. "He is still a powerful man, as well as being most courteous and charming."

"Marta was a lucky woman," said Mistress Estella, "to have gone from that horrible old creature, Gregori, to a handsome sweet man like Raimon."

THE old lady's room opened directly onto the courtyard, and a few rays of the evening sun still made their way into it through her broad doorway. On its windowless north wall was a bed, heavily curtained against winter winds that howled down off the mountains, and scattered about the rest of the room were a comfortable-looking couch, some chairs, and a table. There were windows as well, looking east and south. When they walked in, the shutters had been pushed back, and out her windows Yusuf could see the ridge of mountains to the east and the road he had toiled up so painfully that morning. The sun, low in the western sky, painted the rock of the mountains a rich orange-pink, and gave the room itself a look of opulence.

From this little kingdom, Yusuf thought, one could follow all the activity in the world outside and within the house.

The old lady was lying propped upright on the couch, with the aid of many pillows, listening to a young girl who was telling her a story that she had apparently just heard.

"Mama," said Mistress Estella. "I have brought you the young man who was riding by on his way to Girona. His horse pulled up a little lame outside our gates, and we have been doing what we can for her."

"From what I saw, she looked to need a few days rest, that's all," said the old lady crisply. "Unless she suffers from something very serious that only he would know about."

"No, I don't think so," said Mistress Estella. "But he knows Raimon in Girona. Raimon Foraster. Isn't that amazing?"

"Not really," said the old lady, smiling at Yusuf. "If they both live there, I suppose it is not strange at all. And it is not the first time that someone has ridden by seeking news of Raimon."

"But Mama, that was years ago," said Mistress Estella.

"Not that many years. We have had two or three visitors interested in our neighbor's adopted son, so to speak. The last one who came by from up there in the north was only a few years ago."

"A few years, Mama? That was before my husband died. Remember? And he chased that poor woman away—what was her name?"

"Beatriu."

"That's right—and her daughter—chased them as if they were barn rats."

"They weren't much better than barn rats," said the old lady crisply. "But our guest is not interested in our memories, Estella. What is strange about your arrival, Master Yusuf, is that you should find yourself on this road coming up from the south, and also that your mare should have decided that she could not walk another step in front of our door. As you may have guessed, I watched your arrival."

"And that is exactly what happened, *señora*," said Yusuf, with a bow. "Fate, or my mare's intelligence, has placed me in your generous hands. My mare decided that in reaching your gates, she had reached the fulfillment of her needs and desires and stopped. Poor, brave creature. She has carried me a long distance in the past fortnight."

"You are very welcome," said the old lady graciously, "for we get few visitors here from the outside world, and they are always of interest. Come, young man, sit here beside me, for my limbs are very stiff and painful, although the rest of me is as well as can be. Tell me how you come to know Raimon."

5.

IT turned out not to be a day for carrying messages from his daughter Rebecca—or her friend Sibilla—to His Excellency. Two brief visits to patients turned into two long ones, during which there was much to do, and he had little assistance in his labors from the hapless Jonàs.

Four or five times he was on the point of sending the boy to fetch his daughter Raquel, but he had promised himself that he would only call on her when life and death appeared to hang in the balance. Having made his decision, consideration liberally mixed with stubbornness kept him from disturbing her for his mere convenience. So he sweated and fumbled in his untidily packed basket among misplaced materials for even the commonest of remedies. At every step he had to stop and smell each bundle or vial, or taste them to make sure that he was not giving patients potentially deadly mixtures.

When he finished, he was tired, ill-tempered, and hungry. It was already dinner time and the smell of cooking wafted through the houses they visited. "Let us go home, Jonàs," he said.

"Did I do everything correctly, master?" asked the boy.

Isaac took a deep breath. "Sometimes," he said. "But you *must* learn where everything is placed in the basket. Had Mistress Anna been in a worse state, she would have been dead before I found the drops I needed to give her. That will not do, Jonàs. It is not like working in the kitchen. People do not enjoy a badly cooked dinner, but usually they do not die from it. Medicine is not the same."

"Yes, master," said the child, crushed.

DINNER, served in the quiet of the courtyard, had improved his temper somewhat, but had not resolved his basic problem. Once the board had been cleared, he stayed there, by the fountain, mulling over the question of what to do. The twins, almost nine, had learned their letters and were immensely proud of the fact, but they could not open a letter from a colleague written in a rapid hand, filled with details about diseases or remedies and even begin to read it aloud with accuracy. Judith had never learned her letters nor had any of the servants, except for little Jacinta in the kitchen, but she was only fractionally more expert than the twins.

The children would learn, no doubt, but sitting in his study at that moment was a letter. The seal told him that it was almost certainly from Nisim, his colleague in Montpellier, the one who had promised to send him his son to replace Yusuf and Raquel, but there was little point in opening the letter until Raquel arrived. If she did. And he had no intention of summoning her on such a trivial errand.

The bell at the gate interrupted his reflections.

"Master Isaac," said a familiar soft voice. "It is Sibilla. May I speak to you?"

"Of course," he said. "One moment, and I will open the gate." This at least was something that he could do quickly and without assistance.

"THERE were things I did not say to you this morning," she said, once she was settled on the bench by the fountain. "And on thinking about what I did say—and I have done little else since we spoke—I realized that I must tell you everything."

"What do you mean by everything?" asked Isaac.

"Everything is the history of Guillem and his mother."

"Guillem's mother?"

"Yes, Master Isaac. The bastard, Guillem, is son of Raimon's father, Arnaud de Belvianes, by the serving girl, Beatriu," she said firmly. "His Excellency must ask Guillem why he came here to find Raimon, and what he knows about Raimon's death."

"You tell your tale like an accomplished storyteller, Mistress Sibilla, holding your hearers by giving them a little every day," said Isaac. "But can I rely on your account?"

"I swear that everything I tell you is reliable. Everyone knew Guillem's mother, Beatriu," said Sibilla, "because she was born in the village. And of course, everyone was also sure that Master Arnaud was the father of both Raimon and Guillem. Beatriu herself told my nursemaid, Rosa, that Arnaud was her lover. It was no surprise, for the bastard Guillem was the image of his father, more so than the lawful son, Raimon, whose expression and way of moving was more from his mother's side of the family. Rosa used to say that Arnaud treated Raimon so badly because although the boy looked quite like him, he used to run to his mother every time his father walked into a room. Arnaud and Raimunda hated each other."

"Raimunda was Raimon's mother?" asked Isaac.

"Yes," said Sibilla. "I never knew her, so this I cannot say from my own experience. But people still spoke of Raimon when he was a child, and Guillem the bastard," she added.

"You knew this Beatriu?" asked Isaac. "Was she a friend?"

"Beatriu left the village when I was a baby. Her place in our house was taken by Rosa."

"But Beatriu worked for your family? Did they know her well?"

"She was my grandmother's serving girl. But as for knowing

her well—that is a different question. And not because she was a servant. My closest friend in this world—especially since my grandmother died—has been my maid, Rosa. But Beatriu and my grandmother did not like each other very much."

"And yet she stayed in your grandmother's service."

"She had little choice," said Sibilla dryly. "Soon after she came to work for us—she would have been fourteen or fifteen, I suppose—she was with child and in no position to look for another post. As well, our family had its own difficulties. We were poor and help was hard to find. My grandmother agreed to keep her on, paying her a tiny salary and her keep in return for whatever work she could continue to do. She and her baby lived with my grandmother on those terms until Guillem was twelve and my grandmother forced Arnaud to send him to Toulouse to study the law."

"Did you know Guillem?"

"Unfortunately, yes. He used to come back to the village from time to time, and he would always visit my grandmother. She permitted it because, as she said, he had known no other home but ours. I could not help but know him—it was not a very large house."

"But this Beatriu did not come with him to visit?"

"Certainly not. Two or three years after Guillem was sent to study in Toulouse, Beatriu left. Just like that, in the night, taking all the valuables she could carry with her. Then we heard that Guillem had left Toulouse. Everyone decided that they had run off together, mother and son, to seek their fortune."

"Where did they go?"

"I do not know, Master Isaac. As I said, he came back to the village from time to time for a while, but he never spoke of her, and it is quite possible that he didn't know where she was. After he stopped coming, I neither saw nor heard of him until I saw him at the funeral."

"But he moved in with Raimon's family several weeks ago," said Isaac. "You never saw him on your visits there?"

"Never," said Sibilla.

"Surely he must know who you are, and that you are in the city," said Isaac.

"I don't think so," said Sibilla. "Sibilla is not an uncommon name, and as far as I know, my family's rather distant connection with Francesca is not widely known here—even if anyone here should ever have heard of my family, which I doubt."

"Could he not recognize you?"

"No. When he last visited the village, I had not as yet reached my tenth year. And when I saw him at the funeral, I was partly veiled. I pulled my veil over my face and walked right by him."

"I suspect there is much more concerning Master Guillem's history that you have not told me, Mistress Sibilla," said Isaac.

"There is always much that one does not tell," said Sibilla.

"I mean much that concerns this phantom property, your family, and Raimon's family. I fear that if I ask His Excellency to look into this matter, if I ask him to look into the question of Pau's responsibilities in this terrible happening, he may uncover more than is beneficial to that good family."

"I can tell you no more," said Sibilla. "I know nothing more to tell you. I must go now. Rosa is waiting for me outside the *call*. She will be wondering what is keeping me."

AFTER she left, Isaac sat in the courtyard and considered the whole situation. He was not happy about what he had been drawn into. It was possible that Mistress Sibilla did not understand the background to the family's history, but it was all too clear to him. What Raimon could not tell him, his dreams had. But to tell the bishop—not what you knew that a man had done; not what you had been told that a man had done; but what his helpless mind had revealed about him all unwittingly—this was the starkest betrayal a man could conceive.

On the other hand, he argued, Raimon is dead. To tell what you have deduced in order to save his beloved stepson can be no betrayal of Raimon, for he is beyond betrayal, as he is beyond harm. Surely, if Raimon were still alive, he would wish to help his son.

But he could not forget the voice of his great master, Ibn al-Baytar, in response to his twelve-year-old self pleading that a dead schoolboy companion would have wanted to give his precious book on herbs to Isaac if he had known he was to die so suddenly. "The basest and most selfish desires we have are those that we cast upon the helpless dead, saying that this man or that man—had he known—would have wanted this thing for us that we would not have the temerity to demand on our merits."

If Raimon had wanted his story spread through the streets of the city, he would have done it himself. And why had he not? Perhaps he knew or suspected that somewhere he had family who would suffer greatly if this were done.

He would speak to His Excellency, but only of those things that he knew, not from Raimon's dreams, or Sibilla's village gossip, but from his own observations.

＊⊨ ⊨＊

6.

YUSUF set off the next morning on the lively dun-colored horse, and even his beloved mare back in Girona had never seemed so pleased to be saddled up. The gelding had been dancing in anticipation of being on the road again ever since he had been led out from the stable. Meanwhile, the mare from Granada was being massaged, brushed, combed, fed delicacies, and in general pampered to glossy perfection again. As far as Yusuf could tell, she bid farewell to him and life on the hard open road without a moment's qualm, having reached some pinnacle of horse delight in her own estimation.

He carried a sizable bag of food, fresh water, his clean, if slightly damp linen, a small addition to his store of coins—for Mistress Estella acknowledged that the Arab mare was more valuable than her pretty dun-colored courier pony—and a copy of the document of exchange.

Stuffed firmly into his head were instructions for making his way through the hills and reaching the road east that would take him home, as well as a great deal of very interesting information concerning Raimon Foraster and his father, Arnaud.

FELIP the stable lad came down to the gate to wave goodbye to Yusuf and Fletxa, the dun-colored gelding. He knew, because he had been told several times, that they were going for a long time and might not come back. But a long time was something that he had difficulty grasping, since every day it seemed to mean something else, and for the rest of the day he went to the road periodically to see if they were returning, coming back rather sadly when he was summoned to his duties.

The third time he went, another horse and rider appeared and stopped by the lad. They fell into a long conversation apparently, much longer than Felip usually managed to have with anyone, and certainly longer than he had ever had with a stranger before.

When the rider had gone on his way, the old lady, who had watched all this from her couch with curiosity and some concern, had the boy summoned.

"Felip," she said, "come and sit and talk to me. Maria, bring that bowl of fruit and nuts for Felip, and then you can go until I ring."

The little girl hastily did as she was told and scampered from the room for a few moments of precious leisure.

"Who was that nice man on the horse?" she asked.

"Not nice," said Felip, his eyes filling with tears. "He said a bad thing to me and rode away."

"He shouldn't have done that," said the old lady. "What did he want?"

"Raimon," said Felip. " 'Did Raimon live here?' he said."

"And what did you say, Felip?" she asked quietly.

"I said 'There is no Raimon here.' "

"You're right, Felip, there's no Raimon here. And what did

he say next?" she said, knowing that quiet patience was needed to unlock the knowledge in Felip's head.

"He said it again and again, 'Did Raimon live here?' He shouted at me and said I was stupid."

"That was not a nice thing for him to do," said Estella's mother. "What did you do?"

"I am not stupid, I tell him, and so I tell him the name of everyone here, and of the horses and the mules."

"Can you tell me the name of everyone here and the horses and the mules?" asked the old lady.

With a smile of true pleasure, he ran through all the names in a singsong voice with his eyes shut. Including Yusuf.

"And you remembered Yusuf, too, when the man asked?" asked the old lady.

"I tell him Yusuf, too, but that Yusuf is gone and so is Fletxa but his mare is here, and she is a pretty horse, but she has no name."

"True, and you must think of a good name for her that she will like. You have a good memory, Felip," said the old lady firmly. "The man must have been pleased that you could remember everyone."

"No. He asked me where Yusuf went, but no one told me where Yusuf went. And then he asked me how he went, and I said on Fletxa—he was riding Fletxa. And he kept yelling 'how, how' and then he asked if he went to Lleida, and I didn't know."

"Of course not," said the old lady. "How could you know? No one expected you to know. It wasn't part of your job. But you did very well with the man, and he isn't a nice man, and I don't want you to talk to him if he comes back again."

"Why?"

"Because he said bad things to you, and I don't like that. Now you take the rest of that bowl with you—you may have it—and send me Maria."

"Thank you, mistress," said Felip, clutching the wooden bowl to his chest and going off for the little maid, looking much happier than he had been when he came in.

But the old lady lay on her couch and puzzled over the whole incident at some length.

7.

ON Monday morning, when the sun was still in the east, but high enough in the sky to flood the courtyard with light and warmth, Judith was sitting by the fountain, sewing, in a desperate attempt to keep up with the growth of her infant son. Beniamin slept in a cradle at her feet, a cradle he was soon going to grow out of as well. When the bell rang, she set down her work and walked quickly over to open it. Two strangers, a man and a woman, stood on the other side.

"We seek the house of Master Isaac, the physician," said the woman.

"This is his house," said Judith. "Unfortunately, he is not here, but I expect him any moment. I am his wife, Judith."

"And I am Marta, the wife—the widow of Raimon Foraster, Mistress Judith," she said. "And this is my steward, Esteve."

"Please come in, Mistress Marta. My husband will be back soon. He is visiting the bishop, who will no doubt be too occupied to take up much of his time. Jacinta, bring us something cool to drink," she called, and ushered her visitors firmly into comfortable places in the shade. In a moment or two, they were supplied with drinks of mint and lemon, and small spicy things to nibble on.

For a terrible minute, an awkward silence fell over the group until Mistress Marta's eye fell on the cradle. "What a charming baby," she said. "How old is he?"

"Just three months," said Judith, smiling.

"Only three months old and already he is such a lovely, big baby," cooed Marta, bending over the cradle. "And sleeping like a little angel, too."

"I am very fortunate," said Judith. "My first baby was not so peaceful . . ." and they fell into chatter about babies and teeth and problems and difficulties, so that when Isaac and Jonàs arrived, their presence was scarcely noticed.

"Mistress Marta?" asked Isaac, catching her voice in the discussion.

"I am sorry," said Judith. "Mistress Marta and her steward, Master Esteve, have come seeking you."

At that moment, Beniamin awoke and discovered that he was on the edge of starvation. Judith picked him up hastily, excused herself, and disappeared.

"Did my wife provide you with any refreshment on this hot day?" asked Isaac.

"Yes, Master Isaac, she did. And there is a cup here for you. Let me pour you some."

Isaac drank, set down the cup, and turned to his visitors. "What brings you here in all this heat?" he asked.

"I am concerned," said Marta.

"About your sons, Pau and Roger Bernard?"

"Yes," she said, her voice trembling, "of course, it is about Pau and Roger Bernard. We are given to understand that soon—tomorrow, perhaps the next day, they will be seized for the death of their father, on the word of our maid, Justina."

"But surely that statement of the maid Justina alone could not lead to such an outcome. For one thing, I have heard it, and it is contradictory in many ways," said Isaac. "I cannot believe that anyone has faith in it."

"The problem is that Justina has disappeared, and now they are saying that Pau has done away with her to keep her from accusing them of any more crimes. They are saying that if he had been put on trial as soon as her accusation had been written down, Justina would still be alive."

"Does Justina have family that she could have gone to?" asked Isaac gently, for Marta's voice had been rising with hysteria.

"Family?" she asked. "I do not know. She has someplace where she goes when she is not working. I had always supposed it was family—a sister, or a cousin. Perhaps it is even a man. If we could find my brother-in-law, Master Isaac, then we might find Justina. I think she is hiding."

"Why would she hide?"

"Because she knows that everything she said to His Excellency was a lie, and that she could never defend her statement."

"And you think that she might be with Master Guillem?"

"I do. I am afraid that my brother-in-law, Guillem, for whatever purposes, has been trifling with her."

"What makes you believe that?"

"Because several times I have come across them talking very quietly with each other, as lovers might who were arranging meetings. And I have seen him drop a kiss on her forehead—not a very damning action, perhaps, but extremely odd if they had no understanding between them."

"Your husband spoke of having seen similar things," said Isaac.

"I cannot help but wonder—I always thought that Guillem had something to do with my husband's death, and I wonder if he used Justina to encompass it."

"In order to save him from suspicion of the deed?" asked the physician.

"But why, Master Isaac? What good could his death have done for Guillem? For anyone?"

"Did Raimon ever speak to you about a property that he had a claim to?"

"Not that again," she said. "First Guillem, and then Mistress Sibilla tried to tell him that he had a claim on a piece of property in a village not far from Foix."

"What was his reaction?"

"He laughed and said that he had no desire to dig into his past, even had he the means to do so. He was contented with the present."

"Do you think there is any truth in the claim?" asked Isaac.

"I don't know," said Marta. "I expect that even if there were, it would take years and a great deal of gold to prosecute the claim in the courts."

"You could well be right, Mistress Marta. What do you wish me to do?"

"I don't know," said Marta. "I have the highest respect for your skills, Master Isaac, but I honestly believe that advice from a fairground fortune-teller would do me as much good as yours or the bishop's or that of any other wise man in the city."

"Mistress Bernada, you mean?" asked Isaac.

"That sort of person," said Marta. "And I don't believe she's ever done anyone any good in all her life."

"I have one suggestion," said Isaac. "I think it might be worth your while to find your kitchen maid."

"The kitchen maid?" asked Marta. "But she can't have had anything to do with it. She had left the house at least a week before Raimon died. She left before he became ill the first time, and you came out to help us."

"Nonetheless, mistress, it might be just as well to seek her out. Her absence could have been useful for someone."

"Pau will go and fetch her," said Marta. "Cook knows where she lives."

"PAPA, what is the matter?" asked Raquel, coming into the courtyard a little later and pulling off her veil at the same time.

"Nothing, my dear."

"There must be. You look—almost discontented. And that is a look that I may have, or mama may have sometimes, but not you. You need something cool to drink."

He laughed. "I confess that I was a trifle discontented. I was missing having you right at my elbow, so that I could say, 'Raquel, come here and read me this letter at once.'"

"A letter! Why did you not summon me right away, Papa? I would have come on the instant. Tell me where it is, and I shall read it right now."

"It is in my study, and it is sent under the seal of Nisim of Montpellier. I presume it concerns his son, Amos."

"I will get it at once, Papa," said Raquel.

RAQUEL settled herself comfortably, looked at the envelope and the seal, as she had been taught so long ago it seemed, and broke it open. "It is a short letter, Papa, all written on the inside of the one sheet. It begins, 'My most honored colleague, Isaac. After my last letter, in which I assured you that my scamp of a son would be setting out for Girona as soon as he had his affairs settled here, it troubles me greatly to have to tell you that he will not be coming after all, or at least not for the next few months. I told him that in that time you would in all likelihood have made other arrangements, but as much as he would like to study with you, he mulishly refuses to leave the city right now.

"'I suspect—no, I know—that the cause is a woman, and one not worth the loss of such an opportunity. How our children, in spite of the care we lavish on them, do frustrate our every plan for their advancement and happiness. I hope you will forgive me and my unhappy son for our broken promises. Yours, etc.'" Raquel put down the paper. "What will you do, Papa?" she asked. "And please remember that I am ready to help you whenever I am needed."

"For now, I shall continue to attempt the training of Jonàs, and I shall continue to lean upon your good will, my dear. But I shall also make further discreet inquiries."

"I had thought that by now we should have heard from Yusuf," said Raquel.

"Not only is he a good distance away, my dear, but he is also in a kingdom which is in a state of war with ours. Here, it is almost too easy for us to dispatch a letter, so that we are always wasting time and money sending foolish things back and forth. In Granada, he cannot simply ask if a letter can be dropped in the bag of the royal or the diocesan courier."

"Then they must save a great deal of time and money there," said Raquel, fanning herself idly with a large leaf she had plucked from a nearby plant.

"Not at all," said Isaac, cheerfully. "They have couriers

racing from city to city, and from Granada to the Maghreb by fast galley, and then off to the east again. They are exactly like us in that respect."

"What is it like there, Papa?"

"It is beautiful, my dear. Our gardens and fountains and baths strive to achieve the beauty of theirs. Sometimes they succeed; but not often. They are masters at the art of turning a desert into a paradise, in which song, scent, color, and shape all combine to turn a man's thoughts to greater things—love, beauty, heaven."

"And so they are better than we are?"

"They, too, are every bit as human as the rest of us," said Isaac briskly. "But their architects are dreamers of great dreams. And one can enjoy that. I hope Yusuf does. He has an appreciation of beauty, and the court at Granada will offer him recompense for any loneliness he may be feeling."

"I wonder if we will ever see him again," said Raquel. She jumped to her feet. "Here I am making myself sad when I intended to help you. What can I do?"

"You can straighten out the terrible mess that Jonàs has made of the basket."

8.

THE next morning, Tuesday, Isaac and Raquel were in the courtyard supervising—for the fourth time—the packing of the shallow, narrow, flat-bottomed basket by Jonàs, "No, Jonàs," Raquel was saying, "that is a very strong, very dangerous compound. It must not go on the right hand end of the basket. That is where the mild salves and herbal remedies go."

"But if the basket is turned around, Mistress Raquel, then it will be in the left end," he protested.

"That is why the ribbon is there, tied to one side of the basket. When you are packing it, you must always have the ribbon right in front of you, like this. And whenever you put

the basket down on a table, that ribbon must be facing out."
She was interrupted by a great clatter of hoofbeats outside
the gate, as if a whole regiment of soldiers had arrived at their
door. The bell rang; she laid a hand on Jonàs's shoulder. "I'll
answer it," she said.

Standing in front of her, having turned their horses over to
the stable lad who had ridden with them, was a large part of
Raimon Foraster's household: Mistress Marta, Masters Pau
and Roger Bernard, the steward, Esteve, and a ruffled-looking
young woman whom Raquel had never seen before. "Please
come in," she said, stifling her surprise.

"I'll wait out here with the horses," mumbled the boy after
receiving a significant look from Esteve.

"Papa, it is Mistress Marta and her sons," said Raquel.
"With Esteve and—" she turned inquiringly to Mistress Marta.

"You wished me to find our kitchen maid," said Marta. "Pau
and Roger Bernard did, and a curious tale she has to tell. She
has kindly agreed to come here and tell it to you. Her name is
Sanxa."

"We are very pleased that you have come to talk to us," said
Isaac. "Are we not, Raquel? Perhaps our guests would like
some refreshment. It is a long ride in from the *finca*. You did
come from the *finca*?"

"This morning, yes," said Pau. "And last night we returned to it from Pedrinyà. That is where Sanxa's family lives,
and that is where she was, of course. She has had quite a long
journey for one who is not used to riding very much."

"What have you to tell us?" asked Isaac.

And so, while Jacinta brought in jugs of cool drinks and
wine, and plates of small savory tidbits, and little bowls of
nuts and fruits, Sanxa looked nervously around, coughed, and
began.

"It all started two Sundays ago," she said. "Justina came to
me and asked me if I was ever going to get married. Because,"
she said apologetically, "I have a young man that I've an understanding with, and we've both been working hard and sav-
ing every penny we could. She knew that as soon as I had a

proper dowry, we could marry." Sanxa turned and gave Mistress Marta a nervous look.

"Go on," said Pau, encouragingly. "You're doing very well."

"Well, then Justina asked if twenty *sous* would help and I said that of course it would, but where was I to get twenty *sous*? I mean, that's a fortune, isn't it? It's a reasonable salary for a whole quarter. And she said that a friend was coming by and needed a respectable place to sleep and her board, and that she was willing to work hard for it. It would only be for two or three weeks, but Justina was afraid that if she asked the mistress to take her in, she would say no. So, she wanted me to tell the mistress that my mother was ill and needed me desperately. And then she would bring in her friend, saying that she could do my work."

"Where was Justina going to get the twenty *sous*?" asked Pau.

"She said the friend had given it to her."

"What did you think the real reason was?" asked Isaac suddenly.

"I thought it was a young woman trying to get away from her husband, or maybe a girl waiting until her lover could come for her, and they could get married. It had to be someone from a family with money, didn't it? And someone who was willing to pay a lot for secrecy, because who notices a kitchen maid?"

"Why do you say 'a lot'? Don't you think a girl of good family would consider that a reasonable amount for being safely hidden for two or three weeks?" asked Isaac.

"But clearly, sir," said Sanxa, "you don't know Justina. If she offered me twenty *sous* to leave for two weeks, I'd be surprised if she were getting a penny less than fifty. Not a lot of money gets past Justina without her taking more than her fair share of it."

"And you accepted?" asked Isaac.

"Well, no, I didn't. I wasn't happy with it. It didn't sound right to me, so I said no."

"What made you change your mind?" asked Isaac.

"I thought everyone knew about that. I got a message that my mother was ill, very ill and like to die, and so I went to Justina and told her I'd accept. Then she said that her friend had only given her ten *sous,* so I took that and told the mistress about my mother and went home."

"Was your mother ill?"

"Yes, she was," said Sanxa. "For two or three days she was vomiting and having terrible cramps in her legs and her back. But then it slowly eased off, and after a week she was fine. I was still waiting, though, for Justina to send me a message that I could return when Master Pau and Master Roger Bernard came to fetch me."

"Your mother was fortunate," murmured Isaac.

"Was the person who came in to replace me satisfactory, at least?" asked Sanxa.

"No one came in," said Marta. "Justina did your work as well as her own."

"Which is to say," said Roger Bernard, "that nothing got done that wasn't done by Cook or one of us or the lad out there."

"How very strange," said Sanxa.

"And Justina has disappeared," said Isaac. "Do you know where she might have gone?"

"Oh, no, Master Isaac. I wouldn't know where she's gone to. She wouldn't have told me anything like that." And Sanxa looked around at the people in the courtyard, all of whom, except Isaac, were staring at her as if she were a caged lion.

Raquel noticed the look. She went over to her father as if to offer him more to drink and murmured a few words in his ear. She poured out a little into his cup and went over to sit by Sanxa.

Isaac raised his head. "There are some things that happened in the last few days that I am not clear about," he said. "Would you mind staying for a few moments and going over them with me?"

"Not at all," said Marta firmly, and everyone settled back in their seats.

"You haven't even been around the last few days, have you?" said Raquel quietly to the intimidated kitchen maid.

"No, mistress," said Sanxa.

"We are altering the house next door to live in, and we are about to start on the kitchens," whispered Raquel. "Could you slip out with me and look at them? I'm sure that you could offer me suggestions for making them more useful to work in. It would be a very great help."

"That sounds interesting," said Sanxa, and the two young women went quietly out the gate and around to the new house.

When the contingent from the *finca* left at last, Isaac turned to his daughter. "Did you learn anything from her?"

"A little bit," she said. "Justina rides well, almost as well as Master Pau, and often takes one of the horses from the stable and goes off for half a day."

"One of the horses?"

"Esteve is almost always using the mules, and when he isn't, he insists that they be rested. With the horses, apparently it's more a question of them getting enough exercise on a regular basis than being worked too hard."

"Where does she go?"

"Sanxa doesn't know. She assumes it is to visit a man, but only because she would assume that, I think. If, she—Sanxa, that is—could ride that well and had access to a horse, she'd be off every other day to visit her intended."

"That's all?"

"No—certainly not. From what Sanxa said, I think that Justina comes here when she has free time, because the gossip she brings back is city gossip or gossip about the happenings around the cathedral."

"But gossip about the city spreads very quickly to the villages around and about," said Isaac.

"True enough, Papa, but it seems that two or three times she has brought back sweetmeats that I am sure you can only get from Caterina. Otherwise you'd have to go to Figueres or Barcelona."

"That seems more definite, my dear. What else?"

"In spite of doing little work and leaving most of her tasks for everyone else to do, she will be missed, Sanxa admitted. Not because she is likable, but because she is interesting. She knows a thousand tales of the mountain people, of witches and sorcerers and magic potions. And on dark winter evenings, to pass the time, she reads their futures in cards or flaxseeds or grains of sand. Sanxa said she could talk just like the fortune-teller at the fairground, all kinds of nonsense about a dark-haired strong man with a limp, or the possibility of sudden riches, or beware of a handsome man who has a cleft chin, he will bring you ill luck—that sort of thing. No one believed her, exactly, but it was amusing."

"That is very interesting," said Isaac. "But I would dearly love to know who she rode off to see every week or so here in Girona. Did you discover anything else?"

"She had some excellent advice about the kitchens that has kept me from making several costly errors. I was so pleased I gave her the other ten *sous* that Justina promised her. Now she has her twenty *sous* and can marry all the sooner."

ISAAC was just preparing to make some late afternoon visits to patients, when he was interrupted once more that same day by a polite boy at the gate.

"Master Isaac," he said, "my master, Mordecai, sends his profound apologies and begs that you would come out to visit him as soon as you can. He is not ill, he told me to say, so that it is not necessary for you to bring a heavy basket with you. If it were not important, he said, he would not summon you so inconveniently."

"Run back, lad," said Isaac, "and tell your master that I am always pleased to visit him for whatever the reason. I will be there in a moment."

And indeed, it was only a matter of a few minutes before Isaac was sitting with Mordecai in his courtyard, under a spreading lemon tree in the center of the space. "I am most grateful that you are here, and so quickly, as well," said Mordecai.

"What brought you to sending me that summons, Mordecai? I assume from all this secrecy that you were not merely bored or lonely."

"Secrecy?" Mordecai laughed. "I can never trick you, Isaac my friend. Yes, we are in the courtyard, and I am seated where I can see everything unless someone is climbing over the wall behind me. I am also assuming that you can hear any scrambling on the wall or footsteps on the stones that I might miss. This is one of the few places in the house where I am sure there are not eavesdroppers. This, and my bedchamber. And it is important right now, for what I have to ask you is something that I do not wish to spread around the city. If I am wrong in my fears, and other people hear about them, the consequences for an old acquaintance—an old friend, really— would be severe."

"I shall be silent, at least, Mordecai."

"I know that," he said, and paused. "This is a difficult question to ask, because I violate my own conscience and yours in doing so—but I do not ask out of curiosity or malice. That I swear to you."

"Mordecai," said Isaac. "Ask your question, and in a low voice, and I will answer it somehow. Otherwise night will fall on your protestations."

"You're right, Isaac. What do you know about Pons Manet that I do not? I speak as a man of business. Is he, for some reason, short of money? Is he in danger of losing everything?"

"Why would you ask such a question?" asked Isaac. "What has happened that I have not heard about?"

"Nothing that I know of, but this morning his daughter-in-law, Mistress Francesca, came in and tried to borrow two hundred gold *maravedís*. She was carrying in her hand a leather purse containing all her jewelry to use as security."

"Did you give the money to her?"

"No. First of all I don't usually deal in that sort of loan—a silver ring against five *sous* today, and someone's best dress against five pence next week. There are other people who do that, and they are glad enough of the business."

"What did you tell her?"

"I was too shocked and surprised to make a decision, and so I told her to come back tomorrow. This is the second time she has come to me for money, by the way. The first time was for fifty *sous*. It was for a present for her husband, she said, and she would pay it back in a week. That I gave to her, and she was true to her word."

"She must have expected some money to come in, then."

"Her dress allowance," said Mordecai. "But this time I want to know if Pons is sending his daughter-in-law out to raise money for the business, Isaac. It would be very odd if he did, for his credit is excellent, and we have often financed large shipments of goods for him. He cannot believe that I would not advance him the money if that were the case again."

"I can tell you this," said Isaac, "and I do not believe that I would be violating a confidence—or at least not seriously— in doing so. At the moment, according to Pons, his coffers are full. He has completed some large transactions recently and has been paid. As far as I know, he is preparing for some even larger transactions and seems quite pleased with life. Neither he nor his wife is extravagant; they keep a modest establishment for people in their station in life."

"I know that, Isaac. That is why I was so puzzled. I thought that you might know of some secret worry, or some terrible drain on their resources. As their physician."

"I would guess that the only dark cloud on their horizon is their daughter-in-law herself. She appears to be in a state of profound misery, and no one knows why."

"That relieves my mind, but does not tell me what I should do," said Mordecai.

"When she comes tomorrow, send her off to the least thieving of the small moneylenders," said Isaac. "And in the meantime, I shall speak to Pons Manet."

"Not her husband?"

"Pons is a calmer man," said Isaac.

ISAAC left Mordecai's house and turned toward the cathedral and the bishop's palace. It was time for him to make one of his regular visits there, for he was private physician to His Excellency, and for this he owed him unobtrusive but constant vigilance.

The porter at the gate let him in with an almost civil mutter of greeting and vouchsafed to tell him that His Excellency was in his private study, occupied with the contents of a dispatch bag brought by a messenger.

Undeterred by the ominous sound, Isaac headed up the stairs and along the corridor toward the bishop's study.

"ISAAC!" said Berenguer. "What a propitious time for you to arrive."

"Is Your Excellency having difficulty with your knee again?" asked Isaac.

"No more than usual," said the bishop. "In fact, less than usual at the moment, although your treatments always make it feel better. No, I'm pleased to see you because I have just received a most curious missive from the city of Foix, from a respectable, indeed renowned, notary and man of law, that ties in with our poor friend, Raimon Foraster. Bernat will read it to you."

"Certainly, Your Excellency," murmured the Franciscan.

"You can omit the compliments and such, and go directly to the meat of the letter."

"Certainly, Your Excellency. The letter is addressed to His Excellency," said Bernat, "with the usual compliments and all his proper titles."

"Bernat wishes you to know that this is a serious correspondent who understands ecclesiastical life in this province, Isaac."

"Thank you, Your Excellency," said the physician.

"And it is from a Master Robert de Ganac, a notary in Foix, as His Excellency has indicated. He writes, 'I have been emboldened by pressing circumstances into troubling Your Excellency about a matter involving a considerable property on the River Aude that I am currently administering on behalf of the courts.

" 'This property was seized in a lawful manner at the time of the conviction of one Raimunda de Lavaur, representing a considerable part of the said Raimunda's dowry at the time of her marriage to Arnaud de Belvianes. My honored father was approached by a representative of the family of the said Raimunda to present a petition for the return of this property to her heir, Raimon, who was innocent of wrongdoing, being an infant of five years of age at the time of the conviction of his mother.

" 'My father, with some minor assistance from myself, argued the case all the way up to the papal court and obtained at that time a very favorable decision.

" 'We are currently engaged in searching for the heir to Madame Raimunda's property, Raimon, the lawful son of her marriage to Arnaud de Belvianes, or failing him, his heirs. A member of the family, who has himself no interest in the case, being barred from succession, has claimed to have located said Raimon in Lleida, and then in the diocese of Girona, parish unknown. I suspect that, owing to the notoriety of his mother's case, he no longer calls himself by the family name.

" 'I make bold to contact you, My Lord, because if the property is not claimed within the year, the judgment will lapse for default of an heir.

"And the rest of the letter is closing apologies and compliments," said Bernat.

"I enjoyed his old-fashioned legal style," said Berenguer.

"Perhaps that is because he lives and practices in Foix, Your Excellency," murmured Bernat.

"Nonsense," said Berenguer. "All notaries write letters like that if they are capable of it. What do you think of the letter, Master Isaac?"

"It sounds singularly like the other half of Raimon Foraster's history, does it not?"

"It will be a heavy task, though, for young Roger Bernard to prove that he is 'the said Raimunda's' grandson, I fear. Still, I think I will answer this Master Robert and tell him we might indeed have his missing heir. It will, no doubt, cheer his heart to think that he might be able to present someone with massive account for all the work he has done so far."

9.

THE next morning, shortly after breakfast, Francesca came out of Mordecai's door, still clutching a leather bag in her hand. She looked up and down the street, and then turned from Mordecai's house toward the north gate of the *call*. Several people recognized her and smiled or bowed in greeting. She appeared to see none of them, but walked steadily ahead, out the gate, down to the square in front of the cathedral, and over into the suburb of Sant Feliu. She stopped at last in front of a shop that took up the ground floor of a tall, narrow house. Its door was closed and locked. Shivering, she raised her hand to knock. Instead of touching the door, however, she let her hand fall again and peered into the dark shop through a matching tall, narrow window, only nominally protected that Wednesday morning by a single broken shutter.

Inside she saw a long room, divided into two unequal segments by a narrow table covered with all manner of things. The door led into the front part of the shop, barely large enough for four people to crowd into. There one could either bargain with the moneylender or inspect the sad remnants of people's lives that had not been redeemed as they lay out for sale on the table. From where she stood, peering through the slats of the shutter, she could see an assortment of dishes, a pot, an earthen casserole, a brown woolen dress, muddied at the hem, two shirts, a tunic, and a dirty shift. For an instant, Francesca tried to imagine her jewels on that table—the gold chain, the bracelet, the hair adornment, two rings—things she loved, given to her by her husband, by her stepfather, and by Pons and Joana, carelessly tossed on top of some poor creature's dirty shift, and she began to tremble. She could not walk into that place.

"A sad sight, isn't it, Mistress Francesca?" asked a pleasant voice behind her.

She turned, recognizing the woman, a casual acquaintance of her parents-in-law, and nodded. "I had never noticed it before," she said. "But I suppose it must have been here for some time."

"His grandparents started it when there were few people living out here, and those that were here were very poor. But now all sorts find that they need a little money from time to time, and he does quite well."

"Indeed," said Francesca, turning back toward the city gate. She took a deep breath to steady herself. "Are you coming this way, mistress?" she asked, with an air of assurance dragged from some forgotten corner of her spirit. When her acquaintance nodded, she said, "Then let us walk together. I am on my way home."

FRANCESCA was moderately well-composed by the time she reached her own door. Joana and Sibilla were in the courtyard, chatting idly but working busily at their needles when she came in.

"Did you have a pleasant walk?" asked Joana.

"Yes, indeed," said Francesca. "And I met Mistress Anna—the tall one with the squinty eye, not the other one—and we walked back this way together. She tells me that we are to have a hot summer."

"How does she know?" asked Sibilla.

"Something to do with the behavior of the crows, I think,"

said Francesca. "I wasn't following, really. It seemed a foolish way of judging. How do the crows know?"

"Oh, Francesca," said Sibilla, "you walked so long that your shopping arrived before you did. There's a package over there by the staircase."

"My shopping?" asked Francesca.

"Well, a boy came to the gate," she said, "and handed me a package, saying it was for you. I'll get it." She put down her work, stretched like a cat, and went over to find the parcel. "Here it is," she said, coming back with a more or less cylindrical package, about as long as her forearm. "If it's something to eat, it seems rather lumpy and hard," she added, laughing, and waited, curious to see what it could be.

"I don't know what it could be," said Francesca. She untied the white ribbon that fastened the package of beige linen together and opened it. She stared at it for a long moment, screamed, dropped it on the flagstones of the courtyard, and ran up the stairs.

"Good heavens," said Joana, springing to her feet and hurrying over. "Whatever is in that package?"

Sibilla picked it up, looked at it carefully, and then showed it to her. It was a bundle of twigs and small, dried branches about as thick as a strong man's arm, tightly bound together with more white ribbons. "It's wood," said Joana, touching it to make sure. "That's all. Just a bundle of wood tied up in ribbon. How strange."

"It's a bundle of firewood," said Sibilla. "Look how dry it is."

"Why was it sent to her?" asked Joana. "For she certainly was not expecting it."

"No, she was not," said Sibilla.

"I shall go to her and insist that she explain," said Joana firmly. "I want to know what is going on."

IT was some time later before Joana returned to the courtyard and picked up her sewing. "She is resting," she said shortly. "When I asked her what had frightened her, she said there was a big black spider in the wood, and that she has always been afraid of spiders. It startled her and she screamed, that's all, and she's fine but tired and wishes to rest, for she walked a long way this morning."

"I didn't see a spider," said Sibilla.

"There was no spider," said Joana.

IT was close to dinner time when Isaac arrived to see Master Pons. He was, as usual at that time of day, still closeted in the section of the house that was devoted to the family business, the thriving wool and cloth trade. "Master Isaac," said Pons, sounding relaxed and expansive. "What brings you here? I was under the impression that we were all too well these days to require a physician," he said, laughing. "I suppose you have been summoned by the women. Have you noticed how full my house is with women these days? All pretty and charming, I assure you, with the exception of the cook, who makes up for her lack of physical beauty with her exceptional talent. I live in terror that she will accept one of the many offers of marriage she receives, and so every time I see a man eyeing her, I raise her salary." He walked over to a side table. "Let me stop talking nonsense and pour a cup of wine for you. I worked hard this morning and am delighted to have an excuse to stop."

"A little wine with a great deal of water," said Isaac. "I built up a thirst in my travels this morning."

"Here you are," said Pons. "Yes. A house with many women in it is often a very pleasant and cheerful place. Not only is my Joana clever and shrewd in matters of business, but mostly she has the gift of happiness. And little Sibilla shapes up well, too. If only Jaume's Francesca were not such an unhappy creature," he added. "I have often wondered why that is. It is not Jaume. He loves her dearly and treats her with great gentleness and patience. One can hear in a house of this size if a man is maltreating his wife. He does not have an entire wing to hide bad temper and ill manners in, as some men do. When she is with him, sometimes she laughs and teases him, as happy women do."

"It is about Mistress Francesca that I have come to see you, Pons," said Isaac. "I am glad you broached the subject of her unhappiness. What I am about to say to you is a terrible breach of all which should be kept confidential, and so I beg you to treat it as such."

"What is it?" said Pons sharply.

"Mistress Francesca went to Mordecai yesterday morning and asked to borrow two hundred *maravedís,* offering her jewels as security. He was so shocked, he told her he could not do it right away, and that she should return this morning. He sent for me to find out in all confidence if I knew of any reason for this need for money."

Pons stood up, walked over to the window of his office, and looked out. "He, of course, would wonder if I had sent her," he said, turning back to the physician. "This is how deadly rumors arise, Isaac."

"He and I both realize that," said Isaac.

"And so he wants to know if she needed it for me, or if Jaume needed it to conceal some shortfall in the accounts," said Pons. "I would not like this to become common knowledge."

"That is exactly how Mordecai feels. I assured him that you were in no difficulties. I did not even consider the possibility of Master Jaume needing it to cover borrowing from your strongboxes. He is neither a libertine nor a spendthrift."

"Thank you for your trust in my son. I am sure that Mordecai did consider it, for he does not know him as well as I do. Still—" Pons went to the door of his office and summoned his clerk. "Shall we start the accounting for this quarter after dinner, Pere?" he asked. "They are saying it will be a hot summer, and it is dusty work. Those summaries can wait." There was a pause as the clerk asked something. "Start with a count of cash on hand, and then we will count stock in the warehouse when that is finished."

He closed the door. "I trust my son absolutely," he said. "But still I like to be able to speak with real authority. And that is something we would have done next week, anyway."

"Your clerk will not think it strange?"

"Not at all. I usually do such fiddling tasks whenever there seems to be time for them, and always suddenly like this. It was an early suggestion by Joana, and a good one. But assuming that my clerk's count reveals nothing, we are left with the question of why Francesca wanted such a sum so much that she was willing to sacrifice her jewelry for it. Because she could never pay it back without asking one of us for the money."

"And at the moment, she seems intent on secrecy."

"What, by the way, did Mordecai say to her? Is he going to advance her that money?"

"He said to me that he prefers not to deal with that sort of loan, and that he was intending to send her over to someone else who commonly takes in goods as security."

"So we do not know if she received the money. I will go and speak to her. If she has, the first thing we must do is redeem her jewels, and then I will try to find out why she borrowed the money."

As the two men walked out of Pons's office, they heard footsteps on the stairs that led down to the courtyard. "Pons. I need to speak to you." It was Joana's voice, sounding sharp and worried.

"What is it, my love?" he asked.

"It's Francesca," said Joana. "She is gone from her room."

"She has probably stepped out for a walk," said Pons soothingly.

"Nonsense," said Joana. "She walked for more than an hour—almost two hours—this morning and came back exhausted. She went to her room, saying she needed to rest. She got one of the maids to prepare her a sedative drink that Master Isaac left for her and she locked her door, asking not be disturbed. Now she's gone."

"Do you know where she keeps her jewelry?" asked Isaac.

"It's odd you should ask about that," said Joana. "I do know where she usually keeps it, but it certainly isn't there. It's lying in the middle of her bed, in a tangled heap. How did you know?" she asked.

"Come into the office and let us explain," said Pons. "You might be able to help with this." Swiftly he laid out all the information that Isaac had brought him.

"That's a prodigious sum," said Joana. "And as much as she likes pretty clothes, she has never been extravagant. The only possibilities I can think of are quite unpleasant ones."

"In addition," said Isaac, "she borrowed fifty *sous* two or three weeks ago, saying she wished it for a present for her husband. She then paid it back a week later."

"From her dress allowance," said Joana. "I remember her asking Jaume if she could have it early, since there was some important purchase she wished to make. But as far as I know, she gave no presents to anyone."

"Does any of this make sense to you, my dear?"

"No, because I have questions that must be answered as well. Why would someone send her a bundle of twigs and dried small branches tied up in pale ribbon? She received that this morning, and when she saw it she screamed—in real terror, Pons, I swear it—and ran up to her room. I tried to get her to talk to me, but she locked me out. I am very worried about her. She has eaten almost no breakfast and has had nothing since. So I sent Rosa up—she seems to feel more relaxed with Rosa than anyone else, I don't know why—anyway, Rosa took her some soup and little things to eat that we know she likes, but when she got there, the door was open and she was gone. I don't know how, because we've been in the courtyard all morning. How did she leave the house?"

"Perhaps she is still in the house somewhere," said Isaac.

"No. We've looked everywhere, even in the attics. Where's Jaume, Pons? We need him."

"He went to look at some goods in the warehouse over the river. He should be back very soon."

"Let us go down to the courtyard and see what can be done. Master Isaac, I am glad you are here," said Joana. "You might be able to give us some advice."

SIBILLA was waiting in the courtyard with Rosa when the rest of them came down. "She was not in the office with Pons?" she asked.

"No," said Joana. "Not that I thought she would be."

Footsteps on the street outside and a short burst of conversation heralded the arrival of Jaume through the gate. "Are you all waiting for me?" he asked cheerfully. "I'm not late, am I? And I saw some interesting materials, Papa. I think—What is wrong?" he asked, suddenly aware of the tension in the air.

"We cannot find Francesca," said Joana bluntly. "Would you know where she is?"

Jaume swayed and steadied himself with a hand on the wall. "Francesca? What do you mean you cannot find her? My God, what has she done?" he said in a panic-stricken voice.

"Nothing, that we know of as yet," said Isaac calmly. "But I think you are right, we must find her. You have come in only minutes after we discovered that she was not in the house, and we are all still at a loss what to do."

"Tell me at least what you do know," said Jaume.

Isaac laid out the sequence of events, starting with yesterday's visit to Mordecai. "It is all very strange," he said. "Do you know why she might need money?"

"Money? How could she need money?" asked Jaume. "She has money. In the little silver box. It has a good lock that we both have keys to. Every week I check it and put more money in it, because I know she doesn't like to have to ask for things. I ask for no accounting, and she seems to spend very little most of the time. Whenever she wants more, she leaves the box out because then she knows that I will refill it. Her desires are so modest that there has never been any question of not being able to give her whatever she could lack. Is that not true, Papa? How much did she ask Mordecai for?"

"Two hundred gold *maravedís*," said Isaac.

"I would have found it for her," said Jaume, sounding amazed, "but I cannot imagine what she needed it for. It is a vast sum for someone like Francesca to need." Jaume looked around him. "And I know what you are thinking, but there is no question that Francesca has ever done anything so shameful that she required a sum like that to keep someone's mouth closed about it," he said doggedly. "I know her and her ways. She is shy and modest. She is almost never out of the house without one of us or one of the maids. She has neither the inclination nor the opportunity to bring disgrace to this house, I swear it."

"I think you are right in that, Jaume," said Joana. "That was one of my first thoughts, and it was as quickly banished as it came. Not Francesca. She seems to crave shelter and protection. She has never sought a moment's freedom; a flighty wife would have been driven mad living the way she prefers to live. She must be with a friend. Someone she trusts."

"Whom?" asked Pons.

"Master Isaac, could she be at your house, waiting for you to return?" asked Joana.

"It is possible."

"I'll send the boy to find out," said Joana.

"She might go to Mistress Rebecca, whom she trusts as well," said Jaume.

"Then let us go to ask Rebecca," said Isaac. "But not all of us. Someone has to stay behind in case she returns, saying that it was all nothing. She slipped out to buy some little trifle somewhere."

"It's not like Francesca," said Joana, "but neither were her actions for the rest of the morning. I will stay behind. Rosa, you will stay here with me, will you?"

"Of course, mistress," said Rosa.

REBECCA came to the door with Carles hanging on to her skirt; from inside the house wafted a rich odor of onions, garlic, and spices. "Papa!" she said. "I wasn't expecting to see you—and Jaume, too. And Master Pons and Sibilla. Come in. I was just—"

"We will step inside for the briefest moment, my dear," said her father. "Just so we do not have to discuss our business out in the street. But we have noses and can tell that you are cooking dinner."

"Nicholau will be home in a moment," she said. "If you wanted to speak to him, I mean."

"No, my dear. We just wanted to know if Mistress Francesca were here with you. If for some reason she is and wishes to stay, that is good. But we would like to know because we are very worried about her."

"Francesca? No, she isn't," said Rebecca. "I've seen her around and about this morning, but she didn't drop by to see me."

"When did you see her?" asked Jaume intently. "And do you know where she was going?"

"Carles, go and tell Serafina I'll be a few minutes." As soon as the little boy had bounced his way from wall to wall out into the kitchen, she turned back to them. "I'm sorry to interrupt, Jaume. Carles has been sick, and now he's restless and being rather difficult," she said. "But I saw Francesca around mid-morning. I was out shopping and she was just standing there, staring in the window of the loan shop down the road, probably at something interesting they had up for sale—they do have some good things sometimes. Then someone came along and they started talking, and I was in a hurry to get back to Carles, so I didn't go and speak to her. I am sorry I didn't. And then, just a little past midday, I believe, I was outside, talking to my neighbor, and I saw her go by again. She turned down the road—and this time I ran after her because I hadn't talked to her in a while, but she was walking very quickly, and the last I saw of her she turned toward the road to Sant Daniel."

"Alone?" asked Isaac.

"Yes, she was," said Rebecca, "and that was odd. Both

times she was alone, and she's not one to go around much on her own, is she?"

"Did you notice anything else?" asked Pons.

Rebecca thought for a moment. "She was carrying her broad basket, the one she takes with her to go mushrooming, with her knife and a big bundle of something or other. She looked as if she were going to the woods to hunt for mushrooms, except that midday in the heat of June is not a very good time for it, especially up by Sant Daniel. But I didn't see anything strange in it at the time," said Rebecca.

"That's true," said Jaume. "She loves hunting mushrooms—it is such a quiet, pleasant occupation, and besides, she loves roaming about in the woods."

"Yes," said Rebecca. "And I'd often seen her with that basket and the knife, although not with a bundle. What I should have remarked on was that she was alone," she added, sounding distressed. "She never goes after mushrooms alone. She always brings someone with her—usually the tall maid with red hair."

"Fausta," said Jaume.

"Yes. She's also shy and quiet and makes Francesca feel comfortable. And if I'd been thinking clearly, I would have known there was something odd going on."

"We don't know there's anything odd going on, Rebecca," said her father in warning tones. "She could just have gone out to get away from the noise in the house."

"But how will we find her? It could take us hours to search the woods," said Jaume. "And we must find her. You know she would not go off like that by herself. Something has happened."

"It would be easy to find her if we had a hunting dog," remarked Sibilla. "One that is good at tracking game. All that we would need then would be something that she has worn."

"There is a man who lives not far from here," said Rebecca softly, "who is said to own a hound that can track anything anywhere. He doesn't really like to admit how talented the hound is, however, since people might suspect he uses him to hunt in woods where he has no business."

"Do you know him?" asked Isaac.

"I know his wife," said Rebecca. "And I have spoken to him. He will be home now for his dinner."

"Would you go to him and offer him ten *sous* if he will bring his hound and help us find Francesca?" said Pons. "Double that if we discover her, and no questions asked."

"Then someone must go at once and fetch one of her stockings or boots, ones that have been worn recently and not washed or cleaned yet," said Sibilla.

"I will get them," said Jaume, "and be back before you have negotiated for the hound, Papa."

10.

AFTER the boy left, taking the message back to Joana that Francesca was not at the physician's waiting for him to return, Judith sighed and told Naomi that she had better do what she could to hold back dinner. "It's clear that my husband has been delayed somewhere. He must have told Mistress Francesca that he would be here."

"That's not a problem," said Naomi. "The fish is already cold, dressed with lemon and oil and herbs, and the chicken is cooked. It can sit in the baking dish and stay warm. You should have something to eat now, though," she said. "You can't keep young Master Beniamin growing at that rate on air and water."

"I'll wait for a while," she said, yawning. "Ah, there they are, at the gate. Where's Ibrahim?"

"Jacinta," said Naomi. "The master's locked out."

Jacinta sped down the staircase to the gate, and wrestled it open. "Yusuf!" she cried.

"I'm home," he said, and picking her up around the waist, twirled her around. He put her down and said, "Where is everyone?"

Judith was the next in the courtyard, and then the twins, and then Naomi. "You've grown," said Judith. "You've hardly been away at all, and already you've grown. But we had thought to get a letter from you before seeing you in the flesh. Look at you, you look like something that hasn't washed in a year. Leah, get out Master Yusuf's clean clothes, and you go and wash the dirt of travel off you. You smell like a horse."

"You know, mistress, that is exactly what my cousin the emir said to me when I arrived in Granada. But where is Master Isaac?"

"He's been delayed," she said, "but he might be at Master Pons's house by now. There's been some sort of confusion with Mistress Francesca."

"I must take my horse to the stable," said Yusuf. "I will stop by Master Pons's house and tell the master, if he's there, that he is to return for his dinner. Otherwise, I'll find him quick enough around the town."

"And we will find you some clean clothes to put on," said Judith. "I am so very happy to see you again, Yusuf," she added, with tears welling up in her eyes, and moved smartly away.

"Shall I go tell Mistress Raquel?" asked Jacinta.

"Do," said Judith. "She will want to see him as soon as he returns."

WHEN Yusuf arrived at Master Pons's house, it was in time to see Jaume coming out of the gate with a boot in one hand and what looked like a rag in the other. "Master Jaume," he called down, from the back of the dun-colored gelding, "I'm looking for Master Isaac to tell him that I am back."

"Yusuf," said Jaume in a distracted voice. "He is at Mistress Rebecca's house. Could you ride there as fast as you can and take these with you for the hound?" Jaume thrust the boot and the cloth, which turned out to look like a stocking, into Yusuf's hand. "I will follow on foot."

"Certainly," said Yusuf. He looked down at boot and

stocking, wondered briefly why they were wanted, and then put spurs to his horse. It was not the sort of homecoming he had envisaged, but it was, he thought, the sort of thing he should have expected.

IN the little crowd in the street in front of Rebecca's house, now augmented by two neighbors and Nicholau, Yusuf's extraordinary return was scarcely remarked upon. "Excellent," said Isaac. "And you are mounted? That might be useful," and whispered something to his son-in-law.

"I shall do that at once," said Nicholau and sped off.

The hound was led down to the place where Rebecca had last seen Francesca, and was then presented with the boot and the stocking to think about. After a moment or two, his taciturn handler slipped his leash and said, "Find."

He cast about whining, looking as if he had picked up a few other tantalizing scents, perhaps of rabbits, but nothing that would interest his master. Tension among the onlookers grew.

"When—" started Pons.

"Give him time," said Sibilla, with the confident air of one who had been successfully poaching other's game all her life. "There. He has it."

And indeed the hound loped off. For a while they thought he was going to outrun them completely, but every time the scent became obscured, he paused, hunting back and forth, before starting off again.

By now, Jaume had appeared, also on horseback. "I cannot believe she can have come this far," he said, when he caught up with the others. "Not in her condition or her present state of mind," he said. "We have overshot her."

But the hound had stopped, puzzled. He cast about, whining, first to one side, then to the other, then back again. Suddenly, with a yelp, he started up into the forested hillside. They lost him completely in the trees, until a flurry of excited barking brought them into a little clearing thick with leaves and needles fallen over the years.

There, lying on a rug in the dappled sunshine, was Francesca, her face and throat smeared with blood and a mushrooming knife lying on her open hand.

11.

"SHE is dead," said Jaume. "I cannot bear it. She is dead."

"Wait a moment there, lad," said his father, clutching him around the shoulders to steady him. "Let us be sure of that first before we begin to mourn. Master Isaac, are you there?"

Yusuf had dismounted and was leading the physician up to the clearing. "She is lying on her back, lord," he said, falling into his old habits of speech at once. "There is blood on her throat and her face."

"A great deal?"

"Quite a bit on the throat, just on the left side, her left side, and a smear on her right cheek."

"No more than that?"

"No."

"Not even on the ground around her?"

"A little, no more, that I can see."

"Is she breathing?"

"I cannot tell from here."

"Then we must get down nearer to her."

The two, master and pupil, knelt down beside her. Isaac placed his hand on her chest lightly and held it there. Then he laid his ear to her left side and listened. "She is alive," he said. "Is that wound still bleeding?"

"It is oozing blood, quite a lot of blood."

"But just oozing it?"

"Yes."

"Then she cannot have cut very deeply," he said, as if to himself. "But I would not have expected such a reaction . . . I must—" He felt her face with his fingers and then leaned over and sniffed at her mouth.

"Smell that, Yusuf."

The boy leaned over and sniffed as well. "She's drunk, lord," he said. "And there is a clay bottle of wine, over here," he added, picking it up and shaking it. "It's almost empty. And the cork was dropped right over there."

"Yes, indeed, she has been drinking. But do you not smell something else? Sniff again. Use your excellent nose. Ignore the smell of vomit—she has been sick, no doubt—and smell what else is there."

He tried again and sat back on his heels. "Poppy. A very light smell of poppy juice."

"That is my doing," he said. "I gave her that concoction after she lost her baby, and she has saved it. I should have warned Mistress Joana. Now we must bandage her up and get her back into town, and see if we can rouse her from this torpor."

"Why come out here to drink a bottle of wine with poppy juice in it?"

"She didn't. She came out here to cut her throat, Yusuf, and the concoction of wine was to give her courage and to dull the pain," said Isaac. "But I doubt that she drank the whole thing. Search the ground around you," he said.

Yusuf ran his hands over the leaves, and then pressed the rug she was lying on. He picked up a swatch of fabric from her gown and squeezed it. "The rug and her surcoat are both soaking wet," said Yusuf. "I didn't notice it at first because they are even darker in color than the wine and the mark is hardly visible."

"And that is why she is still alive. We need clean cloths for bandages here, and some water, please," said Isaac, raising his voice. "And then if you would fetch that litter, please, Master Jaume, instead of worrying, it would be much better."

⊹⟩⟨⟩⟨⊹

SOMEONE thrust broad strips of linen into Isaac's hand. He held it out to Yusuf. "Will these do?" he murmured.

"I think they are from someone's shirt," said Yusuf. "They look quite clean."

"Bind up that cut. Firmly, but remember this is her throat. We do not want to choke the breath out of her in trying to stop the bleeding."

Carefully, Yusuf wrapped bandages around Francesca's slender neck. The last and longest piece he used to tie the rest in place, firmly but not too tightly.

Jaume appeared with more cloth soaked in icy water from a stream somewhere, and Yusuf began to wash away the extraneous blood. The cold water hitting her cheek and under her chin made Francesca's eyelids flutter. "Please, let me be," she whispered. "Let me be where I am. I am so tired, and I cannot stand the pain anymore."

"No, Mistress Francesca," said Isaac. He picked up her hand and slapped it gently. "You must wake up," he said in a lively, normally pitched voice. "I'm sorry about this, but you must. You cannot sleep now. Jaume is here, you've been foolish but he is not angry, no one is angry, but he will be very upset if you don't stay awake." He nodded at Yusuf, who sponged more cold water on her face.

"Jaume," she said, "don't let them burn me. I am so afraid of the fire. Please don't let them." Her voice was so low that Yusuf could barely hear the words. "Don't let them." Her voice faded away, and her eyelids closed again.

"Keep mopping her face with that cold cloth, Yusuf. She must stay awake."

"I'm thirsty," she whispered, "and my head aches so. Let me sleep."

"I can believe that her head aches," said Isaac. "Poor creature. We must get her back. Can you sling the litter between the horses? And someone will have to carry her down."

"I will," said Jaume. "She weighs very little." He picked

her up from the rug and frowned. "Her gown is wet," he said, "and she smells of wine most abominably."

"She needed a great deal of courage to do what she did," said Isaac. "She couldn't do it without the wine. Now we must get her home safely."

WHEN Isaac and Yusuf came out of Francesca's bedchamber, the physician waited a moment for someone to speak. "Mistress Joana?" he asked after a silent few moments when all he could hear was the breathing and rustling sound made by two or three people silenty waiting.

"I am here, Master Isaac. As is Pons."

"Good. Mistress Francesca is breathing more easily now than she was when we found her," he said. "That is a good sign. I have left Rosa to look after her—she seems to be a steady, reliable sort of person."

"She is," said Joana. "And very good at handling Francesca when she is upset."

"Master Jaume is staying with her, too, and Mistress Sibilla. I suggest that someone—or two people—stay with her until tomorrow. She must be awakened and given something to drink—water at first, and then broth, at frequent intervals. When she seems hungry, she may eat. If she falls back into her earlier stupor, summon me."

"And the baby?" asked Mistress Joana.

"Whether she keeps the baby is in the hands of the Lord," said Isaac. "We have done what we could. It could be a problem, but remember that many healthy babies are born to mothers who have suffered worse things. Fortunately she was sick, and she may have spilled more wine than she drank—we cannot tell."

"Is that true, lord?" asked Yusuf, as Joana and her husband went down the stairs ahead of them. "That she did not drink much of the concoction she made?"

"All I know is that she spilled some and vomited some; let us hope that it was more than it seemed. But she is recovering from the stupor. She will not feel very well when she wakes up, I fear, but the wine sickness is normal when people drink an unaccustomed amount—especially mixed with something like even a mild dose of poppy juice."

"But why did she do this?" asked Yusuf. "And what was that about fire?"

"That is indeed the question that must be answered," said Isaac. "But let us go home and have our dinner, and you must tell us how you come to be back so soon."

XI
Sibilla

1.

DINNER, that Wednesday afternoon, was served disgracefully late at Master Isaac's house. Raquel and Daniel had come over, having already eaten one meal; they took the places vacated by the twins, who had not been able to hold off the pangs of hunger until their papa and Yusuf had returned, but had eaten and were playing games around the courtyard. There was a great deal of merriment at table.

"How did you get back?" asked Raquel. "By ship?"

"The same way I came the first time," said Yusuf. "Riding overland. I now have another horse, and they looked rather askance at me at His Excellency's stables when I turned up with him. His name is Fletxa, and he is a courier breed. He can keep going forever. That is why I am home so quickly—I left a farm on the far side of Lleida on Sunday morning, and here I am. He seemed to think that we were carrying life-and-death dispatches."

"You came up by Lleida?" asked Isaac. "It is not the route I would have chosen, I think."

"I had very little choice in the matter," said Yusuf. "I was trying to get to the coast so that I could buy passage up to Barcelona, but the roads between where I happened to be and the coast were not very safe, or so everyone kept telling me. The roads I was on were none too safe, either, but I survived quite nicely."

"Tell us what happened in Granada, if you can," said Judith. "Your family—your mother—" She stopped, not sure how to put her question.

"My mother is well, for which I am very grateful, and I discovered as well that she a remarkable woman," said Yusuf. "My sisters are growing up. Zeynab is lovely and is already promised in marriage, but my mother considers her too young to marry as yet. And to my very great surprise, I have a small brother, Hasan, named for my father. He was born after we left for Valencia. My mother was very happy to see me again. Ayesha and Hasan didn't remember me, of course, but at least they had heard of me. They all complained that I spoke Arabic like a longshoreman, even worse than their maid from the deepest countryside, but I was beginning to pick it up again when I had to leave rather suddenly. I have promised my cousin the emir to keep practicing, for the time when things settle down and I can go back. Do you know," he added, more like an excited boy than the world traveler he was trying to emulate, "my mother has spies in her house? Everyone has spies, she said. She said they are like mice; everyone has them but you have to look around carefully for the signs."

"You were moving in important circles, then," said Isaac.

"I think so," said Yusuf, in tones of grave doubt. "The servants and slaves all called me Lord Yusuf. It felt very odd. But the society of the court is very complicated and hard to understand. I don't know how I fit into it."

"*Lord* Yusuf?" asked Raquel. "Are you sure?"

"I would have expected you to have some title of rank," said Isaac. "But remember that the society of the court here is also complicated. It didn't seem so to you, because you learned about it rather more slowly."

"That was it," said Yusuf with a flash of gratitude. "It was difficult to learn all the intricacies of the life there in so brief a time. Ibn al-Khatib gave me his slave for the time I was there, and he tried to explain who it was I was talking to, and where each person fit in, and whether he was really important or just pretending to be. He was very useful, but I did make mistakes. I don't know whether it was something that I said, or did, that someone didn't like, or something else—"

"I suspect it had to do with who you are, and that is diffi-cult because you don't know," said Isaac.

"Yes," said Yusuf. "But in spite of what they called me, it did not seem to me that I was a person of influence. Even so, it was clear that someone was very anxious that I not stay at court any longer."

THE heat of the day was beginning to abate before Yusuf fi-nally reached the description of the farmhouse in Lleida in his account of his adventures. "The most extraordinary thing," he said, "was that because of my poor little mare's sore leg, we stopped right in the middle of the district where Raimon Foraster had his *finca* before he moved here. I must tell him because I bring him greetings from several of his neighbors. How is he?"

There was a sudden hush in the courtyard. "You have not heard?" asked Raquel.

"Heard what?"

"That he is dead, Yusuf," said Isaac. "He has been poisoned. And because of how he died, you must tell us everything you discovered about him in Lleida," he added. "For the world be-lieves that Master Pau and Master Roger Bernard conspired to kill their father, and what the world believes, the law often acts upon."

"All I know is that what he told us of his life there is true. He arrived as a boy of five or six and was raised by a kindly family, who were promised great riches for keeping him."

"Did they receive anything?" asked Isaac.

"Not a penny. But they never expected to. The folk there are practical and hardheaded, and don't believe much in great fortunes coming out of nowhere."

"Did you discover anything else? Anything at all relating to him?"

"Well, I was the fourth person to ask about him," said Yusuf. "Three times before, people had come to find out where Raimon was and to ask other questions about him," said Yusuf slowly, trying to remember all the details that he learned at the horse farm.

"Who were they? Or at least, what sort of people?" asked Isaac.

"The first was a man who came seven or eight years after his father left him there. Raimon was about my age then, they said. The couple who took him in didn't trust this stranger at all—they had been warned by Arnaud that he and the boy would probably have a price on their heads. They decided this man was after the money, and so they told him that Raimon had died of a fever. He went away again."

"And after that?"

"The second was nine or ten years ago, after Master Raimon had left for Girona. She was a woman in her forties and she had her child with her, a girl of between ten and twelve. She seemed more interested in his father, Arnaud, than in Raimon, though," he said. "The third was last fall. He said he was Raimon's cousin. He asked some questions about Raimon, stayed with one of the neighbors of the people who took me in for a few days, and then left again. He called himself Roger, but no one thought that was his name."

"Why not?"

"He never answered to it."

"Nothing else that you can think of?" asked Isaac.

"The woman in her forties stayed in the district for a while. She said she was considering settling down there; she got work as a cook at a prosperous farm, and her daughter was taken on as a kitchen maid, but she was known in the district mostly because of her other accomplishments. She could make charms and philters to trap a lover; she also could put together remedies for sick cattle and horses. Apparently she was very good at curing animals of various problems, but she charged a great deal to do it and so most of the farmers stuck to their old methods."

"An interesting sort of woman," murmured Isaac.

"There's more than that about her," said Yusuf. "She used to tell fortunes and predict the future, and advise on lucky names for babies and that sort of thing, as well, but only for money," he added. "The general opinion was that she had probably been accused of witchcraft in whatever place she came from—possibly deservedly so—and that was why she had moved on and come to Lleida."

"Where did they think she was from?"

"Oh—from the north, of course, because that was where Master Raimon and his father had come from. And although she seemed to be interested in whether anyone had seen Master Raimon's father or not, she also wanted to know what had happened to the son, and where he was now. The little girl looked a bit like Master Raimon when he was a little boy, and so they figured that Master Arnaud was probably her father, too. But no one asked her."

"What did she look like?" asked Raquel.

"I don't know," said Yusuf. "No one said, and I didn't think to ask. Except that the old lady said she was tall and strong, a real countrywoman. She could handle animals of all sizes and was afraid of nothing. Anyway, she stayed until she had received her salary for two quarters and then one night she disappeared, taking everything she owned with her, along with a few things that weren't hers."

"Did they tell her Master Raimon and Mistress Marta had gone to Girona?"

"Yes," said Yusuf. "And the old lady at the farm—the mother of Mistress Estella—said that once she had left, people were a little uneasy that they had told her, because as they got to know her, she seemed to be a little—" He paused, searching for a word that covered it.

"Unpleasant?" asked Raquel.

"Dangerous," said Yusuf. "And almost vengeful, as if she had something against him."

"What name did she go by?" asked Isaac.

"Beatriu," said Yusuf. "I remember that, for there didn't seem to be anything blessed about her at all."

"Beatriu," said Isaac. "That is the most interesting part of all. Perhaps it is a common name in that part of the world, but Beatriu was the name of Master Guillem's mother. And the daughter? What was her name?"

"I'm sorry, lord," said Yusuf. "That was very stupid of me. I didn't ask."

"You could not have known that it would be important, Yusuf. As it is, you have brought us a great deal of fascinating information."

2.

As soon as everyone in both houses had breakfasted, Isaac and Yusuf collected Raquel and made their way over to Pons's house. "We had been hoping you would come soon," said Joana. "Francesca is awake, but she weeps continually and clings to Jaume desperately. Poor man. He has at last gone for his breakfast, and Rosa is with her."

"I will go up to see her," said Isaac.

"Shall I come with you, Papa?" asked Raquel.

"Please, at least for now," said her father, and headed confidently up the stairs.

Francesca was lying in her darkened chamber, and Sibilla's maid, Rosa, was changing the wet cloth on her forehead. Isaac sat by her bed and picked up her hand. It trembled but was relatively cool. "She is not feverish?" he asked Rosa.

"No, Master Isaac," she said. "Right now she only has the headache. And the wound on her neck is painful."

"We will dress that again. Do you think you could find us some clean bandages?"

"Certainly, master," she said. "I will be back in an instant."

"Let's hope not," said the physician. "For, Mistress Francesca, I have a few things that I wish to say to you before we dress your wound."

"Do not berate me, Master Isaac," said Francesca. "If you knew the cloud that I live under—"

"I know something of it," said Isaac cheerfully. "And today I will learn a great deal more, I hope. Enough to banish it altogether, and for all time, I assure you."

"I doubt that," she said. "It cannot be done."

"Of course it can be done," said Isaac. "Have you eaten today?"

"I cannot eat. I feel sick."

"That is because you have not eaten," he continued briskly. "I expect you to eat a little every hour all day today. How else can your baby grow?"

"After what I have done, I have no hope of keeping my baby," said Francesca in a fresh torrent of weeping.

"I would not be surprised if you had a perfectly healthy child," said Isaac. "Some women living in the happiest of times lose babies, mistress, and many women living with famine and the chaos of war have them. There is no rule. But you must do the best you can to help and stop listening to idle chatter. If Raquel will take off those old bandages, we will be able to see what we are dealing with."

"I will need light, Papa. May I open the shutters, mistress?"

"Of course," said Francesca politely. "Rosa kept them shut because of my headache."

Raquel opened the shutters and then took out her scissors to cut away the old bandages, stiff with dried blood. "I will have to soak them to get them off the wound, Papa. Do you want me to do that?"

"Yes. Soak them in wine and water and lift them gently. I want to apply salve to that wound so that it heals properly," he said.

Raquel had just succeeded in lifting the last piece of hardened cloth off their patient's throat when Rosa returned with fresh bandages. Raquel bent over to look at the wound. "It's not so terrible," she said. "The way they talked, it seemed a miracle you were alive, mistress. Not that you won't feel it for a few days, but it could have been worse."

"No, it couldn't," said Francesca, fresh tears running from her eyes. "I have ruined my looks for nothing, for I am still alive—at least as long as I am carrying this baby."

"Nonsense," said Raquel. "And don't move about so. We don't want it to open up again while I'm putting the salve on it. There. Now we can bandage you again, but without quite so much around your throat." And she neatly wrapped and tied the cloths.

"Will you sit with her, Raquel?" asked her father. "Rosa and I need to talk. Perhaps she can help us clear away these doubts, and Mistress Francesca can sleep soundly once more."

"Certainly, Papa."

And as they were leaving, they heard Raquel saying firmly, "We will start with this little piece of toasted bread and tiny cup of broth. If you eat that, I will let you rest for an hour before bothering you again to eat."

When Isaac came into the courtyard with Rosa, he could hear the muted small sounds made by several people sitting together who had nothing to say to each other. "Who is here?" he asked.

"All of us," said Pons. "That is, I am, Pons, along with with Joana, Jaume, and Sibilla. We are too shaken to talk. And no one feels capable of doing ordinary tasks."

"Is Yusuf not with you?" asked Isaac.

"No," said Joana. "I don't know where he has gone."

"He's in the kitchen, talking to Fausta and the cook," said Sibilla.

"Where, no doubt, they are feeding him another breakfast," said Isaac. "But he will have to forgo it, for we need him here."

"Fausta," called Joana. "Send Yusuf in here, will you?" In a moment, Yusuf slipped into the courtyard and sat by Isaac.

"Her wounds are healing," said Isaac, "and she will recover soon from the physical distress of it all. But she has just said something that has angered me greatly."

"Francesca angered you? How?" asked Pons.

"She tells me she has ruined her looks for nothing, because she is still alive—at least as long as she carries this baby."

"She cannot think that because of a scar from a wound I

will cease to love her," said Jaume. "I will go now and tell her—"

"Don't go yet. There will be time for that. Right now Raquel is convincing her to eat. Anyway, she will not believe you fully until you have seen the scar. It was the rest of what she said that caused my fury and made me realize what she fears."

"Clearly she fears execution," said Sibilla. There was a chill in her voice that spread to everyone in the courtyard. "It is one thing that cannot be carried out while she is with child."

"But why?" asked Jaume desperately. "Whatever has Francesca done that would merit execution? I cannot believe it. She was not much more than a child when we met. She was far from being wild or rebellious, yet even so she was watched over with great and loving care. Never in all the time I was in Mallorca did I hear the faintest rumor against her. After all, I had fallen in love with her, and so I asked various people to tell me what they knew of her character and background."

"And what did they say?"

"They told me—and these were serious people, the notary we deal with, the major traders in silk and rare fabrics, not village gossips—they told me that she was a sweet, gentle, and timid girl. Her mother was a widow who had come from the Empordà with her husband, a knight of good family but little wealth, who was hoping to improve his lot in the islands. He died, and she married a wealthy and respected merchant, who raised Francesca as his own. When we heard from her aunt, we were surprised to discover that the family actually comes from near Foix, but realized that her mother and her husband must have gone from there to the Empordà and then to Mallorca."

"And where was she born?"

"Mallorca," said Jaume.

"Belvianes," said Sibilla at the same time.

"Which is it?" asked Joana.

"She was born in Belvianes," said Rosa, speaking for the first time. "I remember the night she was born very well. I must have been thirteen at the time and it was the first time in my life I had helped with a birth. My poor Lady Cecilia had a difficult time—the labor seemed to go on forever—but then Lady Cecilia never had Lady Matheline's strength. But finally she was born. And she was a lovely baby, little Francesca was. Lady Matheline, for all her rank in society, stayed with her sister all the night, helping and encouraging her, as much as the midwife. She brought her up, you know. Lady Cecilia was her baby sister. Their mother died not long after she was born."

"How did their mother die?" asked Isaac.

"We don't speak of that," said Rosa, glaring at the physician. "It brings bad luck, and Mistress Francesca needs good luck right now." She settled back on the bench where she had seated herself, defiantly crossing her arms across her breast.

"The best luck we can bring Mistress Francesca is to find out where her fears come from. Only then can we banish or confront them. Some things, however unpleasant, need to be spoken of. When did Mistress Cecilia leave Belvianes?" asked Isaac.

There was a pause. "When little Francesca was a year old," said Rosa, after weighing the possible dangers of answering. "She wanted to take me with her, but I didn't like the notion of travel, especially not knowing where we would end up."

"Why did she say she was born in Mallorca?" asked Jaume.

"She was probably told she was born in Mallorca," said Joana. "Her mother clearly wished to make a new start and not worry about her family's troubles. A very foolish thing to do, I think—we all need our families—but it happens. Although," she added, "not generally when the woman comes from such a good background—for she did, didn't she?"

"Oh, yes, mistress," said Rosa, back on safe ground. "Important, held in great respect by all the countryside and, until their troubles started, rich."

"Did Francesca do what she did because of what Rosa insists on calling our 'family troubles'?" asked Sibilla. "Because if she did, I agree that it is time we started talking about them before they lead to more terrible problems."

Before any of the puzzled group in the courtyard could answer, a thunderous knocking on the gate interrupted them.

"Rosa," said Joana composedly, "would you be good enough to go to the gate?"

"Certainly, mistress," said Rosa, and opened it to Pau and Roger Bernard. "Good morning, sirs," she said. "I will see if the mistress is in."

"Of course the mistress is in, Rosa. And so is everyone else," snapped Sibilla.

"We came as soon as we heard," said Pau, addressing himself to Mistress Joana. "We would have been here last night but that no one told us that something terrible had happened."

"Nothing terrible has happened," said Joana. "Francesca injured herself; it could have been terrible, but it was not. We were just talking the circumstances over. Fausta, bring some refreshment for the gentlemen. They have had a hot ride, I suspect."

"And I suspect that you should join us for this talk," said Isaac. "It is about Mistress Francesca's family, but it could well be about your family, too."

"It is certainly about about Roger Bernard's family," said Sibilla. "And about how he comes to bear that name."

"If it is about his family, then it is about mine as well," said Pau. "He is my brother, in good times and bad, and his family is mine. Raimon was the only father I knew."

"Master Isaac has been asking us some very simple questions about our family that we have found very difficult to answer. I had just suggested when you arrived that it was time for us to talk about our family's little trouble. And so far, no one has contradicted me," said Sibilla.

"And what is the family's little trouble?" asked Pau.

"I was born twenty-four years after it happened," said Sibilla, "but every day of my life I lived with it, between my grandmother and my father, and everyone else in the village who knew every detail and spoke of it constantly."

"What is this 'it'?" asked Isaac.

"Imagine, if you will," said Sibilla bitterly, "a stretch of sand and gravel by a bend in a river, and a great crowd there— almost forty people, they said, which is a great crowd for a tiny village. The vindictive and the curious were there, of course, along with everyone who didn't want to be there but was afraid not to go. And pushed to the front were four children, since someone had judged that it would be in the interest of their eternal souls to see this salutary event."

"What event?" asked Pau.

"Don't interrupt," she said. "You will understand as I go along. They were Cecilia, Francesca's mother, aged eight, Bernard, my father, aged seven, Raimon, your father, and Beatriu. They were both five years of age. They were there in the name of religion to watch a heretic burn at the stake."

"Raimon's mother," said Isaac.

"No," said Sibilla. "Bernard's father, Roger Bernard. Raimunda, Raimon's mother, had been brought there with the children, for she had not as yet been arrested, and she was forced to watch her twin brother die in that way."

"How horrible," said Joana. "But was he a heretic?"

Sibilla shrugged her shoulders. "Our real crime was that we were loyal to the count and to our lords. But yes, in my family in the old days there were many followers of the Pure Ones. Not everyone, and those who were heretics have all died or disappeared long since."

"But if he really was a heretic, they had no choice—" She stopped. "I do not know any more. It is different if you know someone." Her eye fell on Roger Bernard.

"Yes," said Sibilla. "You, Roger Bernard, were named after your grandmother's twin brother who died at the stake that day, and who was also my grandfather. And that is curious, because of the way each child reacted to the event. Raimon, perhaps because he was the youngest, forgot it completely. When we talked I could tell that he did not remember anything of it."

"Except in his dreams," said Isaac.

"Yes. And when he named his son."

"I remember that," said Pau. "I was at least eleven when Roger Bernard was born, and I remember mother saying 'but why Roger Bernard? Isn't that rather a lot of name for such a sweet little baby?' And he said that he didn't know, but it had come to him, and he liked the name. So Roger Bernard it was."

"The second child, Cecilia, was terrified, and continued to be terrified," said Sibilla. "Grandmother told me that from the day it happened, she lived for the time she would be old enough to marry and leave Belvianes and the County of Foix. By then, all our land had been seized. Our more distant relations were dead or as impoverished as we were. Grandmother arranged a marriage for her with someone from a good family in a different county, who, to her great surprise and sorrow, turned out to be as poor as we were and for the same reason. So instead of taking her away, poor Cecilia's husband came to live with us. Cecilia pushed him into going to the Empordà, apparently, and I suppose when that didn't work out, all the way out to the Islands."

"How did your family survive?" asked Joana.

"My grandmother petitioned some powerful friends and was permitted to keep her dower house, and its little bit of land for her lifetime. We scraped a living from that. But the death of his father and our poverty turned my father, Bernard, the third child, into a silent man. He scarcely ever spoke, and the older he got, the worse he became. I grew up in my grandmother's house, always watching for my father's silences and sudden furies. Sometimes, in a panic, he would wake screaming in the night. My mother spent all her time nursing him and comforting him. Then she died, and my father gave up."

"How horrible," said Joana. "What happened to him?"

"We did our best for him, but he had no desire to live in a world which held so little for him. My grandmother had suffered so much herself that she could not bear to be with him when he was in these states," she said. "Rosa and I nursed him until he died. But it was not his fault," said Sibilla fiercely.

"Whose fault was it?" asked Pons, in a matter-of-fact manner. "In your estimation, I mean."

"After the wars, and the massacres of its followers, the old faith of the Pure Ones was dying of its own accord. There were no Perfects left near us to lead the faithful and administer the final sacrament. It could not have kept going," she said. "No one would have come to our village to investigate if our family had not been denounced. That's whose fault it was. He who denounced us, that is whose fault it was."

"Who was he?" asked Pons.

"Arnaud," she said. "Arnaud de Belvianes, Raimon's father. He betrayed us all. He came from a rather ordinary family; he was ambitious, and he was greedy. He married my great-aunt Raimunda to better his rank, and his wife quickly grew to despise him. He decided to get rid of her—they loathed each other by then—and hoped that by denouncing her and her brother he might be able to seize the family property. Unfortunately for him, I suppose, it didn't work out that way. Other people got the property, and our friends and neighbors made life too uncomfortable for him to continue living in the county."

"What happened to Raimon's mother?"

"She was judged to be less culpable than her brother, but her only hope for seeing her son again was to recant and accept whatever punishment was imposed. She did and was imprisoned for six years. When she was released, she spent every *sou* she had left searching for him. But someone she had sent down to the south came back with the news that he had died of a fever, and she died shortly after."

"Oh, no," said Yusuf. "That must have been the man—"

"Yes," said Isaac hastily. "Such a pity that each died without a chance to find the other."

"What about the fourth child?" asked Pau. "Who was that?"

"That was Beatriu," said Sibilla. "Guillem's mother. People said she enjoyed every moment of the spectacle. They said it was a terrible sight to see this pretty child clap her hands at the fire shooting up. My grandmother claimed that she grew up to be a slut, although that may have been because she had an affair with Arnaud. That, sirs, is all I know, except that if Francesca grew up immersed in her mother's fear, as I grew up immersed in my father's, her reaction is understandable. Why it is different from mine, I cannot say. But I can tell you it was a terrible thing to live with."

"That may be," said Jaume, who had been listening in silence for some time, "but I do not see how it threatens my Francesca in the eyes of the world. Whether she was born in Belvianes or in the city of Mallorca matters not to anyone. Not to the Church, not to me, not to my family."

"You are quite right, Master Jaume," said Isaac, "and if someone were not playing on Francesca's fears, you would not have needed to know any of this. But I think that someone is."

"Why? Why would someone do that?"

"Someone is doing it for the money," said Isaac. "And I believe I know why Mistress Francesca was willing to pay her tormentor. When she first came to her senses yesterday, she was in no state to know what she was saying, and thinking that she was talking to you, she asked you not to let them burn her because she was so afraid of the fire."

"Good God," said Jaume. "How can that be? She is no heretic. I'm sure of that."

"Of course she isn't," said Joana. "That's ridiculous."

"Someone has convinced her that many innocents went to the stake because of their friends and their family connections," said Isaac.

"But who? Who around here would know that much about the family to be able to threaten Francesca?"

Everyone turned to Sibilla.

"Don't be foolish," said Joana. "It cannot have been Sibilla. Francesca was frightened and as nervous as a cat long before Sibilla arrived. Remember? That was why I was so happy to hear that she was coming. In fact, when I got the first letter, the one from her grandmother, I was relieved to think that we would have another young woman in the house, because already Francesca was reluctant to go out."

"But that was losing the baby," said Jaume.

"Losing a baby is a cause for sorrow, not terror, Jaume. And Francesca suffers from moments of terror."

"There's one thing about Sibilla that I've wondered about," said Isaac. "And I will have to ask, for I cannot tell. Who in her family does she look like? Her mother? Father? Grandmother?"

"No," said Rosa. "She certainly doesn't look at all like her mother, who was tall with red-gold hair, or Lady Mathilde, her grandmother, either, not that I could see. She has a touch of her father, but people said she took after her grandfather and his sister, the Lady Raimunda. I couldn't say, because I never saw them, except once, when I was five or six, I saw the Lady Raimunda just before she died. But she had been painted—I saw the picture on the wall at the castle—and the old people remembered her well. She was a great beauty, they said, a small, slender woman, with skin like marble, gray eyes, high-arched brows, and a thin, arched nose with almost flaring nostrils. She had high cheekbones and dark hair that curled, and even in the painting you could see that she looked like an empress."

"That sounds like a description of Sibilla," said Pau. "Especially looking like an empress."

"Your father's dreams started right after the arrival of Sibilla in the city. When did he first see her, do you know?" asked Isaac.

"He was the first person I met when I came through the gates," said Sibilla. "I asked him where this house was, and he stared at me, without answering, in a very strange way."

"As if he had seen a ghost?" asked Isaac.

"Yes," said Sibilla. "But I cannot have caused his death, can I? I would never have come if I had thought . . ."

"You cannot poison a man by looking like his dead mother," said Isaac briskly. "And Raimon was poisoned. But of course no one would realize that you resembled anyone in Raimon's family, for I gather that he looked more like his father."

"Yes," said Rosa. "He did look like his father, except that he had a more open manner, and an open, honest expression to his face."

"You knew his father?" asked Sibilla. "I didn't know that."

"Oh, yes. He was back sniffing around after money and property just before Guillem was sent off to Toulouse. In fact, that was how the old lady, I mean, your grandmother, Lady Matheline, caught up with him. He was in the kitchen, sniffing around after Beatriu again, and she threatened him with I don't know what, but the result was that the lad was sent off to be schooled. And Beatriu got with child again."

"She had another child?" asked Sibilla.

"I don't know if she had it, but when she left, she had a round belly on her, and the old—the Lady Matheline was starting to say things about it. I always supposed that was why she left."

"That would be the child she had with her in Lleida," said Yusuf. "The one that looked like Master Raimon as a boy."

"This woman was in Lleida?" asked Pau.

"Yes," said Yusuf. "Asking for your father. But it was the year after you left. She worked there for six months and left. It must have been her, lord," he said to Isaac.

"It probably was. It seems clear that Beatriu is somewhere nearby."

"Nearby?"

"Close enough that Francesca talks to her while on her daily walks, since she does not often take out a horse to ride for exercise, does she?"

"Never," said Joana. "But why would she become friends with such a woman?"

"They are probably not friends. She could well be someone at the market or in a shop. Someone whom Francesca sees without realizing that this woman knows more about her than anyone else in the city," said Isaac.

"Her dressmaker," said Joana. "Or the herbalist she visits for those creams for her face and hands."

"The fortune-teller, perhaps?" asked Sibilla. "No. She only visited her once, and I think that was to find out if she was pregnant."

"But how can we find out anything from Francesca without terrifying her even more?" asked Jaume. "And I won't have that. I think I will go and see how she is." He rose suddenly and climbed the stairs to their apartment two at a time.

"Until we find who this woman is, there are two people who are at great risk, both of them sitting in this courtyard," said Isaac.

"Who?" asked Joana.

"The two people who can lay claim to the estates that Arnaud went to such trouble to try to get for himself."

"Who are they?"

"Sibilla and Roger Bernard. The great-grandchildren of the father of the twins, Roger Bernard and Raimunda."

"Raimon," said Rosa. "Raimon de Lavaur, that was name of the twins' father."

"We won't find out anything from Francesca—not while Jaume is standing guard over her," said Joana. "I know my son."

"Perhaps someone else could visit the shops and stalls where Mistress Francesca likes to shop and try to find out who might be tormenting her," said Isaac.

"I will do it," said Sibilla.

"No," said Joana. "Did you not hear what Master Isaac said? You and Roger Bernard are in a certain amount of danger."

"Yes," said Isaac. "Until we know more, stay close to home, and be careful of what you eat. Eat plain food, and smell it before you taste it. If it seems strange in any way, eat something else."

"And in the meantime, I shall do my daughter-in-law's shopping for her today. Who else?" said Joana.

"My dear, are you sure that is wise?" asked Pons. "I will go with you."

"Certainly not," said Joana. "No one is going to talk to me with you standing over me growling protectively. I shall take

Pere and the boy. They will stand outside and look their usual useless selves, and no one will be suspicious."

"An excellent idea," said Isaac. "And I would like to talk to Mistress Sibilla for a moment, if I might."

"Certainly, Master Isaac," said Sibilla. "If I am to be confined to the house, there is nothing I would enjoy more."

"Mistress Sibilla," said Isaac as soon as the others had dispersed, "although it will be an excellent thing for my patient if we can discover who is responsible for fueling her fears and prevent him from continuing, I have another obligation. I have promised Mistress Marta to find out for her who poisoned her husband," said the physician. "In a sense, it is simple to know who must have done it, but what I cannot fathom is how it was done. For that I need your help, Mistress Sibilla."

"You know who poisoned him?"

"I know who must have been responsible," said Isaac. "In the sense that one can say that he knows that a message was carried by the diocesan courier, without ever knowing the man's name or ever seeing his face. But I would like you, if you would, to think back to that day."

"If it will help," said Sibilla.

"Please then, close your eyes and think back to that day. You were asked to prepare a concoction. Who asked you?"

"Mistress Marta," said Sibilla, after a pause for reflection. "After talking to Master Raimon, I had been walking in the orchard with Pau—with Master Pau—and when we came in, I came up the stairs to ask if there was any way in which I could help. She came to the door and explained what you had told her—that only a member of the family could prepare anything for Master Raimon, unless it was to be eaten by everyone, and when his herbal preparations were to be steeped, the person doing it must watch it at all times. I said I would do that."

"And?"

"And I did, Master Isaac. I went down and prepared the concoction."

"Tell me every move you made, as far as you can remember."

"Every move? That is a difficult undertaking, but I will try. I went into the dining room and got the packet of herbs."

"Was it locked away?"

"I don't know," she said in a troubled voice. "But I have no memory of being given a key or using one. No—it was in a dresser, on a shelf, in a bowl. It was the last packet of herbs. I brought it into the kitchen. Someone must have handed me a cup—"

"Who?"

"I don't know," said Sibilla. "But I think it was Justina. Yes, because the cook was muttering to herself as she was stirring something on the fire. So it must have been Justina who handed me the cup. Then the cook took the kettle from its hook and poured boiling water over the packet in the cup."

"Were you still holding the cup?"

"Of course not," said Sibilla. "What if her hand had been shaking? I could have been scalded. So yes, I put it down on the table, and the cook poured water over it."

"Did you pick it up again?"

"Not then. It was too hot. I stood nearby and watched it."

"And then?"

Sibilla paused again. "Mistress Marta called down for a jug of fresh water, and I told someone to get it."

"Who?"

"The cook, perhaps. No. She never stopped stirring the rice. It must have been the boy. Or Justina. She was in and out of the kitchen."

"What was she doing?"

"I don't know. Laying the cloth on the table, I think."

"You told me that you smelled the mixture. When?"

"Yes, I did. I picked it up and smelled it. And then I carried it over to the door so that I could see how dark it was. It looked very pale, and I brought it back. I set it down on the table again. And something interrupted me."

"What interrupted you?"

"I know. That was when Mistress Marta asked for the water.

It could not have been at a worse time. The rice in the pot suddenly dried up and began to stick. The cup was in the middle of the table, so the cook couldn't move the pot onto the table until I moved the cup. I was at the door, calling for the boy to get water. Someone else moved the cup to the dresser, the cook put the rice on the table, and the boy got the water. That's how it was."

"And who was obliging enough to move the cup?"

"Justina, of course. And she said she thought it looked ready, so I told her to take out the herbs and give the cup to me. I carried it over to Pau, who took it upstairs."

"Now it is clear how it happened. What I cannot understand is why it happened."

3.

TRUE to her word, as soon as Mistress Joana had straightened her gown, tidied her hair, and given some instructions for dinner, she collected Pere, who was strong and reliable, if not the cleverest of men, and the boy, who was quick on his feet, and if given a specific task, could be counted on to do it. "This way," she reassured her husband, "if Pere hears something strange going on, he will send the boy for you and then come in to help me."

"On what excuse?" asked Pons.

"All he has to say is, 'Did you call, mistress?' He already says that ten or twenty times a day. He's become quite good at it," she snapped.

"Take care," said her husband.

JOANA started with the dressmaker, leaving her two protectors standing on the staircase of the narrow house where that clever woman lived and plied her trade.

"The new surcoat for Mistress Francesca?" asked the dressmaker, looking nervously around her workroom. "I was never asked to make a new surcoat for Mistress Francesca. I would have remembered. I haven't seen her in more than a year," she said. "I was afraid that my last piece of work had displeased her in some way, and then I heard that she—"

"Yes. She fell and injured herself, but fortunately it was not nearly as bad as it seemed, and she was asking about the new surcoat. She can't come out yet, and it seems to worry her, so I thought I'd come and ask." She stopped and looked around her. "You know, she must have intended to order it, and that was what worried her, because until she's well, she won't be able to, and then she won't have it in time for Sant Joan."

"But if I knew what she wanted, I could certainly have it ready for Sant Joan," said the dressmaker. "I know her height and the width of her shoulders. Is it for her dark red gown?"

And some time later, Joana left, having set the dressmaker working on a pale silver-colored surcoat with gold trim that she hoped Francesca would like.

She went into the bootmaker, vowing not to order boots, and discovering once more that their business was languishing for lack of Francesca's custom. Joana promised that poor Mistress Francesca would be by soon. At the glover's establishment, there actually was a pair of gloves that she had left to be mended, but in Daniel's view, the lady really needed some new gloves, and they had not seen her for a year or more.

"Except when she dropped off the gloves," said Joana.

"No," said Daniel. "It was the maid who dropped them off. The new one."

"Rosa," said Joana. "I am sure Francesca will be by soon," she added. "She was just mentioning the other day that she wanted a new pair of gloves."

Joana also discovered that Francesca had not ordered any silver chains or buckles, although she had brought a gold chain in for valuing, in case she decided to sell it. She had not been in the cloth warehouses, nor had she commissioned any pieces of furniture.

She was standing in the cathedral square, considering where

to go next, when Pons came up. "Have you found anything out?" he asked.

"I discovered that, for all the money Jaume gives her, she has not bought a single thing for herself in more than a year. She has sent one pair of gloves for mending, that is it. Where is all that money going?"

"Come home, Joana. I worry about you."

"It is not quite midday, Pons. I have two servants with me, and only one or two people to see."

"Who is that?" he asked.

"The herbalist and the perfumer. Beyond that, I cannot think of anyone."

"What about all these shops?" asked her husband.

"Cook is in charge of all the food," said Joana, "supervised by me. Francesca has nothing to do with it, unless she has a fancy for something special, but I've never noticed it in her. Away you go. I'll be back soon."

The herbalist had apparently also been languishing because of Mistress Francesca's lack of interest in her products in the past twelvemonth. "I have a particularly good ointment for the hands that Mistress Francesca always loved."

"I will buy her a small pot of it," said Joana. "Until she can get out and look at your wares for herself."

"Is she better?" asked the herbalist cautiously.

"From her little accident? Yes, indeed. Almost well, but the physician feels that she should rest for a few days."

"This ointment is very helpful for scars and marks on the skin," the herbalist whispered, taking a tiny pot from her shelf. "Especially if you start using it when the scar is fresh." Joana nodded, and it was added to her purchases.

The perfumer smiled cheerfully when Joana entered; with a sigh she said that she had come in to collect Mistress Francesca's order.

"I have it right here," said the perfumer, taking a small pot from a shelf under the counter. "That will be two *sous* for the scent, and the usual amount for Bernada."

"Bernada?" asked Joana.

"Did Mistress Francesca not explain? Bernada makes the wonderful cream to smooth the skin that Mistress Francesca so likes. After she has made it, I beat the client's favorite scent into it and then put it into a little pot. But Bernada prefers to be paid separately. Usually Mistress Francesca puts her payment in a small cloth bag, and it goes into the special strong box here for Bernada's money."

"Now I understand," said Joana. "I wondered what that money was that she gave me, wrapped in a little cloth." She opened her pursestrings and carried everything over to the window for better light. After considerable fumbling, she pulled out a small kerchief wrapped around some coins. "There you go. Can you tell me where I can find Bernada? There was something else—for me—that I'd like her to make."

"YOU see—I was perfectly safe," said Joana when she came in the gate to her waiting husband. "Where is everyone?" asked Joana. "Master Isaac, Sibilla, Mistress Raquel?"

"I am here," said Isaac. "I heard you at the gate and was most anxious to ask whether you discovered anything at all."

"I certainly did," said Joana. "I discovered that Francesca has not spent a single penny of the money that disappears from her allowance on anything she needs for herself. It all goes regularly to the perfumer, where she buys a special cream for the skin, for which I suspect she pays an absurd amount of money. It is made up by that fortune-teller, Bernada, especially for Francesca."

"I think it is time to speak with this Bernada," said Isaac.

"I agree," said Joana. "I will go and fetch Jaume. He must know of this, too."

"WHEN I lost the baby," Francesca was saying, more tears pouring down her face, as Joana slipped quietly into the room, followed by Pons and Isaac, "I went to Bernada, the fortune-teller, because someone I knew had gone to her and said that she was extraordinary. And she was. All I wanted to know was whether I would have another baby, but she seemed to know everything about me."

"What sorts of things, Francesca?" asked Raquel gently. "If you can tell us."

"When I first went in she greeted me by my father's name, not my stepfather's name, and said that she saw great mountains around the place of my birth. And then she said that she saw danger, especially danger from fire, and that I should take care to avoid the fire. What could I think, except that she really did have magical powers? I almost went mad, for I am terrified of fire." She sipped a little warm broth and went on. "She knew all about my family, where we had come from, what we had done, what our problems were. Everything. It was terrifying."

"And then?"

"And then she said that people were still going to the flames if they were thought to be trying to hang on to the old ways, and if I didn't want this to happen to me, it would be expensive. And since then, I've been paying, but I can't pay any more."

"Why pay?"

"My mother was faithful to the Pure Ones to the end," said Francesca. "And so were other people in the family."

"How did you know?"

"Bernada told me. I knew Mother was, in a way, faithful to the end, and Bernada told me about the others. They were all people I knew, and she promised to wipe the memory of my mother's beliefs from the minds of her neighbors and friends so they couldn't denounce me. But to do that, she had to travel closer to where they lived and do each group separately. It's expensive, she said."

"And you believed her?"

"Yes," said Francesca. "No. Not exactly. I was afraid it was all true. Anyway, I knew that she, at least, could denounce me."

"Not for having a foolish mother, dearest," said Joana. "Not for that."

A discreet knock and the entry of Fausta, the maid, interrupted them. "Master Pau and Master Roger Bernard are in the courtyard and would like to speak to Mistress Sibilla," she said quietly.

"I'll go now," said Sibilla.

"Alone? Someone should——" said Joana, looking desperately around.

"Don't worry, Joana," said Sibilla. "I promise not to misbehave in the courtyard this morning. And both Pau and Roger Bernard seem moderately trustworthy."

"Of course they are," said Joana. "But——"

And the door closed on Sibilla's retreating figure as well as Joana's faint-hearted objection.

"Gentlemen," said Sibilla. "You summoned me, and here I am."

"How is Mistress Francesca?"

"Sitting up a little, drinking broth, and talking. Where have you been that you do not know?"

"We have been to see His Excellency," said Pau. "We told him everything, and then thought—rather late—that it was not entirely our tale to tell, and that we should have consulted you. So we are now. Consulting you."

"Or rather, telling you that we've done it already," said Roger Bernard.

"In case I wish to ride like the wind to catch the first boat out of the country?" she asked.

"Of course," said Pau, "should you so desire."

"Well, I don't so desire," she said. "But I might have. You could have asked me before. What did you tell him?"

"The history of your family—our family—and how Papa and all of us fit into it, including Guillem," said Roger Bernard. "He seemed quite interested."

"I expect that he was," said a deeper voice from the staircase. "Very interested. And since you have gone that far, you might as well go back and tell His Excellency that this Bernada is dealing in magic and spells," said Isaac.

IN the end, it was Isaac and Yusuf, Rosa, Sibilla, Pau, and Roger Bernard who went down the street past the *call* and then up toward the bishop's palace. They met His Excellency in the hall, just as he was heading toward the door to leave. "And what are you doing back?" he asked. "I thought I had settled your difficulties already."

"While we were speaking to you, Your Excellency, Mistress Joana was asking all the shopkeepers and tradesmen that Mistress Francesca used to deal with whether she had been in recently," said Pau. "And only one, the perfumer, still did work for her. That work is in conjunction with one Bernada, the woman reputed to be a fortune-teller who lives above the shop. I think that—"

"Yes, indeed. She shall be questioned. I have wondered from time to time about this Bernada."

"I have never spoken to Mistress Bernada directly," said Sibilla, "but I have heard her speak. Her manner of speech seems very familiar to my ears, as if she might come from my part of the world. My maid thought it possible that she might know her, did you not, Rosa?"

"I did not get a clear look at her, mistress," said Rosa in some confusion. "I would not like to take my oath on it."

THE task of collecting Bernada for questioning was left for the bishop's sergeant and one of his guards. "It would be helpful to have someone go ahead to play the part of a client," said the sergeant. "She turns as shy as a little woodland creature at the sight of me, and she always seems to keep an eye on the street to see who's coming. Perhaps Mistress Sibilla could come with us, and her maid, of course, just to make sure that she does not disappear as we are coming up the stairs."

"Of course we will come," said Sibilla. "Won't we, Rosa?"

"Yes, mistress," said Rosa, sounding subdued.

"I will come with you as well, Sergeant," said Pau at once. "And bring my brother. We might be able to help."

"Certainly," said Roger Bernard, sounding amused.

"I think there may be another woman living there now," said Gabriel, the guard who was along to do the actual seizing, if seizing had to be done. "Not the maid, but someone younger than Bernada, tall and strong-looking. I have seen her going in and out as if she lived there, all veiled like a great lady."

THE street in front of the perfumer's shop was quiet for the moment. The sergeant looked around. "There must be a courtyard in back, is there not?"

Gabriel nodded. "I think there is, Sergeant. With a gate into the little alley that comes out over there." He looked distinctly uncomfortable.

"Then you will guard that back exit. Make sure that nothing larger than a cat gets out of it without me knowing about it."

"Yes, Sergeant," said Gabriel, and ran off.

"The trouble with that lad," said the sergeant, "is that he knows some pretty girl in every house in and outside of the city. Sometimes it's handy, so I don't like to embarrass him too much. Let us go up."

"Which floor does she live on?" asked Sibilla.

"The perfumer lives behind his shop," said the sergeant. "She lives above. Let us waste no more time."

"All of us?" asked Pau.

"You and your brother will wait on the stairs and request anyone leaving to wait," said the sergeant. "Mistress Sibilla and Rosa will go in first and look like clients. I will slip in behind you."

THERE were only two women in the sitting room of the flat above the perfume shop. Bernada and a younger one, in her twenties. When Bernada answered the door, the younger one was heading toward the back of the room. Bernada took one look at her visitors and started to slam the door closed in their faces, but the sergeant, just as experienced and somewhat stronger than she was, slipped between the two visiting women and planted himself in the doorway. One substantial heave against the door and he was inside, closely followed by Rosa and Sibilla. "Stop that one, will you?" he asked, nodding at the younger one. Then he whistled and called, "Master Pau! We could use you."

Both young men appeared; Roger Bernard stayed in the doorway; Pau rushed into the room. "We're here," he said.

"Catch me that one if you can," he said, nodding toward the younger woman, who was making it very difficult for Rosa and Sibilla to keep a firm hold on her.

FINALLY, with the sergeant holding Bernada, Pau in control of the younger woman, and Roger Bernard investigating the back rooms out of curiosity, a certain peace settled on the room. "Well," said the sergeant. "Mistress Bernada. I have been looking forward to this day."

"But, sir," said Rosa, pointing at the woman he was holding. "That woman isn't Bernada. Her name is Beatriu. As God is my witness, that is Beatriu."

"Nonsense," said the sergeant. "She's Bernada. I've had my eye on her ever since she arrived here, and she's always been Bernada."

"I've known her since I was a baby," said Rosa. "She's Beatriu."

"Then who's this one?" asked the sergeant.

"That one?" said Roger Bernard coming back into the room. "That's Justina, our useless maid. And I can testify that this flat does not contain another being, man, woman, or child, Sergeant."

Suddenly the sergeant raised his hand for silence. They

heard boots on the stairs and a cheerful voice crying out, "Mama. I'm back. And you can forget all this you're doing. I've got a new idea—it's worth a king's ransom . . ." His voice drifted off and stopped when he walked in.

"And who are you, may I ask?" the sergeant inquired.

"Guillem de Belvianes. Just dropping by to pick up a horoscope I was having read. Is it ready?" he asked innocently.

"I distinctly heard you address this woman as 'mama,' Master Guillem. Are you sure you just dropped by to pick up a horoscope?"

"I call all women over a certain age, 'mother,' don't you?"

"That may be. But I don't call them 'mama.' Let us go and have the bishop sort this out."

BUT when the sergeant turned Beatriu over to Sibilla and Rosa to hang onto, in order to go to the back window and summon Gabriel, the guard, she suddenly snapped herself free of their embrace and flew down the stairs like the wind. Bystanders said that she came running by them like a boy, racing, going out the gate, down the road toward the bridge and out to its middle. She threw herself over, heavy skirts, apron, surcoat, and all. Even had she been able to swim, she would not have saved herself, everyone said. The water swallowed her up, and the current threw her back onto a sandbank downriver two days later.

"HOW could she drown herself in the river?" asked Sibilla, when the news had been brought to Master Pons's house that Beatriu's body had been found. "It's not that deep."

"There have been others," said Pau. "They panic, and in the spring—even as late as June—the water is still very cold. She went in at its deepest point, and the river is full this year."

"I wouldn't have drowned in there," said Sibilla.

"No—I don't think you would," said Pau, in a voice filled

with admiration. "But how did she get away from you? I would have thought that between the two of you," he added, nodding toward Rosa, you could have held her."

"She was very strong," admitted Sibilla. "But it wasn't that. You let her go, didn't you, Rosa?"

"No harm was done by it," said Rosa, from her post near the door to the kitchen. "I knew what she'd do."

"How did know that, Rosa?" asked Pau.

"Because she used to talk," said Rosa impatiently. "Especially about how stupid people were to face the fire when all they had to do was escape."

"But she didn't escape."

"Beatriu was never as clever as she thought she was. She used to say," said Rosa, "that if you threw yourself in the river where the current was strong, and let yourself be carried downstream, then all you had to do was climb out again and everyone would think you were dead. And she said she would never face the fire, for she knew what it did. She'd seen it."

"Face the fire?"

"They would have had her for witchcraft, you know, and while hanging is usual, she was afraid they might go back to the fire."

"So it was pure kindness on your part, then," said Sibilla.

"Kindness!" said Rosa. "It wasn't kindness. There were a thousand stories in that head of hers, and her soul was filled with malice. She wanted to see every one of you dead, mistress. That is how stupid she was. She never understood the law, or that there was a difference between a lawful child and a pair of bastards. She always thought she'd get the property if you were all dead, you know. The boy knew, but he couldn't make her understand."

"Guillem, you mean," said Pau.

"He was the only son she had," said Rosa.

AND at the bishop's palace, Berenguer was watching his physician massage his troublesome knee. "They will be tried tomorrow," he remarked. "The judges were only waiting until the old woman was fished out of the river."

"And hanged?" asked Isaac.

"In all likelihood. Or at least the woman will be. But it is the most amazing thing," said the bishop. "The only thing the two of them agree on is that Beatriu, whom we knew as Bernada, was their mother, and Arnaud, Raimon's father, was their father. The sister, Justina, says it was her mother's idea that she work for Raimon and Marta, and that when Raimon fell ill, her mother concocted remedies for him. She had always been famous for her herbal remedies, both for people and for animals."

"And bribing the kitchen maid to go home?"

"That was her mother's idea. That way she would have access to the kitchen and could prepare soothing, healing dishes for her half-brother, Raimon. She would never harm him, she insists, because she respected him so much. Her mother was full of ingenious ideas like that, she said."

"And Guillem?" asked Isaac.

"Guillem told us that all he wanted was to make a living for himself and his mother, and to find the means for his sister to marry respectably. He knew a bit about the law, having spent two or three years in a notary's office. Since then, he worked here and there as a clerk until he had the idea for the land claim. He heard about the case of the young viscount who reclaimed a great deal of his property in a papal court, using the argument that, having been very young when his family was arrested, he hadn't been responsible for his parents' and grandparents' errors. Guillem made some inquiries to find out how the viscount had done it. He soon discovered that a similar claim had been pursued by someone else in the family already on behalf of the missing Raimon, and so he offered to find the heir instead. He hoped that if he did, he would be offered something in compensation."

"I wouldn't be surprised if that were true," said Isaac.

"Nor would I," said Berenguer. "But I don't believe a word of Justina's tale. Mother and daughter were in it up to their necks. We will see."

❧❧❧   ❧❧❧

"I'M going to marry Sibilla," said Pau to his younger brother the next morning.

"Does she know?" asked Roger Bernard.

"Not yet," said Pau confidently. "I'll tell her this afternoon. Down by the river where we first walked."

"Where Beatriu threw herself into the water?"

"No—downstream from there," said Pau. "I have some feelings, you know."

"And you'll move away and leave us all alone, Mother and me?" asked Roger Bernard.

"I don't think so. We'll stay here, for a while at least. I hear you stand to inherit a handsome property in the county of Foix, so I wouldn't like to leave Mother alone."

"Mother will never be alone," said Roger Bernard. "She needs a husband, and she attracts men the way a rose attracts bees. I think she should marry Esteve. He adores her, and we both get along with him."

"Have you told them that?"

"Not yet. I, too, have proper feelings sometimes."

"And you?"

"I shall go to the wild mountains of the county of Foix and marry some poor, clever girl of excellent family who, like Sibilla, is landless and dowryless because of the sad fate—or perhaps, folly—of her ancestors, and the circle will be complete."

"Folly?"

"Don't you think that clever families must have survived?"

"No—it was pure malice that destroyed Sibilla's family. Our family. No matter how clever they were, they couldn't escape that."

"Then they should have turned the malice against their accusers . . ." And still arguing, the two brothers rode companionably into Girona.

❧❧❧   ❧❧❧

"THIS is where we walked when we first met, is it not?" asked Sibilla.

"It is," said Pau. "I enjoyed that walk; I wanted to repeat it."

"I must be honest with you, Pau," said Sibilla. "Whatever you may think, you cannot marry me."

"Why is that?" he asked.

"I am the granddaughter—the penniless granddaughter—of a man of gentle birth who was burned at the stake for heresy. That—his father's death, the loss of our titles and revenues, our terrible poverty—drove my father mad before he died. The whole family was ruined. Your own stepfather, Raimon, was the son of my grandfather's sister Raimunda, who was imprisoned for the same reason, and that destroyed Raimon's life. It is an infection. A deadly infection. Stay away from me, Pau," she said, beginning to weep, "or the world will judge you not only a murderer but a heretic."

"Do you know," asked Pau. "It is amazing, but that is the first time I have ever seen you in tears? All the other women I know, except for my admirable mother, are fountains of tears all the time, it seems."

"Did you hear me?"

"Of course I heard you, and I think your view of it is noble but foolish. I admire the nobility, and I am still going to marry you. You speak of events that killed your grandfather and ruined your family as an infection. I agree. Those four unfortunate children who were brought to watch that terror were infected by it without a doubt."

"Except Beatriu," said Sibilla viciously.

"Especially Beatriu. Who knows how much evil sprang up in her soul that day that otherwise would not have taken root? But you speak as if infections were eternal, but they are not. Even the great plague has faded."

"It, too, destroyed families."

"In different ways. Those four children were profoundly affected, Mistress Sibilla, by something not of their making. They are now dead—all of them. Even Beatriu. We are left, you and I and Roger Bernard, grandchildren of the twins, Raimon and Raimunda, brother and sister who clung so strongly to their faith. And Francesca, your grandmother's niece, she, too, has survived. We are all saddened and touched by it, but we did not see what they saw. We did not hear the screams or smell the burning."

"It is surely folly to cause such suffering, because it is not forgotten, generation after generation."

"It is folly, I agree. But not the first to have destroyed so many people, and no doubt it is not the last. But I am sure that the next round of death and destruction will be for different reasons that we cannot predict. And so we must put this to one side, Sibilla, to grieve over quietly from time to time, and make a life for ourselves."

"How can you dismiss it like that?" Her voice shaded between wonderment and anger as she spoke.

"By looking at you. When shall we marry? We have no one to please but ourselves, and the bishop, who has already given his permission. Lady Matheline, to give her her proper title, your grandmother, wrote him before she died and said that any honest, upright young man who wished to marry you, and whom you wished to marry, who had means to sustain you, received her blessing. I am honest and upright and can keep you, and His Excellency agrees."

Sibilla looked at him gravely without answering for some time. She turned and stared down at the water as if seeking answers among the fish. "Have you finished what you wanted to say?" she said at last, still looking down.

"I have," said Pau.

"You are a stubborn man, Pau," said Sibilla. "So stubborn, that in time, you might make me forget all my hard-won common sense."

"Nonsense. We will give my mother long enough to overcome her grief and anger. September is a good month, don't you think?"

And Sibilla began to laugh. "At least you won't have to waste weeks arguing with notaries about my dowry. And

September is a lovely month. But don't you think we should tell your mother first before fixing a time and day?"

4.

"I am glad to have Yusuf back with us," said Judith, dreamily. It was night, and they were sitting in the courtyard, listening to the gentle sound of the fountain.

"So am I," said Isaac. "But you know that we will not be able to keep him here, don't you? Remember that he tells us he is addressed as Lord Yusuf among his own people. And the emir is going to want him back. His father was a loyal and trustworthy courtier of the old Emir Yusuf."

"But he does not have to go back right away," said Judith.

"No. We will have time now to make other plans. And to set our lazy son, and his almost as lazy sister, to work a little harder. At the rate they are learning, their little brother will catch up with them soon."

"You are right, Isaac. They must both work harder, for it is only family that you can trust to stay with you these days, isn't it? And not betray you for their own good."

"Sometimes," said Isaac. "And sometimes not. Thoughtless children or hard-hearted parents can be deadly."

"Surely, you do not speak of our parents or children," said Judith, shocked out of her revery.

"Who is speaking of parents and children?" said a voice at the gate. "When I have come all this way to visit you?"

"Good evening, my dear," said Isaac to his daughter. "I do not speak of our own family. We are very fortunate. But I have seen rather too much of the other kind recently."

"Where?" asked Judith. "Where have you seen such families?"

"At poor Master Raimon's. Look at his death."

"Did someone in his family poison him? You did not say that. Surely not his wife or his sons."

"No," said Isaac. "He was poisoned by his sister, acting on her mother's instructions."

"Not by the housemaid?" asked Raquel. "I was sure it was Justina. I did not know how, but I was sure of it."

"Justina is his sister."

"How could Master Raimon have his sister working for him as a housemaid?" asked Judith. "I have never heard of such a thing."

"Likely he would not have done so had he known she was his sister, and she would not have worked for him in such a position if she had been able to find an easier way to get near enough to him to add poison to his food."

"Did she hate him that much?" asked Raquel.

"She had never met him before," said Isaac. "But her mother hated him and all his family, and thought that by killing them she could be a rich and powerful woman."

"But you told me Justina had no access to the cup that was poisoned, Papa."

"I was wrong. She did, Raquel. That was my carelessness, and Mistress Sibilla's memory. She insisted that no one could have been near the cup because she had been told to keep it away from anyone, and felt that she had not been careless. But when she retraced every movement she made, it was clear that Justina had ample opportunity to poison the cup. We remember often what we mean to do, rather than what we do. And Mistress Sibilla is more accurate than most people."

"How did you know it had to be her, Papa?"

"I knew that Raimon's family, which includes Mistress Sibilla and Mistress Francesca, had all their property confiscated. When I discovered that one estate, Master Raimon's mother's dowry, had been returned to her innocent heirs—"

"Master Raimon?" asked Raquel.

"Yes. Therefore, I wondered about Master Raimon's heirs. Or potential heirs. His son, Roger Bernard, seemed unlikely, since he didn't know about the property. My attention then turned to his half-brother, Guillem. And since he was far away when Raimon died, perhaps it was some other person connected to him. It was. It was Guillem's mother, with the help of his sister."

"But surely no court would give them Raimon's lawful mother's dower property," said Raquel, shocked.

"We know that, my dear. And so did Guillem. He was hoping for some crumbs from the table for helping Raimon get his land. But his mother and his sister were convinced that they could have it all if only Raimon were dead."

"And his son? And his cousin?" said Raquel. "Would they die too?"

"If necessary," said Isaac.